Also by Christopher Miller

Sudden Noises from Inanimate Objects

THE
CARDBOARD
UNIVERSE

A Guide to the World of Phoebus K. Dank

Christopher Miller

HARPER PERENNIAL

NEW YORK • LONDON • TORONTO • SYDNEY • NEW DELHI • AUCKLAND

A B C D E F G H I J K L M N O P Q R S T U V W X Y Z

HARPER ⬤ PERENNIAL

FIRST EDITION

Designed by Justin Dodd

Library of Congress Cataloging-in-Publication Data

Miller, Christopher.
  The cardboard universe : a guide to the world of Phoebus K. Dank / Christopher Miller.— 1st Harper Perennial ed.
      p. cm.
   ISBN 978-0-06-168636-8
   1. Biographers—Fiction. 2. Literary quarrels—Fiction. I. Title.
   PS3613.I533C37 2009
   813'.6—dc22

                                                         2008047698

09 10 11 12 13   OV/RRD   10 9 8 7 6 5 4 3 2 1

In memory of Donald Miller

"It's a cardboard universe . . . and if you lean too hard against it, you fall through."

—Philip K. Dick

"Wherever the corpse is, there will the vultures gather."

—Philip K. Dick (quoting *Matthew 24:28*)

THE
CARDBOARD
UNIVERSE

ABOUT THE AUTHORS

WILLIAM ("BILL") BOSWELL's books include *Fastest Pen in the Galaxy: The Fiction of Phoebus K. Dank* (1994), *Pass the Brains: The Table Talk of Phoebus Dank* (1999), and *Dank!* (2006). Boswell has lectured on Dank at conferences throughout the nation, and is widely recognized as the nation's leading Dankian. He lives in Hemlock, California, where he heads the Dank Studies department at Hemlock College and edits *What Next?: The Journal of Dank Studies.* Boswell is also a notable novelist in his own right and a winner of the Melville Prize for neglected writers.

OWEN HIRT, the poet, was a friend of Dank's and a firsthand witness to his career.

PREFACE

From his humble beginnings as a scribbler of generic science fiction to the night of his horrifying death, Phoebus Kinsman Dank was probably the only real genius of our time, and certainly the most prolific. His fifty-seven books present a daunting challenge to prospective readers. Not even his most ardent fans are likely to have read more than a few of those books, since most are out of print. One reason for this guide is to provide the basic knowledge of Dank's life and work that his ideal reader should bring to any particular book.

At first blush, Dank's life was not a happy one. To the shame of our illiterate age, none of his novels ever really made him famous or (notwithstanding four ill-fated marriages) won him the enduring love of any woman he loved back. He ended his days in bachelorhood and neglect. Some of his novels sold well enough, but none of them sold faster than poor Dank could spend the money. The world saw him, insofar as it saw him at all, as a fat, badly-dressed, and mild-mannered nobody.

His neighbors, to be sure, knew him all too capable of floridly silly behavior. At one time or another, he built a time machine and convinced himself it worked, got himself arrested for public urination and then four years later for public *defecation*, decided that he was a robot and asked the police to arrest him again, decided that the man next door was beaming a death ray at him and took to wearing a suit of aluminum foil while working in the yard, formed a short-lived punk-rock band called Idle Threat, was questioned in connection with the murder of a critic, wore his wristwatch on his ankle ("to give my wrist a rest"), adjusted his refrigerator so the little light would stay on when the door was shut, called the vet at home in the middle of the night because he'd accidentally fed his cat a can of dog food (which for all he knew might just prove fatal to a cat), exploded a coconut in his microwave oven, took so many vitamins his tongue turned black, and mowed his lawn every day for a month and half with his new ride-on mower, till the neighborhood association made him stop. Not even his neighbors, though, seemed to credit Dank with any inner life to speak of, much less to recognize a genius in their midst.

But if his life was sad and often ludicrous, his art is immortal. And the two are connected, of course, even when his novels question the reality of "real life," even when the so-called real world is revealed as a sham, or a mass hallucination. (Dank's favorite pick-up line—though I'm afraid it never worked—was "What if we're just disembodied brains suspended in a vat of nutrients, and this bar is our hallucination?") But even when he wondered if his memories were implants or worried that his senses had been tampered with (one of his early stories is set in a dismal near-future where everybody is fitted at birth with a pair of permanent rose-colored contact lenses), Dank's fiction was a lifelong effort to make sense of his own life. And you need a knowledge of his life to make sense of his fiction, since even at its most lurid (bug-eyed monsters, two-fisted space cadets, three-breasted alien babes), his fiction was always heartfelt, and even the tales he set in other galaxies were usually provoked by doings in his own backyard.

This guide is a complete Encyclopedia of Dank. Except where otherwise stated, titles in italics are novels and those in quotation marks are stories. The rest of the headings refer to that colossal work of artlessness that was Dank's day-to-day existence. Entries are in alphabetical order, so the book can be consulted like the reference work it is, or read from cover to cover, or browsed at whim. The cross-references (in SMALL CAPITALS) suggest all sorts of forking paths—paths that correspond, I like to think, to likely bifurcations of the reader's curiosity.

Some of the entries are mine and some are Owen Hirt's. Cynthia, our editor, finds the difference in tone between our entries "positively jarring," and adds that Hirt's are often "murderously cruel." Indeed. Hirt, a onetime friend of Dank's and (like everyone these days) "an author in his own right," is best known now not for his thirty years of inglorious toil at the foot of Parnassus but for his week of tabloid notoriety after the appalling bloodbath in Dank's bedroom, since Hirt was and is the prime suspect. (As to how exactly I wound up collaborating with my best friend's killer, see my entry for "The Collaboration.") You'd think that bashing in the head of a writer you envy and hate would make it easy, later, to discuss that writer's books without excessive rancor, but evidently not if you are Owen Hirt.

Even if Dank's books weren't so hard to find, there would still be reasons for providing summaries. One point on which his fans and foes agree is that what's best about his fiction is the premises—the astounding ideas that gave rise to his stories and novels. Good ideas are more common than good books, of course, and not even Dank always succeeded in erecting structures worthy of the plots on which they stand. I have devoted my life to the praise and exegesis of his novels, but I sometimes wish I could just hold one up to my forehead, like the megacephalic Martians in "Abbie's Babies," and extract its gist, its ever-thrilling "concept," without having to read two hundred pages of Dankian prose. This guide does its best to fulfill that wish: It presents the concentrated essence of Dank's genius, minus the impurities and the inert ingredients, providing an ideal starting point for readers who want to know what all the fuss is about.

—William ("Bill") Boswell,
October 31, 2007

A PHOEBUS K. DANK CHRONOLOGY

1952   Born in Chicago with twin sister Jane, on December 16, to Edmund and Dolores Dank

1952–1964   Boyhood: obesity, truancy, bullies

1958   Edmund and Dolores divorce; Dolores and the twins move to Berkeley, California

1959   Earliest surviving writings (see JUVENILIA)

1965   (William Boswell born in St. Louis, Missouri)

1965–1970   Adolescence: science fiction, masturbation, vertigo, first course of psychotherapy

1970   Meets Owen Hirt in senior English class at Golden Gate High; resumes psychotherapy

1971   Parents remarry and move to Los Angeles; Dank stays behind, enrolls at University of California–Berkeley: roommate troubles, Science Fiction Club, writes "Barrett's Bargain"

1972   Drops out of college and moves into rented house in Oakland with Hirt and several other young writers; "Barrett's Bargain" published in *Shocking Science Fiction*;[*] writes *Boost*

1974	*Boost* published by Trickster as paperback original
1975	Marries Jessica Teller; moves into basement apartment in Oakland
1976	*Appointment Book* published; stillbirth of son; divorces Jessica Teller
1978	Misdiagnoses self with terminal illness; marries Molly Jensen; moves to Eugene, Oregon
1979	Still not dead; divorces Molly Jensen; moves back to Oakland; writes "Wacko!"
1980	(Boswell, fifteen, reads "Wacko!"—first encounter with Dank's fiction)
1981	Arrested for throwing a microwave oven out the window of his apartment
	(Hirt moves to Hemlock, California, to teach at Hemlock College)
1982	Follows Hirt to Hemlock; writes *Fastland*; turns thirty
1983	MacDougal praises *Fastland*; beginning of their friendship
1984	Quarrels with MacDougal
1988	(Boswell enters graduate school in Santa Cruz)

---

[*] This thumbnail chronology doesn't list *all* of Dank's stories and novels, of course—just a few landmark publications.

1991	(Boswell's *Midnight of the Soul*)
	Dank and Boswell meet at a science fiction conference
1992	Meets and marries Gabriella Febrero; turns forty
1993	Exit Gabriella; heart attack, two suicide attempts, and four arrests; jailed briefly for drunk driving; resolves to "go legit"; fails Mensa entrance test; mental exercises; a divine (?) revelation; embarks on what will grow to a four-thousand-page exegesis or transcription of his revelation
1994	(Boswell earns his doctorate with thesis on Phoebus K. Dank, moves to Hemlock)
1995	*The Man in the Black Box*
1996	*The Selected Poem of Phoebus K. Dank*
1998	Meets Pandora Landor; Punk Rock phase; assorted drugs; arrested for public urination; marries Pandora; evicts Boswell; marriage fails, Boswell returns; second heart attack; stage-diving accident; exit Pandora; *The Demolition of Phineas Duck*
1999	Leopold Lips moves in with Dank and Boswell, then moves out again
	Quarrels with Hirt; fourth suicide attempt; enter Billy Ray Ruefle
2000	MacDougal publishes *Peter Pan in Outer Space*; death of MacDougal; beginning of La-Z-Boy phase and assembly-line approach to writing
2002	Wildcat strike by Dank's assistants; end of assembly line; turns fifty

2004   Death of Edmund Dank; Dank writes final novel, *Virtually Immortal*

2006   **January–March**—Boswell attempts to interview Hirt

March 3—Hirt and Boswell come to blows

May 10—Boswell moves out after twelve years under Dank's roof

June 14—Dank murdered (by Hirt) in his sleep; Boswell retreats to Portland, Oregon

June 15—Boswell starts work on this encyclopedia

June 22—Hirt contacts Boswell from whereabouts unknown; joins Boswell as co-author

December—Boswell moves back to Hemlock and back into what is now his house

2007   **January**—Boswell inaugurates Dank Studies program

June—Boswell fires Hirt and single-handedly completes encyclopedia

October—Boswell revises encyclopedia, writes preface and chronology

A B C D E F
G H I J K L
M N O P Q R
S T U V W X
Y Z

"Abbie's Babies": After the birth of her child and the simultaneous desertion or abduction of her husband—last seen gazing skyward from a local hilltop—Abbie gets to wondering. She wonders why her children are so puny, when her pregnancies all lasted upward of ten months. She wonders why none of the kids look like her, why they all bear such a striking resemblance to her short, slight, pop-eyed, pointy-eared, bigheaded husband. She wonders why she was so irresistibly attracted to the man, whose personality—cold, aloof, superior—was as unappealing as his physical appearance. She wonders why her seven children have inherited those traits, along with their father's high, toneless, "unearthly" voice and cold, clammy "reptilian" flesh. Can it be (as her gynecologist suggests) that Abbie's chromosomes are "just too wimpy to assert themselves"? No. It turns out her husband was actually a Martian, one of hundreds impersonating earthmen as part of a scheme to infiltrate humanity. (Martians, we are told, reproduce asexually but viviparously, the male of the species depositing an egg inside the female, whose job is just to incubate it.)

Things are not what they seem: If I had to reduce Dank's metaphysics to a simple formula, that would be it. *And*, I'd add, *not everything that looks like a human actually is*, since that was the deception Dank found most disturbing. "It's bad enough when some dumb bug impersonates a twig," as the narrator of another story says, "but when you find out that your roommate is really a Venusian, then you don't know *who* to trust." Dank's fiction swarms with seeming humans who prove really to be androids, simulacra, clones, hallucinations, holograms, extraterrestrials, or worse. Usually extraterrestrials. Dank, I think, sometimes suspected that *everyone* but he was only posing as an earthling.

"Abruptophobia": Jim is an audio repairman in a Dankian near-future. After his hot-tempered wife hits him on the head with a rolling pin, he develops a morbid sensitivity to everything *sudden*: a camera's flash, a thunderclap, even a violent sneeze (and even when he is the sneezer). Jim also has a bad heart, so his new allergy to surprises endangers his life, and reduces him to a bedridden invalid in a soundproof room (a room that also functions as a refuge from his marriage). He is thrilled the day his doctor tells him of a wonder drug named Graduall. Originally developed for the drivers of the superfast and frequently colliding helibuses that are now the standard form of mass transportation, Graduall makes everything appear to happen in slow motion. Jim gets a prescription, and his abruptophobia clears up at once, since when you're on Graduall, nothing *is* abrupt. Not even the explosion of a toy balloon:

> One time Julia [Jim's awful wife] tried to surprise him, *or maybe*, mused Jim with a cold chill, *to kill me by inducing a deadly heart attack*, by sneaking up behind him when he wasn't looking with a red balloon and sticking a big pin in it, so it would pop. Except, on account of Jim's altered perception of Time, due to the drug that he was on, it took so long for the balloon to pop, seemingly, that it sounded more like when you open a creaky door, slowly. Gruffly, Jim wheeled

around and saw Julia wincing from the loudness of the noise even though it paradoxically didn't bother *him* one bit, ironically. He derisively laughed at her so-called "prank."

So far so good. The following day Jim is feeling so perky that he tiptoes up behind his spouse, as she stands "making noises" at the kitchen sink (Dank was still unclear at that point as to just what women do there), and startles *her* for a change by pinching her rump, as he hasn't dared to do since their honeymoon. Julia jumps, but Jim gets the bigger surprise: thanks to Graduall, he witnesses for the first time her transformation, *almost* instantaneous, from her real self into the ugly and shrewish but seemingly human woman he married. Her *real* self turns out to be "some kind of hideous Thing, the color of a rotten avocado, with fangs instead teeth and eyeballs dangling from long slimy stalks." Jim clutches his heart and drops to the linoleum, and "Julia," with no further need for concealment, reverts to her fanged and avocado-colored self the better to gloat at his death agonies.

"Abruptophobia" was written in 1976, during Dank's first marriage (to the ill-tempered Jessica TELLER). In the spring of '76, when his AMPHETAMINE habit first got out of hand, Dank himself developed an abnormal and unhealthy sensitivity to the abrupt—to everything that rudely claimed his attention or rerouted his train of thought. All at once he was so sensitive to noises, even his own, that he glued a circle of felt to the bottom of his favorite coffee mug (SCIENCE FICTION WRITERS DO IT WITH A SENSE OF WONDER), to keep it from startling him each time he set it down. He also modified his toaster to eject his toast in slow motion rather than a spasm of mechanical panic. He had to give up his favorite pastry, those "poppin' fresh" biscuits packaged in a special cardboard cylinder designed to burst open at the seams, with a never-quite-anticipated POP!, as you peel off the helically wrapped label. No, it was all too much for him—the POP!, the leap of the can, the instantaneous expansion of dough into daylight like an angry mollusk surging from its shell, at once thoroughly expected and utterly surprising.

After a few weeks, Dank reduced his daily ration of amphetamines and his abruptophobia vanished, but not before he had a chance to take down all the mirrors in his house in order to avoid the jolt of sudden confrontations with his image. He even squandered a day in the basement trying to invent a new kind of mirror in which it would take a minute for his image to materialize, as with a Polaroid snapshot. Though he never managed to patent his "gradual mirror," a slowly-brightening-video-screen-and-camera combination, Dank convinced himself that his invention was destined one day to replace the old-fashioned unelectrified variety.

For some reason, Dank's first wife took umbrage at "Abruptophobia." It gave them one more thing to get divorced about. The disturbing thing for me about this early story, though, is its premonition, as if Dank foresaw, from a distance of three decades, his final year of hypochondriac withdrawal from the real world. If he did, he saw it darkly, saw it backward. In real life, his final bout of womblike isolation in a dim and soundproof room was not caused but rather crowned by a blow to the head, or succession of blows, the ones that ended poor Dank's life last night, about twenty-four hours ago.*

---

* Almost exactly, since (according to my diary) I finished the entry on "Abruptophobia" in the wee hours of June 15, 2006, and (according to the coroner) Dank was murdered around two AM on June 14.

Unless otherwise specified, the footnotes in this guide were written just after the corresponding entries (which were written in alphabetical order), but I added a few more during revision—i.e. this month, October 2007.

Since moving up to Portland yesterday, I too have developed some abruptophobic tendencies: I jump every time a pedestrian walks by the front window of my rented house (impossibly small and impossibly close to the street—there's no front yard!). If someone knocked, *I'd* have a heart attack. Though I don't know what I'm afraid of. The worst that could happen happened already, happened last night. The carnage in Dank's bedroom put an end to the happiest phase of my life, and this encyclopedia is all I have to live for now.* As E. M. Cioran said, "Every book is a postponed suicide."

The Academician: A family rents out a room in their house to a quiet, inoffensive assistant professor at the local college. There ensue all kinds of minor mysteries: a bad smell in the basement, a new noise from the microwave oven, the dismemberment of a Barbie doll, evidence of tampering with a box of tampons, neurotic misbehavior by the formerly good dog, etc. Gradually the wife becomes convinced that her new lodger is insane and maybe dangerous. Her brother thinks so too, and he's a top psychiatrist. It turns out, however, that Professor Zaxon isn't a lunatic after all, merely an extraterrestrial, and that none of his strange acts mean what they would if committed by an earthling. In the end his superhuman powers come in handy to fend off a pair of burglars (modeled, I believe, on the pair in *Home Alone*).

---

* (October 2007) All I had to live for *then*, that is, in June 2006, when I moved to Oregon and embarked on this encyclopedia, still in shock from its subject's brutal slaying. I'm glad to say that the despair afflicting me at the time, and afflicting certain of my early entries, has lifted by now. I'm even tempted to revise the entries in question—since from this distance my despair looks a little like self-pity—but I think I'll leave them as they are, as a testament to the grief I felt on losing my best friend.

The Academician was begun September 1, 1994, the day I moved in with Dank. I'd discovered his books in my adolescence, at a point in my reading life when I was not only keenly appreciative of their many merits, but blissfully oblivious to their few faults. A decade later when I entered a graduate program in English at U. C. Santa Cruz, I was still a big Dank fan—big enough to make him the focus of my dissertation. In April 1991, I had just embarked on that project, and hadn't yet gotten around to contacting its subject, when I happened to meet Dank in person at a science fiction conference—not a convention, an academic conference. He'd shown up for a talk by some comic-book artist, but the conference was running behind schedule, so he had to sit through my talk on "The Greatest Living American Writer." Dank was at least as surprised to discover that he was the Greatest Living American Writer as I'd been, minutes later, to find out that the fat man in the second row, who'd unnerved me with his expression of slack-jawed incredulity (causing me to qualify my brazen claims on his behalf with some anxious last-minute *perhaps*es and *arguably*s), was none other than the subject of my talk.

When the organizer introduced us afterward, Dank was touchingly flattered to learn that I was writing a book about him.

"A whole book!?" he exclaimed, with that same incredulous expression, causing me again, for just a moment, to wonder how wise it had been to hitch my wagon to his particular star.

"Well, for now it's just a dissertation, but I hope to publish it some day."

Dank looked disappointed, or maybe only puzzled. "So which is better, then—a dissertation or a book?"

The organizer laughed.

"Is a dissertation like an essay," Dank persisted, "like a column on the op-ed page or something? Is it short like that?"

I told Dank that dissertations can be just as long as books, that if anything they tend to be longer (mine would run to 1,111 pages, more than thrice the length of the book I pared it down to), since no one reads them or expects them to be readable.

The organizer added: "It's called a dissertation till it finds a publisher."

"Oh," said Dank. "Like a bill before they make it a law." (He was, I later learned, a longtime fan of *Schoolhouse Rock*.) After a pause, he added: "I think a book is better."

"Speaking of unpublished books—" I started, but before I had a chance to mention my own novels, we were interrupted by another fan, a severely palsied teenage boy in an electric wheelchair who said that Dank's most recent novel, *S.P.U.D.*, had changed his life.

Dank and I, though, kept in touch, and a few months later he invited me to visit him in Hemlock. I came to know his shady redbrick house so well that I forget what it was like to see it all for the first time—the giant conifers out front, the yard that looked more like a forest floor, the long redbrick veranda, the handwritten notice (DANGER: DO NOT PUSH!) above the doorbell, the vestibule crowded with boxes of books, the working water fountain in the living room, the stairway equipped with one of those motorized lifts that enable the crippled, enfeebled, or lazy to ride upstairs instead of climbing.

That first visit was such a success (notwithstanding my ill-boding first encounter with Hirt—see COFFEE TOWN) that I made two more in the next two years. In 1994, the year I became Dr. Boswell, a position opened in the English department at Hemlock College. Dank wrote a recommendation calling me "the nation's number one authority on Science Fiction," which of course I wasn't—as of course he knew, since the day before he'd scolded me for saying "sci-fi" instead of "SF." If I dwelled in the same town as Dank, though, I could at least secure my claim as the number one authority on *his* science fiction.

There was a housing shortage in Hemlock that fall, as in so many college towns at that time of year, and Dank offered me a room in his house while I got my bearings. I accepted the offer, though I had some reservations the day I moved in and got my first glimpse of Dank's HYPOCHONDRIA. That day it took the form of a bad headache with a running commentary focusing on his particular pain ("like someone keeps on hitting me in the head with a stick") but sometimes broadening its scope to describe the genus of headaches in general, as if I might have reached the age of twenty-eight without firsthand experience of headaches.

By the end of my first semester, when I finally got around to house-hunting, Dank and I had formed such a cozy household that he seemed a little hurt by my talk of moving out: Any misgivings he'd felt the day I moved in were long gone. I should mention that Dank had completed just one semester of college, and it was no doubt his unfamiliarity with academia that suggested a *professor*, of all things, as the sinister figure of mystery in *The Academician*. The great "outsider" artist Henry Darger, a grade-school dropout, often painted mortarboards—"college professor hats," as he called them—on the heads of the sadistic child-killing soldiers in his pictures. Not that Dank and Darger were so wrong to fear professors. Professor MACDOUGAL—a sometime book reviewer, onetime friend of Dank, opponent of my hiring (and later of my tenuring), and head of my department from 1996 until his sudden gruesome death in the year 2000—was so hateful and so widely hated that even a man as peaceable as Dank was questioned in connection with that death.

Dank was more gregarious than the average novelist, and liked having me around. Or having *somebody* around. Later I learned I was part of a pattern: Whenever a wife left him (as number three had lately done), Dank invited a friend or quasi-friend to move in, to share his house and food and beer and help ward off the terrors. He was afraid of living alone, and fretted about burglars when I was out of town. I fretted too, since it was I who made the house look occupied. In 1997, on the eve of a trip to St. Louis, I bought some of those timers that crafty vacationers use to turn the lights on and off back home. Though rudimentary in their programming capacity, the timers still created a more convincing illusion of life than Dank, who had once received a bad shock fresh out of the bathtub and was liable to go for days without touching a light switch, content to use the rooms that happened to be lit and forgetting about the rest.

And so I stayed put. For the next twelve years, the last twelve of his life, Dank and I shared the house, in a living situation that I still have trouble explaining to outsiders. Except that we never had sex, it was like a happy marriage, or so I imagine (I wouldn't know—and neither would Dank, I'm afraid). Generous to a fault, he refused year after year to let me give him rent, but I did my best to lend a hand around the house, especially during the various crises of his later years. It was the least I could do, considering the way he gave me the run of the house. *He* spent most of his waking hours holed up in his study, a stuffy little room adjacent to the kitchen and soundproofed by the shelves of science fiction paperbacks that lined its walls. He even had a chamber pot in there, so he wouldn't have to leave the room to use the toilet. Sometimes I pretended the house was *mine*, and Dank my eccentric but studious lodger.

Over the course of a dozen years in Hemlock, I grew very fond of the house, and even of my gloomy bedroom—the big guest bedroom on the third floor, at the southeast corner. That's a sunny corner in most houses, but due to the giant pine outside my window, it was always dusk indoors when it wasn't midnight black. When I arrived, the room hadn't seen a guest for a while, to judge by the fossil bar of soap I found in the adjoining bathroom, a brittle, dull-green oval, striped with grimy black fissures, that looked like it had been there longer than Dank—looked like a stone you'd find on the beach. The old two-faucet sink had what must have been its original white rubber stopper, also petrified by age, but still tethered to the site by a tarnished bead chain. The built-in toothbrush holder dated from an earlier and less expansive era of dental hygiene: Its slots were too narrow for my toothbrush.

My room came with a single bed, a desk, and an old wooden swivel-tilt chair that in its day—the day of Dictaphones and mimeos—must have been the latest word in ergonomic comfort. I didn't get a chest of drawers, but there was a big closet, vacant except for a few ancient paper-clad hangers. Above the hanger dowel was a little shelf, just too high for me to see the top of. Wanting to make sure, before stacking my clean underpants up there, that the shelf was clear of dead bugs, mouse droppings, and such, I inspected the upper surface in a series of glimpses by hopping up and down. On my third hop I spotted a *Playboy* dating from the very month—April 1982—that Dank had moved into the house. Had my bedroom once been his? When I asked (not mentioning the magazine, of course), he said no, so I conclude that, just as he later zoned different bathrooms for urination and defecation, Dank must at one time have used different bedrooms for masturbation and for sleep. One reason he'd invited me to share his house, he told me once, was an uneasy sense that he wasn't making full use of it single-handedly. He even tended to forget that certain rooms existed.

But back to my window, with its close-up view of several giant pines. Thanks to the trees and the eternal shade beneath them, there wasn't a blade of grass in the yard, just needles, mushrooms, pinecones, twigs, and moss. Especially moss, of which our author seemed to have more than his share—and this in a town so gray and rainy that moss was routinely groused about in the same breath as mildew, and the supermarket sold big bags of "moss killer." Dank's roof was striped with moss, which seemed to take root (if that's what moss does) where the shingles overlapped. The brown sisal doormat by his seldom-used side door was so overgrown that for months I mistook it for a moss-green carpet fragment. The crumbling concrete driveway that sloped down to Dank's built-in garage was carpeted in moss, as were the rising concrete walls that flanked the driveway. My pine's trunk was moss-padded, and so was my front window's rotting outer sill, where I used to rest my elbows as I gazed, when I wasn't resting my cheek on that cushion of moss, with its individual spore capsules rising on slender stalks above the main growth and reminding me of the alfalfa sprouts in the Organic section at Food Planet. Once while gazing at the moss like that, from inches away, my cheek on the sill, I saw Owen Hirt strutting up the street with his customary self-importance; from my odd perspective, he looked no taller than the moss-sprouts in the blurry foremost foreground of my field of vision. And that's how I like to picture him (though in fact he was the same height as I): a tiny, haughty, unsuccessful, envy-maddened poet.

When Dank was murdered a few nights ago, I found myself homeless, and somehow I wound up in the tiny rented house where I am writing these words—this uninhabitable hovel with its too-low ceilings and its windows that don't open and its decades of cigarette smoke exhaling night and day from the liver-colored carpet, in an ugly, almost treeless part of Portland whose only claim to fame is as the birthplace of a flamboyantly misbehaved Olympic figure skater. Quite a comedown from Dank Manor. Back there I wasn't paying rent at all, and it's been a rude awakening to realize just how much less spacious my life will be from now on, now that Dank is gone and I have to pay through the nose for the mixed blessing of being alive. Alive and extremely alone.

"Adam Able, Astronaut": Not, despite its title, a picture book for boys, but a breathtakingly mindless and hagiographic short story about strong, silent, square-jawed Adam Able—unafraid of Martians, unimpressed by hyperspace, and irresistible to women— and his space adventures.

Dank's worst stories tend to telegraph their badness in the first sentence. No one who keeps reading after a sentence like *this* has any right to complain about the ordeal that follows:

> If there was one thing Adam hated, a top astronaut and winner of the prestigious Armstrong Award, that they only awarded every decade, it was when Sheba, his spaceship, started making funny noises that drove him up the wall—literally, for there is no gravity in Space.

As Mencken said of Warren G. Harding's inaugural address, "It is the style of a rhinoceros liberating himself by main strength from a lake of boiling molasses." And that's *after* copyediting. At one point the piece was even worse. Dank wrote it, originally, in the future tense, reasoning that since it was *set* in the future, the story should be worded like a prophecy—albeit an unusually elaborate and longwinded one—and not a chronicle:

Adam will enter the flight deck just as Quisix-9 is in the process of shape-shifting into the form of Lt. Zadar.

"What the hell is going on?" Adam will demand, striding purposefully toward the Venusian.

Quisix-9 will pause in mid-transformation to draw his plasma gun . . .

It was his editor (at a magazine called *Flabbergasting Science Fiction*) who ordered Dank to return the rusty and sputtering time machine of his syntax to the present, thereby saving him, this once, from making an ass of himself. Or an even bigger ass. A few years later, though—in 1980, soon after the Pioneer space probes sent back their disappointing news about the odds of life on Venus—Dank (still proud enough of "Adam Able" to permit its reprinting in some fatuous anthology) re-verbed the story *again*, this time in the subjunctive mood:

And then, if life were possible on Venus—that torrid ball of barren rock and deadly greenhouse gases—Adam would have encountered a native in the hold of his spaceship during his routine pre-launch systems check.

"Who the hell are you?" he would have demanded, drawing a bead on the stowaway with his matter annihilator.

"My name is Quisix-9," the creature would have warbled in its unearthly voice—a voice that would have seemed to come not from its mouth but from its dozens of frantically waving green tentacles. "Think of me as an emissary from my people to yours."

"I wouldn't exactly call you guys 'people,'" Adam would have retorted, stubbing out his cigarette. (OH)*

---

* Readers who want an unbiased assessment of Dank should skip the entries by Hirt, since—as should be obvious already—Hirt doesn't play fair.

Agoraphobia: Dank and his twin sister, Jane, were born "six weeks too soon" (his words). All his life, Dank blamed the trauma of his premature eviction for his fear of the outdoors. He didn't like to leave his house because he hadn't liked to leave the womb. Daylight, fresh air, freedom, wide-open spaces, sensory data—he'd been exposed to those good things too soon and had acquired lasting allergies to them, as other babies do to strawberries.

And so—unlike the manly action-craving heroes of his fiction, or the rugged outdoorsy persona he cultivated as his PUB-LIC IMAGE—our author settled for the pleasures of the great indoors. Like so many writers, Dank was happiest in his imaginary worlds, and as much as possible he shunned the real one, though it often served as a setting for his daydreams. With his high-resolution, hyperreal imagination, and his frequent inability to cope with real events, Dank took for granted, at the prospect of a movie or a concert or a party, that he'd enjoy it more, and remember it more vividly, if, instead of actually enduring the experience, he stayed home sipping coffee from his favorite mug (not the sense-of-wonder mug but the one with the Nietzsche quotation: I WANT HOBGOBLINS AROUND ME, FOR I AM COURAGEOUS), and *imagined* the outing in question. Toward the end he even came to think of sex that way—as something better imagined than endured.

Dank's agoraphobia got worse as he got older, though even as a child he had suffered flare-ups that kept him out of school for weeks, forcing his poor mother to explain, to a succession of skeptical teachers, the difference between her son's af-

---

To make his entries easier to skip, I have set them in a different font, or rather left them in the font he favors. Readers seeking information on a particular novel or story, of course, may have no choice but to sift through Hirt's slanders for whatever facts they may contain. (BB)

fliction and old-fashioned truancy—a difference of which she herself was never quite convinced. Many of the characters in Dank's fiction share his phobia. One of them (see BIG DICK and DICK, PHILIP K.) is repeatedly housebound by fear of the world outside, while another (see THE TOE) is finally afraid to leave his bed because he knows that he could die if he stubs a certain toe.

It wasn't until the end of his life that Dank's own agoraphobia became quite that crippling. I first met him, after all, at a science fiction conference in Eureka, three hundred miles from Hemlock. Until the turn of the millennium, Dank worked up the nerve to leave town several times a year. In the end, though, a series of misfortunes caused his world to shrink catastrophically. In July 2000, he returned from a disastrous week in Hollywood, and that proved to be his last trip out of Hemlock. In April 2002, he was knocked down by a speeding moped and resolved never again to cross the street—in other words, never to leave the block he happened to live on. In the summer of 2005, after being attacked first by a stray dog, then by a rival author, he vowed never again to leave the safety of his house. But more about all that, no doubt, in other entries.

In 1999, Dank spent a lot to have a little swimming pool installed in his basement, a so-called endless pool. It was really less a pool than the aquatic counterpart of a treadmill, with the water running steadily westward, so that although the thing was only ten feet long, you could swim against the adjustable current as long as you wanted. Dank—a famous taker of long baths, and already the proud owner of a sensory-deprivation tank—took endless pleasure in his endless pool, though he seldom used it as directed. More often he turned off the current and just floated on his back for hours, naked as a fetus, dictating his novels to a handheld recorder. (His physique enabled him to do all that without a float—as it had already enabled him in 1982 when, a few weeks after moving to Hemlock, he was arrested for backfloating naked in Lake Granite.) He tended to lose track of time in there—to overbathe as others oversleep—and one of my duties was to remind him when he had an appointment that required him to climb out, towel off, and get dressed. I hated the task because I felt so cruel: Nowhere else was Dank as happy as when floating in his pool. Once or twice he even started crying, silently, when forced to leave that heated, over-chlorinated uterus and face the triple terrors of activity, responsibility, and gravity.

"Allergic!": In this story, dating from the time of Dank's second divorce, a bizarre "new virus" (of the kind Dank so often invoked in his pseudo-science fiction, to get the ball in motion) causes a bizarre immune disorder, leaving certain people lethally allergic to certain other people. The hero, Bud Thrust, is a dashing young writer (and back then, though already a good hundred pounds overweight, Dank still had delusions of dash). Bud contracts the virus and finds that overnight he has become allergic to his wife. Unless he wants to risk anaphylactic shock each time he sets foot in their bedroom, he has no choice but "to sadly leave her" for one of his worshipful groupies.

Dolly, the obese and allergenic wife, is clearly—even litigably—based on Molly JENSEN, Dank's own loathsome second wife, the one who once handcuffed him to their bed for fear that he would leave her. I myself have no wife, no attachments, no commitments. I can go wherever the hell I want, so here's a tip to the hounds trying to pick up my scent: At any given moment—as you read this sentence, say—it's safe to say that I'm exactly where I want to be. Someone with a good enough sense of my psychology could unfold a world map and put his finger on the spot where I sit now in my beach chair, sipping my Campari, savoring the perfect weather, and only intermittently putting my pleasure on hold for a minute to type another sentence, on this state-of-the-art laptop, about poor Dank's poor writing. (OH)

The Amazing Green Powder: In this rare foray into the world of young-adult fiction,* a boy receives a chemistry set whose little jars of chemicals include an unlabeled jar of green powder. The set also contains a booklet of experiments, but none of them make use of the green powder. After working his way through the book, though, the boy tries mixing a pinch of that powder with each of the other, labeled compounds, one by one, and each time, something happens: One combination bursts into flames, another glows in the dark, another vanishes into thin air, another keeps changing colors "like a hyperactive chameleon," another expands to a hundred times its original volume, another gives off an overpowering smell of freshly mown grass, another is powerfully magnetic, and so on. But the boy has only an ounce of the magical powder to play with, and all too soon it's exhausted. He scrapes together the money to buy another chemistry set, but this set, though otherwise identical to the first set, doesn't include the green powder.

Dank seldom spoke about his childhood. (When he did, his voice assumed the solemn, elegiac tone of a *National Geographic* special on endangered species—"These gentle giants will soon be extinct"—or primitive cultures succumbing to modernization.) He seldom wrote about it either. *The Amazing Green Powder* is as close as he ever came to writing about his boyhood

---

* Rare? Dank wrote next to nothing that an exacting critic *wouldn't* call young-adult fiction, given the level of emotional maturity his novels demand from the reader. Not that he was alone in that respect—most of the novels sold to adults nowadays are addressed to their inner adolescent—but Dank's books are unusually puerile even for a science-fiction writer, and sci-fi is at the forefront of the young-adulteration of the American novel. (OH)

obsession with chemistry, though he still owned his first chemistry set and at my request once dug it out of a closet. On the box lid was a photo of a boy and a girl with their cheeks retouched to a shocking red that looked more chemically induced than the artist probably intended. Both kids were gazing raptly at a wisp of smoke arising from a test tube that the boy held up as if proposing a toast. Inside the box were several of those test tubes, and a special brush to clean them with, and a plastic test-tube rack, and a real Pyrex beaker, and a little booklet, and a bunch of little plastic jars with red plastic caps and red labels, along with several little glass jars that didn't look like part of the original set. The glass jars had never been opened, and each contained a different white powder.

As *The Amazing Green Powder* suggests, its author's obsession with chemistry had less to do with curiosity about the way the world works than with the magic of eye-catching transformations. One of Dank's anecdotes reveals where he got the idea for the book, and also how unscientific his interest in chemistry was. As a boy, he'd received his allowance every Friday after school, and every Saturday morning he walked over to the Rainy Day Hobby Shop on Haight Street. Inside, he always headed straight to the back of the store. On the back wall, behind the counter, was a pegboard display of all kinds of Pyrex glassware, and below it a case with perhaps a hundred different chemicals in six or eight tiers, all packaged in little one-ounce jars by a company called Perfect, which also printed a checklist of the chemicals it sold. Phoebus would consult his copy of the list, ask the frowning man behind the counter for (e.g.) a jar of potassium carbonate, and then hope that potassium carbonate turned out to be something interesting. Most of the jars contained boring white powders, and Phoebus had enough of those already. For weeks he obsessed about a pistachio-green powder on the third or fourth tier, but the print on the little jars was too small to read from his side of the counter, and week after week he would guess wrong and leave the store in disgust with another unwanted jar of white powder.

Dank was unable to explain either his fascination with the green powder—he does not seem to have had any special plans for it—or the qualm that had prevented him from simply requesting "the green one." (Decades later it occurred to him that the jars on the rack were almost certainly arranged, like their names on the checklist, in alphabetical order, so he could have zeroed in on the elusive powder by its position on the list.) Maybe he'd already sensed that there was something wrong with his approach to chemistry. When he first got interested in the subject, his mother—momentarily deranged at the thought of having produced a prodigy—bought her eleven-year-old son the thick, close-printed, navy-blue *Fundamentals of Chemistry* used at U. C. Berkeley for introductory courses. Never had he seen a book with so many pages, such fine print, or such a pervasive absence of warmth, but more than anything it was the constant irruptions of mathematics that had convinced him, after a minute or two of slack-jawed skimming, that he wasn't destined to win a Westinghouse Science Award (like the one-eyed boy in the *Boys' Encyclopedia* entry on Science), or wear a bright white lab coat and work for Bristol-Meyers (like the Scientist on the following page of the volume, grimly pouring some unidentified liquid from a test tube into an Erlenmeyer flask).

And he proved to be right: His interest in chemistry peaked by the time he turned thirteen, when it gave way to another hobby. When I knew him, Dank no longer played much with his chemistry set, though neither had he ever quite outgrown his Boy Scientist phase. Once in 1996 he spent a whole afternoon microwaving everything he could think of (this was before he developed his phobic DELUSIONS about that appliance), to see what would happen: a sugar cube, a kiwi fruit, an avocado, a Brazil nut in its shell, a charcoal briquette, a hard-boiled egg, an M&M, a Reese's cup, a malted milk ball, a coconut, a pomegranate, a pumpkin, and so on. Not that he'd had all those foodstuffs handy, but in the name of science he made three trips to Food Planet as more and more things struck him as microwavable.

Amnesia: A new virus causes everybody to develop a "rolling" amnesia: all but their latest memories disperse like vapor trails. As the novel opens, the epidemic is a *fait accompli*; the book is set in a wacky post-apocalyptic world populated by incurable amnesiacs. People are afflicted with different degrees of "mnemonic myopia"—X can't remember anything that happened more than a month ago, Y a week ago, Z a day—and the disorder has all sorts of ramifications for art, ethics, law, relationships, and so on. We're told, for example, that most people seek out mates with the same focal limits to their memories, though some favor partners with longer or shorter ranges, just as some of us are attracted to mates distinctly taller or shorter, smarter or dumber than ourselves.* The actual plot concerns a cabal of unscrupulous and power-hungry Commies (which in *Amnesia* is short not for Communists but Commemorators, the elite few who somehow eluded the virus, as opposed to the billion of Fogies or Forgetters) and their scheme to enslave the mass of humanity by means of superior memory power.

The book was written at a time (the winter of 1994-5, soon after I came aboard as his live-in biographer) when Dank thought he was losing his memory, and so his mind, and that soon he'd be a basket case. He'd reread the manuscript of his

---

* Similarly, Dank himself had a thing for women with bosoms bigger than his own, a precondition that—as anyone who ever saw him in a swimsuit will attest—did in fact thin out the field a bit. (OH)

previous book (THE ACADEMICIAN, one of his hastier efforts) and found that he'd inadvertently written the same scene—the one where Joan discovers the condom in the jar of mayonnaise—*eight times*, at eight different points in the novel. (He managed to fish out five of the redundant condoms before publication, and the two he missed can almost pass for artily deliberate repetitions.)

This ugly surprise spelled the end of his brain-a-day diet. Dank decided he was being punished for that diet (a brain every morning for breakfast) with a dose of Mad Cow Disease, though he'd mostly eaten pig brains. His own brain was so forgetful (he insisted) because it was riddled with spongiform voids where the memories had been. Doctors told him his forgetfulness was due to nothing worse than overwork, but Dank was not so easily reassured. More than once I saw him listening to his own head with a stethoscope bought for the purpose, while percussing his temples with the little rubber-headed reflex hammer he'd bought years before, from the same mail-order medical-supply store, in connection with another self-misdiagnosis. One morning I watched from the kitchen window as Dank buried a coffee can in the back yard. He dug it up again the following morning, but not before I'd discreetly determined (since he'd refused to explain what he was doing) that the can contained a slice of burnt toast left over from breakfast, a *Hi and Lois* strip torn from the funnies section of the morning paper, a fan letter that had come in the morning's mail, and (in a zippered plastic sandwich bag) a mole his cat had killed that morning. The coffee can, as far as I could tell, was an extremely short-term time capsule.

Amphetamines: Many great writers were substance abusers. Balzac had his coffee (fifty cups a day!), Faulkner his whiskey, Kafka his roughage. Many terrible writers, too, have relied on drugs to numb the pain of sheer ineptitude. In Dank's case, the poison of choice was methamphetamine, $C_6H_5CH_2CH(CH_3)NHCH_3$, which as everybody knows is used—and has been at least since 1961, when *Webster's Third* appalled the educated world by legalizing "ain't" and so participating in, if not precipitating, the madness of the all-permissive sixties—as "a stimulant for the central nervous system and in the treatment of obesity."

It was as a treatment for obesity that the drug first came to Dank's attention. He had enlivened a dull adolescence by sampling the pills in his mother's medicine chest, and from her he inherited not just his faith in pharmaceuticals but his obesity. He liked her diet pills so much that he got a doctor to give him his very own bottle, and though they couldn't stop his steady transformation into the lumbering blob that he finally became, he soon discovered that the pills enabled him to write his shoddy fiction faster. I'd go so far as to say that amphetamines were to blame for one of the forms the shoddiness assumed: the insanely cantilevered, pathologically tangential plots of his novels. Not only *doesn't* the laser gun described on the first page, above the holo-hearth, go off in the course of the book, but its hapless owner, his wife, his mid-life crisis, and his job repairing spaceships—all are forgotten forever as soon as their hopped-up creator embarks on a subplot which promptly gives way to another, so that in the course of an average potboiler (or toaster-oven warmer, to give a better sense of Dank's attainments as a chef), a whole nest of parentheses open, never to be closed.

In addition to enabling Dank to stay up writing schlock around the clock, the amphetamines were responsible for the inane "experimentation" in some of his books—a feature that had less to do with the Modernist program of making it new, or the Post-Modernist program of making it zany, than with a speed freak's compulsion to keep doing things long after anyone else would call it a day. And of course that compulsion carried over to his extraliterary life (where one of the things the pills made him keep doing was eat, thus defeating their purpose). Dank's drug-addled inability just to sit still, to leave well enough alone, got him into all kinds of mischief, especially in the days when he shared a house in Oakland with me and several other students (see Dog House). One night the rest of us returned from a bar to find that Dank had removed *all the interior doors*, even the one to the bathroom, because of some epiphany about the need for "openness." It is eloquent of the anything-goes mentality that still reigned in those days, in those parts, that we didn't evict him on the spot, though in the special house meeting that followed our discovery (and from which Dank, as the occasion for the meeting, was excluded), a vocal minority—I—insisted that he should be.

Dank, in those days, had more than his share of addled epiphanies. Once he "realized," and for several days went around insisting, that "everyone is either a lever, a pulley, a wheel, a wedge, or an inclined plane." On another occasion he contended that everyone was either a rock, a piece of paper, or a pair of scissors. And yet he shunned the drugs we usually associate with such illuminations. He was the only one in the house who didn't smoke pot, for example, or drop acid. I guess if your mind is already predisposed to spurious epiphanies, even amphetamines will do the trick.

Another consequence of the pills was paranoia. Dank once stayed indoors for three days straight, convinced the minivan some neighbor had parked in front of our house was waiting to abduct him—though *why* anybody would want to abduct him is anybody's guess, and Dank changed his own theory half a dozen times in the course of the siege. Sometimes I'd come home on a perfect summer day to find all the windows down and all the curtains drawn. Once he went so far as to shut all the shutters. And he was convinced, on no evidence at all, that our telephone was tapped, though he couldn't decide who was listening in. His two chief suspects were the Black Panthers and the Aryan Nation, depending on which way his latest bout of paranoia had him leaning, left or right, but he also mistrusted the Feminists, the Communists, the Freemasons, and of course the Government. Whenever a phone conversation turned to anything subversive or illegal—his suspicion that President Ford was a robot; his illegal purchase of more diet pills than even his far-out physician would prescribe—Dank had a disconcerting habit of interrupting himself to address imaginary eavesdroppers: "Are you getting all this, officer?" or "Like me to spell that name, comrade?" (OH)

And How Will I Know You?: Dank's prodigious output is even more astounding when you reflect that in addition to the books discussed in this encyclopedia, he also wrote some hundred other books, in his mid-twenties, under such pseudonyms as Steve Rockhard, Dirk Manning, and John Slaughter. I have reluctantly acceded to his wish not to include entries for those novels. Most, in any case, are impossible to find. But judging from the few I've managed to track down, Dank was unfair to himself—or to his square-jawed alter egos—in dismissing his pseudonymous output as "speed-written trash." The books do appear to have been written rather hastily, but even the fifty-seven to which Dank signed his name were written faster than those of his more fussy, less inspired fellow authors. The unstoppable, almost incontinent gush of Dank's imagination far outpaced *any* novelist's ability to convert ingenious premises into well-turned sentences and well-crafted narratives.

And How Will I Know You? is unique in that it started off as a John Slaughter novel (the protagonist is Slaughter's trademark hero, astronaut Brock Headstrong), but one with such a fertile premise that its author found himself unable to toss it off in two weeks as usual. He kept vowing not to sweat the details, but he wound up sweating them profusely, spending two *months* on the novel and producing something he was proud to sign his name to.

The book opens with an astronaut's return to earth after twenty years of tooling around the solar system. He worries that he'll no longer recognize his wife and children, and it turns out he was right to worry: In his absence, a new virus called "the Proteus strain" has infected the entire human race, causing people to change their physical form, involuntarily and unpredictably, every night as they sleep. Some constants do survive the transformation—gender, mass, apparent age—but the rest is up for grabs. Every time two people—even twins— arrange to meet, they have to ask each other the title question: "And how will I know you?"

Dank refused to talk about his pseudonymous books, and we may never know just how many there were or how he managed to write them so fast—faster than most of us can *type*. In top form, in fact—and though he'd taught himself touch-typing—Dank wrote even faster than *he* could type. An average session ended with a good hour of data entry from memory's buffer after his inspiration dried up. He took most of his speedwriting secrets to the grave with him, but we do know he had dozens of abbreviations for frequently-used phrases, abbreviations he'd expand at the last moment in the final draft. As a result, his speedwritten manuscripts can be pretty cryptic. A few years ago, by comparing first and final (i.e., second) drafts of three Dirk Manning paperback originals whose paper trails Dank neglected to sweep up, I determined that in the mid-1970s the following abbreviations were standard for him:

agd = anti-gravity device

ba = benevolent alien

bb = big-breasted

cblf = carbon-based life form

cdcswffc = at the CDC, scientists were working feverishly to find a cure

ew = earth women

gf = galactic federation

hsb = he said brusquely

hsg = he said grimly

hsgx = he said gruffly

hwc = her womanly curves

il = intelligent life

mi = memory implant

pp = protein pills

pu = parallel universe

sc = space colony

sj = square-jawed

spu = striding purposefully

ss = spaceship

thah = threw herself at him

tsswd = threw the spaceship into warp drive

vx = videophone

waa = was actually an alien

waar = was actually a robot*

wmfw = was a man of few words

waw = was actually a woman

wstvr = was still trapped in a virtual reality

wcip = "We come in peace"

wfhi = women found him irresistible

Because Dank used a typewriter in those days, he did eventually have to spell out the full version of each and every occurrence of phrases like "galactic federation" in the final draft. By the time he switched over to a word processor in 1986, he was no longer writing much straight science fiction. But he still found abbreviations useful, and indeed the ease with which he could get his computer to expand every instance of "aishfft," for example, to "as if seeing her for the first time," or of "ycrap" to "you can't run away from your problems"—that dangerous ease led Dank to construct his books as much as

---

* *That* one must have saved a lot of time: Dank, whose eagerly-awaited mail-order love doll had proven such a bitter disappointment (unlifelike, unladylike, and so leaky that he had to reinflate her during sex), loved to fantasize about a future era when it will be impossible to tell the robots from the humans. And certainly *his* humans—with their push-button emotions, prerecorded dialogue, and tiny repertoire of jerky gestures—are impossible to distinguish from robots. (OH)

possible from prefabricated phrases. It took him a while to realize that his computer couldn't distinguish (for instance) between the "bb" that stood for "big-breasted" and the "bb" in "robber." Since neither he nor the publisher of his first word-processed book had been especially zealous about copyediting, that book—SIGHT UNSEEN—is marred by such monstrosities as "'Hand over the money!' barked the robig-breasteder gruffly, brandishing a pistol." But even with misprints, a novel by Dank is better than one by anyone else.

Appointment Book: Dank's first novel*—like the first dead rat at the onset of a plague—channeled his anxiety about his own personal future into a dreary dystopian nightmare that owes as much to *1984* as a bad book *can* owe to a good one. The book is set in a totalitarian society whose citizens are forced at age eighteen to plan out their entire lives, right down to what they'll have for supper on Citizen's Day seventeen years hence, or which state-run holiday resort they'll visit with their spouses to celebrate their silver anniversary. As soul-killing dystopias go, this one grants its citizens a surprising range of choices during the big Planning Week, but once their Appointment Books have been officialized, people are forced for the rest of their lives to stick to their initial plans. Violations, ridiculously, are punished by prison or death, and citizens are constantly spot-audited by the Ministry of Choice with the aid of two-way video screens straight from Orwell. The hero of this rehash is a Winston Smith type who decides that his plan is all wrong—that he really wants to be a solitary artist, not a family man with a full-time job at the fertilizer factory.

Dank jotted down the idea for *Appointment Book* on June 8, 1971, during our high school graduation, while—or more pre-

---

* His first-*written*, to be accurate (as Hirt so often isn't). Dank's first published book was BOOST. (BB)

cise, instead of—listening to the valedictorian's address, which would have been delivered by this commentator if not for a spiteful B minus from one of my more comically insecure teachers. Instead I wound up sitting in the cheap seats, next to Dank, and I remember his furious scribbling and stage-whispered interjections of self-congratulation ("Yes!" "Right on!" "Ha!" "Far out!") throughout Amanda Oh's painful and painfully thorough account of prevailing—with straight As—over Hodgkin's disease. I remember the scowls directed at Dank by nearby parents. *He* didn't notice: He was too busy watching his own fertilizer factory produce its first batch of manure. He saved the program from that ceremony—its original data barely legible beneath the budding author's frenzied memos—and kept it paper-clipped to a big photo of himself in cap and gown, facing eagerly into a future that no longer scared him, now that he had the plot for his first book. By then I knew him well enough to foresee how little he had to be eager about.

I'd met Dank nine months earlier in our senior English class at Golden Gate High (to which I'd just transferred from a better school in Santa Cruz). On the first day he arrived some fifteen minutes late, red-faced and winded from his heroic ascent of a full flight of stairs without a single breather. (By that point he already weighed some 220 pounds.) His fly was wide open and one of the cuffs of his ugly mustard-colored corduroys had gotten tucked into his sock.

"Phoebus!" someone shouted, and the class burst into raucous applause.

Dank's entry was so clownish that I joined in the applause—took charge of it, in fact, and turned it into a standing ovation. Later it occurred to me that our classmates (most of whom had known him, or known *of* him, for years) hadn't been applauding poor Dank's present laughability so much as his whole history—his appearance at the Junior Prom the year before (with the only girl in the Physics Club) dressed as a robot and flummoxed to discover a semi-formal gathering and not a costume party; his ungovernable seventh-grade erections, or erection (he seems to have spent that year in a single continuous state of tumescence); his science-fair volcanoes, bigger every year till he was using a full box of baking soda and a quart of vinegar; his claim, in second grade, that his missing father was a famous astronaut en route to Jupiter; his legendary tantrum, the first day of kindergarten, when bullies stomped on his brand-new *Fantastic Four* lunchbox.

From the first day of twelfth grade, in any case—from the moment I corrected poor Miss Endive's definition of "dramatic monologue"—Dank conceived a slavish and embarrassing devotion to this commentator. He made a point of sitting next to me, and saving me a seat when I was late. Because in those days I wore Izod sweaters, he too started wearing them, thus obliging me to stop, like the elite Star-Belly Sneetches who wisely have their stars removed as soon as the arriviste Plain-Belly Sneetches get stars of their own. He applied to U.C. Berkeley because I did (and also, to be sure, because it was so close to home, though as it happened his mother moved away the month he started college, forcing Dank to live in a dorm, where he told everyone he was an orphan). Eleven years later he followed me to Hemlock. If I'd moved on to Europe sooner—while he was still alive and not yet housebound by his phobias—he'd have followed me across the ocean too.

The germs of Dank's novels (and if that makes the books themselves sound like so many diseases, so be it) can generally be traced to real life, insofar as Dank had a real life. *Appointment Book* is no exception. Even at eighteen, Dank was a pathological planner. It wasn't only in his fiction that his eye for inert and unnecessary detail was 20/20. For about a week in January 1973, after receiving a stopwatch for Christmas, he attempted, for the hell of it, to micro-plan each day the night before—accounting not just for every minute, but for every *second* ("7:45:00-7:45:15—hear alarm clock and wake up; 7:45:15-7:45:18—turn off alarm clock; 7:45:18-7:45:25—yawn and stretch; 7:45:25-7:45:35—get out of bed; 7:45:35-7:46:05—walk down hall to bathroom; 7:46:05-7:47:00—pee; 7:47:00-7:47:02—flush toilet . . .").

He was less scrupulous, though, about *adhering* to his plans, and often expressed the wish—sometimes in terms that sounded outright sadomasochistic—that someone or other would "make" him do what he'd said he would do. The police state he imagined in *Appointment Book* was as much a daydream as a nightmare. (OH)

"The Architect": Spunky young reporter moves to small town for newspaper job, buys big red house suspiciously cheap, promptly "senses" something wrong with it. Asks around and, sure enough, house has "checkered history": suicide, infanticide, castration, vivisection, bestiality. Former tenants all in prisons, coffins, mental institutions. Turns out house was built by evil real-estate mogul still bitter over failure, as young idealistic architect, to get young idealistic houses built. Now designs malignant houses, builds at own expense, sells cheap, and conducts unholy "psycho-architectural" experiments on unsuspecting tenants.* Tragical, tragical

---

* Whether or not a house can really drive its occupants to the sort of excesses imagined in Dank's story, it can certainly affect their moods as much as the weather outdoors does. I'm painfully aware of that today, July 7, 2006. It's a beautiful blue summer day, but my mood and I are stuck inside this tiny dingy rented house (in what I now know to be the ugliest suburb of Portland) that I moved into after Dank's death a few weeks ago, when—seeing no good reason to remain in Hemlock, and several good reasons to leave—I took my show on the road. I ended up in a house, and in a neighborhood, where there's truly nothing for a thinking man to do but kill himself, and I'd have done so by now if I weren't determined first to finish this guide. (BB)

stuff. Lest reader fail to realize story is sad and not funny, author uses saddening adjective, "tragical," twenty-seven times, a cue card telling audience when *not* to laugh. (OH)

Aromarama: Dank was blessed or cursed with a keener than average nose. He could tell by scent alone if I was up and about, though no one else has ever remarked on my scent. You'd think he would have found it hard to bear his stinkier acquaintances, but Dank exhibited an almost canine lack of squeamishness where odors were concerned. He seemed to like them all—to like it whenever reality reached him by way of his nostrils. He liked works of art that smelled. In general he liked works of art that stirred the humbler senses and not just the eye and ear. Jaded by attention, by efforts to impress them, the eye and ear, like proud coquettes, are hard to please; but the other senses, so seldom asked to dance, respond with touching eagerness, grateful to be acknowledged at all.

Dank had first conceived *Aromarama* as a picture book, a "scratch-and-sniff" volume with clip-art illustrations. Unlike any book that he had ever scratched and sniffed, though, Dank's was written for adults, which meant it could include all kinds of R- and X-rated odors. When Tom, his agent, told him such a volume was "unfeasible" (Tom's favorite word, I sometimes think), Dank resigned himself to an unscented (and unillustrated) book of stories making their appeal to the *mind's* nose: a boy-meets-girl story called "Love at First Sniff"; a detective story told from the perspective of a bloodhound; a comedy of manners about a stuffy butler with terrible body odor; a brief foray into Social Realism using odors to evoke the squalid working conditions in a sewage-treatment plant;* two science fiction stories, one about

---

* One is reminded of Valéry's quip: "If a perfume manufacturer were to adopt the 'naturalistic' aesthetic, what scents would he bottle?" (OH)

a parallel world where smell is the most important sense, and the other a space operetta written earlier but retrofitted with the smells of outer space; a rags-to-riches story of a visionary chef who starts a chain of restaurants serving only aromas; a moralistic tale à la Hawthorne (though Thoreau supplies the epigraph: "Behave so the aroma of your actions may enhance the general sweetness of the atmosphere"), about the corruption of a once-virtuous man who despite obsessive bathing smells worse and worse as he becomes a worse and worse person; a scary story about a murderess (modeled on poor Dank's third wife) who *smells* a ghost, recognizing her victim by his favorite aftershave; and another scary story in which a woman who was raped years ago by a man in a ski mask recognizes the rapist—by his scent, the first time she has consensual sex with him—as the gentle, soft-spoken, unthreatening *litterateur* (modeled on the third-rate writer for whom Dank's third wife left him) who befriended her after the rape. (As to why the woman never recognized the telltale scent before, the story seems to assume that you can't tell what people smell like until they take off their clothes.)

I was especially annoyed by Tom's rejection of the scratch-and-sniff approach because it had been my idea—one I'd first considered for a book of my own but then bestowed on Dank instead. Experimental fiction is such a laughingstock, in our culture, that I won't be seen as boasting if I say that formally my own writing was more venturesome than Dank's. His *plots* were among the most original ever, but when it came to form he mostly settled for the tried and true, perhaps because the fiction where he did try something different suffered the same fate as mine: to remain unpublished.

August and April: Dank, though plainly born to churn out shoddy genre fiction, yielded from time to time to his touchingly hopeless ambition of being a legitimate or "literary" author. The sheer unsalability of his "serious" fiction spared him much embarrassment, but one or two examples made it into print due to unscrupulous publishers hoping to hoodwink Dank's modest but brand-loyal mob of science fiction fans by mislabeling the stuff as if it were the interplanetary crap they craved. That's what happened with this dismal would-be-mainstream novel, the story of a fat astronomy professor's ill-starred romance with a student half his age: despite the novel's studious avoidance of all science fiction elements, its cover shows a sexy hugging couple in silhouette against a stark unearthly sky whose points of interest include several comets, the moon (but so close we see its craters), Saturn with its rings aglow, and—small but unignorable—a fleet of flying saucers.

The novel's hackneyed plot—already tired if not chronically fatigued when Dank took a whack at it—unfolds here in two acts: the idyllic dawn of the affair in early spring, and its parched conclusion four months later. The hero is poor horny August Traurig, the professor. Dank, as a myopic but trigger-happy marksman who liked an easy target, was forever making fun of German pedagogues. He gave German surnames, ancestors, and accents to most of the many evil geniuses, mad scientists, and absent-minded professors in his fiction. And yet his portrayal of Herr Traurig is surprisingly "compassionate," either because Dank had seen that virtue praised so often in reviews of third-rate novels like the one he was trying to write, or because the character and story were suggested by one of Dank's pathetic crushes on a girl half his age.

"*Traurig* is German for *sad*," I heard him explain once to a yawning interviewer. Many of his characters have Meaningful Names (usually borrowed from the one foreign language that Dank had ever studied—and just for a semester). Dank himself had a Meaningful Name, or so he insisted. All his life he attached a portentous importance to the fact that "Dank" means "thank" in German. He gave the author-figures in his fiction idiotic names like Sol Grateful, Solar Thanx, and Sunny Thanker (since of course—and this too was supposed to be Significant—Phoebus is the sun god). He liked to say that his entire oeuvre was just a way to thank his lucky star—the one he happened to find himself in orbit around—for enabling intelligent life. In our Oakland days (see Dog House), Dank affected to pronounce his name the German way, so that it rhymed with "wonk" and not with "crank," but he failed to persuade the rest of us to follow suit. Indeed, I made a point, when forced to mention him at all, of stressing the thankless nasality, the rankness and dankness of "Dank." (OH)

Automobiles: By the time I moved to Hemlock, Dank was no longer permitted to drive, and possibly one reason he let me live with him for free was that he needed a chauffeur. Drunken driving was to blame for the final revocation of his license, but even when sober he'd always had moments when the road skills his mother had taught him would suddenly forsake him. There was a whole week in 1980, for example, when he repeatedly confused the accelerator of his Gremlin with the brake. His insurance premiums were never the same. In 1988 he almost lost his life by running a red light—barely clearing the path of an oncoming truck—in the honest if sudden and short-lived conviction that red meant "go." For a month or two in 1991, at the height of the addiction to British television that followed his discovery of *Dr. Who*, Dank kept forgetting which side of the road to drive on, and once caused a low-speed but head-on collision with an ice-cream truck whose sullen teenage operator refused to yield his right of way to Dank's confusion.

For such a bad driver, Dank was surprisingly ready to take other people's reckless driving personally. In 1995, in the course of an after-dinner walk, he was nearly run over while crossing Hegel Street. Though he'd been jaywalking, Dank became convinced that the government was out to silence him.

Not only was the car that almost hit him big and black, but the driver had been wearing the kind of suit and sunglasses worn in action films by sinister government operatives. As for why They were out to silence him, Dank couldn't say—he had published dozens of books, and there was no telling which had earned him enemies in high places. None of his fiction was explicitly "political," but Dank was convinced that at one point or another (in AMNESIA? in LA VIE EN ROSE?), he had unknowingly stumbled on a truth that the government was determined to hush up.

Some of the drivers he feared were a bit closer to home. One winter afternoon in the final innings of their marriage, Dank's second wife, Molly, returned from the beauty parlor in their old red VW Beetle and pulled slowly into the driveway, which Dank was shoveling at the time. And even though she pulled in just far enough to clear the sidewalk, and he was back by the garage, some forty feet away, he became convinced, before she cut the engine, that she was about to run him over—to finish the big argument they'd had that morning, and finish it more finally than mere words could ever do. Throwing down his shovel, he sprinted for the safety of their house, and through the house to the front door, reaching it a moment before Molly did and chaining it against her.

A B C D E F

G H I J K L

M N O P Q R

S T U V W X

Y Z

"Bacterial Rights": Many of Dank's stories would be better if they were shorter—the shorter the better. Often their very titles exhaust whatever interest their premises hold. "Bacterial Rights" is a perfect example: Dwell on that title for ten or fifteen seconds and it's safe to say you just thought up a better story than the one with which Dank, unencumbered by any real knowledge of biology or sociology, eked out the title to the length of something salable (though only, be it said, to a magazine called *Twat*). "Bacterial Rights" is a cautionary tale about misguided hippies who, convinced that "Germs are Living Beings Too" (their battle cry) break into the R & D wing of "a top antibiotics factory," smash all the beakers and flasks, and are infected with a strain of meningitis so lethal that it barely leaves them time, before dying in excruciating pain, to beg for the life-saving antibiotics they sought to destroy. Except perhaps as evidence that when he wrote it in 1972, Dank liked prescription drugs more than he liked hippies, the story is worthless.

Dank's early lack of promise could be the subject of a dissertation: Why, when all the signs said no, did he continue to impersonate an author? Even his Magic 8 Ball returned that answer—"SIGNS SAY NO"—*three times in a row* when an eighteen-year-old Dank asked the oracle, one evening in a Berkeley coffee house, if he had "what it takes" to be a "real writer." Each time the polyhedron bobbed up to the surface of the inky liquid (which stands in its opacity for the murky future's unknowability) and settled into focus behind the little window, Dank winced as if reading an unwelcome telegram. Afterward, of course, he dismissed the Magic 8 Ball as a toy, its pronouncements as toy pronouncements. But it was clear that he'd been ready to take those pronouncements as omens, if they'd told him what he wanted to hear. (OH)

"Barrett's Bargain": The year is 2049, the USA has colonies throughout the Milky Way, and modern medicine has discovered how to transplant limbs as well as organs. One day Bart Barrett's spaceship is shot down on lawless planet X-19, and though he isn't injured, unscrupulous black-marketeers force him to give up an arm and a leg—literally—in payment for the small but necessary part, a plastic gizmo costing only pennies back on earth, that Barrett needs to get his spaceship airborne again.

Written in late 1971, when Dank was eighteen, and inspired by his mother's frequent complaints about the cost of car repairs, "Barrett's Bargain" appeared in the March '72 issue of *Shocking Science Fiction* and was not only Dank's first published story, but the first he ever wrote with a view to publication. He'd been an avid reader of SF since puberty, but until he met Hirt in a high-school English class, he'd always planned to turn that passion to account by helping to install and service the future his favorite writers had already envisioned. Somehow that had seemed more realistic than aspiring to join the ranks of those writers himself, the more so as Dank had never shaken off the theory—one he'd first encountered in *Shocking Science Fiction*—that science fiction writers are actually mouthpieces for enlightened extraterrestrials hoping to educate the human race in the rudiments of its future. So he couldn't simply *choose* to write science fiction, any more than a megaphone can choose what messages, if any, will be bellowed through it. I'm not sure if Dank ever did abandon that theory, not altogether, even when he started writing. Artistic inspiration, after all, is mysterious enough, and alien enough to the everyday operation of our brains, that until recently even the sanest poets saw themselves as mouthpieces for superior beings. Dank's muse just happened to be an extraterrestrial.

The Big Book of Problems: One reason for this reader's guide is that Dank's seven greatest novels have never been published at all. He was really two different writers: a passably well-selling churner-out of quirky genre fiction, and a shamefully unpublished dreamer-up of brilliant literary fiction. The seven novels for which he'll be remembered long after posterity has forgotten all about _____, _____, and _____ (fill in the blanks with your favorite living authors)—those novels are still ratty typescripts patiently awaiting their admission to full bookhood, like petitioners in Kafka thwarted by inscrutable and arbitrary regulations. If this encyclopedia serves no other purpose than to stir up a demand, among Dank's staunchest fans (or "fen," as SF buffs prefer to pluralize the word) for the unpublished novels (THE BIG BOOK OF PROBLEMS, HOW JOHN DOE GOT HERE, A KNOCK ON THE HEAD, PANTS ON FIRE, PLANET FOOD, THREE-WAY BULB, and WORD GAME—all discussed in the pages that follow), and to prompt some visionary publisher to print even one, or better yet all seven, I'll feel compensated for my efforts.

Till then, you'll have to settle for a synopsis of *The Big Book of Problems*, an autobiographical novel in the form of a mathematics textbook. Or is it a teach-yourself-math book in the form of a *Bildungsroman*? Hard to know just what to call this *jeu d'esprit*, a chronological series of stories pretending to be math problems pretending to be stories. The problems (each accompanied by the math you'd need to solve it) span the years from birth through college graduation, and span the range of math that an average non-math-major might acquire in those years, from simple arithmetic through trigonometry. As the hero and his mind, emotions, ambitions, and real-life problems grow more complicated, so do the equations in the story problems, just as if there were a correlation between existential and mathematical complexity. Or as if you needed a certain amount of life experience to understand the trickier math.

An early problem:

If Phoebus was conceived on the morning of April 22, 1952, and his mother's pregnancy lasted exactly thirty-four weeks, when was he born?

A later problem:

Phoebus and Kevin [Phoebus's freshman roommate, introduced in the previous problem as a difficult person to live with] have decided to divide their dorm room by painting a line on the floor so that each will have the same amount of space. Phoebus's bed is against the north wall and his roommate's is against the south. The room is 12 feet long (north-south), 9 feet wide, and 8 feet high, but there's a 3' x 2' projection in the northeast corner corresponding to a utility closet in the hallway outside. The only free outlet for their refrigerator is also in Phoebus's territory, so the fridge is there too. This refrigerator is a perfect cube, 3 feet to a side. Its inner dimensions are 2'8" per side, and two-thirds of this storage space is allotted to Kevin, who isn't on the meal plan. The space inside the fridge counts toward their respective totals, but at Kevin's insistence the responsibility for the space occupied by the fridge itself (minus the space it encloses) is shared equally. Exactly how far from the north wall must

Phoebus and Kevin paint the line (assuming it to have no breadth) in order to give each roommate equal space?

The Big Book was written in 1992, or soon after I met Dank at an SF conference in Eureka, California (see THE ACADEMI- CIAN). The novel may have been inspired by the questions I was asking Dank back then, by phone and mail, about his childhood and youth, or perhaps by my account of a brief but recent and painful stint composing story problems for a maker of standard- ized tests (the only time *my* fiction has ever earned me a cent).

The result, in any case, is a brilliant *tour de force*: power- ful, original, and educational—and yet (or therefore) still un- published, like all of Dank's best novels. I still hope that that will change, though today (July 14, 2006) my hopes received a blow when I finally heard back from Tom Wainwright, my agent and formerly Dank's, a month after Fed-Exing him the manuscripts of the Magnificent Seven, as I like to think of the yet-unpublished novels on which Dank's lasting fame will finally rest. (Dank himself had never gotten around to send- ing them out—I think he still considered them unfinished, by some mysterious criterion, though in terms of polish they surpass the books he did send out.) As soon as I saw Tom's name in my inbox, I knew it was bad news: *good* comes by phone. Tom wrote that though he hasn't "had a chance to really read them yet" (!), his impression at first glance is that the seven manuscripts "aren't very good," and that *that's* why Dank never showed them to him. (And yet Tom the Inconsis- tent added that he *had* seen "one or two of them" already.) He said that if I wasn't in a hurry, he would "try to take a closer look at them" when he had time, "though that might not be for quite a while yet." I can't say his message leaves me feeling terribly optimistic as to the health of literature in our day. But our day will pass, and sooner or later the worthiest books get a hearing. Those seven novels *will* be published. A pity I may not be here to see it happen.*

Big Dick: A characteristically silly example of the dull subgenre that sci-fi fans insist on calling "*alternate* universe" fiction. The novel is set in a parallel world exactly like ours except that there is no Phoebus K. Dank. What they have instead is a stout, prolific, serially monogamous science fiction writer named Philip K. Dick. This Dick—a queasy compromise between the way Dank saw himself (already a comically grandiose misperception) and the way he wished he were—is one of the more implausible figments of Dank's imagination. Dick, indeed, is almost as implausible as the three-breasted stripper in PALS with the degree in particle physics (Dank's ideal woman?), or the armless and legless but telekinetic heavyweight-champion boxer in TOUGHIE. Dank asks us to believe, for instance, that a character modeled on himself could be a thriving womanizer, regularly trading in his latest young and pretty wife for another even newer. Dank also asks us to believe that this surrogate—this flawed reflection in a somewhat slimming fun-house mirror—is destined for belated recognition as the greatest sci-fi writer ever.

Since (or if, or insofar as) cosmology is a science, parallel-universe tales are a type of science fiction, so *Big Dick* (1996) can be

---

* Ugh. Not *another* suicide threat. Here's the only pep talk you're going to get from me, Bill (and if it's as empty as your threats, that serves you right): Chin up. We all have problems. I too sometimes grow weary of my post-Hemlock existence—the restaurants, the mistresses, the beaches, yachts, aperitifs. For the record, people kill themselves in Europe too. It's just that over here we don't cry wolf for years beforehand to everyone in earshot: We know that even if the *loup* is real, it isn't one that anybody can protect us from. (OH)

seen as a relapse into a genre Dank had renounced in 1993 after his third wife, Ms. Gabriella FEBRERO, left him for another author. In his own opinion, though, Dank had never *stopped* writing science fiction. His stories didn't always star a Martian, to be sure, but he thought of even the most "realistic" and most earthbound of his books as taking place, not here and now, but in some parallel universe where the imaginary people, places, and events were real. He once said, in fact, that he thought of *all* fiction that way, from Chaucer to Cheever (not that there's much evidence of his ever reading either), and had thought so ever since he first encountered the idea of parallel worlds, as an adolescent, in some pop-astronomy book. One reason he'd done no worse than he had in our high-school honors English class was that he'd found a way to transform the readings into true accounts of doings in other real worlds. "After all," he told me once, "the alternative is thinking that it's just a bunch of made-up lies." So much for Dank's philosophy of fiction.

In *Big Dick* (and, yes, that atrocious title alludes to one of the many daydream endowments Dank confers on his fictive counterpart), our Philosopher foregrounds the parallel-world tomfoolery. What makes it especially tomfoolish is that, though Dick himself is only loosely and wishfully modeled on Dank, his *world* is *identical* to ours. They have the same breakfast cereals, the same TV shows, the same politicians that we do. (Or that we did: In order to savor his counterpart's posthumous fame, Dank shifted the timeline a quarter-century backward, having Dick exit the womb in 1928 instead of 1952.) It could be argued that the sameness of their worlds shows humility on Dank's part, shows a lucid recognition that—unlike George Bailey, say—*he* had made no difference whatsoever in the scheme of things, and that it wouldn't have mattered a bit if he'd never been born, if some other fat and wacky sci-fi writer with the same initials had been born instead. We all know that one of the hazards of time travel is stepping on a prehistoric butterfly and thereby altering the course of history, but Dank may have sensed that he, for one, had made less of an impact on the scheme of things than any butterfly. Either that or else the novel's "parallel universe" gimmick is just an unusually lazy attempt to qualify for the Science Fiction label with one of those self-fertilizing novels about novelists that all card-carrying hacks try their hand at sooner or later. (OH)*

"The Block": A fortune-teller with honest-to-goodness psychic abilities loses them when a disgruntled client—a carver who can't think of anything to carve—bonks her on the head with a block of wood for telling him unwelcome truths about his future as an artist.

Dank insisted that the story was an allegory for the fate of honest writers in a world that just doesn't want to know the truth. Maybe so, but (as the title implies) the clouding over of the fortune-teller's crystal ball is—like the carver's failure to picture a sculpture inside his block of wood—first and foremost a metaphor for writer's block, a problem Dank complained of on occasion, always after reading some especially savage review of his fiction. (Chekhov: "Critics are like horseflies that prevent the horse from plowing.") Most of these kinks in the hose were easily fixed, and followed by a surge of pent-up creativity.† Now and then, though, a reviewer's enmity dovetailed so precisely with Dank's own insecurities as to make our author fear that he'd ever write again.

---

* For a more thoughtful and evenhanded discussion of this significant novel, see my entry on its protagonist, Philip K. DICK. (BB)

† Bad metaphor: It suggests a talent for waiting patiently that Dank completely lacked, along with all the other talents indispensable to writing well. Like a jogger running in place at a stoplight, Dank kept writing even when his inspiration failed. (OH)

Though "The Block" dates from 2001 (the height of Dank's brain-damage phobia), his worst case of writer's block occurred in 1998, when the uniformly bad reviews of THE LIFE PENALTY shut him down for several months. He tried everything he could think of to win back his ex-muse. He tried fasting, he tried binging. He tried sleep deprivation. He tried sense deprivation, floating for an hour every morning in his special tank (this was before installing the pool mentioned in my entry on AGORAPHOBIA). He took a brief vacation from caffeine in hopes of lowering his tolerance. He got back on AMPHETAMINES. He started chewing Nicorette—because he didn't like the smell of cigarettes—and wound up addicted to the stuff. He grew more and more frazzled and unhappy. He kept telling himself it was all grist for the mill (as he'd read somewhere that writers ought to tell themselves whenever they're unhappy), but as another Phoebus laments in James Russell Lowell's *Fable for Critics*:

> *What boots all your grist? It can never be ground*
> *Till a breeze makes the arms of the windmill go round*
> *(Or, if 'tis a water mill, alter the metaphor,*
> *And say it won't stir, save the wheel be wet afore) . . .*

So the grist piled up, and the miller sat and waited for a breeze. I'd glance into his study and find him sitting on the floor and playing glumly with his Star Wars action figures, making Chewbacca do something obscene to Princess Leia, or to Yoda, while Darth Vader awaited his turn. Or he'd be slumped in his recliner scowling at the laptop he had bought the month before in hopes that it would make his writing easier. So far it hadn't, despite all the selling points—so fast, so much memory, and so forth—enumerated on a sticker he left on the computer to remind him what a deal it had been.

No, his laptop had been jinxed a week after he bought it, when CompuTown offered a newer, faster one, with still more memory, for less than Dank had paid. Now he knew, he said, how the early Christians felt when the New Testament came out, after they'd spent their bottom dollar on a copy of the Old one.

Unable to make any headway on his fiction, Dank busied himself with other tasks: sharpening pencils, alphabetizing his bookshelves, cooking big batches of chili he then poured into old Cool Whip tubs and stuck in the freezer, and even catching up on his correspondence, since his writer's block didn't extend to that. One day he wrote, addressed, and stamped a dozen letters to his mother—a whole year's worth. Each alluded to the season when Dank planned to send it ("The days are getting longer"; "It's hotter than 'blazes' this summer"; "The days are getting shorter"), and was otherwise so vague in its "news" that when the time came to post it he could trust it to be, if not true, not too flagrantly false. Dank kept the postdated letters—neatly stacked in the order they were meant to be sent—on top of a teetering tower of books in his study. He'd sent only two, though, when Dookie toppled the tower and scrambled the letters—which Dank sent anyway, at random, one per month, hoping it wouldn't be August when his mother got the one about us building a snow fort in his back yard.

Boost: In a way, I'm to blame for this excruciating novel. At least Dank later claimed he got the "inspiration" (!) the day I told him—in a candid answer to his anxious question—that yes, as a matter of fact, he *was* "boring." Designed to prove that boring people have emotions too, the book begins when Schubert Pharmaceuticals develops a "mood-amplifying" drug called Boost and tests it on six members of its target market, the pathologically mild. Just as a sonic amplifier can make the faintest sounds not merely audible but earsplitting, so (we're solemnly informed) Boost turns up the volume of whatever faint stirrings of passion the clinically dispassionate can muster. The novel, or "novel," traces the adventures of each subject, lurching artlessly from storyline to storyline. One subject commits murder and her lawyer blames the drug. One quits his job as an accountant and starts painting lurid abstract expressionist canvases, but then goes back to accountancy once the trial ends and the pills run out. One commits suicide rather than revert to her old boring self. And so on. It must be admitted that Dank, writing about what he knows for a change, convincingly depicts the inner life of crashing bores. Too bad the book itself is such a crashing bore.*

Boost was Dank's first published novel. He feigned embarrassment that his debut was science fiction and not the "literary" fiction he was also doggedly trying to write and sell in that era. I remember the day (in September '75) when he received his author's copies and waddled over to my house (where he too had lived till recently; see DOG HOUSE) with a copy just for me—and a big dopey smile on his face, no doubt, though Dank took a moment to readjust his features before knocking, so as to present

---

* With all due respect (if any) to my fellow commentator, Dank himself was anything but "boring." Mild-mannered, if you like, but not unfeeling. On the contrary, he felt his life so vividly that what for most of us would be annoyances for him were real torments. But it is true that he was prone to moments when he knew he should be feeling something but he couldn't—when his sole emotion was embarrassment at not achieving any others. I remember him listening politely but with patent boredom to his cleaning lady's tearful account of her granddaughter's cancer, only to be moved to tears himself a few days later by an after-school special on the same subject, a child with cancer. I guess some people, like some objects (statues, grand pianos), can only be moved by professionals. (BB)

the would-be-nonchalant expression I encountered on opening the door. He held up the book for a second, rolled his eyes, and dropped it in the wastebasket we kept by the door for unwanted mail.

What to make of that ostentatious gesture? Granted the book deserves all the contempt it can get, why did Dank himself treat it so dismissively? Because it was sci-fi rather than hi-fi (to invent a fittingly crass and tacky name for his laughable idea of literary fiction)? Because it was a shoddy paperback original—tiny type, stingy margins, pulpy paper, lurid cover? (Not till 1988 did Dank persuade somebody to release one of his books—THE PAGEANT, of all things!—in cloth.) Because its publisher sold *only* sleaze and schlock, stuff like *Nympho Nuns in Outer Space* and *Randy Mann: Intergalactic Swinger*? Because they'd dared to change his original title (*The Call of the Mild*), as publishers would dare throughout poor Dank's "career," as if his Novels were so many soulless products to brand and package as they pleased, and not high-minded Works of Art? Because, in a rare moment of good taste, he'd seen his book for what it was? We'll never know. I do know that a few days later, on his next visit, the first thing Dank did on arrival was to glance into that wastebasket, and when he saw his Novel exactly where he'd tossed it, he sulked for several weeks, like someone who makes an insincerely self-derogatory comment and then gets offended when you don't contradict him. Come to think of it, Dank used to do that too. (OH)

"Boswell the Burglar": An unauthorized biographer breaks into his reclusive subject's house and steals every single curtain, blind, and window shade—and nothing else.

My biography of Dank (see DANK!) was fully authorized, and far from needing to break into his house, or peer in through the windows, I had the run of the place. That isn't to deny that Dank, in giving the obsessive, overcurious biographer my surname, was laughing at me and my own sometimes overweening curiosity. Of course he was, and with my full collusion. It was I, in fact, who suggested making the burglar a biographer and giving him my surname: Initially the character was based on Dank himself and was not an overzealous scholar but a lovelorn stalker. The occasion of the story was Dank's passion for young TAMMI (the supermarket checker who gets an entry in this guide though our author never knew her surname), his curiosity about the life she led in her apartment when off-duty, and the extremes to which that curiosity drove him.

Though he never went so far as to break into her apartment, in April 1990 he rented one in the building opposite, and for several weeks he sat there at his window every evening, after dark, in the dark, with his telescope. I hasten to say that even though Dank's attraction to Tammi was frankly sexual, his voyeurism wasn't. From his rented lookout he could survey neither her bedroom nor her bathroom, just her living room and kitchen. But he could see her TV screen and watch with her, over her shoulder, while his own set provided the soundtrack. He could see which CDs she picked to listen to, and since he'd made a point of buying copies of them too, he could listen along with her. (Tammi, like all supermarket checkers maybe, liked soft rock—less of a stretch for Dank than the punk rock favored by another, later, even sadder passion, the unspeakable Pandora LANDOR.) He could read the memos on the little board suction-cupped to Tammi's refrigerator door ("BUY TAB"; "CALL SIMON"—and if there was anything Dank hated more than Tab, it was Simon, whoever Simon was), and when she opened that door he could see what she was eating. For a while he made a point of buying the same groceries she did—veggie burgers, baby carrots, diet TV dinners, cottage cheese, and even Tab.) He could see her answering machine, and though of course he couldn't listen to her messages, he could tell by the red indicator light whether or not she had any. Dank had no phone in the apartment, but sometimes when Tammi was out he'd go down to the pay-phone at the corner, call her number, and hang up as soon as he had activated the machine, just to see the blinking light when he got back upstairs, and know he'd made a difference, from a distance, in Tammi's surroundings.

But sometimes she would close her shades (hence his fantasy of stealing them, like the burglar in the story), and after a month she moved out, maybe to move in with Simon, and Dank was stuck with the remainder of a one-year lease on an apartment he had no use for. And he was afraid to break the no-sublet clause, so for the next eleven months he paid rent on an empty apartment. Now and then he went and sat there for an hour, no longer looking out the window (he had no interest in Tammi's successor), but just sitting in the chair he'd left there, in an otherwise bare room, since it seemed too sad to pay rent on the apartment and not use it at *all*.

Though I don't approve of violating people's privacy, I myself am not immune to fits of overwhelming curiosity about the insides of my neighbors' homes, as I was forced to admit to myself the morning I snuck into Hirt's by way of the tunnel connecting his basement to Dank's (see THE MYSTERY). The tunnel itself I'd already explored the day Dank showed it to me, but that time I'd turned around, with difficulty, on reaching the hinged wooden flap—it looked like a big pet door—at the far end. One rainy day in April 1999, though, a few days after my infuriating first visit to Hirt's house (see PASS THE BRAINS), I was emboldened by the sight of him loading a suit-case into his car and driving away, and I decided to sneak in.

Actually, I think I was counting on the door at his end of the tunnel being locked or blockaded. I was more alarmed than pleased when the little door swung open to a rat's-eye view of Hirt's tool room. Still, I crawled out, stood up, and took a look around.

What was I looking for? Anything: a Fleetwood Mac album, a package of hair dye, a jar of Miracle Whip or carton of Hamburger Helper, a subscription to *Writer's Digest*, a telltale URL on his computer (www.hotgrannies.edu? www.peefun. gov?), a complete collection of *He-Man* action figures still in their original boxes—something, in other words, to convince me that Hirt was as fallible, and laughable, as everybody else. We tend to be intimidated by our equals, and sometimes even our inferiors, because we are relentlessly aware of our own weaknesses but only now and then catch sight of theirs. And what goes for minds is just as true of diaries, attics, medicine cabinets: We are only too conscious of everything embarrassing or compromising in our own, but seldom have the chance to rifle our neighbors' in search of *their* shameful secrets.

By now my fellow commentator is purple with rage, I imagine. But don't worry, Hirt—I'm not going to tell our readers about any of the various embarrassments I did find. (I can't resist revealing—sorry, Owen!—that the list included at least one, and maybe more, of the sample embarrassments listed above. But I won't say which.) Hirt, in any case, must see that I was paying him a compliment by sneaking into his house in search of a chink in his armor. I wouldn't have bothered if I hadn't been a bit in awe of him—and an aging, unsuccessful, lonely poet* needs all the awe he can get, in whatever form it takes. Aside from Dank, who'd been imprinted on him at a tender age, I was probably the first person in decades to pay

---

* Since I'm not paid for these footnotes, only for actual entries, and since I don't care what Boswell—or, for that matter, the reader—thinks of me, I can't be bothered to respond to my collaborator's slanders, though, of course, I don't concede them either. (OH)

Hirt the compliment of envy, and all because I'm easily impressed by people who seem to despise me.

Not that all I did was poke around in search of secrets. I also
got the feel of the house, as if that would tell me how it felt to
be its owner. In the living room I reclined in Hirt's recliner—
not as deep or relaxing as Dank's—and thumbed through the
latest issue of *Quotient*, a publication of the high-IQ society
to which Hirt evidently belonged. I went into the kitchen (in
whose cupboards food and liquor mingled freely—a bottle of
vermouth between a jar of peanut butter and a box of cereal;
a mob of canned goods milling around a fifth of scotch) and
made and ate two pieces of dry toast, and washed them down
with a small bottle of imported water. Wow, *classy*. Upstairs, I
urinated, and considered dipping Hirt's electric toothbrush in
the toilet. The air in the neglected poet's bedroom was stuffy
and stale, and a squeamishness prevented me from lying on his
unmade bed, though I sat down heavily on its edge to try its
springs. I tried on one of his Armani blazers: It fit passably,
but made me look like I was Dressing for Success, a ploy that
clearly hadn't worked for the poet who owned it.

I still hadn't seen a study, by the way, or any other evidence that Hirt was still writing, and after almost two hours I
headed back down to the basement, resigned to leaving without gaining access to that innermost sanctum. Probably he
had a laptop in his suitcase. As I was about to duck back into
the tunnel, though, something prompted me to investigate
the laundry room, which earlier I'd been content to glimpse in
passing from its doorway. And there, sure enough, was Hirt's
computer, at a little desk beyond the dryer and the washer, up
against the same windowless cinderblock wall as those other
appliances, as if writing were just the first step of a three-stage
process that subsequently laundered and tumble-dried the
cling-free, lightly scented fabric of Hirt's poetry. The com-

puter was just hibernating—some people leave them on all the time, like refrigerators or clocks—and woke up when I hit ENTER. I found myself looking at page 43 (of 480) of one of Hirt's fine readables—a novel, to judge by its length and by the texture of the page in front of me:

> . . . perfect breasts, and even if she wasn't quite as bright as Anna, she made up in tact what she lacked in quickness. More than once that afternoon she'd responded to one of his more subtle witticisms with polite laughter that suddenly became the real thing when she finally got the joke. Rowan, anyhow, could always read a book when it was *intelligence* he wanted. . . .

This is not the place to enumerate the reasons why I hated Hirt so much by April 1999 (as if Hirt's native hatefulness weren't already evident in every sentence he writes), much less to describe the acts to which that hatred later drove me. But I will mention *one* reason: Dank had told me that the Bard of Hemlock was taking a break from poesy ("From reveries so airy, from the toil/Of dropping buckets into empty wells/And growing old in drawing nothing up"—William Cowper) to write a novel. And the novel, according to Dank, featured a portrait of me. No doubt an unflattering portrait. I hit Ctrl+F and searched for my forename, my surname, my nicknames, my initials, but Hirt had encrypted me better than that. Or maybe there were other novels in his computer, but—according to its clock—I was already late for the faculty meeting I'd been rebuked for missing completely the previous week. Ewan MacDougal, the head of my department, had been rebuking me a lot of late because he hated Dank, and hated me for liking Dank. Before getting up from the computer, though, and heading back into the secret tunnel I would come to know so well in a later chapter of my life (and Hirt's!)—the chapter culminating in Dank's assassination—I hit Ctrl+H and replaced every instance of "subtle" (thirty-eight in all) with "heavy-handed."

"Brain Damage": A "top philosopher" has spent a decade working on "a monumental book" about appearance and reality. When finished, it will be "one of the hardest books ever written," or so Dank solemnly assures us, in his customary knock-kneed and flat-footed prose:

> With a hearty chuckle, Brennschluss pondered the ironical fact that the more time he spent on his monumental treatise, making it even better, the less readers there would be that could appreciate the final product when it was done. Not that he ever expected to write a "bestseller," naturally! But it made him wanly smile to reflect that there were less than fifty people, probably, in the entire galaxy that could comprehend the subtle complexities of his complicated thesis—and the more he "polished" it, the harder it kept on getting. Yes, it was time to "wrap it up" and send it to the publisher.

Before he has a chance to do that, though, the philosopher incurs "extremely mild brain damage, not even one IQ point" by shaking his head too vehemently during "a high-powered intellectual debate with another leading thinker"—and spends the rest of his life attempting to complete a book he no longer understands.

With its neo-Jamesian quotation marks and its perfect pitch for the awkward turn of phrase, the story is one of the funniest Dank ever wrote, though the humor was not intentional. (Dank's *attempts* at humor are painfully *un*funny.) In any case, intelligence was no laughing matter for him, any more than height is for a midget. When a witless man insists on living by his wits, his fear of getting even dumber can be almost touching, like a bag lady's rabid solicitude toward the contents of her shopping cart.

Once, in the era when we shared a house with several other young "creative" types, Dank took an IQ test, watched TV for sixteen hours straight, and then took another IQ test, all to refute a roommate's claim that TV makes you stupid. To Dank's dismay, his IQ fell by seven points (and he hadn't done all that well on the *first* test). He blamed the difference on exhaustion and lumbered up to his bedroom. The next day, though, he took the test *again*, now fully rested, and this time he did even worse: *eleven* points lower than his middling original figure. After that, for several years, Dank refused to watch TV at all, though until then he'd been the house's most devoted viewer. He campaigned to have the TV set evicted, or banished to the basement. We refused, and Dank had to content himself with avoiding the living room when the set was on, averting his face when he had to pass through on his infrequent trips outdoors. It was right around then that he developed his lifelong fear of damaging his brain—a fear so obsessive (and so *excessive*, when you consider how little he had to lose) that Dank couldn't bump his forehead on a door jamb without fretting that his IQ had just dropped a tenth of a point. One night in that same era he shook his head so hard, to waken himself from a nightmare, that for the next week he walked around as gingerly as if bearing a jug on that head, and—though he didn't dare to take another test—finding introspective evidence of brain damage in every thought he succeeded in thinking. (OH)

A B C D E F

G H I J K L

M N O P Q R

S T U V W X

Y Z

"The Camera": Sick of buying batteries for his power-draining digital camera, a Sunday inventor (during the week, he's a particle physicist) builds himself a special camera with a tiny nuclear reactor, guaranteeing an inexhaustible power source. The camera works, but it produces images that differ from their originals in bewildering ways. The first picture, a self-portrait, shows the clean-shaven inventor sporting a big bushy beard, of the sort he hasn't worn since graduate school. (Since I moved to Portland, I've been growing one myself, from sheer demoralization: In a town where there's nothing to live for, there's certainly nothing to *shave* for.) After fiddling with the lens, he takes another picture of himself: This time his image is beardless, all right, but it's also nearly bald, though in reality the inventor still has all his hair. Gradually it dawns on him that his new nuclear camera is capable of taking pictures of the past and future. The climax of the story involves his efforts to avert the future foretold by one especially gruesome snapshot, a snapshot of his wife and daughters as dismembered corpses on the living room floor, rather than a smiling trio on the living room sofa.

As for *how* the camera takes its pictures of the past and future, Dank has an impressive if imperfectly convincing paragraph about its nuclear flashbulb, which instead of generating photons seems to be shooting out tachyons, those hypothetical faster-than-light particles so beloved of science fiction writers. Dank relies, in other words (as SF writers are allowed to), on the average reader's inability, where modern physics is concerned, to tell the difference between true and pseudo-science. And since writers also must suspend their disbelief in order for fiction to happen, it can't have hurt that cameras as such were magical to Dank. (And they *are* magical, those microtomes we use so matter-of-factly to prepare wafer-thin slices of time for protracted inspection.) All his life, Dank was as dazzled by photography as some aborigine watching his first Polaroid develop. Once, in the course of an infuriating argument, I failed to persuade him that no earthly technology existed, or could ever exist, to resolve a blurry photograph into a sharply focused one. Dank contended that "as long as you still have the negative," you (or rather "they") could take a blurry snapshot—one of his father reading the newspaper, say—and enhance it to the point where you could read the articles on the side facing you. Dank went even further, speculating that it would be possible one day—"when computers get stronger"—to turn corners in snapshots, as in video-games, so that Dank could read the *other* side of the paper—the side his *father* was reading—over his father's shoulder.

For a science fiction writer, Dank didn't always seem to know much science—to have much of a sense of how the world works at present, to say nothing of its future. Once he insisted that if only the cap on his Thermos could be screwed on "tight enough," the coffee inside would never cool down, "not even in a thousand years." But perhaps it isn't fair to expect a writer with so much imagination to be as well-endowed with common sense, for the same reason that few high-jumpers moonlight as sumo wrestlers, or vice versa: different excellences can be mutually exclusive. Dank's endearing and childlike vagueness as to the limits of the possible—to say nothing of the probable—was precisely what enabled him in his fiction to take such liberties with reality, to mold it as easily as Play-Doh, while other novelists must set their chisels to the cold hard marble of reality seen realistically.

The tradeoff was that Dank lacked the reassurances of a commonsensical worldview. He lived in a strange and terrifying universe where (depending on his current theory) his microwave oven could either make him sterile or enhance his creativity, and where he couldn't step outside without braving death rays, tractor beams, and killer bees. But he was safe as long as he stayed in his study. One reason he was so prolific is that he was afraid to leave his desk.

Chat Rooms: For about a year or two near the end of his life, Dank was addicted to Internet chat rooms. Like the rest of us, he was intrigued by the anonymity of e-communication—by the boundless possibilities for self-misrepresentation. He used to say that if they ever remade *The Wizard of Oz*, they'd have to change the title character's most famous line to "Pay no attention to that man at the computer." Lying about his weight, his height, his age, and now and then even his gender, Dank reinvented himself every time he went online. Sometimes he'd pretend to be one of his characters—the sadistic soccer mom from LAUGHING MATTER, for example, or the title character from ADAM ABLE, ASTRONAUT. But far from neglecting his writing to gossip all night with invisible strangers, he was (he said) using his e-chats to refine his characters, to perfect their voices and learn new things about them and their ways of relating to others. And maybe he was, though none of what he learned thereby was shared with his readers, since with the exception of a few short stories and the novel prompted by his father's death, Dank by then had pretty much retired from the writing racket.

In any case, his favorite online persona was not a character but one of his own alter egos, Steve Rockhard, the two-fisted author of some of Dank's early pseudonymous fiction. Dank told me once that from the age of fourteen he'd fantasized about being Steve Rockhard, and that he still lulled himself to sleep, some nights, with that fantasy. Even after all these years, though, he sometimes forgot Steve's vital statistics, and since a good impostor has to keep his story straight, Dank, for the duration of his chat-room addiction, kept a cheat sheet taped to the side of his computer to remind him of those stats. In reproducing that sheet for the curious, I've added Dank's own stats for comparison:

	Rockhard	Dank
Gender:	hyper-male	male
Age:	34	51
Profession:	astronaut/ex-Green Beret/writer	writer
Height:	6'3"	5'7"
Weight:	198	331
Body type:	mesomorph	endomorph
Eyes:	steely blue	brown
Marital status:	single; women find him irresistible	divorced
Drink:	straight whiskey	domestic beer
Ambition:	to set foot on Mars	to write a bestseller
Distinguishing marks:	square jaw; five-o'clock shadow; washboard abs	double chin; eyeglasses; appendectomy scar

Clothing: Since his writing betrays in every sentence an astounding lack of style, it should come as no surprise that Dank was not a snappy dresser. He went surprisingly far, though, in his indifference to public opinion, for an author whose *books* were so many more-or-less inept attempts to *cater* to public opinion. Back in the days before he concocted his official PUBLIC IMAGE (a laughably inadequate stab at no-bullshit machismo), it wasn't so unusual to see Dank mowing his back lawn in nothing but his Jockey shorts and a pair of fuzzy pink slippers* clearly meant for the opposite sex. One hot summer day I saw him at the public library in safety goggles and a heavy hooded parka: He was about to photocopy a mirror, to see what would happen, and he wasn't ruling out an explosion.

His dowdiness, if that's the word, was exacerbated by the fact that Dank was always getting fatter; he outgrew a pair of pants, for instance, long before he wore them out. To wear a favorite pair for longer than a year, he had to undo the button, unzip the zipper, and loosen his belt (in a way that may remind the reader of various unseemly slackenings in our author's garish, gaudy, badly tailored novels), adding inches to his waist's sphere of activity and exposing an expanse of yellowed underwear. He did this even before the pants in question got really tight—to one accustomed to the joys of looseness, evidently, even snugness is experienced as pain—and not just around the house, but at the supermarket and for most other errands. In 1998 he switched to sweatpants, and in 1999 to pajamas for round-the-house use and for all but the dressiest public occasions. He routinely wore them to Food Planet, though as a rule his pajama bottoms fit so loosely that if

---

* I remember those slippers, and the day Dank bought them at the Dollar Store on Main Street because they were the only ones his size. There's a snapshot dating from his second marriage that shows Dank at the kitchen sink, washing dishes in a frilly pink apron that must have belonged to his wife. Though now and then the tight-lipped, square-jawed, hard-assed hero of his non-canonical "Steve Rockhard" books hauls off and slugs a broad for asking him to launder her undies or pick up some Tampax, Dank himself had no such phobia about feminization, perhaps because he—unlike Steve Rockhard?—was secure about his sexuality. (BB)

he bent over with his back to you, you were treated to the sight of the dim cleft between his massive buttocks. (Fat as he already was, he kept getting fatter, and with the foresight of a frugal parent made a point, on his yearly visit to the Big Boy's shop on Main Street, of buying clothes he could grow into.) When he did wear real pants, he wore them, too, so low that, given his lifelong obsession with big-breasted women, it was hard not to suspect him of cleavage envy. No wonder I preferred not to be seen with him in public.

The only time he dressed more carefully was for his beloved sci-fi conventions. If he was the guest of honor, he'd squeeze himself into a three-piece suit of some hideous color like marmalade or mustard. If not, he went in a space suit. Science fiction fans, though seldom noted for their fashion sense, do like to get dressed up, as I discovered the time I let Dank drag me to something called a Worldcon, a convergence of nerds from all over the planet. The fashion statements I witnessed that day, in that Hilton, were much louder and more urgent than the pair of pointy plastic Vulcan ears Dank bought me so that (he said) I'd "fit in." Needless to say, I didn't wear them (the only fashion statement *I* made that day was "No comment"), but I must have stuck out more *without* the ears, in that saturnalia of Darth Vaders, semi-nude space hussies, and loin-clothed barbarians. Among so many primal screams, even Dank's astronaut getup amounted to no more than a genteel clearing of the throat.

On a recent jaunt to London to be fitted for a dinner jacket, I reflected on the similarities between a good sentence and a good suit. Neither can exist without both taste and patience—the taste to know and care what a good suit or sentence looks like, and the patience to measure and sew as if the fate of Man depended on the outcome. With your clothes, of course, you can pay someone else to be patient for you (and it's no coincidence that tailors as a class are the only artisans as irritable as writers). Still, if your sentences are as rumpled, ill-cut, and ill-fitting as Dank's, chances are your wardrobe too will be a mess of solecisms, barbarisms, catchwords, diction shifts, clichés, ignoble slang, and malaprops. (OH)

Coffee Town: A coffee house on Democritus Street, right around the block from our house. Coffee Town was a home away from home for Dank, who went there every Tuesday for the weekly meeting of the MELVILLE BROTHERHOOD, and went with me on evenings when he didn't feel like writing. We also went there every Friday afternoon after our weekly trip to Hemlock Books-n-Such, the better-than-nothing bookshop next door to the coffee house. And sometimes I went alone to work on my own fiction: Though I felt a little pretentious writing in public, it's easier to court the muse when you're among so many other people pursuing the life of the mind, just as it's easier to proposition someone when you're in a singles bar, in the midst of so much other recklessness and lust. (Needless to say, there's no counterpart to Coffee Town in the soulless suburb where I'm living now.) Even Owen Hirt sometimes staked out a corner table, in his glowering pursuit of "Choice word and measured phrase, above the reach/Of ordinary men," though his muse preferred whiskey to coffee.

It was at Coffee Town, by the way, that Dank introduced me to Hirt, on a chilly afternoon in November 1991, on my first visit to Hemlock. I'd like to say I despised and pitied the poet the moment I met him—and in fact that's what this sentence used to say—but just now I'm feeling candid to a fault, so I'll admit that I was as dazzled by him at first as Dank was to the last. Hirt wore expensive custom-tailored London suits, and his speech was bejeweled with German, French, and Latin words that always sounded as though he was saying them right. I should have realized at once that the imported words and clothes were the consolation prizes of artistic failure, but it took me surprisingly long to see through Hirt, especially since he made no effort to ingratiate himself with me. That first day at Coffee Town he ignored me the whole time, and somehow managed to imply that though he found Dank himself barely worth talking to, he found *me* so much *less* so that by comparison his indifference to Dank felt like enthrallment. At one point, the third or fourth time he refused to acknowledge a comment I'd addressed specifically to him, I pictured myself punching Hirt in the nose, as if to say "Ignore me now!" I don't mean I had an *impulse* to hit him, just a vivid image of how satisfying it would feel. In retrospect, that flicker of violent aversion strikes me as ominous, as if my whole dismal history with Hirt could have been predicted at that point. But in fact it wasn't until I moved to Hemlock that I really came to hate him.

"The Collaboration": Tad and Tod, identical twins, decide it's too much trouble to maintain separate identities and lifestyles, so they take advantage of their identicality to pretend to be just one person, Ted. By pooling their efforts, they are able to project the illusion of a single omnicompetent and indefatigable overachiever, with a single high-paying but highly draining job, a single stunning but high-maintenance girlfriend, and so on. Some days Tad goes to the office and some days Tod. Some nights Tod romances their unsuspecting girlfriend and some nights Tad. (We're told that the brothers' elaborate imposture started in college, when it became clear that despite the same genes, they had different strengths academically: together they formed an A student, though either alone would have been hard-pressed to maintain a B average.) Though "Ted" is a workaholic, his component twins are both pretty lazy, and while one is active, the other naps or watches TV, except at those times when an ordinary person might wish to be in two places at once—at which times the extraordinary Ted can do just that.

If the story sounds absurd, that's not an accident: The twins' impossible "collaboration" is a metaphor for Dank's no-less-unlikely collaboration with Hirt on a murder mystery they had planned to sign "P. K. D. Owens." That project was an act of charity on Dank's part—a way to initiate his poet friend into the well-paying art of genre fiction—but as usual where Hirt was concerned, Dank was repaid for his kindness with scorn. Hirt was willing to hear Dank's advice on mystery-writing, but not to hide his contempt of Dank for having mastered that lowly genre in the first place. Hirt insisted, naturally, on making *their* mystery artier, tricking it out with pretentious stream-of-conscious interludes, silly "existential" non-events, pointless disruptions of chronological order, and the reddest of red herrings—objects (an abandoned Buick, a torn-and-mended photograph) and incidents (a pigeon's odd behavior, a drunken beggar's death) described in so much detail as to assure the reader that they must be crucial clues, when in fact their only function is to symbolize whatever Hirt the Thinker thought he had to "say." Thanks to Hirt's ambivalence about the mystery genre, and to his repeated overriding of his friend's much sounder storytelling instincts, the final product, *Weltschmerz* (!), is an unreadable hybrid of honest lowbrow page-turner and brainy highbrow head-scratcher. And as fond as my co-commentator is of finding fault with Dank's own prose, the prose of *Weltschmerz* balks and falters, lunges and lurches and stumbles and staggers, in a way Dank's solo writings never do. When your Standards are as high as Hirt's, I guess, lowering them from one book to the next must be as hard as running down a tall steep hill.

The history of their doomed collaboration was one reason for my reluctance to team up with Hirt on this encyclopedia. Another reason was the recent trauma of my "interviews" with Hirt in the beginning of 2006, when instead of answering my inquiries about his oldest (if not only) friend, the sullen drunken poet just baited and insulted me. An even better reason (and one to keep in mind while reading his opinions): *Hirt killed Dank.*

A lurid murder trial might have resurrected Hirt's career— might at least have prompted some disreputable publisher to dredge up one or two of his books, each of which had sunk without a trace after a single printing—but their author didn't stick around to find out, vanishing without a trace himself the night Dank was killed.

But then, one rainy day about a week later, as I was surfing the World Wide Web from my rented hovel in suburban Portland, I received an e-mail from the fugitive. I'd left Hemlock partly out of fear that I'd be his next victim, but I hadn't thought to change my e-mail address. Hirt more or less admitted to the murder, blaming his "recent behavior" on a head injury, though he didn't have enough confidence in that defense to come out of hiding, or even to tell me where and how he was living. I gathered that he'd fled the country and assumed an incognito. I also gathered that he'd written me (in one those sans-serif fonts so popular among the class of bullshitters who cultivate a plainspoken no-bullshit image) only because he'd somehow ascertained that Dank hadn't changed his will since their big falling out in November 1999. In other words, the document still stipulated, as it had since 1998 (when the *memento mori* of a second heart attack persuaded Dank to draw up a will in the first place), that if Hirt outlived Dank, Dank's estate would pay him to write a guide to all things Dankian—pay him enough that the money itself might have served as a motive for murder.

It was sickening to think of Dank's own money paying his assassin to write a book about him, especially when I knew that the book too would be murderous. By that point I had started work, *pro bono*, on a reader's guide myself, figuring Hirt was out of the picture. And wasn't he? Though perhaps still technically entitled to the job, he was not in a position to enforce his claim. Actually he didn't want to write the book all by himself. What he proposed was that we split the job, and split the payoff.

At first I rejected that idea as absurd—as if I'd collaborate with my best friend's killer! No, I wouldn't even acknowledge his message, though I did forward it to the Hemlock police, who like everyone else these days are online. The detective who responded told me that they had no way to trace the message, but that I should let them know if I heard from Hirt again. That seemed unlikely, since my first reaction to Hirt's unwelcome epistle had been to click the little box that said "block sender."

The more I thought about his odd proposal, though, the more it tempted me. I was just then realizing what a Herculean task I'd let myself in for: rereading and discussing everything Dank ever wrote. The prospect of sharing the labor was certainly appealing, especially as Hirt had offered to focus on Dank's less triumphant works, leaving me to sing the praises of the greatest. What's more, for all his prize-winning neglect, Hirt was at least a little better known than I am in the world of letters, and "all publicity is good publicity." After a night of thinking it over, I lifted the embargo on his messages and took him up on his offer after all,* but only on condition that

---

* (October 2007) I would never have teamed up with Hirt if he hadn't happened to e-mail me at a point when I was crazed by loneliness: I'd just lost my best friend, and had no friends in Portland. Though I'd hated Hirt for years, at least he was a

his initials appear after each of his entries: No way was *I* taking the blame for the sentiments I knew those entries would express.

I warned Hirt at the onset that if I learned anything about his whereabouts I'd pass it on to the police. He said he'd take his chances. As for *his* conditions, they forbid me to delete or change a single word of his, though they do allow me to object, in footnotes, to his more outrageous misstatements—a compromise that I accepted with misgivings, since it also means that he gets to footnote *my* entries. And since of course I can't point out *everything* unfair to Dank, readers may assume that I endorse those libels to which I don't object at the bottom of the page. So I'll say once and for all that I object to *all* Hirt's cavils, quips, and quibbles—to quibbling in general. Quibbling is for pipsqueaks. When all is said and done, the fact remains that Dank is a colossus and towers over his critics, hostile and friendly alike. There are really only two attitudes for us to take toward him: that of terrified Lilliputians shooting tiny arrows at a fallen Gulliver, or that of Tom Thumb gratefully hitching a ride in a friendly giant's pocket.

Come, Sweet Death: Over the years, Dank wrote a series of slightly futuristic thrillers about an FBI profiler, Agent Bronson Harder, who tracks down serial killers. Dank shared Agent Harder's fascination with the criminal mind, though like most writers of crime fiction, Dank himself was law-abiding to a

---

link to Hemlock, a town for which I was already terminally homesick. Our attitudes toward Dank were diametrically opposed, but at least Hirt had an attitude. (The few people in Portland to whom I'd mentioned my author had just looked at me blankly.) I was desperate, in a word—desperate enough to need Owen Hirt, though I kept reminding myself that he was the one to blame for my desperation. Idea for story: Lonely man befriends his best friend's killer.

fault (notwithstanding several arrests for various endearing misdemeanors). Once, in the course of an after-dinner stroll, he stood for half an hour waiting for a light to change before a cop in a passing police car—dispatched for the purpose?—told him it was stuck on red.

In *Come, Sweet Death*, which dates from 1998, Agent Harder must explain the murders of a dozen men, from as many walks of life, who seem to have nothing in common but a penchant for goatees and sweater vests. In the end, Harder discovers that what *look* like murders were in fact suicides: the "victims" were all members of a secret death cult. For various reasons they wanted to die, but—to spare their families, or for insurance purposes—didn't want their suicides to be recognized as such. And so they not only made sure their deaths would look like murders, carefully avoiding any evidence of suicide, but even framed a nonexistent serial killer, leaving clues that had detectives hunting for a tall, left-handed white male in his thirties, one who drove a windowless red minivan, favored defenestration as his M.O., and bore a pathological grudge against men with goatees and sweater vests. In the months before their "murders," the members of the death cult made a point of sporting sweater vests and pointy beards—just as Dank's enemy MacDougal did, for reasons of his own, in real life. As far as I'm aware, though, MacDougal's vests weren't woven out of spider silk—which, as recently as 1998, Dank predicted as the leading "fashion" fiber of 2006.

The first Agent Harder novel, NEVER MIND ME, was set in what was then the present, 1979. Soon, though, it occurred to Dank to broaden his fan base by relocating Agent Harder to the future, thus enabling publishers to cross-market Dank's crime novels as SF. There have been countless definitions of that genre (my favorite is the one pronounced by John Campbell, founding editor of *Astounding*: "Science fiction stories are whatever science fiction editors buy"), but Dank felt that any story set in the future fit the bill. So he set the last four Agent Harder novels in the future, but such a *near* future— five or ten years down the line—that even if we grant futurity itself as sufficient grounds for the SF label, most of the Agent Harder novels have by now reverted to "mundane" or mainstream fiction, since (as with *1984*) their futures are behind us. And other than postdating them like checks the real world wasn't quite ready to cover, Dank did very little to futurize Harder's surroundings: a cyborg here, a ray gun there, a few coinages like "serkil" (short for "serial killer") and "foocaps" (food capsules, the favorite meal of hard-driving FBI agents in 2006, again according to Dank in 1998). And even those few touches seem a little grudging: The Agent Harder novels were written as vacations from the rigors of full-throttle science fiction.

Soon after *Come, Sweet Death* was published, Dank became convinced that a certain Hollywood thriller (here to remain nameless, lest we revive the studio's indignant legal threats) was a "total rip-off" of his novel, though as far as I could tell the movie was a standard serial-killer shocker, with no sweater vests, no goatees, and nothing like the book's inspired twist. But—to list the highlights of Dank's case for plagiarism, a long litany of damning parallels and overlaps he cited and recited heatedly to anyone who'd listen, even stopping perfect strangers on the street as if he were the Ancient Mariner—both book and movie do begin with the discovery of a murder victim; both assign a gruff, no-bullshit cop to the case (if Agent Harder can be deemed a "cop"); both develop a love interest between that cop and a gutsy young female cop; both have a scene where the cops must no-comment their way through a mob of pushy reporters; both involve windowless minivans; both have a tearful corpse-recognition scene in a morgue; both have a cop wondering what kind of crazy sonofabitch would kill all those innocent people; both bring in a psychiatric expert to answer that question; both experts attribute the malefactor's crimes to his childhood; both narratives have a suspenseful scene near the end where the gruff cop saves the cute one from the bad guy in the nick of time; both leave open the possibility of a sequel; and both appeared the same year. To those who know how long it takes to turn a book into a movie, that last circumstance alone might seem to rule out plagiarism—except that *his* book, Dank was quick to point out, had knocked around in manuscript for several years before publication.

Though not himself suicidal when he wrote *Come, Sweet Death*, Dank never found it hard to think of reasons for dying. No more than I do. Today's: the gray and rainy Portland weather, the impossibility of moving back to Hemlock, the knowledge that I'll never find another friend like Dank.

Conference Call: Dank's one foray into playwriting is a futuristic radio drama described by one reviewer as "an interplanetary comedy of manners." Somehow inspired, I think, by his phone-sex misadventures, the drama consists of a long-distance chat among space colonists whose outposts are so far apart that an outrageous delay intervenes between any remark and any reply. And since the far-flung characters are stuck at different distances from one another, there is a *different* transmission delay—thirty seconds, or five minutes, or fifteen—between each pair of speakers. Thirty seconds elapse between the instant when A says "I like bacon" and the instant when B hears it (and, yes, "instant" is a problematic concept in case of distances so great the speed of light seems sluggish), but five whole minutes elapse before C hears A's avowal, and by that point B has already replied, said what *she* likes, and sent the conversation in a whole new direction. To say nothing of poor D who, fifteen minutes from A and almost as far from the others, never hears a question, outburst, joke, confession, boast, or flirtation until the talk has moved on, has changed its subject, and the other speakers have long ago forgotten the words that have finally reached D. This being the future, the phones transmit live images as well as words, but of course the images too are long out of date by the time they arrive, like the images of distant stars.

The Consequences: Begun the day Dank's first wife announced her pregnancy—forcing his friends to imagine the two having sex—this unedifying novel features a man who discovers an odd correlation between his behavior and events in a stranger's house a block away. As with some of Dank's other "magical" premises, the book begins by showing how a sane and sensible protagonist (insofar as Dank could picture sensibility or sanity) gradually becomes convinced of the magic in question. Once he *is* convinced, he can no longer budge without considering the consequences for the strangers, a single mother and her infant twins, since an act as trivial as scratching his nose could cause her to get mugged or them to die of SIDS. We're not told how the hero manages to care so much about three strangers who leave the reader indifferent. Sheer heroism, maybe.

The Consequences expresses its author's two most pressing concerns at the time: the problem of living with someone who was either pleased or, much more often (we're speaking of the shrewish Jessica TELLER), annoyed by everything he did, so that he couldn't lift a finger without anticipating her reaction; and the problem of impending parenthood. Anxious for more money like all expecting fathers, Dank produced *The Consequences* in less than a month, or before the stillbirth of his baby put an end to one of his pressing concerns and then, with the divorce the baby was going to avert, to the other. But maybe Boswell should have written this entry, since, bad as it is, *The Consequences* may have been the high point of poor Dank's career, the least horrible novel in his *oeuvre*, both because it's the shortest and because of a rare relaxation of whatever mental muscles were to blame for the strenuous badness of Dank's other, riper, ranker books. There's nothing memorably *right* about *The Consequences*, but it lacks the laborious wrongness that is the hallmark of Dank's prose—the hard-won infelicities, the effortful ineptitude, the frantic flapping of a flightless bird that hasn't faced the fact. From then on it was all downhill: His books got worse and worse (or, as Boswell would probably say, with his knack for putting a positive spin on a damaging fact, "each book was even better than the next"). (OH)

Constipation: In 1998, Dank was punished for one of his more drastic alimentary experiments, a zero-fiber diet, with his first-ever case of constipation. Up to then his gastrointestinal tract had always tended toward the opposite extreme, processing food as fluently as his brain converted life into fiction. Now, though, he seemed to be spending less time at his desk than on the toilet (the one by the kitchen, since he'd decided the one off his study was jinxed). I couldn't help but follow the accelerating progress of the *Star Trek* bookmark boldly going through the swollen paperback that Dank kept on the toilet tank, *Immortal Poems of the English Language* (a book that tended to open, I noticed, to the ample selection of poems by the anthologist himself, as if the paperback were still astounded, after all these years, by the hubris of the never-famous, now-forgotten poet-in-his-own-right who put it together). Dank tried all the standard laxatives to no avail. He invented a laxative "milk shake" by adding Hershey's syrup to milk of magnesia. Sometimes he flavored his milk of magnesia with fruit, in blender concoctions predating the vogue for smoothies. He wrote to the makers of Feenomints urging them to make a bubble-gum variety of their Chiclet-lookalike laxative gum, and a month later he received a coupon good for one free box of Feen-a-Mints. He even tried a little reverse psychology on his recalcitrant bowels with a homeopathic dose of Immodium, which only made things worse. *Immortal Poems of the English Language* was succeeded by a book of great short stories, which in turn gave way to a fat omnibus collection of classic science fiction novellas.

Dank's tribulations on the toilet lasted several months and finally entailed a surgical procedure called fecal disimpaction—an operation "better imagined than described" (as the Johnson Smith catalog used to say of the noises produced by whoopee cushions)—as well as a stern lecture from his doctor about the allowable parameters of any future diets.

A B C **D** E F

G H I J K L

M N O P Q R

S T U V W X

Y Z

Dank!: The authorized biography, on which I worked through-out the final dozen years of its subject's life. It was one reason I lived in his house: I wanted a ringside seat for the big fight, the slugfest between the irresistible force of Dank's imagination and the immovable object that most grown-ups are resigned to call reality. With so much firsthand access to the man himself, I never felt the need to track down other people in his life, past or present. I did attend two of his family reunions (see How John Doe Got Here and Insomnia), but that was it as far as legwork. I couldn't bring myself to travel just to talk to his ex-wives, of whom all three sounded awful (though not half as bad as number four would be), but in 1996 I sent each one a postcard, an invitation to tell her side of the story. The only one to take the bait was Molly Jensen (number two), and she didn't tell me much I hadn't gleaned already—though I did learn that Dank had been an hour late for their wedding (he had overslept, and then overshowered), and that he sometimes blurted out his own name during sex. As for his friendship with Hirt, I knew more than enough about that, since they reminisced every time they got together.

My book remained unpublished in Dank's lifetime because I couldn't bring myself to round it off and write The End as long its subject was adding a new postscript every day to what-ever conclusions I'd reached the day before. But the book was all but finished when he died, like those obituaries of famous living people—or maybe only famous dying people?—that our leading newspapers rather crassly keep on file, lacking only the date and cause of death. I sent a presentable draft to my agent on the day poor Dank was buried (it helped that I had written the whole thing in the past tense, just as those overeager obituarists do), together with the seven immortal manuscripts that Tom *still* hasn't found the time to "really read" (see THE BIG BOOK OF PROBLEMS), though two months have now passed since Dank's death. I was eager to start work on this encyclopedia, since what should really matter to posterity is not the frail, fallible, and maddeningly self-effacing mortal, but his immortal creations.

Dank! will be published in March 2007* by the Hemlock College Press, whose editor, Cynthia Olin, lives right around the block from me, across the street from Coffee Town— though in order to sell her the book, I had to route it through Manhattan so that Tom could take his cut of my princely thousand-dollar advance.†

Dank (*née* Gernsback), Dolores (b. 1931): Our author's mother and second-biggest fan. She herself was totally uninteresting and insignificant, as she is to this day, but Dank's love-hate relationship with her could be the subject of a dissertation. Dolores was the model for all the model moms and happy housewives in his fiction,

---

* (October 2007) When it finally appeared—in May instead of March— *Dank!* was well received by those who noticed it at all, though most of the reviews so far have been in fanzines and blogs. I'll perhaps be forgiven for boasting if I mention that MouthBreather.com described the biography as "a book more readable than any of its subject's."

† (October 2007) The HCP will also publish this encyclopedia, though I brokered *that* deal myself, since Tom and I are no longer speaking.

and the reason for his palpable, implacable, and often inexplicable hostility toward all those characters.* Not that his feelings for her were restricted to hatred. It's no accident that his second wife was the same age as Dolores and *looked* enough like her that more than once someone mistook that wife (the massive Molly JENSEN—who, as luck would have it, insisted on frequent, elaborate, disgusting, and public displays of affection) for Dank's mother, or vice versa.

As for Dank's other heartthrobs, one reason he kept chasing, if not catching, younger women—women young enough to be his daughters—was to flee his unholy feelings for his mother. And even then those feelings steered him, more often than not, to prematurely *motherly* young women. Or else those were the only ones who ever smiled at him. (He had a knack for deluding himself that the maternal and pitying smiles elicited from women by his pudgy-little-boy physique—or by the bewildered expression with which he encountered fellow earthlings, on his rare excursions out of his house—were clear signals of sexual attraction.) (OH)

Dank, Edmund (1930–2004): Our author's father. Phoebus was five when his parents divorced and Edmund disappeared for thirteen years, forgoing his right to see his children and in fact forgetting them entirely, to judge by his steadfast non-payment of child support. When Phoebus was eighteen his father reappeared and Dolores married him again, for reasons known best to herself. (She'd kept his surname in the meantime.) Thirty-three years later, their dutiful son did his best to decipher the nightmare "reminiscences" written by Edmund on his death bed, or, rather, typed in his death chair, at his death desk.

---

* A rare true observation from my fellow commentator, who knows all about implacable hostility. Too bad everything *else* he says in this entry is nonsense. For more on Dank's resentment of his mother and its consequences for his fiction, see LAUGHING MATTER. (BB)

Edmund and Phoebus had nothing in common, unless you count the fact that Edmund worked for the Department of Agriculture, for several decades, as a *fraud investigator*. Phoebus never knew just what that job entailed, or what would count as fraudulent (mutton dressed as lamb?) to a USDA investigator. Still, you can't help wondering if Dank's lifelong obsession with illusion and reality originated with his father, who made a living by distinguishing between the two.

Not that Dank simply followed in his father's cowpat-dodging footsteps: He distrusted all Departments, Ministries, and Bureaus, and the notion of Big Brother ordaining what is false—and thereby what is real—must have struck him as especially sinister. In his readiness to doubt what he once described as "the official version of Reality presented by the Government-approved mass media," and in his own freelance probings into what is real, Dank was actually rebelling—like the title character in "The Anesthesiologist's Son" (unfinished and unpublished), who rebels by becoming a top esthetician.

Dank himself avoided judgmental words like "phony," "fake," and "fraudulent." Even when reality fell short of his expectations, he rejected the traditional dichotomy of Real and Illusory, preferring to distinguish subtle shades of actuality or "realness." Although grammarians insist that the adjective—like "pregnant" or "dead" or "unique"—has no comparative form, much of what commonly passes for "real" struck Dank not as outright bogus, but rather (as he said once of the faintly perforated "PRESS HERE" arc on the macaroni-and-cheese box) as *insufficiently* real.

Dank, Phoebus K. (1952–2006): American writer. In the biographical sketch that follows, I will focus on Dank's early years—what I like to think of (and like to think *he* thought of) as the

Pre-Boswell years. The final twelve years of his life—the years we shared—are covered in many other entries.

Phoebus Kinsman Dank and his twin sister, Jane, were born in Chicago, on December 16, 1953, to Edmund and Dolores Dank. When Phoebus was six, his parents divorced and he moved with his mother and sister to Berkeley, CA, where Mrs. Dank's parents lived. From an early age, the future author suffered the persecution that is the lot of the genius, as when the other kids on his block formed a secret club with the sole purpose of excluding him. Eventually that persecution drove him, as it does so many misfits, to the solace and succor of science fiction, but as a boy he was at least as interested in bug collecting, chemistry, chameleons, and those big street-cleaning trucks with the rotary brushes. His obsession with the SF genre really began at age thirteen, and seems to have served the fat and unathletic boy—screamed at by gym teachers, laughed at by girls, tormented by bullies—throughout his adolescence as a steady source of compensatory fantasies.

In his later teens, Dank suffered from intense AGORAPHO-BIA that often kept him home from school, and from bouts of vertigo that may have been to blame for his lifelong sense of unreality—his sense of the everyday world as a Potemkin village, a cardboard imposture, a *trompe-l'oeil* backdrop that at any moment was liable to rip and give him a glimpse of some appalling truth beyond. In tenth grade, because of these and other problems (such as his panic attacks, or the swallowing disorder that made it hard for him to eat in public, or his mother's fear that he might be a homosexual), Dank saw a psychiatrist on Tuesday afternoons, explaining his absence to classmates by claiming that he was attending a special class for teenage geniuses.

Around that time he also developed his lifelong fear of schizophrenia, from time to time convincing himself that he had actually contracted that famous disease. Dank, of course, was attracted to the most lurid, terrifying, novelistic diagnosis he could think of (in preference to some dingy social maladjustment problem or boring personality disorder), but in fact he never really lost his mind. No, as precarious as his mental health may have appeared—to Dank himself and to his mother, neighbors, wives, and many others—and notwithstanding his many endearing DELUSIONS, he never did develop a full-blown psychosis, unless that's how we choose to think of his withdrawal from reality in the last year of his life. (He did have more than his share of *hermeneutic* episodes—times when the otherwise reassuringly tedious world began to seem a little *too* meaningful and interesting.) In any case, his problems didn't stop him from getting decent grades, or from holding down a part-time job as a salesclerk at Berkeley Audio while he was in high school. After a year or two on the job he was even allowed to perform some minor repairs, since he'd always liked taking things apart and figuring out how they worked.

In his senior year at Oakland Senior High—in Miss Selma Endive's honors English class—Dank met Owen Hirt. Hirt's work had already been published (in some vanishingly little magazine with a name like *Gnarled Stump* or *Weedy Bog* or *Dying Pond*), and yet he was already bitter, almost as bitter as if he foresaw the decades of Neglect awaiting him. He and Dank struck up an unlikely friendship, of which one long-term result would be Dank's bloody and tragically premature death. A more immediate result was that Dank himself began to write for publication. (Till then, remarkably, he'd never even considered writing as a vocation, though he'd recently taken to writing "fan fiction" based on *The Jetsons*.) Before the school year was out, he'd had his first story, BARRETT'S BARGAIN, printed in a magazine called *Shocking Science Fiction*.

In 1972, Dank started college at U. C. Berkeley, living in a dorm because his mother had just remarried his father and moved to LA. (For the rest of his life, Dank claimed to feel "abandoned" by his mother, and blamed her abdication for the failure of his four marriages.) He'd planned to study engineering, but immediately changed his major to English—a change he later blamed on the layout of the college catalog, which instead of segregating the arts from the sciences, as the wisdom of the ages recommends, listed them in simple alphabetical order; scanning the descriptions of engineering courses, Dank was lured astray by the English courses, and specifically by Introduction to Creative Writing. In any case, he dropped out of college after one semester, to focus on his fiction.

Dank's first novel, BOOST, appeared on April 1, 1974, and fell stillborn from the press (as Hume said of his *Treatise of Human Nature*), sending him into an eight-week depression as florid as his eight weeks of euphoria *before* the book was published. In the following decades, Dank tried all kinds of things (many of them illegal without a prescription) to recapture the elation of "2-3-74," as he referred ever after, in his notebooks, to those weeks when he fully believed he was on the brink of sudden world fame. What with the cherub of painful experience guarding the gateway to that fool's paradise, Dank never did recapture the elation of his first prepublication, but at least he got over the disappointment that followed.

Publication prompted Dank to make two life decisions: He quit his job at Berkeley Audio, vowing to support himself exclusively by writing (a vow he would keep for the rest of his life, though it reduced him once or twice to eating dog food),[*]

---

[*] That dimwitted vow was yet another reason for the badness of Dank's fiction. Not only did it force him into frantic hackwork, but it severely narrowed his view of the human comedy: Except to buy more food or waddle to the

and he got married, to Jessica TELLER. In all, he was married four times: in 1975, for a year and a half, to Ms. Teller; in 1979, for roughly a year, to Molly JENSEN; in 1992, for half a year, to Gabriella FEBRERO; and in 1999, for three weeks, to Pandora LANDOR. (Jessica reverted to her maiden name even before she filed for divorce; none of the other wives deigned to take Dank's surname in the first place.)

He went on to write fifty-seven extraordinary books, including such high-water marks of recent American fiction as AMNESIA, THE BIG BOOK OF PROBLEMS, THE DEMOLITION OF PHINEAS DUCK, HAPPY PILLS, A KNOCK ON THE HEAD, THE MAN IN THE BLACK BOX, THE PAGEANT, PANTS ON FIRE, PLANET FOOD, THE PLAGUE OF CANDOR, ROCKET ROY, THE SALT FACTORY, TESLA'S REVENGE, and VIRTUALLY IMMORTAL. Other notable events include his move in 1983 to Hemlock, California, where he lived for the rest of his life; his first meeting with his future biographer in 1991; and his violent death on the night of June 13/14, 2006. The definitive biography is DANK!, by the present commentator.

Dank, Phoebus K., Jr. (1977–1977): No cruel book review is quite complete without a cruel title, and the cruelest of all, for our author, headlined a savage review of THE PAGEANT: "Dank's Pregnant Silence Ends with Yet Another Stillbirth." Or maybe the reviewer didn't know that Dank's one foray into literal parenthood had been terminated by the stillbirth of the son he

---

nearest mailbox, he seldom ventured out of doors once he no longer had to leave his house to earn a living. For the rest of his life, Dank based most of his male characters on co-workers at Berkeley Audio, his only on-the-job exposure to the real world. That's why so many of the hapless ninnies in his fiction make a living selling or repairing stereos. (As for the *women* in his novels, most of them are modeled on his wives.) (OH)

fathered on his first wife, Jessica TELLER. (His second wife had had a hysterectomy before they met, the third never showed much interest in bearing her husband an heir, and the fourth didn't even let him consummate their marriage.) Dank never spoke about the tragedy but returned to it again and again in his fiction, as if the only way he knew to come to terms with such a loss was to imagine characters coming to terms with such losses themselves.

Dank Studies*: An undergraduate concentration offered by the English department at Hemlock College as of 2007. I'd been lobbying for such a concentration—or better yet, for an autonomous Dank Studies *department*—for more than a decade, but just as the USPS has a policy of not depicting living persons on its postage stamps, and the Baseball Hall of Fame of not inducting active players, so professors of English have a policy of ignoring living writers (especially those with any popular appeal), only to canonize them after death. In the case of Dank, this process can already be observed. During his lifetime, only one serious critic—yours truly—ventured to write about him or, so far as I know, to include him on a syllabus. Since his death, however, Dank's stock has soared: more than a dozen articles (and I mean solemn academic ones, with colons in their titles) have appeared or are forthcoming in WHAT NEXT?: THE JOURNAL OF DANK STUDIES.

---

* (October 2007) Though as a rule the entries in this volume were written in strict alphabetical order—the order in which they appear—this entry is an exception: I went back and added it last week. In August 2006, when I wrote the rest of the *D*s, it seemed doubtful that there'd ever be a program in Dank Studies, since I'd quit my job at Hemlock College and left the Edenic surroundings of Hemlock itself for the exile of Portland.

"Delmore": A fat undergraduate slowly realizes—several pages after the dimmest of readers have done so—that his strange and difficult roommate is really an extraterrestrial. No, Dank's·bag of tricks was not a large one, and like a retarded ten-year-old with a new joy buzzer, he used the "really an extraterrestrial" trick ending every chance he got. "Delmore" dates from 1983 but recalls Dank's difficulties with his college roommate, who continued to inspire rabid hatred, and tepid fiction, more than a decade after their single semester together. After that semester, Dank announced that college wasn't for him, and so ended his formal education. In adulthood he may have seemed a bit more literate than most high-school graduates, but he was all too plainly self-taught, with the autodidact's typical naiveté, credulity, and undiscriminating taste for trivia. He may have known a few more words than the average high-school grad, but he mispronounced them all. The only grown-up words he ever learned to say correctly were the ones he heard *me* using—and not even all of those, since I had a game of mispronouncing certain word in his presence, knowing he'd adopt my version. By that means, for instance, I got Dank saying "ineVIT-able," and he went on saying the word that way—convinced that everyone else was saying it wrong—long after I grew tired of the joke and reverted to the correct pronunciation. (OH)

Delusions: Dank started college as an engineering major, and his little learning in the sciences had proven a dangerous thing—not so much for his fiction (whose flights of fancy might have been shortened, or grounded altogether, by a more thorough knowledge of scientific principles) as for his mental health. His astonishing imagination was not something he could simply unplug when off duty, and he knew just enough science to frame his crazier notions about the real world in terms too technical for an English major like me to refute. Over the years, he dabbled in all sorts of delusions, though most were mercifully short-lived. At one time or another, Dank convinced himself:

—that his hated next-door neighbor, Jock JABLONSKY, was beaming a death ray at him via a satellite dish

—that he had contracted Alzheimer's disease by wearing a suit of aluminum foil next to his skin for more than a week during the death-ray episode

—that his computer not only tracked his websurfing, but also beamed his image to the webmaster of whatever site he was viewing

—that government spy satellites could see what he was doing even when he was indoors with the shades down (his back-yard writing bunker—see THE MAN IN THE BLACK BOX—doubled as a zone of privacy, and long after ceasing to use it to write fiction, Dank shut himself in there to jot down subversive thoughts)

—that his microwave oven was making him impotent

—that the radioactive dial on his first wristwatch was making him impotent thirty years after he'd stopped wearing it

—that every piece of bubble gum he'd ever swallowed as a kid had not only remained in his gastrointestinal tract but continued to form bubbles in there, when the winds were auspicious

—that dogs laugh, and laughed at him

—that microwaves cause brain damage

—that sneezing causes brain damage

—that shouting causes brain damage ("that's why the loud-est people are the dumbest")

—that Jablonsky was stealing his mail

—that Hollywood was stealing his plots

—that he was nothing but a character in another science-fiction writer's novel

—that the cash registers at Food Planet had a discount pedal analogous to the "soft" pedal on a piano, and that if the cashier liked him, she'd ring up his purchases with the pedal down, and everything would wind up costing him a little less.

The Demolition of Phineas Duck: One of Dank's best novels, even if the title makes it sound like a Disney cartoon. His original title for this tale of "ego transfusion" was *Thanks for the Memories*, but that title had its problems too, since the technology on which the book is premised—an operation that enables the entire contents of a brain to be copied to another brain, the way you burn a CD—was designed for dying people wanting immortality, not for amnesiacs wanting someone else's memories. (Who wants other people's memories? Who even wants to sit through their home movies?) So the problem isn't finding donors but *recipients*—empty heads to house the selves of dying clients soon to be evicted from the bodies they were born with. Dank's solution (not the most original, I realize) is to set the novel in a grim near-future that uses death-row prisoners as surrogates, after wiping their own memories so thoroughly as to satisfy even the staunchest proponents of capital punishment.

After the transplant, the new body that now houses X's mind resumes his life where it left off—sleeping with X's wife, rearing X's children, bowling for X's team, working for X's employer in X's cubicle, and so on. Not surprisingly, people refer to the procedure not as a memory transplant but as a *body* transplant—and sometimes the very rich undergo the operation even when they're *not* dying, just to relocate to someone younger, healthier, or better-looking. (The novel was in fact an outgrowth of its author's fantasy of trading in his body for a more attractive one—of remaining Dank, deep down, but no longer looking like him.) One absurdly rich woman, whose lifelong eating disorder is an inextricable part of what gets transplanted from host to host, treats herself to a new slender body every other year, using the transplant as a sort of radical liposuction.

Sometimes, of course, things go wrong. Sometimes a transplant doesn't "take" because the initial wiping of the recipient's own memories was incomplete. (Some psychologists insist that the former self and its memories are *never* actually deleted, just driven out of sight.) In those cases, the former self shows through, as when a layer of white primer fails to hide the undercoat. And so some recipients wind up with two sets of memories—two *pasts*—that are equally vivid but mutually exclusive. And that's what happens to Dank's newly transplanted protagonist, Dodsworth J. Worthington, Jr.: One day he sees his own picture on the jacket of a science fiction novel that he has no memory of writing, just as he has no memory of being called Phineas Duck. And though he's better off as Worthington—a billionaire whose life consists of Lamborghinis, yachts, champagne, servants, mistresses, cocaine, and (perhaps improbably) an enormous library of science fiction—curiosity gets the better of him. Worthington tracks down all eighty-seven of Duck's novels—some of which he'd read already, since he was a fan of Duck long before his psyche wound up in Duck's body. Gradually, assisted by those novels (which, like Dank's, are semi-autobiographical), Worthington manages to reconstruct his "other past," his body's past, right up to the heartache, lust, betrayal, murder, and arrest that led to the erasing and reformatting of Duck's prodigious brain.

After several years of daydream opulence, the protagonist decides that his old life was more fun, and makes up his mind to go back to being Duck. By that point, though, it isn't clear *whose* mind has been made up—it's been unclear for a good hundred pages whether the viewpoint character is Duck already or still Worthington. It's hard to know, in other words, if the ending should be understood as a semi-erased writer's triumphant exorcism of the demonic mogul who'd possessed him, or rather as a jaded billionaire's decision to defect to the more interesting self that once inhabited his adopted body.

Deutsch (*née* Dank), Jane (b. 1952): Many grown-ups—notably the most pathetic—still resent their siblings for offenses dating back to early childhood. In Dank's case, the resentment went back even further: He claimed to remember his twin sister's mistreatment of him in the womb, months before the two were born. Even in those days, according to Dank, Jane was "pushy" and "bossy" and "obnoxious." His first memory, he told me once, was of "bobbing around in the dark and feeling crowded."

Dank blamed his sister's intrauterine behavior for his lifelong nervousness: Everybody who is destined to be born at all [he used to say with idiotic indignation] has a right to a womb of his own, to nine months of rest and relaxation in that fool's paradise, and to the lingering complacency that such an easy start—such beginner's luck—instills.

Dank also blamed his overeating on Jane, or on Jane and their mother, who hadn't had enough milk for both twins, and, forced to choose, had favored her daughter. And in fact his earliest medical records show that, a month after his debut, little Phoebus was admitted to the hospital weighing *less* than the day he was born. The diagnosis: "Failure to thrive." It was one of the few failures he ever overcame: By his second birthday, he'd thriven his way right up to the first percentile for weight.

As for Jane, she too continued to thrive. By the time her brother introduced us (in the high-school cafeteria), she was already the obese, opinionated troll she remains to this day. If, as

Helen Rowland claimed, "the chief excitement in a woman's life is spotting women who are fatter than she is," Jane's life cannot be a terribly—or frequently—exciting one. (OH)

Dick, Philip K.: Although it is regrettably impossible, in a guide to the worlds of a demiurge as inexhaustible as Dank, to include entries for each of the thousands of imaginary people in his fiction, there is one who demands such attention: the semi- or sesqui-autobiographical Philip K. Dick, the hero of BIG DICK.

Dick seems at times to realize that he is nothing but a fictional character. His own novels, by the sound of them (Dank summarizes dozens), are haunted by a sense of unreality, a suspicion that what passes for the real world is actually a dream from which at any moment he might awaken. Dank himself was not immune to such suspicions: In his final year, he became convinced that he himself, and probably I, and certainly Hirt, were nothing more than characters in someone else's novel. Maybe one of Dick's: In BIG DICK, we're told that one of Dick's abandoned novels features a writer named Phoebus K. Dank, a paradox recalling that famous Escher lithograph of two hands drawing each other.

Dank doesn't give us any samples of Dick's writing, but he tells us it's terrific, and by the end of the novel the world agrees. That world—a parallel one, identical to ours except for the absence of Dank and his books and the presence of Dick and his—is unforgivably slow to acknowledge Dick's merits; not until after his death does he achieve anything like the fame we're assured he deserves. The narrative is strictly chronological, and up until his death at age fifty-three, Dick's life corresponds (imperfectly) to Dank's, but the novel then continues for another twenty years, and another sixty pages, because Dank liked to daydream of posthumous glory.

In many ways, in fact, Dick is a daydream version of Dank—an even faster typist, a more celebrated writer, a more energetic reader (he not only reads but *likes* the tricky stuff—the *Critique of Pure Reason*, *Ulysses*—that Dank got no further than wishing he wanted to read), and a more successful lover. Dank had never *not* been fat, and had never been good-looking in the conventional sense, but Dick—as a young man at least—is "tall and well-knit," according to Dank, "with a shock of blond hair and two piercing blue eyes irresistible to women." And like so many authors—though not, alas, *his* author—Dick has the knack of trading on his status, parlaying his art into sex, though for most of his life he is almost as sadly neglected an artist as Dank.

The daydream aspects of this Dick are not restricted to his looks and knacks. They affect his circumstances, too. Dick, like Dank, starts life with a twin sister, but unlike Dank's detested sister, Jane, *Dick's* sister Jane obligingly dies as an infant. And though Dick, too, in his lifetime, is denied the level of fame he deserves, he is at least more highly regarded than Dank ever was. Dick, for instance, wins a Hugo for one of his parallel-universe novels. Dank was never even nominated for the prize.

Overall, there's so much wishful thinking in his flattering self-portrait that you wonder why there isn't more. Why give *Dick* a weight problem, toward the end of his life? Why give him Dank's bad heart? Why torment him with the vertigo, agoraphobia, and fear of madness that tormented Dank? And why give him so much trouble—as Dank had so much trouble—when it came to selling anything but science fiction? Why not make him rock-star famous in his lifetime, rather than obliging him to wait—as Dank eventually resigned himself to waiting—for the consolation prize of posthumous fame?

The answer, I think, is that Dank was a complicated person, incapable of yielding to simple wish-fulfillment even in his daydreams, needing all his pleasures spiced with pain. (He once complained that when he tried to fantasize about invisibility—about all the mischief it would let him get away with—he got sidetracked by logistics: Would the food in his intestines also be invisible? And what about his shoes?) Dick was as much of a stretch as Dank's imagination—otherwise boundless—was capable of where he himself was involved.

"Did I Miss Anything?": Not a story but a sort of mantra for our author. Dank was haunted by a fear of missing out on things—of being asleep, or out of the room, or facing the wrong way, when something big happened. I found this worry so endearing that I started a list of unlikely occasions on which Dank asked the question we all ask at the movies on returning from the rest room or the snack bar. To cite a few:

—On stepping back outside (after a wrong number summoned him into the house) to resume his admiration of a sunset.

—On emerging from general anesthesia after having all his wisdom teeth extracted.

—(Repeatedly) On returning to his surroundings in the middle of something I was saying, after something I'd said a few sentences earlier set him off on some private train of thought.

—While watching TV, or at the movies, since Dank was so easily distracted by his pesky imagination that he didn't need to leave his seat to lose touch with the story unfolding on the screen.

—On car trips through picturesque landscapes, and even while driving, since of course it's possible to drive—and drive a lot better than Dank did—without really seeing your surroundings. (By the time I moved to Hemlock, Dank was no longer allowed to drive at all, but once or twice on longer trips I swallowed half a Valium, thanked heaven for my El Camino's passenger-side airbag, and, with great misgivings, let him take the wheel.)

—As the first words out of his mouth on bumping into an ex-classmate he hadn't seen in more than twenty years. (By that point the question had become a reflex, part of Dank's one-man campaign to make it the standard greeting, in place of "How are you?")

Dank's determination not to sleep through anything "good"—his reluctance to relinquish consciousness and miss whatever happened next—was one reason for his decades of amphetamine abuse. Popping pill after pill, he reminded me of a slot-machine junkie dropping coin after coin into that addictive stupidity detector, more convinced each time he loses that the record-setting jackpot is just a tug away. The irony is that, after all that tampering with his circadian clock, Dank ultimately needed heavy-duty sedatives to fall asleep at all. *Those* pills knocked him out so effectively that there's reason to believe he slept through—"missed"—the last and most momentous event of his life: his death. And it wasn't a quiet one, either.

Diet: Some people can't help wondering, each time they see a fat man, whether or not he "deserves" to be fat. Dank ate less than I did, though. He was not a glutton, just a sluggard, and cursed with a sluggish metabolism. He was always on a diet, always trying to lose weight or boost his energy or make himself smarter or saner or calmer. In the years I knew him, Dank went through a long succession of odd dietary fads.

For a week or two in 1995, for instance, he ate nothing but spherical foods. I remember him returning from Food Planet with a cantaloupe, a coconut, a container of cherry tomatoes, a bag of pearl onions, a box of Kix, a box of Peanut Butter Cap'n Crunch, a package of heat 'n' serve meatballs, a carton of malted milk balls, a cheese ball rolled in ground nuts, a jar of capers, and a jar of those little silver cake decorations that look just like BBs.

One day in 1998, as he sat down to eat a pork chop, Dank had some kind of epiphany and became a vegetarian (though first he ate the pork chop—sometimes these epiphanies need a minute or two to sink in). Our refrigerator cleaned up its act overnight, going from a meat locker to a peaceable king-dom of roots and sprouts and leaves, soy milk and bean curd, strange juices and plain yogurt. After a week, though, Dank's epiphany wore off in mid-meal: he pushed away his plate of tofu, hastened to the kitchen, and came back with a tube or chub of liverwurst he'd overlooked—or providently spared—during his purge of meat products. For the next year, Dank, when he ate meat, ate only *organ* meat, and for a while only brains. Since in our household Dank did most of the cooking, I was subjected to these diets too. Still, I was happy to choke down the results if the alternative was eating dinner by myself, as I do these days in the various fast-food infernos with which my new neighborhood is graced.

As for what Dank ate while writing, for years he started ev-ery session with a dozen sandwich cookies, preferably Hydrox (or, after they were discontinued, the less-scientific-sounding competition, Oreos), eating all twelve before he typed a word. Not that he couldn't type one-handed, but the cookie feast itself was a two-handed operation: He needed to unscrew each cookie and scrape off the space-age kreme with an expired credit card he kept handy for the purpose, flicking the gunk into his dented metal *Battlestar Galactica* wastebasket. Only after thus eviscerating all the cookies did he eat the chocolate wafers, all twenty-four, one after another, and only after that did he begin to type. More than once I'd offered to scrape off the gunk myself, anxious to save Dank from wasting precious moments of peak creativity on such a mindless task, but apparently the task itself was an important part of his larger writing ritual.

To get himself in the mood while working on novels set in the near future—as so many of Dank's were, probably because that's where he located the fame the past and present had denied him—he played, over and over, a futuristic Bach-on-synthesizer recording, and observed a special "science-fiction diet" that consisted exclusively of foods he could imagine an astronaut eating: TV dinners, Lunchables, Carnation Instant Breakfast, Tang, cheese in spray cans, protein powder, caffeine pills instead of coffee, vitamins, and, for dessert, artificial sweetener straight from the jar. Sometimes, to make the messy and embarrassingly biological business of eating itself seem more "scientific," he even drank his Tang from Pyrex beakers or graduated cylinders, and, when winding down for the night, his alcohol—pure ethyl alcohol, of course—from test tubes.

Dog House: In January 1972, after dropping out of college, Dank remained in the Bay Area, moving into the big ramshackle house in Oakland where I was already living with several other students too savvy to live in a dorm—a painter, two more poets, a future editor, and a composer. (Dank was the least gifted person in the house—and to those who understand the way the world works it should come as no surprise that he's now the most famous.) The previous owner, an old maid named Miss Love, had been one of those sad people who hoard pets—in her case dogs, of which she'd acquired more than a dozen when the landlord kicked her out. The neighbors still called it the Dog House, and we adopted the name, since the smell of dog had so thoroughly saturated the stained carpeting that five years of cigarette and reefer smoke, stale beer and bong water, turpentine and oil paint—and three years of Dank's own body odor—never succeeded in displacing it. Dank tried to get us to call it the Slan Shack instead (some kind of nerdy sci-fi allusion that I'm unable to explain, though he explained it constantly, as I never listened to his explanations), but we told him to shut up.

Because I was short on funds at the time (I'd just quit my job at a used bookstore, no longer willing to humor my semi-literate employer's pathetic poetic ambitions), I agreed to let Dank share my room and pay my rent. In those days, before he came to think of himself as a Serious Author, he still struck me as a likable enough nonentity—"a modest little person," as Churchill said of someone, "with much to be modest about." My memories of our cohabitation boil down to a single vivid image of Dank on his back in his bed with a book. I suppose he must have sometimes lumbered over to his desk to type his little spaceman stories, but I never caught him in the act. No, unless his fellow nerds from the Science Fiction Club were there, debating the relative strengths of the Superfriends and the Fantastic Four like blockheads in a sports bar arguing about their favorite teams, I never saw Dank in any position but belly up in bed like a beached whale—most often in his underwear, since he was always hot, and raptly reading some craptastic paperback with a title like *She-Warriors of Zardoq-Eight*. Sometimes he'd be staring at the ceiling, putting a new book down long enough to fantasize that he'd written it himself. (As far as I can tell, the secret of Dank's "irrepressible imagination" is that he didn't just *enjoy* his daydreams, he was afraid to face life without them. Fantasy for him was a way of making frantic small talk with himself, for fear of something real being said.) One day I came in to find him huffing and puffing and "reading" a *Playboy*. After that we partitioned our room with a heavy curtain down the center, though I still had to pass through his zone to get to mine, since the door was on his side.

When a room opened up (after one of the poets transferred to Bennington), I made Dank move across the hall. Worshipping me as he did, *he* would have been happy to share a room forever—to share a bunk bed, even, and fall asleep each night discussing Literature in the dark. But I wasn't having that, for many reasons. (For one, Dank's sleeping pattern was irregular to the point of nonexistence, in part because he'd started his romance with AM-PHETAMINES.) Sharing a *house* with him was already hard enough, and I don't know how I put up with him as long as I did—longer than anyone else ever would except for Boswell. (And Boswell, in his slavish devotion to his master, has more in common with the tail-wagging, anus-sniffing former tenants of the Dog House than with any self-respecting biped.) Finally, on marrying Jessica Teller in the spring of '75, Dank moved out—at her insistence and that of his housemates, since none of us could stand her, and by then we were all sick of Phoebus too*—and into a basement apartment a few blocks away.

Readers who think I'm too hard on Dank's works may be surprised to hear that Dank and I were old friends, and may even charge me with duplicity, but I was always candid with him about my low opinion of his talents. That we remained friends nevertheless is testimony both to his affable nature (until he got too

---

* So "sick of" him that in 1977, after his first divorce, two of them moved in with Dank and took advantage of his hospitality for several months—paying no rent, eating his food, and encouraging his drinking so they could drink his booze. For more about the various parasites, lowlives, and grifters who preyed on Dank over the years, see HAPPY PILLS, HENRIETTA'S PERFORMANCE, and PRAISE THE BIG BOTTLE. (BB)

big for his britches) and to his somehow endearing doltishness, since in general—sorry, Boswell—I don't befriend anyone I can't respect.* (OH)

Don't Say I Didn't Tell You: In 1997, at a big sci-fi convention, Dank was voted the author *least* likely to be proven right about the future. Sci-fi fans have strong opinions about the shape of things to come, and in a rare consensus, they agreed that the future, whatever it looks like, will bear no resemblance to the one Dank foresaw.

Over the following month, in a pathetic attempt to vindicate his futurology, Dank compiled this tellingly slender selection from his oeuvre—a handful of stories, and excerpts from novels, that in his opinion had already proven prophetic as of 1997. There wasn't much to compile, and even his luckiest guesses managed to be wrong about the little they got right. In 1980, for example, in one of his "day-after-tomorrow" stories (PALS), Dank had predicted—as anyone could have—that network TV would continue to grow even raunchier and ruder. Yet Dank failed altogether to foresee the triumph of cable and videotape, though by then both trends were already well underway. (I find it emblematic that the only VCR to appear in his fiction of the eighties is a Betamax: Dank always bet on the loser.) Likewise, *Don't Say I Didn't Tell You* reprinted a long dull digression from APPOINTMENT BOOK, which back in '75 had imagined something vaguely resembling the World Wide Web, though in the book it's called the "Information Ocean," and the computers used to surf that ocean are the same low-octane slowpokes that seemed so fast in '75.

---

* Hirt should ask himself why, if his friendship is such a hot commodity, his quarrel with Dank in 1999 left him utterly friendless. Not that their friendship had ever amounted to much. By the time I moved to Hemlock, Dank and Hirt had known each other for so long they had nothing left to talk about. For more about their reminiscence sessions, see PALS. (BB)

His booby prize for Wrongest Prophet was awarded for career achievement, but it's fun to wonder which of Dank's predictions clinched the title. Was it the vogue for time-lapse pornography? The emergence of vegan bulimics (who eat all the meat they want, but then bring it right back up)? The thermo-pills that take the place of coats in winter, air-conditioning in summer? Was it the Institute of Time Travel in TIME VANDAL, a think tank staffed by well-paid centenarians—since the elderly are experts on Time and its perils—though aside from those few lucky ancients, everyone is euthanized at thirty-five? Was it the shopkeepers in that same time-hopping world, who, knowing their own personal futures and those of their shops, don't boast "Since 1983" on their signs but "Till 2094"? Was it the weight-watching future in which Osmo's—a nationwide chain of olfactory restaurants where patrons "dine" on aromas—is more popular than McDonald's? Was it the over-regulated future that requires an environmental impact study just to plant a flower? Was it the future where mirrors are a luxury only the very rich can afford, and others must pay by the minute to see themselves in special coin-operated mirrors ("like you have to pay to use those big binoculars at scenic overlooks")? Or the one where the *outdoors*—the surface of the earth—is a luxury, where the world is so crowded that people live in tiny subterranean apart-ments, and time above ground is strictly rationed? (In *that* future everyone must wear a monitor—"like the ones that perverts on probation wear, and people under house arrest," except that this one ticks "just like the meters in the hover-cabs.")(OH)

Dookie (1995–?): Our author's cat. Dookie was the first pet Dank had ever owned, unless we count the fish in his aquarium, or the series of short-lived and disappointingly colorfast chame-leons he'd had as a boy, since his mother was allergic to any-thing with fur. Everything that Dookie did was new to Dank, and it was touching to hear the leading writer of our time marveling over typical feline behavior: ". . . and sometimes when I'm revising, he gets up on the desk and sits right on my manuscript, like he wants me to pay attention to *him* instead!" Dank even bought a teach-yourself-art book called *Draw 50 Cats*, and taught himself to draw the one that looked the most (though none looked much) like his.

Dookie was just three weeks old when Dank adopted him, in 1995, from a neighbor with a litter to get rid of. At first the cat was small enough to fit in one of Dank's (size 13) shoes, which is where he spent his first few weeks. I recall an exchange from that era:

> Dank: "Why does he like my shoes so much?"
> Boswell: "They smell like you."
> Dank: "Like my feet, you mean. . . . Do *I* smell like my feet?"

When he wasn't lurking in a shoe, Dookie was usually rolling around—or just napping—in his litter box, which is how he earned his name. He was the least intelligent cat I've ever encountered, and would sometimes walk around for half an hour making the anxious low-pitched moaning sounds that normal cats will make for a few seconds before vomiting—but instead of vomiting, he'd finally come across his litter box and bring forth an especially large and fragrant stool (which Dank would hasten to bury, since Dookie never bothered), and all would be well: he'd known there was *something* in him wanting out, but was too dumb to distinguish between the need to vomit and the need to defecate.

As a kitten Dookie had looked normal enough, but he soon developed an eating disorder. By his second birthday (celebrated with a double ration of canned salmon), he was so fat he no longer resembled a cat, though I guess he might have passed for a Venusian cat, or some giant South American rodent. And he always looked for chances to grow fatter. He'd spend hours in Dank's study watching the aquarium, now and then spastically thrusting a paw into the water in an always-unsuccessful effort to snag a betta or a tetra.

Sometimes Dookie tried to catch birds, but he never succeeded. The birds didn't even bother taking wing, just strode away at Dookie's lumbering approach—whereupon he'd either flop down on the grass in defeat or trudge back to the house, squeeze through his cat door, and head for his food dish. He was always hungry when he returned from the hunt, as if his failure to catch a meal had made him more appreciative of store-bought cat food. Like Dank, after any disappointment he consoled himself with food.

Dookie disappeared in 2001, during the LA-Z-BOY era. I can't say I was sad to see him go, though Dank was—to the point of shedding tears over the loss—a few months later, once he'd recovered the strength for strenuous feelings like grief. I told him that Dookie had probably found himself a better deal elsewhere, since by the time he vanished his owner hadn't had the strength to pick him up in months (this was the nadir of Dank's appalling, record-setting bout of laziness), and I was too busy running Dank, Incorporated (see PRODUCTION LINE) to pay attention to a pet I'd never cared for anyhow. Or pay attention to his litter box, which remained, to the end of Dank's own life, in its place of honor in the basement, as a sort of shrine to Dookie's memory, in the supersaturated state in which he'd left it.

Dank envisioned a more dignified memorial: a novel whose protagonist unwisely buries *his* dead cat in an unholy pet cemetery, and lives to regret it. When I pointed out that Stephen

King had written that novel already, and that Dank and I had seen the movie adaptation, Dank resolved to write a *renovelization* of King's novel—one he hadn't read, and made a point now of not reading. He soon abandoned that bizarre and unpublishable project, but not before reading the rest of King's enormous *oeuvre* in the name of research and watching every movie adapted from that *oeuvre* as of 2002. Luckily for Dank, he had taught himself speed-reading as an adolescent, and now he solved the question of what to do first—read the book or watch the movie?—by doing both at the same time: He read each book *while* watching the corresponding movie. (Back when he was still allowed to drive, Dank had experimented with reading while *driving*. He claimed to have read all 256 pages of *Have Spacesuit, Will Travel* on the five-hour drive from Hemlock to Eureka—to the conference where we met—in 1991.)

"Double Jeopardy": Written—in the form of a legal brief—during the last inning of Dank's second marriage, and set in a toxic near-future where birth defects are the rule, "Double Jeopardy" is the tale of a man named Floyd and his decision to sue his Siamese twin. Floyd accuses Lloyd of thoughtless behavior that affects them both: drinking that gives them both hangovers, after-dinner coffee that keeps them both awake (though anything, even a private worry, that keeps one awake—tossing and turning as much as a Siamese twin ever can—tends to keep the other one awake as well), overeating that makes them both obese, smoking that puts both at an increased risk for cancer, and so on. At one point, Floyd even makes a citizen's arrest of Lloyd.

In 1995, or soon after I moved in, Dank revised the story to make the legal language still more legalistic. A few years earlier, during a long stretch of immobility, I had passed the time by reading a textbook of criminal law, and for the last twelve years of our author's life I served as his consultant on all legal matters. In the year 2000, the year Dank took to putting a copyright notice in the upper right-hand corner of every page he produced, his fear of plagiarism also led him to add a sentence to his cover letters, warning editors not to "even think" of stealing his stories because his best friend was "William Boswell, the leading copyright lawyer." I was more touched by the "best friend" part than annoyed by the fib that followed, though the fib implied (correctly, I'm afraid) that no editor would recognize that William Boswell was a writer, not a lawyer. Dank himself kept forgetting that I was not a lawyer, bursting into my room at one AM to ask about the difference between assault and battery. Could there be battery *without* assault? If not, wasn't "assault and battery" redundant? Why not just say "battery"? Same questions, on another night, for "cease and desist."

After his arrest for public urination (see VOID WHERE PROHIBITED), Dank spoke of writing a legal thriller à la Scott Turow or John Grisham. Rather than serve as his round-the-clock law lexicon for the project, I bought Dank a law dictionary. After that he made a point of peppering his conversation with terms like "usufruct," "cross-complaint," "ambit," and "tortfeasor." He was especially fond of "tortfeasor." For a while there he used it in any context where a normal person—even an off-duty lawyer—would have said "asshole": "As you know, my brother-in-law is a real tortfeasor." "If that tortfeasor doesn't stop letting his dog go to the bathroom in my yard, I'll call the cops."

In his long and systematically unjust indictment of Dank's works, MACDOUGAL, sounding even angrier than usual, denounces "Double Jeopardy" for "flagrant lawyer-bashing." At first this struck me as gratuitous, this anger on behalf of sharks and shysters, but now it seems appropriate. MacDougal, like so many critics and reviewers, had less in common with a conscientious judge than with a self-promoting lawyer—in his case, a lawyer for the prosecution, more interested in winning than in seeing justice done. Like the cheerfully amoral court-room lawyer who doesn't care about the truth and can't afford to, MacDougal built the strongest case he could against the books on trial, ignoring or dismissing with a condescending shrug any evidence that didn't serve to prove his point.

"Dugan's Daring": What if the bad guys had beaten the good guys in World War II? I'm told that several sci-fi writers have imagined such a world in their "alternate history" novels (though no one seems to know why such books count as "science fiction"—or why sci-fi fans insist on saying "alternate" when they mean "al-ternative"). In Dank's hands, such a world looks a lot like *Hogan's Heroes*:

> As happened every morning, Jim Dugan was stopped at the checkpoint outside of his place of compulsory employment, Arbeit, Inc.
>
> *"Guten Tag, Heinrich,"* he said sarcastically to the scowl-ing Nazi guard, rolling down the window and thrusting out his bicep to show his employee tattoo. *"Wie gehts?"* he added with disgust, being forced to use the hated tongue of the op-pressor, German, the Germans having won the war and oc-cupied his country. Now it was the *Bundesrepublik Amerika*, thought Dugan with disgust.

Throughout the story, Dank takes a courageous and outspo-ken stand against all grumpy strudel-eating Nazi killjoys:

> *"Alle Musik ist verboten!"* thundered Heinrich, sporting shiny black boots and a hateful Nazi uniform as he patted his Luger omniously [*sic*].

"Jawohl, Herr Kommandant," said Dugan, adding "you lousy little kraut, I could take you with one hand behind my back if you'd put down that gun and fight like a man!" under his breath before he grudgingly turned off the eight-track player in his hovermobile.

How did the bad guys wind up in control? Simple, says our alternate historian:

"As you know, the Nazis won the Second World War, having murdered Winston Churchill back in 1939 and beat the Allies 'to the punch,' atomically, with the lethal V3 missile that, it being both transcontinental and atomic, brought us to our proverbial 'knees.' Now they rule our country, forcing real Americans like you and I to use the German language for official business, Jim, as you know," snapped Rossiter.

When a writer's limitations are as obvious as Dank's, it is easy to lose sight of his *genre's* limitations. Of course, the biggest problem with sci-fi is that it's mostly written by people like Dank and mostly read by people who don't know enough to insist on something better. Maybe that's two problems, in a cozy symbiosis. The next-biggest problem, though, is dialogue, and not because the writers have no ear for speech. Some do, some don't, and some, like Dank, sound like Martian or Venusian writers trying to imagine Earthling conversation. And often—as in DOUBLE JEOPARDY, when Floyd informs his brother, "As you know, Lloyd, we're Siamese twins"—Dank's ineptitude is so conspicuous one hesitates to blame his genre.

Read enough sci-fi, though, and you'll discover that one form of badness that at first might seem like Dank's invention is in fact endemic to that genre, or at least to its clumsier authors: Characters are constantly *explaining* everything to one another, telling

one another all about the brave new worlds they would take for
granted if they really lived there. That's because a novel set in any
other world than the here and now requires so much *exposition*—
and a sure sign of a third-rate author is to cram that exposition into
dialogue. (OH)

A B C D E F
G H I J K L
M N O P Q R
S T U V W X
Y Z

"Embers": The story of man destroyed by sexual rejection. The man is August Traurig, hero of August and April, which ends, of course, with August setting fire to his house after April dumps him at the worst possible time for an unbalanced college professor, the last week of summer vacation. "Embers" may be thought of as an epilogue or coda to the novel. A year has passed and August now lives in a psychiatric group home on a possibly symbolic hilltop. One day he takes a long and aimless walk downhill. When the time comes to head back up for dinner, he decides he's too sad to walk *up*hill, so he continues downward, "taking the path that water would take," and ends up at the edge of the river that runs through his city. Only a chain-link fence prevents him from walking straight into the river. August can't go farther in any direction, in fact, without heading back uphill, so he lies down instead, among the liquor bottles and discarded condoms, resolving to die on the spot. Before he manages to do that, though, two cops show up and wearily return him to his group home—as (we gather from the conversation in the squad car) they've been doing for a year now, several times a month. The *next* time he takes his favorite walk, though, someone has cut a big hole in the fence at the very spot where it's been stopping August, so this time he does continue down into the river, where he promptly drowns.

When Dank left the house for an aimless walk, he too always headed downhill, westward, though that meant he'd later have to trudge back up, an ordeal he too sometimes found unbearable. "Embers" was suggested by an incident in 1993—soon after Dank's third marriage self-destructed—when a solo walk marooned him in a neighborhood well downhill from his home. On that occasion, it was indeed the police who returned him to his normal altitude after a complaint from the old lady in whose small front yard Dank's walk had petered out, leaving him flat on his back in the middle of her lawn, drenched by the sprinklers she'd turned on in an effort to make him go away. After that he was more prudent, and in his blackest moods he'd either ride a bus or (after I arrived) have me drive him to the top of the nearest summit, in order to be *up*hill from his house for the walk home.

But he sometimes came to grief even when walking downhill. For one thing, Dank had never learned how to steer clear of oncoming pedestrians. The little dance you sometimes find yourself engaged in with a stranger on the sidewalk, where you both move first this way, then that, attempting to bypass each other—on a busy street Dank could get caught in that dance several times a block. He should have been a linebacker, he was so big and hard to get around. More than once a neighbor accused him of purposely stepping into the way, like an after-school bully, but that wasn't true, unless the purpose that prompted Dank to do it was unconscious. Consciously, he hated and dreaded these encounters. Some days he couldn't even work up the nerve to leave his property.

The irony was that we lived two blocks away from a park with wide-open spaces, where not even Dank would be likely to come to many standoffs with his fellow earthlings, but he never set foot in that park, content to hug the residential shore across the street. As a rule, he found nature (even the domesticated "nature" of a public park) too depressing in its vegetative mind-lessness, its emptiness. I think he was afraid of wide-open spaces as such—a surprising phobia for a famous science fiction writer. One can only wonder how he would have fared on a spaceship hurtling through the icy black infinities of interstellar space.

Sometimes I joined Dank on walks, to keep him company and keep him out of trouble. On one excursion, I recall, he told me all about his plan for an electric corkscrew. On another we debated whether (as Dank claimed) Clark Kent is "really" Superman or (as I contended) Superman is really Clark. But Dank seldom spoke on walks, or seldom spoke to me. More often he relived old conversations, sometimes audibly, winning arguments he'd lost in real life or berating absent (sometimes dead) acquaintances who, days or decades earlier, had done him wrong. Now and then he grew especially agitated, forget-ting me completely, gesticulating with both hands, and ev-ery fifty feet or so exclaiming "That's *your* problem" or "Your turn to cry, babe." When that happened, I could tell he was retaking favorite scenes from an elaborate revenge fantasy in which Gabriella, finally realizing how wrong she'd been to leave him, tried to rekindle his interest, only to find that Dank had risen so far above her that he could muster nothing but a lofty Olympian pity.

When *I'm* depressed, I find it often cheers me up to climb a hill, as if I were slowly but surely rising above my sorrows. Maybe I'd be less unhappy in my new surroundings if the ground were hillier, or just if it were possible to walk more than a block, in this pedestrian-unfriendly neighborhood, without getting run over or choking to death on exhaust fumes.* Dank,

---

* (October 2007) I've decided to ignore my editor's request that I remove allusions to the circumstances in which certain of the entries in this guide were written. After all, the *raison d'être* of the book is to relate Dank's writ-

however, was never a climber—not even as a child, when his favorite pastime was to go to a department store and walk down the "up" escalator endlessly (or until some grown-up told him to get off), like a Sisyphus in reverse.

The Encyclopedia of Perversion: Dating from the long and lonely interregnum between Wives Numbers Two and Three, this mercifully abandoned book was to have featured lubricious descriptions of every possible object of sexual arousal. Dank had planned to tackle not just the more celebrated fetishes (midgets, livestock, amputees), but every known perversion in the annals of sexology, and even some still undiscovered but whose existence Dank's science of the lewd had led him to infer—as physicists infer new sub-atomic particles—and then from curiosity to see if he couldn't produce them, if only for a nanosecond, in the atom smasher of his own libido.

I was always glad, for posterity's sake, when Phoebus K. Dank abandoned a book, but especially glad when he abandoned *this* one, and I think I speak for the whole neighborhood. Imagine living two doors down from a fat man, badly dressed and barely socialized, who has suddenly taken to leering—like an adolescent boy with his first centerfold—at everything he sees, or at least at everything beginning with an "A," since he was writing the book in alphabetical order. Aardvarks, abridgments, accountants, accordions, Adam's apples, aerosol sprays, air conditioners, alligator clips, ankles, arms, armbands, armchairs, armpits, ashtrays, athletic supporters, automobiles—

---

ings to his life—to reveal *traces* of that life in those writings, as a detective finds traces of blood in the most meticulously wiped-up murder scene. I'd feel hypocritical pretending that writers of reference books have a unique ability to clean up after themselves so thoroughly as to leave no DNA on the page.

none was spared the cosmic rays of Dank's *I'll-try-anything* lust. (I think the Alps were in there too, though in their case—as in the case of women, more often than not—Dank had to content himself with simulacra. With pornography, in other words, such as the postcards for sale at the foot of the alp I just climbed—I'm in Switzerland this week—and at whose peak I am writing this note, when I'm not gazing out at the astounding view, or breathing the lung-cleansing air.)

After a few weeks, though, in the midst of *Avocado* (". . . especially when it's nice and ripe, and the hateful pit can be removed like the seed of a previous lover, leaving only the soft and yielding flesh—so tender and self-lubricating . . ."), Dank set aside the idiotic project, possibly sensing that he would go crazy, or crazier, if he didn't focus his lust a little higher up the food chain.

Maybe the reason Dank published so little nonfiction is that, even when off duty (that is, even in his "real," extraliterary life), he had so much trouble recognizing and complying with reality. As an endless source of unwelcome information and unpleasant stimuli, the real world was the last thing Dank wanted to think about when he retreated to his study, closed the blinds, and booted up his word processor. (OH)

The Erasures: A suicidal man attempts, before he kills himself, to eliminate all evidence of his existence. He chops down the apple tree he planted as a boy, buys and burns as many copies as he can of the book he once published, hacks into computers to delete all sorts of data about himself, swipes pictures with his image from his siblings' photo albums, and so on. He refers to all this in his diary as "Cleaning up my mess" or "Picking up after myself."

Though you wouldn't know it from my synopsis, the novel is set in the year 2020. Nickels and pennies no longer exist, science has developed a seedless pomegranate, the cars all run on water, and telephones signal an incoming call by a single brief earsplitting blast.

Despite or between these reminders, however, it is easy to forget that the year is 2020. One reason that Dank's vision of the future sometimes seems a little blurry is that, like all great writers, he had more to say about the present and the past. Though most of his novels were sold as science fiction, Dank was never really happy with that label, and accepted it only because he found it so hard to sell anything else. Much of his SF began as mainstream fiction. Dank retrofitted it with futuristic trappings only after failing to interest mainstream publishers. Not surprisingly, the futuristic touches in his fiction often seem extraneous, like whiskers scribbled on the Mona Lisa.

The Erasures dates from 1983 and was the book that cost Dank his library card. It was the first book he wrote after moving to Hemlock and into the big old house where he lived for the rest of his life, and where the traces of past occupants—a child's crayon marks on a bedroom wall, a forgotten box of corn flakes in a kitchen cupboard, a pair of black lace panties in an unlit corner of the laundry room—so fascinated Dank that he also wrote a story (THE HOUSE) about a man who falls in love, sight unseen, with a former tenant of his house.

As of 1982, the Hemlock Public Library didn't own a single book by Dank, but much of *The Erasures* is *set* in Hemlock, and after months of campaigning Dank finally persuaded the library to order it. After the book had sat on the New Fiction shelves for a month without tempting even a single borrower, Dank himself took to checking it out every couple of weeks, so that the date due slip pasted in the back would bear (false) witness to an avid readership. At length, however, he misplaced the book before he could return it. When the overdue notices came he ignored them, and when a bill for the lost item came a few months after that, he refused to pay: After all, it was *his* book. And that refusal cost him his borrowing privileges.

Dank seems never to have understood the difference between physical and intellectual property. Years later, in a big chain bookstore, he was arrested for vandalism, and his felt-tip pen impounded, after a floorwalker caught him defacing—or, as he insisted, "revising"—a shopworn copy of A MIDWINTER NIGHT'S DREAM that he'd found in the literature section. Again he insisted that he'd done nothing wrong, since after all the book was "his."

"Everybody Dies": A group of humans living in a colony on Mars sit around the rec room of their compound and bicker about what to do next. Harvest the lichens? Mend the canals? Throw an orgy? Kill a Martian? Play charades? Reminisce about the good old days on Earth? The omniscient narrator tells us that these people have been bickering like that for better than a decade now; that all they *ever* do is bicker, because they can't agree to do anything else; and, in an odd authorial intrusion, he adds that the people in the room are all "incredibly annoying" and that they "don't deserve to live." There follows an even odder authorial intrusion as the door bursts open and in walks a dead ringer for Dank, as he saw himself in 2001 ("a stocky, no-nonsense type whose gold-rimmed spectacles focused his exacting gaze to an unbearable intensity"), brandishing a ray gun. He yells "I HATE YOU ALL!" and opens fire. Everybody dies—everybody but the gunman, who strides out cheerfully, "wishing he'd done that a long time ago."

Though only seven pages long, "Everybody Dies" is the work that gave Dank the most trouble—gave him a taste of what other, less-inspired writers suffer all the time. Not that Dank had never gotten stuck before, but in the past he'd seldom wasted more than a month on an ill-conceived project before cutting his losses by ditching it once and for all. This time, though, his project wouldn't let him off so easy. He gave up on it as often as his mother had given up smoking, but with as little lasting success. In the years I knew him, Dank must have abandoned "Everybody Dies" a dozen times, always vowing never to look at it again . . . only to tell me, after an hour or after a year, defiantly or sheepishly, that he had "reopened the file on" the piece, as if it were an unsolved homicide.

What ended up as a short story was conceived as a long novel about a series of suspicious deaths among a group of enterprising farmers on a Martian lichen farm. At its longest, the novel had approached the five-hundred-page mark, but then something happened: The plot wasn't right, and Dank couldn't figure out how to fix it. Instead he merely replaced it with a plot that was equally faulty, and that with another, and so on. He must have felt like an artist painting a series of pictures—one over another—on the same canvas. As the years went on, the novel got no better. It didn't even get *bigger*. On the contrary, it dwindled: few sentences, few scenes, however sound they first appear, can withstand as many rereadings as Dank inflicted on the sentences and scenes in "Everybody Dies." All told, he struggled for more than a decade, off and on, with what finally cooked the story down to a seven-page story.

Dank always fantasized at bedtime—about flying; about invisibility; about winning arguments he'd lost in real life; about defending fortress towns, in olden days, with fewer troops but better guns (often anachronistically better—AK-47s, say) than the besieging army; about abduction by extraterrestrials who exhibited him for the rest of his days in a cage in the alien zoo—in a cage with several big-breasted and nymphomaniacal earth women. Over the years, one fantasy rose to the top of the playlist: Dank woke one day and found the finished manuscript of *Space Tundra* (as he'd planned to call "Everybody Dies" back in its glory days as a long novel about a serial killer, before it dwindled to a short story about a mass murder), in a neat stack of twenty-pound bond beside his typewriter (or, once his fantasy caught up with technology, as a beautifully spell-checked and formatted file on his computer). All he had to do was sign his name, send it off, spend his advance, and take all the credit, since the brownies who'd done all the work didn't expect anything in return, not even a nod in the acknowledgments.

Dank alluded to that fantasy so often, especially during his (brief and infrequent) bouts of writer's block, that I once jokingly, or semi-jokingly, offered to make it come true. Or half-true: although I didn't dare offer to finish his novel for him, I did have several other worthy manuscripts gathering dust, and I gladly offered to let him to send one out under his own name. Dank, however, laughed so loud and long at my idea— as if to say that nothing I had written could possibly be worthy of *his* name—that I almost took offense. Even now it almost makes me angry (though not as angry as the gunman in "Everybody Dies"!). Maybe I shouldn't have asked, but simply sneaked into his study one night, while he was snoring and snorting overhead, and left a manuscript for him to find, read, love, and publish in his name.

Over the years, Dank's feelings toward *Space Tundra* grew more and more ambivalent. He told me of the panic he'd experienced one day on arriving home from Coffee Town and realizing he'd forgotten the battered old laptop (containing the novel's latest draft and all previous drafts), and how that panic had given way to disappointment when he trotted back to the coffee house and found his computer still there. Yes, disappointment—as even the most loving and devoted father might feel, for a fraction of a second, on learning that his difficult, rebellious, ungrateful runaway son has been found, safe and sound, and will be back home soon with his attitude, his acne, and his electric guitar.

The most striking manifestation of Dank's ambivalence—or better say his flat-out hatred for the story—is the plot he finally settled for, which has nothing in common with the one he started with except the characters. He assured me that the massacre wasn't the first time—just the bloodiest—he'd written an unhappy ending to revenge himself on characters who had been making *him* unhappy.

A B C D E F
G H I J K L
M N O P Q R
S T U V W X
Y Z

F for Fatal: In the spring of 1981, during a ridiculous one-year appointment at a small, expensive private college, our indefatigable hack dashed off a novel about a professor at just such a college who murders a bunch of his students. This "disturbing coincidence" (rather than the novel's sheer ineptitude) was later used to deny Dank a teaching position at another college, Hemlock College, as if Dank were any likelier than any other pedagogue to run amok, or as if the school's liability would be greater if he did, because they had failed to heed the novel's warning.

That novel, anyway—the vengeful bedtime fantasy of a justifiably unpopular professor[*]—reprises Agent Bronson Harder, the no-bullshit FBI profiler with the heart of gold. Harder fires up his private hoverjet (Dank envisioned one in each garage by 1991, the year the book takes place) and flies to Oregon to do his thing. Who is killing all the rich kids? As in every College Novel, and notwithstanding the rigamarole on the copyright page about how "Any resemblance to actual persons is just coincidental" (has that *ever*

---

[*] Odd to see *Hirt*, of all people, invoking the tribunal of Popularity. I wasn't all that "popular" myself as a professor, though my uncontested position as the leading expert on Hemlock's most illustrious adoptive son secured my teaching post during my years in Hemlock, and will no doubt help me to retake that post, if circumstances ever permit me to return. (BB)

been true?), the characters are clearly based on people the author met and detested as a teacher. As in any whodunit, we are shown a whole rogues' gallery of "memorable" suspects; from their number, we can sense how many colleagues Dank must have antagonized in just one year, antagonized enough that they returned the favor. Could the killer be Knute Rangler, the noisy little scientist whose bossiness, abrasiveness, and coziness with management cause his fellow teachers to call him Alpha Lapdog? Could it be Rufus Carr, the sexagenarian sculptor, whose endless mid-life crisis is funded by his crowd-pleasing porcelain cowplops and Carrara-marble cat turds? Timothy Tosser, the lily-white expert on Afro-American lit? Kristoph Ermueller, the candy-bar-wrapper-collecting buffoon who teaches Intro to Pop Culture when he isn't laughing Sanka out his nose or masturbating at faculty meetings?

Time will tell. A lot of time. (As another critic said of another volume, it is "a book to kill time, for those who like it better dead.") After chasing all sorts of false leads down all sorts of dead ends (and tailing many a "shadowy figure" on the moving sidewalks that Dank foresaw in widespread use—at least in northern Oregon—by 1991), Harder determines that all the victims were enrolled in classes with a certain Dr. Bland, a seemingly drab and unflappable man, assistant professor of something or other. (It is typical of Dank that, though he takes pains to make us see each spike of manly stubble on his hero's chin, he forgets to tell us what his villain teaches.)

Agent Harder gets a warrant to search the teacher's office and confiscates a grade book, where, in addition to the usual attendance, quiz, and homework grades, he finds—ho hum—a mystery column headed "Obnox." Most students have at least one check in that column, many have several, and the murdered students all have ten.

In retrospect, the newspapers and other media would later come to wittily refer to this as the "Obnoxiousness Score," being as the students testified that the notorious professor never showed the least annoyment in the classroom, but, instead, that any time that a pupil said or did something in class that was obnoxious, the poker-faced professor would thoughtfully nod and, then, make a cryptical notation next to the offending scholar's name in his notorious grade book.

Where to begin with such a sentence—such an embarrassment of poverties? The redundancy of "later" and "in retrospect"? The solitary "this," shipwrecked an ocean away from the homeland of its antecedent? The self-congratulating "wittily" with which Dank splits his infinitive? The clunky repetition of "notorious," or the even more ham-fisted effort to *avoid* a repetition of "students"? The way that those on the far side of the lectern—be they students, pupils, or scholars—know not only that the poker-faced professor's notation concerns the most recently obnoxious of their number, but also that it is "cryptical"? The annoyment of the non-words that made up so big a part of Dank's vocabulary? I could go on, but suffice it to say that *F for Fatal* is composed entirely of sentences, or "sentences," like the above, and so it's quite a slog—"like wading through glue," as Tennyson said of Ben Jonson.

In his ability to hide—or inability to show—his anger, Bland reminds me of my fellow commentator,[*] but since Dank wrote *F for Fatal* before Boswell came along, any resemblance must be coincidental, or clairvoyant. It transpires, anyway—after another hundred pages of uniquely turgid, bloviating prose—that once a student's Obnoxiousness total hits 10, the notorious professor records his final grade (always an F, even if the victim deserves an A) and then murders the student in question.

---

[*] Nonsense. I can show my anger when I need to—as *Hirt* of all people knows only too well—even if I don't face life, as he does, with a sneer as my default expression. (BB)

It will come as no surprise that as a teacher Dank was a disaster. If he'd been allowed to teach sci-fi and nothing but sci-fi, he might have done okay, but his colleagues insisted that he take on some real courses too, feeling it would be unfair if Dank were allowed to teach nothing but "fun stuff." But the fun stuff was the only stuff he understood, and by the end of the year his cluelessness was legendary. Dank was one of those miseducators who, in the words of Thomas Reed, "never open their mouths without subtracting from the sum of human knowledge." In his Intro to Literature course, he told his students that "blank verse" is another name for "free verse," and that it was invented by T. S. Eliot "on account of the war." In his Great Books course, he raised eyebrows by adding *Starship Troopers* to the tail end of his syllabus, as if Robert Heinlein were the culmination of the tradition that produced Plato, Dante, and Shakespeare. In a composition course, he mixed up "its" and "it's" for the better part of a semester, and trained a roomful of freshmen to do the same, in cases where they hadn't been doing so already. Even Dank himself knew he was out of his depth, and he soon gave up all thought of a career in academia. Too bad he was no better qualified for a career in literature. (OH)

Fastest Pen in the Galaxy: The Fiction of Phoebus K. Dank: So far, the only full-length study of Dank's work (not counting—and we shouldn't—the appalling PETER PAN IN OUTER SPACE). Released in 1995, *Fastest Pen* is a revision of my doctoral dissertation, which featured a sketch of Dank's life to that point and also served as the basis for last year's DANK! (the authorized biography), and for much of the encyclopedia in hand.

(My own pen is slower than Dank's, I'm afraid. *Fastest Pen* was my first book; it appeared when I was thirty. By that age, *Dank* had published more than a dozen volumes. The disparity is only partly due to the infertility of my imagination, the

more leisurely gestation of my brainchildren, the more traumatic parturitions, the longer breaks between successive pregnancies, the higher incidence of miscarriages, the absence of
multiple births. There's also the fact that none of my novels
has ever been published. All my *published* books are books
about Dank, as this one will be. Like a hapless character in
one those old stories whose moral is "Be careful what you
wish for" or "Be careful how you *word* your wish," I've been
granted the power to write, but evidently only about another
writer. The gods have not allowed me to be a novelist, only to
sing the praises of one.)

We biographers are suckers for chronological order, and
having already recounted Dank's life in that famous order
three times, I've been finding it hard not to tell it that way
once again in the present volume, despite its alphabetical format. My subject would have made my labors easier if he'd
been so kind as to write his books and stories in alphabetical
order, beginning with ABBIE'S BABIES and ending with THE
ZOO, so that chronology and alphabet could march side by
side from cover to cover, rather than constantly leapfrogging
each other.

Speaking of labors, today is Labor Day, and my neighbors are out in their tiny backyards, in their barbecue aprons,
celebrating (though as far as I can tell the only "labor" they
perform is cashing unemployment checks—and of course the
yearly labor pains of nearly every female between the ages of
puberty and menopause) with burnt steak, domestic beer, and
classic rock. As for me, I'm in no mood to barbecue, can't
bring myself to spend another holiday at Arby's, and have
nothing in the house but a jar of instant coffee, a few crème-
filled snack cakes, and a can of that aerosol cheese. Oh, and
some insecticide. Let's see what happens next.

Fastland: Fastland is "a planet much like Terra," except that it spins a lot faster, completing a rotation in three hours. The circadian cycles of its humanoid inhabitants also last about that long: People stay up for two hours and then sleep for one. The narrator stresses, however, that the Fastlanders live as long as we do, and log as many hours awake. It's just that their periods of wakefulness are interrupted eight times as often. They eat only every other "day" or so, and bathe just once a "week." All trains and planes have sleeper compartments for every passenger.

Like the Lilliputians who take for granted that six inches is the normal height for a human being, the inhabitants of Fastland naturally assume that their world is the norm (though oddly they still call it Fastland). They would never credit the idea of a planet where people routinely stay awake for *sixteen* hours. To be sure, a reckless writer named Danx has just written an epic pamphlet (for on Fastland there are no books, only pamphlets, most divided into paragraph-length chapters) imagining just such a world, but the Fastland reviewers denounce the pamphlet as so much irresponsible nonsense, and in the end Danx is sentenced to death by the Minister of Culture, one Ewxan Maqdox, whose job it is to stamp out artists guilty of wasting the citizens' time—a capital offense on Fastland, where the days are so short. (Here Dank seems to forget his earlier insistence that, since the Fastlanders live as long as earthlings, and spend the same proportion of their lives awake, they have as much time as we do.)

Febrero, Gabriella (b. 1964): The third of our author's four wives ("but the first pretty one," he used to say). They met in 1992 at the annual awards dinner of the Science Fiction Authors of Northern California. Dank's most overrated book, THE PLAGUE OF CANDOR (written in 1986 but not published until '91), had been nominated for the organization's Best Novel award, incredible as that will be to anybody who has read the book. Somehow the tastemakers on the prize committee decided that of all the bloated carp and other bottom-feeders in that small and stagnant pond, our own Dank was one of the big fish. Or maybe it was just his turn. As for Gabriella, she'd been working for the outfit that catered the event. And even though *The Plague of Candor* lost to a book called *Robo-Slut*, Gabriella had been visibly in awe of Dank (who, as the only man among the nominees for the top prize, must have struck her as the evening's alpha male). Her awe was so visible that even Dank picked up on it, and by the time she cleared away the dessert plates, he'd overcome his shyness, with the aid of much free wine, and mustered the courage to ask for her number, ostensibly to tell her what science fiction masterpieces she should read. Reader, I was there that evening—dragged along for moral support—and I can truthfully say that, in my considered opinion, Dank was as polished a ladies' man as he was a literary stylist.

Their courtship consisted of lectures by him, in assorted local eateries and drinkeries, on the bewitchments of sci-fi. That's not a topic that gets many women "hot," but it worked on Gabriella, who came from a background as illiterate as Dank's—so illiterate that anybody who could summarize the plots of half a dozen books, no matter what books, struck her as a genius. After a week of listening to Dank hold forth on bioports and faster-than-light spaceships, Gabriella told him he was the smartest man she'd ever met, though that may have been the sangria talking. They were dining, at the time, at the local Olive Garden, which both she and Dank considered real classy, just the place for a big date. At the conclusion of that date they slept together, and Dank proposed to her as he ejaculated (or so he told me later), and again the next morning at breakfast, since Gabriella hadn't acknowledged his first offer, probably assuming it was just the orgasm talking. A week after that they were married—Gabriella for reasons of her own, and Dank because he was eager to close the deal that would link him for the first time ever to a pretty woman, and lawfully entitle him to nightly sex with her. That, at least, was Dank's understanding of the law, even with two marriages behind him—but if there really is such a law on the books, Gabriella wasn't a law-abiding wife. Given his obsession with citizen's arrests (see DOUBLE JEOPARDY and THE MAN WHO SUED HIMSELF AND SETTLED OUT OF COURT), it wouldn't half surprise me if Dank tried one on her.

The biggest difference between this marriage and the first two was Dank's fear, ongoing and finally prophetic (though hardly self-fulfilling—it would have happened anyway) of losing the prize he had won. With the first two wives, he'd wasted part of every day trying to persuade himself that he hadn't made a big mistake—that all the obvious drawbacks of marriage were somehow offset by its fabled advantages. With Gabriella, his fear was that *she'd* made a mistake and sooner or later would notice.

As for why their marriage fizzled as fast as it did, I know it would be psychologically correct (since psychology no less than politics has its moralizing *bien-penseurs*) to say that Dank's insecurity and jealousy drove her away, but he was *right* to be insecure: He was just a dorky fat guy, after all, who'd lucked into something he couldn't hope to keep. He took to humming, and sometimes even singing, a lugubrious popular song—from the seventies, no doubt—called something like "When You're In Love with a Beautiful Woman." When you are, according to the song, one thing you do is "watch your friends," and sure enough, Dank watched me narrowly whenever I tendered Gabriella some unmeaning compliment or showed up at their house for dinner wearing aftershave. But of course Dank overrated Gabriella's charms: As trophy wives go, she was barely an honorable mention. Besides, I found the thought of sleeping with a woman who had stooped to sleep with Dank—with poor flabby, floppy Phoeb—physically repulsive. (OH)

"February": Hilarity ensues, or tries and fails to ensue, when an "exotic-looking" dark-haired model on a nudie calendar is miffed at being chosen for the shortest month, since it means she doesn't get to show her stuff for quite as long as all the other hotties. Dank puts a distinctive hourglass-shaped birthmark on the forehead of the bitchy, frigid, petulant, illiterate, manipulative heroine of this embarrassing story (one of several in his oeuvre that must be called pornography, and in fact it first appeared in a magazine called *Dugs*), a mark just like the birthmark on the forehead of his third ex-wife. When I asked him, Dank denied—though unconvincingly—that Miss February's breasts and genitalia, which the narrator goes on about for two full pages, also correspond to those parts of his ex-wife. (OH)

Food Planet: Not a novel (though it did serve as the setting for a brilliant one—see PLANET FOOD) but the supermarket across the street from our house. Especially in his later and less mobile years, Dank went there almost every time he left the house. His love of supermarkets wasn't simple gluttony, though it may have been a factor in his fatness, especially as Food Planet was open around the clock. If Dank woke at three AM with a craving for butterscotch pudding, he wasn't forced to resign himself to a night *without* butterscotch pudding. It was quicker to put on his slippers, pad downstairs, and cross the street—in his pajamas, during the summer—than to lie awake for an hour convincing himself that he didn't want pudding that much after all.

Even when he wasn't hungry, Food Planet cheered him up. Sometimes Dank went there just to gaze, as people go to galleries, with no intention of buying. Sometimes I joined him on these gazing sprees, and as we walked the aisles we compared the memories evoked for each of us by particular products—Nilla wafers, Armour hot dogs, Lipton onion soup mix. Not that those outings were purely for pleasure: Dank also had to satisfy himself that no misguided entrepreneur had reissued one of the defunct food products to which Dank had devoted a nostalgic passage in one of his books, since a reissue would spoil both the passage and the nostalgia—as it had in the case of flavored peanut butter, taco chips, red M&Ms, and Space Food Sticks. It's maddening, the way the world fidgets, the way it can never sit still for its portrait. That's why all portraits of the present moment are at least a little blurry—especially the novelist's, since a novel's shutter speed is so ridiculously slow.

On his non-shopping visits to Food Planet, Dank had a habit of snatching some random item (a can of dog food, a head of cauliflower, a "family pack"—six rolls—of toilet paper) as soon as he arrived, so as not to be seen an hour later walking around empty-handed. When he finally left, he'd ditch this unwanted prop on some random nearby shelf. He did the same thing while actually shopping. I could always tell Dank had been to Food Planet before me. After a dinner of creamed corn and Sloppy Joes, I would cross the street to buy us some chocolate dip and strawberries. (This was in the era when Dank took care of dinner and I was in charge of dessert.) In the produce aisle I'd spot a can of store-brand creamed corn lost among the unshucked ears, and mentally congratulate Dank for opting to make it from scratch, even as I gently reproached him for leaving the can there. More often he switched vegetables *within* a given format (frozen broccoli for frozen Brussels sprouts; fresh cabbage for fresh cauliflower) rather than opting for the same vegetable in another format (fresh for canned or frozen spinach), maybe because in a sense all canned vegetables (for instance) have more in common with one another than with their respective frozen, fresh, or dehydrated kin.

By the same token, Dank seldom made it through the store without ditching several groceries he'd thought better of, leaving each item at the spot where he'd suddenly, or finally, decided against it, as a monument to his change of heart. He told me once that he never put anything back in its proper place because he could never remember where anything was shelved. The stock boys must have hated him, but his biographer welcomed the clues to Dank's state of mind. Some displacements hardly counted—a box of Corn Chex fraternizing with the Rice Chex—but other substitutions were more thought-provoking: a big bag of barbecue potato chips abandoned in a freezer case among the half-gallons of Food Planet ice cream, presumably because Dank had decided to permit himself either a sweet or a salty snack, not both, and had finally opted for the sweet. But he didn't always muster that much self-control: once, in the breakfast cereal aisle, aisle 7A, I found a jar of wheat germ slumming among the granolas and a box of granola fraternizing with the Kudos; in another aisle, I found a box of Kudos in the space vacated by a pack of Nutter Butters—the traces of poor Dank's snowballing demoralization. Once he started breaking his own dietary laws, he found it as hard to stop as cheating at solitaire.

"Funny Peculiar": A popular stand-up comedian loses his sense of humor after the death of his son. For a while, like a fluent speaker who has lost his sense of hearing, he's able to coast on old habits, remembering what *used* to strike him as funny. But just as the speech of the adventitiously deaf deteriorates, so does this comedian's ability to simulate mirth.

Written in 1982 but haunted by the stillbirth five years earlier of Dank's only son, "Funny Peculiar" is a fragment of an abandoned book that Dank had planned to call *Career-Ending Injuries*: stories of people from all walks of life each undergoing the worst possible affliction for his or her profession: a composer going deaf, a painter blind; a human statue developing the shakes; a preacher losing his faith in God, a psychic her clairvoyant powers (see THE BLOCK, another fragment), a restaurant critic his sense of taste, a model her looks, a mugger his nerve.

I'm writing this at Dunkin' Donuts—the closest thing I've been able to find, in the strip mall that has been my "neighborhood" since I left Hemlock, to a proper coffee house. The resemblance is slight. The welfare mothers, sex offenders, cops, and loud obnoxious kids who make up the clientele seem to think I'm a weirdo for writing when I could be eating doughnuts. I've got a lot of coffee in my system and I need to urinate, but I don't dare leave my laptop unattended. If I take it in there with me, someone's bound to snatch my booth, since it's the primo one with the view of the liquor store, the 7-Eleven, and the eighteen-wheelers hurling by. I don't even *like* doughnuts. I expect that surly girl at the counter to storm over here at any moment and forbid me from eating the peanuts I bought at the 7-Eleven.

"The Future Tense of 'Ouch'": The yawn-inducing story of a world just like ours, except that pain takes longer to arrive—a full hour, in fact. If someone stubs his toe, he thinks, "Oh no—*that's* going to hurt." If he winces, it's not a wince of pain, just a wince of irritation at a painful prospect—the wince I used to wince each time Dank asked me to examine the latest symptom of his chronic graphorrhea.* The toe-stubber might not even notice at the time that he *has* stubbed his toe, though an hour later he surmises it as he sits reading the paper and feels, suddenly, "a painful agony" (as Dank puts it, with his genius for *le mot juste*). "People make sure

---

* According to Webster's, "a symptom of motor excitement consisting of continual and incoherent writing." Hirt was always vain of his vocabulary. (BB)

they don't hurt themselves before important meetings or occa- sions," Dank informs us in the ponderous eleven-page preamble to the "story" proper—a page and a half of comic-book fisticuffs and interjections. (As usual with Dank, you can tell where the throat-clearing ends and the "action" begins by the irruption of— bad—dialogue, like bubbles in the surface of a cesspit.) Fights end, by the way, not when one party is incapacitated by pain, but when one party prudently judges himself to have incurred too much future pain. What else? Oh yes—as I say, there's even a "plot" tacked on at the end, to reward readers of special persever- ance. But never mind that. As Poe said about the work of some forgotten poetaster, "We look in vain here for anything worth even qualified commendation."

As I write these lines, or jot them on my new Palm Pilot (now and then I treat myself to some such amusing toy as an incentive to persist in the distasteful task of discussing Dank), I await my *crème brûlée* and *café au lait* at a restaurant that, judging by the truffled sweetbreads I just finished, and the *bouillabaisse noire* and s*alade frisée* that proceeded it, fully deserves its three stars in the *Michelin* guide. The waiters, too, are every bit as attentive and deft as it says in the book. Funny that an eater's guide should be more judicious than a reader's guide. (But you can correct for the absurdly-inflated ratings in this one by subtracting 2.5 stars, as it were, from each of Boswell's appraisals.) It's a perfect evening and I'm sit- ting out on the terrace, like all but a couple of my fellow diners. Who sits *inside*, at a place like this, where you have a choice, on a night like this? Maybe people who've been out enough already. Sometimes when you've been out all day you do begin to feel overexposed, no matter how perfect the weather, and to long for a roof and four walls, as even I do by this hour, some days, in my balmy southern-European paradise. But I'll never understand how Dank could *stay* indoors, as if he'd never once opened the window and noticed how much nicer it was outside than in the stuffy, smelly confines of his "art."

Dank's tragedy, or one of them, is that he never left the house. He spent his whole life in his cell, attempting with his fiction to garner love and glory, fame and fortune, but—even apart from the fact that he had no talent and nothing to say, and so was like a madman trying to cook a banquet without either heat or food— his seclusion finally made him unfit for the world and its awards, i.e. for life *outside* his cell. When now and then the world noticed him and lured him out, what it saw was something as pale, blind, bewildered, and unsightly as if it had evolved in the depths of a cave. Or as if it had never left the womb. (OH)

A B C D E F
G H I J K L
M N O P Q R
S T U V W X
Y Z

"Gray Eminence": All rejected lovers dream of turning the tables, or so I'm told. Dank once estimated that in the time he'd wasted on daydreams of getting back his third ex-wife—of being in a position to reject *her* for a change—he could have written another novel .or two. (Not that *that* was saying much, considering that he squeezed out his fictions with the rapidity and regularity of a well-functioning gastrointestinal tract.) As he grew older, though, and the objects of his lust grew younger, and his infatuations accordingly more hopeless, it became harder and harder to imagine *any* state of affairs in which he'd gain the upper hand romantically, and so the fiction driven by that fantasy grew more and more farfetched.

Written in the summer of 1990, at the height of its author's farcical infatuation with a woman half his age, "Gray Eminence" is the story of a world just like ours—except that there not youth but age is sexy. Teenagers dye their hair gray and use makeup to simulate liver spots. Plastic surgeons specialize in "gerontogenic" surgery—adding rather than subtracting wrinkles, inducing quasi-arthritic limps, performing "face drops" rather than face lifts, and so forth. *Right.* Few men under forty can find lovers, while a sixty-year-old man can take his pick of younger women . . . unless some tubby *septua*genarian rival comes along. (Dank—who weighed an appalling 301 pounds at his 1990 checkup—doesn't come right out and say so, but it is implied that obesity is another competitive edge in this unlikely universe.) It's against the law to sleep with anybody over eighty—the age at which senility officially sets in—but the oldest people are "so irresistible" that "any younger man or woman that has a chance just goes ahead and risks arrest for statuary [*sic*] rape." Luckily, few of these *fogies fatales* condescend to sleep with anyone much younger than themselves—after all, they've waited all their lives to be so delectably ripe—but now and then an elder afflicted with low self-esteem will stoop to taking a young lover. Such old-timers are despised by their contemporaries, though, and the youngsters who luck into their deathbeds are ostracized by *their* contemporaries, out of envy, as "grave robbers."

Near the end, the story switches gears, with a lurch, from one kind of idiocy to another, as "top scientists" discover a "portal" to a bizarre mirror universe where youth and not age is fetishized. "Gray Eminence" ends with a glimpse of that hard-to-picture portal ("no wider than a typical suburban sidewalk") thronged with two-way traffic as young people surge through into the youth-friendly universe, and old people hobble through in the opposite direction. (OH)

A B C D E F
G **H** I J K L
M N O P Q R
S T U V W X
Y Z

Happy Pills: A dozen stories each concerning some imaginary drug, and often sounding like so many product placements, or out-and-out endorsements. The stories date from 1981, the year of Dank's first real spree of reckless drug abuse. He'd recently divorced his second wife, Ms. JENSEN, and moved back to Oakland. All his life poor Dank was scared of solitude— scared to be alone with himself, that sketchy stranger, when he turned off his computer—and after the divorce he hastened to invite a friend to stay with him rent-free, as he'd also done after his first divorce and would again after the two to come. This time the lucky sponge was a sculptor named Jimmy, an aging beatnik Dank had met at City Lights. Like most artists, Jimmy didn't have a lot to say, and so the two shared drugs instead, of which Jimmy did have quite a repertoire.

Up to then, what with his morbid fear of damaging his brain, Dank had never even smoked a joint (though he was a bit too fond of his prescription diet pills—see AMPHETAMINES). But in April 1981, he had just recovered from a bout of deep depression roughly coextensive with his second marriage, and for a while his brain no longer thought of itself as a delicate computer, but more like a torture chamber. That he still had any brain cells left by 1982 is thanks to the Berkeley police, who put a period to that unhealthy chapter of Dank's life by busting Jimmy for possession (and also busting several dozen biomorphic blobs of spray-painted papier-mâché that were to have been Jimmy's legacy to a hushed and curatorial posterity—busting them, like so many piñatas, in search of a stash).

Soon after Jimmy's handcuffed departure from his life, Dank consulted a neurologist to ask if there were any wonder drug to undo whatever damage all the other drugs had done, or at least to rid his system of the foreign substances he'd introduced it to, which he listed for the doctor's benefit. Considering that Jimmy's tenancy had lasted just six weeks, Dank had worked his way through an impressive pharmacopoeia: absinthe, amyl nitrate, animal tranquilizers, banana skins, catnip, cold capsules, cough syrup, deadly nightshade, hashish, magic mushrooms, mandrake, marijuana, morning glory seeds, nutmeg, nitrous oxide, paint thinner, patio sealant, peyote buttons, poppy seeds, quaaludes, rubber cement, scopolamine, toluene, and Valium.

So he soon regretted his spree, but first he dashed off a dozen stories celebrating psychogenic drugs. Though several of those drugs sound distinctly futuristic, *Happy Pills* is set in 1967, in San Francisco during the Summer of Love.* A

---

* "I was *there*," says Dank, in a self-important preface, as if his clichéd and inaccurate portrayal of the Haight-Ashbury in its druggy, huggy heyday were an eyewitness account. In point of fact, young Phoebus, still reeling from his middle school's fervid anti-drug indoctrination, sat out that famous orgy, declining the few invitations that came his way, and so passing up the only chance that he'd ever get (slim enough in any case) for easy sex. So, no, he *wasn't* there. He was never anywhere, but especially not there. What with his fear of bridges and his fear of tunnels, Dank never crossed the San Francisco Bay if he could help it, then or later. If he did set foot in Frisco during the Summer of Love, Dank was dragged there by his mother. The few semi-accurate details about that place and time in *Happy Pills* were gleaned from other books. Like all historical fiction, no matter how recent the history, it smells of the lamp—in this case, the lava lamp. (OH)

frame tale explains that the pills in question are made by a visionary firm called Seuss Pharmaceuticals, hippie-owned and Berkeley-based—a sort of Ben and Jerry's of the pharmaceutical sector.

I won't summarize the stories (except to say that each one features a chemically assisted happy ending), but readers may be interested in what kinds of drugs Dank perceived a crying need for as of 1981. Among other happy pills and magic potions, he proposes:

—A logic drug that makes illogical thinking physically painful.

—A wisdom pill that doesn't eliminate dangerous passions (jealousy, rage, lust) but accelerates them to the point where the impassioned person no longer has time to act on them. Moods succeed one another in their natural sequence, but so rapidly that each obliterates the one before it, nips it in the bud. After the loss of a loved one, for instance, people on this drug still go through the usual stages of grief (denial, anger, bargaining), but in a matter of minutes rather than months.

—A still-faster-acting wisdom *spray*, since even a minute of pure hatred or despair can lead to tragedy. This spray speeds up emotions almost to the point of non-existence. Whenever something terrible happens—the death of a child, the desertion of a spouse—users whip out their inhalers and inhale. Their faces blur for just a moment, as if the normal play of expressions over a period of days or weeks had been compressed by time-lapse photography into the space of a second. Then their features come back into focus, but now the people look sadder and wiser, as if they'd been brooding for weeks but had finally resigned themselves to the calamity and resolved to put it behind them.

—Several other narrow-spectrum nasal sprays, including "Happy Spray," a fast-acting anti-depressant in a special dispenser (like the ones used by asthmatics), developed for patients prone to attacks of sudden life-threatening sadness, and "Dowse," a fast-acting aerosol anaphrodisiac for sex offenders turning corners in a world of abrupt temptations.

In addition to all these and several other drugs—pity pills, emotion potions, capsules to enhance the sense of humor, injections to suppress the sense of guilt, suppositories enabling the user to forgive but not forget anything done to him or her the day before—Dank proposes novel modes of delivery. Before the days of Nicorette, he envisioned several psychiatric chewing gums: a bubble gum that also functions as a mood elevator; a sugar-free tranquilizing gum with a special liquid "serenity burst" at the center of each piece; a mint-flavored breath-freshening anti-shyness gum. Dank also introduces a topical over-the-counter anti-psychotic called Sane, a sky-blue cream to be applied directly to the scalp of the afflicted head.

Happy Pills seems to have been conceived as a get-rich-quick scheme: letters to his agent, Tom (from whom I'm *still waiting*, as of September 19, to hear back about the seven manuscripts I sent him in mid-June), show that Dank was convinced, and could not be unconvinced, that if any of his fictive drugs were ever actually invented, he and not the chemists who invented them would own the "rights," just as he owned the film rights to his novels. Anyone who wanted to market "his" drugs would have to pay him for the privilege.

The Happy Young Men: A literary movement started in October 1972, during our author's one semester at college. The movement was co-founded by the fledgling novelist and three other members of the Science Fiction Club to protest the gloomy "mainstream" novels they were forced to read in their modern fiction courses and the scorn they were encountering in creative-writing seminars. The Happy Young Men claimed to be proud of the very aspect of their fiction most ridiculed by their snooty classmates: its optimism, its conviction that sooner or later Science would fix everything (as it does, e.g., in HAPPY PILLS). And the leader of the movement was none other than the subject of these pages.

It's easy to see why his fellow members deferred to the portly fictioneer (lately the "K" key on my laptop has been jamming, and though I can still get it to function if I jab it hard enough, I'd rather just avoid the letter, even if I'm forced to find all sorts of synonyms for the budding wordsmith's surname, like that cartoon pig whose stammer plays so big a part in his choice of words). Though his life itself was not a happy one, his art was a way of transmuting his life, turning lead into gold. I don't just mean that writing was what Dank, like Kafka, did for kicks, when he wasn't telling knock-knock jokes or watching *Kojak*. (There, I've finally fixed the "K" by pulling off the plastic cap—there was a bit of peanut shell in the works. Now, though, I can't get that cap back on.) No, I mean that Dank was a true artist—and art may be the only way available, for some of us, of being glad about the world, glad to be alive.

"The Headache Factory": An ordinary man in a repressive and humorless future is arrested, one afternoon, for cracking a subversive joke at work. He is taken to a torture chamber, strapped into a special chair, festooned with electrodes, and subjected to some kind of high-tech, high-voltage reprogramming. He's released an hour later—but from then on, anytime he thinks of something funny, he gets a splitting headache.

Despite its resemblance to such dystopian nightmares as *A Clockwork Orange* and *1984*, Dank insisted that "The Headache Factory" was based on nothing but the headaches that tormented him in 1999. For a while there he was convinced, and made no secret of it, that his brain had just developed "special sensors" to punish him whenever he thought an illogical thought ("You know, like how the teachers in the olden days would hit kids with a stick if they made a dumb mistake"). Not even Dank could explain *how* his brain had grown all those new sensors midway through its career, but I liked his explanation of *why* it had happened: His mind had detected its own instability, its anarchic elements, and the headaches were like a police state clamping down on subversives. By the time they went away, Dank had come to think of his new capacity or incapacity—the inability to think an illogical thought without instant negative reinforcement—as an evolutionary advance. The human species was beginning to outgrow its irrational nature, and his headaches were no more or less than growing pains.

It wasn't the first time he'd suffered from headaches—or the first time he'd confused them with mental events. The day I moved to Hemlock (see The Academician), Dank complained of a "murderous" headache and then—not wanting me to think he was a whiner—explained that he was good at tuning out most other pains, but that a headache is harder to ignore than a stomachache or toothache because "it takes place *in* your brain, so how can you *not* think about it?" Dank added that "even those yogis that can meditate while lying on a bed of nails" would get no meditating done if afflicted with headaches like *his*. And he went on to describe, at great length, what sounded like an ordinary headache. That struck me as even crazier than Dank's conviction that such pains partake of the nature of thoughts—his assumption that I might not have suffered a headache myself at some point in my life, and so might need him to describe one to me. It was a strange world he lived in, and what's even stranger is that Dank managed to write fiction other people understood, given how unclear he was about what is and isn't common knowledge, what goes without saying and what doesn't. Alluding to his hemorrhoids, he'd take for granted that I was as familiar as he with that affliction. Then he'd turn around and describe a bloody nose at length, as if life might have spared me any firsthand knowledge of a nosebleed—the taste, the stinging in the throat, the sodden Kleenex used to stanch the flow, and so on.

Heat Wave: Dank's favorite movie of 1974 was a predictably dismal disaster film whose only selling point was something billed as "Sensurround"—a gimmick consisting of massive subwoofers and a massive ad campaign to convince the credulous that they would not just see and hear but *feel* the disaster, an earthquake. Nothing if not credulous, Dank was so thrilled by that prospect that he saw the film the night it opened. I allowed him to drag me along, and of course I quaked no more than you do when you crank up the bass on your stereo. Even Dank admitted that, after what the ads had led him to expect, the actual experience of Sensurround was disappointing.[*] But that didn't stop him from becoming obsessed with movies that appeal to more senses than the usual two. That fall he and Elliott, one of the many like-minded nerds he'd befriended three years earlier, during his single semester at college, used Elliott's Super-8 camera to make their own disaster movies. In *Tornado*—which I've deemed unworthy of a separate entry—a trailer park is menaced by a twister. At the first screen-

---

[*] In fairness to a movie that I haven't seen, Dank had been at least as disappointed, many years before, by his first *real* earthquake: a novelist's imagination amplifies events so much that few live up to expectations. (BB)

ing, in the basement of the house we shared in those days, the windier scenes were enhanced by half a dozen oscillating table fans set to full blast. (Or so I'm told—I'd left town for the weekend.) I wasn't as lucky with *Heat Wave*, another thirty-minute epic meant to be enhanced by extra-filmic effects. This time the gimmick was an array of portable electric heaters whose thermostats Dank turned up, grimly and little by little, in the course of the film. The story concerned a future overheated by the infamous greenhouse effect (one of whose direst consequences, seldom mentioned, has been a spate of hot and bothered science fiction). At the first screening, the world was saved from lethally rising temperatures, and the audience from lethal boredom, not by top climatologists working feverishly to find a solution, but by the *deus ex machina* of a tripped circuit breaker. (OH)

Heirloom Clinic: A Los Angeles sperm bank for Nobel Prize winners and other geniuses. In 1989, feeling that the time had come to assert himself genetically, Dank presented himself to the receptionist as a prospective sperm donor. The childless author had made a special trip to southern California for the purpose, armed with an ancient and much-handled piece of paper documenting his SAT scores, a snapshot of him shaking hands at some convention with a Nobel-winning physicist, and a paperback copy of FASTLAND bearing a blurb (by his ex-friend MACDOUGAL) pronouncing the book "a work of genius." Despite these credentials, the Heirloom Clinic rejected our author due to a policy—one he might have ascertained by telephone before booking a flight to LAX—of refusing to consider unsolicited emissions.

Given his unfair reputation as a "mere" science fiction author, it is not surprising that Dank himself never received a Nobel Prize. Indeed, he never won a prize of any kind (not counting the booby prize discussed so gleefully in Hirt's mean-spirited entry for DON'T SAY I DIDN'T TELL YOU), and this was a sore point with him. Even late in his career, with dozens of published books to his credit, he entered writing contests intended for much younger and less-established writers, including several for high-school students. I think he was driven by a sort of masochism—a despairing joy in casting pearls before swine—rather than any desire for ill-gotten gain. Few of the contests offered a prize more substantial than bragging rights, rights that Dank would of course be unable to exercise if he won, since in order to enter he had to use a pseudonym and lie about his age. In any case, he never won—though in 1999, at the age of forty-six, he did receive an honorable mention in the Kudzu "New Voices" competition (ages fifteen to eighteen). He'd never placed first in *any* contest, not even the science fairs in junior high, and no doubt it was a wish just once to come in first, no matter where, that drove his lifelong quest to enter competitions for which he was absurdly overqualified.

"Henrietta's Performance": An aging science fiction writer discovers that his beautiful young wife is a performance artist, and that their marriage has been nothing more—as far as she's concerned—than a grant-funded piece of art. The story begins when the man finds an unmarked videocassette in the VCR, one day while his wife is out. He watches the tape and sees a two-hour montage of himself at his worst—picking his nose, kicking the dog, gorging on lasagna, trying in vain to jiggle his penis into a usable erection, and so on. What surprises him is not that such footage exists. After all, his wife is a film-school dropout who never goes anywhere without her camcorder, and in his middle-aged infatuation he has given her permission to film him any time she wants, even when he's straining and blaspheming on the toilet. No, what surprises him is that she's clearly taken great pains to splice together, into an artfully paced and cumulatively devastating sequence, all the most compromising footage that a year with him has yielded, as if to produce the most damaging and one-sided portrait she possibly could.

When his wife returns that evening, camcorder whirring, he waves the cassette in her face and demands an explanation, but she just mutters something about art. He blows his top and calls her a poseur, a so-called artist who never paints or draws or sculpts or even photocopies. Given such an opening, she can no longer resist the temptation to tell him that their whole *relationship* is nothing but a work of art, the postmodern kind that he's too square to recognize. He doesn't believe her at first, but after she storms out he goes through her papers and finds a draft of her grant proposal: "I'll pick a man at random, some really boring, bland, complacent dork, and . . ." He goes through her old bank books and find a large deposit—for just the sum of money named in her proposal—dating from the day they met, a day whose date he's memorized, the day he was approached in Starbucks by a stylish, unnervingly hip, unreadable woman. At the time it all seemed too good to be true, and so it was.

Dank wrote this story in November 1992, soon after his wedding to a woman who resembled Henrietta as closely as the plump and bespectacled husband in the story resembles its author. Just like that husband, Dank never knew, and never ceased to wonder, just what *his* wife, Gabriella, saw in him. He had the impression, throughout the six months of their marriage, that other people, and not always strangers, were wondering too. Soon his wife herself began to wonder, though when Dank wrote "Henrietta's Performance" she hadn't yet confirmed his deepest fears by leaving him. She did that a few months later—in April 1993, by which point she'd written him off as a "schlub" (her word).

And yet in the beginning she'd considered Dank a genius. Where had he gone wrong? Since her initial attraction to him remained a mystery, it followed that her subsequent repulsion must remain one too. But he speculated endlessly about it. Had she left him because he wrote science fiction and not literary fiction? Was he no good in bed? Did she want a man her age? (But Dank's replacement was even older than Dank.) Had she gotten sick of his nocturnal snorts? Was he too funny-looking? Was she more superficial, more hung up on appearances, than her initial interest in Dank had led him to hope? But she claimed that for six years she'd dated a one-legged man, a drunken amputee named Sam. *Six years.* How had Sam managed to stay in the saddle so much longer—a dozen times longer—than Dank? Did Gabriella only stay with men she pitied? Was Dank not pathetic enough? *Too* pathetic? Too ambulatory? Had Gabriella resented his walks, as she might've resented a rival?

In any case, their last official quarrel had been triggered by one of his walks—by Dank's failure either to see or to hear Gabriella when, out running errands in her Toyota, she'd spotted him striding up Pine Street, more than a mile from home, talking to himself and gesturing emphatically, probably winning an argument he'd lost, days or decades earlier, in real life. Gabriella claimed that she'd pulled over to give him a lift, but though she'd honked repeatedly, and called his name, and crept along beside him for a block, Dank had continued to walk, talk, and gesticulate, either failing, as he later claimed, to notice her or else refusing to acknowledge her, as she assumed at the time. In truth he hadn't noticed her, though in retrospect he recalled a muted honking and the peripheral blur of a car impinging on his daydream conversation. Dank, indeed, had been conversing with Gabriella herself—reliving (and, yes, winning) the argument they'd had the day before about pornography. And even if he'd noticed her—the flesh-and-blood original of his imaginary companion—driving alongside him, Dank couldn't have accepted a ride from Gabriella that day: He'd been seeing if he could walk around all afternoon without once crossing or retracing his path, as in those brain teasers where you have to run a pencil through a maze, and past certain checkpoints, without crossing or retracing any lines. Getting in a car would have felt like cheating—like lifting his pencil from the page.

I moved in with Dank the year after Gabriella moved out, and in an odd, nonsexual way, I think I served him as a sort of Platonic "rebound" relationship. (Later I learned that this was a pattern with Dank: After a marriage fell through, he would put away his cologne, break out the booze, and regress for a couple of years to a presexual phase.) Gabriella had dealt his self-esteem a blow from which it would never recover, and what he needed most, around the time I came along, was the sort of unconditional admiration I offered.

In exchange, I got a home—not just a place to stay, a *home*. I doubt I'll find another. The other night, while watching some depressing docudrama about a homeless family, it occurred to me that I too am homeless: Although I'm renting this ugly little houselet in suburban Portland, there's no way I could call *it* home. I'd be better off in a cardboard box myself. Or better yet a pine one. It's a measure of how far I've fallen that I watch as much TV these days as my obese, flag-waving, tabloid-reading neighbors. I've finally come to understand why people *watch* TV: When you're alone, when the view from your front window is as desolating as the view from mine (a wide and noisy street, a used-car dealer, and a Taco Bell), when the day is as dull and dark as this one, and a cold rain has been falling all week long from a gray sky—when that's how it is, who can blame you for sitting around drinking whatever beer is on sale and gazing through that other, magic window, at the brighter world on the other side?

Hirt, Owen (b. 1952): Dank's oldest friend and later his most deadly enemy. As far as I can tell, the origin of their friendship was Dank's touching veneration of the first writer he'd happened to meet—of Hirt's pedigree, the books on his shelves, and the confidence of his opinions where books were concerned. Hirt would make some loftily contemptuous remark—"the sort of idiot who still reads *Hem*ingway"—and Dank, whose own opinions in those days concerned things like the relative merits of Heinlein and van Vogt, would hasten to purge all Hemingway from his shelves, hoping that Hirt hadn't seen it there. (Hirt was even harder on Heinlein than on Hemingway, but Dank was too addicted to SF to break *that* habit.)

Tall, good-looking, self-possessed, with the confidence of a third-generation author (his parents and *their* parents were all published writers), Hirt outdid poor Dank in everything but talent. And for the longest time, they shared the assumption that Hirt was more talented too, and more likely to succeed. That was the axiom from which their friendship was derived, so it was predictable that Dank's success, when it arrived and such as it was, destroyed the friendship. It took Dank decades to realize that he, not Hirt, was the real writer. I'm not sure he *ever* realized it—certainly Hirt never did. Dank, with his endearing modesty (enlivened, to be sure, by episodes of a no-less-endearing grandiosity, when he invented time machines or spoke of starting his own nation), never really got over his initial awe of my fellow commentator. By 1983, Dank had published nine or ten novels and Hirt one slender book of po-ems. Yet that year Dank moved to Hemlock, because Hirt was there, and bought a house two doors away from Hirt, because the house next door was not for sale.

Dank used to tell me that Hirt was "independently rich." Be that as it may, Hirt clearly sees himself as a natural aristocrat, one who by rights *ought* to be rich. His parents were mere academics like me, but no doubt Hirt nurtures fantasies of being switched at birth—fantasies of actually being a prince, or at least a baronet. I can see him courting a rich heiress by pretending to be even richer than she. And he did own some nice objects—cufflinks, rugs, and such—and liked to imply that they were only the tip of the iceberg. And Dank said something once about Hirt's "classy vacations" in spots like the Côte d'Azur. Yet he lived in a smaller house than Dank's, on a not-so-classy block, with Jock JABLONSKY right next door and a supermarket right across the street. And he was famously frugal. If he hadn't lost his teaching job due to the touchiness, contentiousness, and arrogance that make it hard to picture him lasting long in *any* job, sooner or later he'd have been fired for his compulsive thievery of office supplies, library books, printer paper, toilet paper, paper towels, liquid soap, and even a bottle of ketchup from the school cafeteria—infractions for which Hirt is legendary among his ex-colleagues more than a decade after fouling out of academia.

Though he tried his hand at fiction once or twice (and with predictably pompous, opaque, and pretentious results), Hirt was best known—or best neglected—as a poet, perpetrator of such books as *Final Notice*, *Yaddo D-Day*, *Neighbor's Wife*, *Last Call*, and *Occupation: Other*. I've tried to read his poems, but they're unreadable, in the strictest sense of the word: Hirt must add a special anti-caking agent to his lines to prevent them from clumping together to form something larger. And yet one component of his arrogance vis-à-vis Dank (and vis-à-vis this commentator, too, since I too write novels, though I've yet to publish one) was the age-old snobbery of the poet toward the novelist. Hirt made no secret of how he felt about the two camps, and once quoted ("jokingly," but with obvious approval) the words of that no-longer-lionized but still-overrated turncoat W. Somerset Maugham: "The crown of literature is poetry. . . . It is the sublimest activity of the human mind. . . . The writer of prose can only step aside when the poet passes." As far as I'm concerned, of course, Dank was more of a poet than Hirt, at least by any intelligent definition. Isak Dinesen's, for instance: "A poet's mission is to make others confound fiction and reality in order to render them, for an hour, mysteriously happy." It's safe to say that Hirt's effusions have never made anyone happy, unless it be some rival poet pleased to see a colleague founder.

Hirt's first book was well enough received, by the little magazines where its poems had first appeared, but the world would pay less and less attention to each successive volume. The world may be stupid, but like a cat it can tell if you like it or not, and often that determines how much it likes *you*. Although you'd never guess it from his entries in this guide, Hirt had started off as a love poet, or at least a celebrator, now flattering his neighbor's wife, now singing the praises of a forest or a statue or a bird song. Because he'd been hailed, early on, as "a poet in love with the world," he'd felt obliged in later books to continue his public displays of affection, when in fact Hirt would have liked to wring the world's neck—torch the forests, smash the statues, poison the birds. One reason Erato favors the young is that most poets do grow angrier as years go by, and soon are too full of hatred to write persuasive love poems. ("Anger raiseth invention," as Lord Halifax remarked, "but it overheateth the oven.") Hirt should have lived in the age of Pope and Swift, when love poems were less popular than hate poems.

For some reason, Hirt resented Dank's success more fiercely than he resented everyone else's—which is ridiculous when you consider how meager Dank's success was in proportion to his genius. It is understandable that Hirt should envy that genius, but absurd that he would envy Dank's official stature in the world of letters—like the 5'1" MacDougal (whose Lilliputian arrows Hirt is so fond of retrieving and reshooting with his own puny bow) resenting Dank's 5'8".*

"Hobson's Choice": After many years of persecuting misfits, a tall, blond, handsome, heartless jock named Hobson is abducted by a pair of Rectifiers—aliens who kidnap, try, and punish the most hateful earthlings. Coming from "a more sophisticated planet" where brains have triumphed once and for all over brawn, to their author's plain approval (since, for all his bulk, poor Dank had no brawn at his disposal), the Rectifiers, Fiawol and Fijagh, have no sympathy with this beater-up of bookworms. They offer Hobson a tough choice: Over the next year, he can either grow obscenely and irreversibly fat, or insufferably and irreversibly smelly. At that point, the dreary story forks, and we get to see the dreary consequences of each choice, the smelly and the fat—both of which result in just the sort of persecution Hobson used to dole out to others. (Dank himself, by the way, was no lily of the valley, especially in the periods of fevered drudgery he mistook for inspiration, and so for an excuse to neglect such things as bathing.)

Although the handsome, confident, and virile Hobson bears a droll resemblance (up until his Rectification) to this commentator as an adolescent, Dank insisted that the bully was based on one named Hansen who'd tormented him in junior high; Phillip, the poor little fat boy tormented by Hobson, is patently modeled on Dank. Even in his forties, decades after his last wedgie, noogie, charley horse, swirly, or Indian rope burn at the hands of Hansen, Dank

---

* There must be a psychiatric term for Boswell's compulsive-quotation disorder—something like Bartlett's Complaint. (OH)

had nightmares of the running-through-molasses sort in which the thirteen-year-old bully chased a grown-up Phoebus, threatening to beat him up and shouting things like "pussy," "dweebus," "flabbus," "fat-ass," "fetus," "geek," and "homo." And it must be stated, in fairness to the bully, that (judging from old photos) young Dank did fit the standard adolescent definitions of "pussy," "geek," and "dweeb," though he was never a "homo." No, he was always clear about his sexuality, such as it was—surprisingly clear, for a man whose mother often called him "Phoebe" (as *her* mother had been named), though he hardly ever got a chance to exercise that sexuality.

As for "fat-ass," just how fat *was* Dank? His will stipulated that I should have access to all documents pertaining to him—or as many as he himself had access to—including his medical records, and with their help I've been able to chart his height and weight through the years:

Age	Weight	Height
Newborn	5 lbs., 8 oz.	1'6"
5	52 lbs.	3'6"
10	143 lbs.	4'10"
15	187 lbs.	5'6"
20	241 lbs.	5'8"
25	257 lbs.	5'8"
30	278 lbs.	5'8"
35	296 lbs.	5'8"
40	319 lbs.	5'7"
45	333 lbs.	5'7"
50	387 lbs.	5'7"
53*	399 lbs.	5'6"
Average	**242 lbs.**	**5'0"**

---

* According to the coroner. (BB)

Quite a butterball, then. The correlation between body fat and science fiction has always intrigued me, insofar as anything to do with science fiction can be said to intrigue me. It isn't a strict correlation, of course—not all science fiction fans are fat, or not initially, and not all fat men will admit to reading science fiction. But there's clearly *something* about obesity that predisposes adolescents to the genre. Simple escapism, maybe: I'm told that for people less attractive and athletic than myself, that time of life—that time of such relentless body consciousness and peer evaluation—is a painful one. And for adolescent *boys*, classic science fiction must be a perfect escape, either disregarding women altogether or relegating them to brief and pornographically pliant appearances (since even the meekest, most cerebral, most asexual fourteen-year-old still needs to masturbate every hundred pages or so). And even fans who aren't fat to begin with tend to put on weight as they lie there on the couch, weekend after weekend and summer after summer, turning pages and eating Doritos. As the fat son of fat parents, though, Dank never had a chance: He would have grown up fat no matter what he read, or even if he'd never learned to read at all (as some would say he never did). (OH)

"The House": Written right around the time Dank followed me to Hemlock and moved into the house where he was to live for the rest of his days, this is the story of a lonely bachelor who buys a house and falls in love, sight unseen, with the single mother who lived there before him, and traces of whom—forgotten panties and the like—our hero keeps coming upon (an ambiguous expression in this context, but I'll let it stand), like an overgrown child at an Easter-egg hunt. At (needless) length he tracks her down and wins her heart . . . but then decides, on the eve of their wedding, that he doesn't want to share his house with the flesh-and-blood woman, but rather with his ghostly first impression of her. (With her panties, in a word.)

Before his falling-out with Dank, MacDougal called this story "Henry James on acid." In truth it's more like Henry James on antacid, but a thousand times more creepy (and of course Dank's fiction was only ever creepy—as it was only ever funny—inadvertently). I should be much harder on "The House," condemning and demolishing the creaky, leaky, shoddily constructed hovel, but today I'm in a mood to temper justice with compassion. It's hard to feel anything but pity for poor bumbling Dank when you're sitting in a beach chair savoring the sunset and sipping your third Campari and soda. At the risk of revealing my whereabouts, I'll add that the sand on this beach is as white, the water as blue, and the bathers as attractive as in a travel brochure. In fact, they're *better*—not as if merely retouched by a clever art director, but as if ardently wished into being by someone in a gray and rainy, sad and landlocked place. (OH)

How John Doe Got Here: Dank observed March 18, the anniversary of his third divorce, with an annual day of self-hatred. On March 18, 1996, he told me glumly that his greatest accomplishment was being born, that it had been all downhill from there. I replied that birth may be the single biggest event in anyone's life, but that as a biographer I couldn't afford to think so, or my biography of him would itself be one long anticlimax. That conversation may have given Dank the idea for the book he wrote that summer, one of his most innovative works, and one that's still disgustingly unpublished.

Most biographies, of course, start before the subject's birth, sketching the lives of his or her parents and even grandparents. *John Doe* is a fictional biography, and with no limit to the omniscience of fictional genealogy, the narrator is able to go back much further—back to the generation of the John's great-great-great-great-grandparents, all sixty-four of them.* The brilliant book begins with page-long sketches of each of those sixty-four lives, capsule accounts that would be even briefer—brief enough to carve on tombstones—if they didn't slow down at what for our purposes is the important point: the mating that produced one of the subject's thirty-two great-great-great-grandparents. And so on for each successive generation, except that for each generation the biographical sketches are twice as long, so that by the time we get to John Doe's parents, we are not surprised to see them allotted thirty-two pages apiece. The emphasis throughout is on the iffy moments in John's prehistory, the near-engagements of his ancestors to non-ancestors, the marital problems that came close to estranging two forebears before they'd had a chance to engender another, the near-fatal illnesses (and other pre-parental brushes with death or celibacy) that if not for hairbreadth recoveries would have broken the chain, the timely demises of irrelevant older siblings that made room for more children. The saga ends the day of John Doe's birth, with his emergence from the womb: the important thing about him, the amazing thing, is not what he may go on to accomplish, but the simple odds-defying fact of his existence. Never has an author expressed so unforgettably the central mystery of life, the one underlying all other mysteries and certainties, grievances and gratitudes—what a miracle it is to be here at all.

By the time I met Dank, three of his grandparents were dead, but his parents were still hanging in there, having gauchely stuck around for more than forty years after serving

---

* Dank never dug any deeper into his own past than the generation of his grandparents, thanks to his habit of throwing down his spade as soon as the ground began to get hard. (OH)

their genetic purpose. I had a chance to meet them and all sorts of other branches, blossoms, buds, and blights on Dank's family tree in August 1995, when I chauffeured him to the Dank family reunion—a yearly gala held that year in Sacramento at his sister's house. So I'm able to report that Dank got his looks from his mother, his fashion sense from his father (who rose to the occasion with what looked to be a brand new sweatshirt and a freshly laundered pair of sweatpants), and his physique from both, since both were as big as him. So were his sister and most of the other strangers milling and moiling around her tiny smoke-filled bungalow. They must have shared a gene for fat, or else the fault lay with the Swedish meatballs, scalloped potatoes, lasagna, fried chicken, baked ham, buttered biscuits, and pie they all seemed to associate with a good time.

More important than our author's physical similarity to the rest of his breed, though, was his spiritual *dis*similarity. Unlike Hirt, that son and grandson of *litterateurs*, Dank was a first-generation intellectual, and clearly the last bookworm the Dank line would ever produce. When his sister and her husband Stan accused Phoebus of being "some kind of stuck-up highbrow, always reading Asimov," you'd assume they were being sarcastic, calling him a *low*brow, but far from it: In that house, even a subscription to *TV Guide* was seen as an egghead affectation. ("He can't just watch TV, he has to *read* about it," I once heard Stan complain of some snooty coworker.)

Stan, a brawny, brainless junior-high phys-ed instructor, was what Dank dreaded most about reunions. Junior high, the low point of Dank's life, had plainly been the high point of Stan's, in part because he'd spent those years tormenting kids like Dank. Stan never missed a chance to regale his brother-in-law with tales of an adolescence blissfully spent copping feels, sniffing glue, and beating up weaklings and bookworms and fatties.

Even more than Stan's anecdotes, though, Dank dreaded Stan's bone-crunching handshakes. He dreaded them, each year, for a good month before the reunion, and I couldn't blame him, having suffered the handshake myself. It was as if Stan had channeled all his adolescent sadism into the one form of physical contact sanctioned in civilized life between men. Especially men as homophobic as Stan: When, in 1998, at the second and last reunion I attended (see INSOMNIA), Dank tried, on my advice, to preempt the handclasp with a manly long-time-no-see hug, Stan shoved him away roughly and asked, at head-turning volume, if Dank had "gone gay or something." For the rest of the day, the gym teacher referred to me as "Phoebe's date," and even, once, as "Phoebe's bitch."

But Dank had warned me about Stan, and I'd been "training" for that reunion for several months with one of those red-plastic-handled A-shaped hand-exercisers. When we left that evening, I made a point of squeezing Stan's hand even harder than he'd squeezed mine that morning. His expression of surprise was priceless. I like to think I injured that sadistic hand of his, though I didn't stop him from promptly squeezing Dank's again. The next day, back in Hemlock, Dank did the math and determined that, at a rate of two handshakes per reunion (on meeting and on parting), he would have to endure another fifty if both parties—both forty-five at the time—lived to be seventy. Was it possible that all those handshakes, past and impending, wouldn't do lasting damage to the delicate bones in his pen hand?

Hypochondria: As befits a science fiction writer, Dank did much of his suffering beforehand, in anticipation of ordeals that often seemed anticlimactic when and if they arrived. This was especially true of diseases. Aside from and in spite of his obesity, he enjoyed adequate health for most of his fifty-three years. An old-fashioned down-to-earth physician, one with no time for neuroses, mood disorders, or psychosomatic symptoms, would have said that Dank, though he'd been *injured* once or twice, had barely been sick a day in his life. There is even reason to believe that Dank's two heart attacks were—like certain pregnancies—hysterical. What caused him to lose so much sleep, toward the end of his life, was not Fatal Familial Insomnia or FFI, the bizarre disease that killed his father (see INSOMNIA), but what might be termed *FFFI: fear* of Fatal Familial Insomnia. Even the AGORAPHOBIA that plagued him all his life, and made its final chapter so bizarre, may be seen as an invalid's avoidance of something (in this case, reality), that he believes, superstitiously and in defiance of medical science, to aggravate his illness (life).

Dank was one of those constant consulters of the *Family Medical Guide*, the *Color Atlas of Incurable Diseases*, the *Merck Manual,* and the American Psychiatric Association's *Diagnostic and Statistical Manual*—and as anyone knows who has looked at those books, and specifically the last-named, it is hard to flip through without seeing yourself, or someone you know, on every page. For a while there Dank kept his copy of the *DSM* on the toilet tank in the blue bathroom, and once, in the course of a single bowel movement, I diagnosed myself successively with Intermittent Explosive Disorder, Paranoid Disorder, and Psychogenic Fugue! As for Dank, with his supreme suggestibility, *he* saw himself in nearly all the nebulous shapes in that massive cloud atlas.

His worst misdiagnosis occurred on his twenty-fifth birthday, minutes after he finished a memoir of his life up to that point. He had ended with a sentence predicting that he'd live to be a hundred, then headed to the bathroom of his rented house in Oakland to answer a call of nature he'd been too busy till then to acknowledge. He opened his *Complete Encyclopedia of Signs and Symptoms,* that week's toilet reading, at random. (If anything is random.) It may be that his cocky centenarian ambitions annoyed the god in charge of the future's mystery, the god who makes fools of astrologers and weathermen, to say nothing of science fiction writers. Maybe Dank's prediction (and his title for the never-published memoir: *First-Quarter Report*) had struck the god in question as a form of hubris meriting at least a wrist slap. All we know for sure is that Dank happened to open the book to a discussion of something called Hepatolenticular Degeneration, and left the bathroom, half an hour later, insanely convinced that he was dying of that almost-always-fatal disease. His doctor failed to persuade him otherwise, and after some more research at the public library Dank gave himself six months to live. Happily for readers everywhere, his self-diagnosis proved to be another of his DELUSIONS, though one that lasted long enough to prompt his might-as-well marriage to Molly JENSEN.

A B C D E F
G H I J K L
M N O P Q R
S T U V W X
Y Z

"If Looks Could Kill": Short-short story. Should be shorter. Title says it all.* (OH)

"The Ill-Advised and the Inadvisable": As retirement approaches, a high-school guidance counselor starts to wonder if anyone has ever heeded his advice—and, if so, who fared better, those who did or those who didn't. To find out, he tracks down several dozen students from two decades earlier. To his horror, he discovers that the ones who listened to him have all come to bad ends: prison, suicide, insanity.

The advice in question isn't specific career counseling, but general wisdom, or what till now the counselor has always mistaken for wisdom. Each chapter features, and takes as its title, one of his favorite ill-considered maxims ("He who hesitates is lost"; "If at first you don't succeed, try, try again"; "In for a penny, in for a pound"; "The road of excess leads to the palace of wisdom"; "A stranger is a friend you haven't met yet") and its consequences for advisees who took it to heart. Each

---

* If my collaborator didn't want to summarize the piece in question, he should have let me. "If Looks Could Kill"— inspired by my explanation of a game called Laser Tag to which I'd just been introduced by my students—imagines a terrifying world where people can kill one another just by glaring hard enough. (BB)

chapter shows the many ways that a particular bit of unwisdom has ruined lives, given twenty years to rage unchecked. In the end the counselor sends out a sort of product-recall letter, urging everybody to discard the malfunctioning maxims he sold them on so long ago.

I too had my doubts about the advisors who oversaw my education—especially, I'm ashamed to say, the PhD adviser, Dr. Handler, who persuaded me to write my dissertation on Dank. I once hurt Dank's feelings by confessing that he hadn't been my first choice for a dissertation topic. He'd always been my favorite *writer* (though by a wider margin in my adolescence than after), but I'd had some wrongheaded notion, when I entered graduate school, that I had to focus on "someone serious" like T. S. Eliot in order to be taken seriously myself.

Dr. Handler, though, insisted that T. S. Eliot—and all the other Serious authors I named—had already been done, and overdone: There was nothing left to say about that bunch. Why not write instead about that science fiction author I'd once mentioned as a guilty pleasure? The prolific one? I was probably the only person in the world who'd read all his books, and so far *nothing* had been said about *him*. I'd have the first word, and every scholar who came later would have to reckon with me in order just to get a word in edgewise.

At that point I was of two minds concerning Dank: Part of me knew I'd much rather read him than read Eliot or any of the other writers I was now supposed to want to read, just as deep down I knew I still preferred grape juice to wine. Part of me, though—the part that tends to get the upper hand in graduate students—was convinced that any book I actually enjoyed, any book that *allowed* me to enjoy it, must be unworthy of serious study. So at first I resented Dr. Handler's insistence on Dank, especially since my friends were being steered toward heavyweights like Joyce and Shakespeare. Had my advisor sized me up as a lightweight? Some of my resentment even rubbed off on poor Dank, when I sat down to reread him—the first time I'd read a word of his from duty instead of for pleasure. I couldn't help comparing him unfavorably to Eliot and Joyce and Shakespeare. I'm ashamed to say I thought—and said, over pitchers of beer, to the fellow graduate students I groused and caroused with—all kinds of appallingly snide and ungrateful things about books I had loved for a decade. (I'd give an example, but I've repressed that shameful era of my intellectual development and can't remember a single criticism.)

But then, one stormy night, just like the one outside my window now (but in Santa Cruz instead of Portland, and in spring instead of fall, so with the prospect of much better weather up ahead), I had a change of heart. My advisor was right: If literary scholars serve a purpose, it is not to count the adverbs in *Ulysses* or to prove that Charlotte Brontë was a hermaphrodite or that the same versatile theory can enshroud both Henry James and Steven King in jargon so interchangeably opaque as to obscure any reason for reading one and not the other. No—our *raison d'etre* is to call the world's attention to unnoticed beauties and profundities. I'd had my winter of discontent with Dank because I'd been demanding that he give me what I got from Joyce or Shakespeare (though in truth I've never had much use for either), rather than the thrills that Dank alone could give, and had always given me so generously when read on his own terms. In a midnight of the soul I date to March 18, 1991 (or about two months before I first met Dank), I vowed to love my fate, to love my dissertation, and to love the odd niche my advisor was driving me into. In other words, I vowed to love Dank, through thick and thin (and at his thickest—e.g., the 936 pages of LISTENING TO DECAF—he did put that love to the test), in sickness (artistic) and in health, for the rest of my life. I took my vow so seriously that a few nights later I got into a fistfight with a drinking buddy who'd ventured to disparage Dank, though he was just repeating sentiments he'd heard me expressing all winter.

And, yes, I know how odd it sounds to *vow* to love an author, but after all I'd loved him all along, ever since I first encountered his fiction at the age of fifteen. All I was doing now was solemnizing our relationship: putting a sacramental stamp on a teenage crush.

Influences: Dank's taste in books—if we can speak of Dank and taste in the same breath—was formed way back in junior high, at an age when fiction served as an escape from the world of sneering phys-ed teachers, menacing bullies, and snickering girls. Afterward he seldom felt the need to leave the ghetto of his chosen genre. In a way, his ignorance of real fiction was a blessing. Writers as derivative as Dank are often haunted by anxiety of influence, by the nagging sense of merely making shoddy knockoffs of the great works they admire, like those phony Rolexes. Not Dank: *He* was happy counterfeiting Timexes. His favorite writers were already so debased that no matter how flagrantly he stole from them, no matter how often he turned his hand to things they'd done already and done better—describing motion sickness, say, in zero gravity—none of his reviewers in the mainstream press was apt to catch him out.

If Boswell ever coaxes or coerces some unlucky grad to write a dissertation on Dank's "influences," at least the budding scholar will know where to look, assuming that Dank's "library" is still intact. Dank himself never discarded a book. He was such a hyperactive highlighter, moreover, that it wouldn't be much work to find out just what parts of just what paperbacks he thought worth plundering. He even highlighted *The Joy of Sex*, a book he went for years on end without occasion to consult. (A certain page was dog-eared:

When he did get a chance to try out the procedures recommended by *The Joy of Sex*, Disco Dank seems to have been especially partial to, or curious about, the one called *Negresse*.)

So if he lied about his favorite authors, it wasn't to conceal his shameless thieving but to hide his shameful taste. When interviewers asked about his reading habits, he never mentioned any sci-fi authors, but rather recited a list of red herrings like Homer and Virgil and Goethe. (I don't think he fooled anybody, though those interviews—the few I deigned to glance at—took place in Dank's living room, near the shelf that showcased all the books he was proudest to own: Homer and Virgil and Goethe and so on, but all in mint condition, patently unread, though dating from Dank's freshman course in Western Civ.)

To know what he *really* read, you had to step into his study, as I did just once in all our years as neighbors, since it stank in there—stank as I imagine it must inside a marsupial's pouch. The walls were lined from floor to ceiling with the vile paperbacks of Dank's never-ending adolescence, books with garish covers (big-breasted women, spaceships) and titles like *Earth Unaware, Planetoid 127, The Man Who Folded Himself, The Man Who Shrank, The Man Who Melted, Dawn of the Mutants, March of the Robots, Thing From Another World, Virus X, The Microscopic Ones, The Reaches of Space, The Corridors of Time, Gateway to Limbo,* and *Stowaway to Mars*. "Books think for me," said Charles Lamb— and those were the books that thought for Dank. You could tell that all the tawdry, tattered, swollen, dog-eared reading matter in his study—unlike the highbrow volumes in his living room—had been read cover to cover and over and over, and that its owner hadn't skipped a single bug-eyed monster, flying saucer, ornithopter, time machine, supernova, tractor beam, benevolent alien, galactic federation, tentacle, replicant, biochip, teleport, telepath, bioport, hive mind, warp drive, solar wind, exosuit, overlord, underling, anti-matter factory, antigravity device, if-the-South-had-won-the-

Civil-War scenario, intelligent fungus, rebellious computer, sinister eugenicist, jet pack, or death ray. What would poor Goethe have said, if he had left the living-room shrine to see what Dank was up to all day in the study? "There is nothing more dreadful than imagination without taste."* (OH)

"Insomnia": The diary of a man with a rare degenerative brain disorder that appears at first to be routine insomnia but progresses in a matter of months to total sleeplessness and finally to death. The entries get longer and more incoherent as his nights get shorter.

Although the story first appeared in *Flabbergasting Science Fiction*, the lethal sleeplessness that Dank inflicts on his protagonist is a real—though rare—condition known as FFI, or Fatal Familial Insomnia. (The piece's only science fiction feature is its setting, a future abuzz with robots and moving sidewalks.) The story was written the day Dank discovered that his father had the gene for the disease, which as its name suggests is heritable. That didn't prove that Dank too had the gene, but it was worrisome, especially as he'd never been a gifted sleeper, or not since the catastrophe of being born. (He was convinced that he'd slept better in the womb than ever again. He used to say that sleep was like returning to the womb—like pretending that he *hadn't* yet been born and was still exempt from all anguish of the post-natal condition.)

---

* Granted that Dank's models weren't always the loftiest, the important thing is that he improved on—and so earned his squatter's rights to—every weedgrown plot or vacant premise he chose to inhabit.

Notice that as much as Hirt objects to my quotations, he has a weakness for quotations too, though the sort *he* favors are not thought-provoking so much as thought-*preempting*, like the sort of music—Strauss, Rachmaninoff—that doesn't inspire emotions so much as have them for you. (BB)

No matter how fantastic the worlds they imagine, all great writers take a lively interest in the real world, and some nights Dank found himself unable to lose interest to the point of losing consciousness. Even at his best, he tended to lie awake for an hour at bedtime, savoring the lack of stimuli and brooding on the problems posed by whatever book he was writing at the moment, before downshifting to the erotic fantasies that usually escorted him to dreamland. And some nights he fantasized till sunrise without ever drifting off—sometimes consciousness pursued him like a noxious body odor no amount of bathing would remove.

Dank tried his luck with half a dozen sleeping pills, but the only one that proved a match for his tenacious mind also suppressed REM sleep, and yet (or thereby? furthermore?) gave his waking hours a nightmarish tinge. Even after Dank discontinued that pill, it took a long time for his night life to get back to normal—long enough for him to speak of filing a lawsuit against the pill's producer and demanding a million dollars for the loss of his ability to dream.

We expect prodigious brains to have some trouble shutting down at bedtime. I've been sleeping poorly too, these past few months, though it's a miracle I ever sleep at all in this earsplitting neighborhood, with its raucous residents (who seem *not* to sleep at all) and heavy traffic roaring past. Dank made his own noise. During his third marriage, he was diagnosed with disruptive sleep apnea, which meant he stopped breathing now and then, only to resume a minute later with a snort. The doctor told him to stop sleeping on his back, and Gabriella, in a heartwarming expression of tenderness toward the spouse whose snorts kept disrupting her own sleep, sewed a special pouch into the back of one of Dank's old T-shirts and sewed a tennis ball into that pouch, so that if he rolled over onto his back, he would feel the ball between his shoulder blades and either wake up or roll back onto his belly. (He still had this T-shirt when I knew him, and—though he slept alone now and could snort and snore to his heart's content—sometimes wore it to bed for old time's sake, as I know because he sometimes stayed in his night clothes well into the following day. More than once I found him up and about—eating lunch or reading mail—in his special T-shirt, with that unsightly bulge between his shoulder blades like an enormous carbuncle.)

But though it helped his apnea, the tennis ball was not a match for Dank's insomnia. In 1996, he finally spent a (sleepless) night in a sleep lab. The finding was "poor sleep hygiene": bad habits like amphetamines (though Dank had understated the magnitude of *that* bad habit), after-breakfast naps, after-dinner coffee, a beer or two at bedtime, now and then a midnight snack, and no fixed hour of arising—no alarm clock. Dank cleaned up his act, and for the next two years his problem went into remission, but then came the awful family reunion of 1998, held that year at some random cousin's house a hundred miles away, on a rainy day in early March. Most years the reunions were in August, but that year the tribe met early because Dank's aunt was dying fast of some mysterious disease. For the second time in three years, I attended too.

This time the whole Dank clan was awfully glum, compared to the high spirits of the other, sunnier reunion I'd attended. We soon learned the reason for the gloom: In the two weeks between the invitation and the day itself, Aunt Edna's doctors had diagnosed her with FFI. Five other Danks had already been tested for the gene, and two—including Dank's father—had tested positive. As for the rest of the tribe, some were still steeling themselves for the test, others insisting that there was no point, since there wasn't a vaccine, and the disease was neither contagious nor curable. Only Stan, the gym-teaching brother-in-law with the bone-crushing handshake, was in high spirits, candidly cheerful about his exemption, as an in-law, from the family curse. Right before we left I even heard him quip, within earshot of Aunt Edna (admittedly well on her way to the serenity of a vegetable), that he'd taken out a big insurance policy on his not-yet-tested wife, and got his hopes up every time she had a restless night.

Dank himself had quite a few after that dismal reunion. It took him a month to submit to the test, and two weeks to learn the results. He tested negative, but never felt quite reassured by the report. Perhaps the lab had accidentally switched his blood with some luckier man's; perhaps the technician (whom he pictured as a beautiful young woman—a fan of the fiction of Phoebus K. Dank—with a big heart, bigger breasts, and wisdom well beyond her years) had decided to hide the ugly truth from him, knowing there was absolutely nothing he could do about it. He didn't dare to have *another* test, though—that would have felt like courting disaster. And so for the rest of his life he lived in authentic, if manageable, fear of suddenly developing a quickly fatal illness.

His initial reaction to the news, though, was to sleep for a week, from sheer relief or maybe—just in case the lab was wrong—to store up as much unconsciousness as possible in preparation for the lean years ahead. (No more crazy, after all, than the day he laundered all his clothes a dozen times in the hope, or rather the conviction, that they would stay clean twelve times longer.)

"An Insomniac in Somnolia": Somnolia is a land where people sleep their lives away because their religion promises an afterlife of eternal wakefulness for good and bad alike, and they want to rest up while they can. The hero of the story is a heretic who doubts the existence of this afterlife, doubts it to the point where he stops taking his state-issued "vitamins"—

actually sedatives dispensed intended to keep the populace asleep. Written in hopes of selling the film rights, the piece reads a little like an action movie, with the hero chased through swamps and sewers, parking garages and derelict factories, by the wide-awake special police. He also has to fend off the dreamily violent, drowsily murderous onslaughts of his fellow citizens, especially those who are repressing doubts of their own, and who hate the hero because his rebellion implies that they have wasted their lives.

Inventions: When he was thirteen, Dank saw a documentary on Thomas Edison. For the rest of his life, off and on—though most fervently in adolescence—he styled himself an inventor. For a while he insisted that his mother (and his sister, who refused) call him "Tom" instead of "Phoebus." A photo of his boyhood bedroom, circa 1967, shows posters of Edison and Tesla rather than Asimov or Bradbury. None of young Dank's inventions ever worked, but some of his ideas were ingenious: a tickle-proof vest; an insect *com*pellant, an altered Etch-a-Sketch he dubbed the Etch-a-Curve for its ability (in theory) to draw perfect curves, not just boring verticals and horizontals; special food perfumes and food deodorants for smelly foods like fish and cabbage; a variable-speed stink-activated bathroom fan; and felt-tip pens with scented ink for use with "odoring books"—like coloring books, except that the user would add odors and not colors. See AROMARAMA for more on Dank's abnormally sensitive nose, even keener in his teens.

Dank was not content to be the most inventive author of his era. He had a workshop in the basement, and every now and then, encouraged by all the talk of his "inventiveness" (a virtue even hostile critics granted him), he reverted to invention in its more tangible Thomas Edison sense—the sense, after all, in which he'd encountered the word as a boy.

The first of these Edison phases I witnessed occurred in the summer of 1995. I knew something was up the day I spotted Dank at the public library, checking out an armload of books with titles like *The Big Book of Inventions, The Young Inventor's Handbook, Pulleys and Gears, All About Magnets, Prize-Winning Science Fair Projects, Thomas Edison: Boy Inventor,* and *How Does a Refrigerator Work?* (I'd secretly paid the fine that had cost Dank his card, and even got him a new card, persuading a friend in the reference department to mail it to him. Dank never knew why he was forgiven but may have assumed that after all those years the library had finally come round to his point of view.) By that point he'd outgrown his guilty taste for young-adult fiction (half the paperbacks in his SF collection were intended for young readers, and not all those young-adult novels dated back as far as Dank's own young adulthood), but he still had an embarrassing penchant for juvenile *non*fiction. Any time he grew curious about a subject—automobiles, meteorology—he consulted a children's picture book about it, as well as or, often, instead of a sober grown-up volume. For someone so smart (and, sometimes, so grandiose), Dank was oddly lacking in intellectual confidence. Or maybe the kind of knowledge he wanted was so superficial that it could be found only in children's books, since only there is the impossibly intricate real world portrayed in such broad strokes, such bold cartoonish outlines.

The upshot of this particular Edison phase (the first of several during my tenure as Dank's *aide-de-camp*) was a combination laser printer/paper shredder, configured in such a way that each sheet would begin to feed into the shredder even before it finished printing. An alert reader could still scan each line in the seconds between its emergence from the printer and its disappearance into the shredder, but unless you had a photographic memory, that would be your one and only chance.

Dank was convinced that sooner or later one of his inventions was bound to make him rich, and he tended to head for the basement any time he felt besieged by practical concerns—an overdraft notice or an odd persistent tingle in his elbow or the nagging fear that no one would ever consent to have sex with him again. By the end of his life, he had filed applications for seventeen patents, including three that dated from the heat wave of 1996 (when he went through a brief "refrigeration" phase): a self-cleaning freezer; an electric cooling blanket (with a compressor to circulate refrigerant through a network of slender and flexible coils); and an energy-saving refrigerator with a duct to the outdoors, so that on cold days owners could harness the cold to chill their food, rather than paying to chill a special compartment in the house they were already paying to heat. (Dank actually adapted our own fridge along these lines, but his invention wasn't perfect, and sometimes on cold days everything froze—the milk, the mayonnaise, the lettuce, the lunch meat.)

My favorite Dank invention, though, was a fully automated confessional that looked just like an ATM. The device, a sort of Automatic Priest Machine, dated from the era of Dank's marriage to Ms. FEBRERO, a practicing Catholic. To use it, you'd insert your "SoulCard," punch in your PIN and then the alphanumeric codes corresponding to your sins, and receive both a penance and a printed statement. The statement would tell you your spiritual balance—what shape your soul was in and what your odds were for salvation, according to the church of your choice (each machine would belong to one particular denomination, but people of other persuasions would still be able to use it for a small service fee). You could lie to the machine, of course, just as you could to a flesh-and-blood priest in a conventional confessional, but you wouldn't fool God; you'd only hurt yourself and waste your time, defeating the purpose of confession and of spiritual counsel in general, live or automated: not to bluff your way into heaven, but to discover where you stand and how to improve that standing. Finding no takers for this invention in the real world, Dank contented himself, in the end, with installing it in a novel (see THE PRAY-O-MATIC).

But for all his tinkering and taking things apart, and fooling with the plumbing, and fiddling with the toaster, and claiming that he could have been the modern Edison if he hadn't found a different channel for his talents, Dank never struck me as very mechanically gifted. For years he slept with an electric blanket his sister had given him, but he used it like a conventional blanket, not plugging it in, because he'd never figured out how to operate it. In 2002, when he bought a new microwave oven to replace the one he'd wrecked by microwaving the blender (to test a sudden hunch that the taboo on metal was nothing but an old wives' tale), he was so bewildered by the new appliance and its multitude of buttons that for the next year he cooked everything on the one-touch Popcorn setting, whether he was making popcorn, baking a potato, boiling a cup of water, or reheating a slice of pizza.

"It'll Come Out in the Wash": Dank wrote many stories, but this is the only one narrated by a sentient washing machine. The piece is set not in some distant future where such things might be routine, but in late twentieth-century suburbia, and Dank doesn't tell us *how* this particular washing machine came to possess intelligence, a decent grasp of English, and the ability to see, hear, feel, taste, and smell (though only inside the machine). It uses these endowments to infer the lives of the family it serves on the basis of their laundry—the kinds of garments, their sizes, their stains. When the story begins, the machine has already developed an amazingly detailed picture of the people upstairs; the plot involves its unraveling of a domestic murder mystery.

In a way, it's funny that Dank didn't write *more* about laundry, considering how much he liked to do his own, once he got his own washer and dryer. Owning machines that would wash and dry his clothes *for free*, and under his own roof—it seemed almost too good to be true, after all those years of doing his laundry in public and paying for the privilege (even with his freedom: *twice* in 1977 he'd been arrested for indecent exposure after stripping down to his underpants in a Berkeley laundromat so as to wash the clothes he was wearing). More than once Dank compared those machines to the gumball machine he'd received one year for Christmas, after months of lobbying, that dispensed a regulation gumball *for free* every time he turned the handle. Sometimes he would wash a single pair of socks as a pretext for running his washer and dryer, just as sometimes he'd bake a single cookie in his oven, or run his dishwasher when it contained nothing but one mug. He liked big appliances. While they were running, they gave Dank himself an illusion of gainful employment, even if he was just petting the cat, or watching a game show, or polishing an old brown wheat-ear penny to make it look freshly minted. (After he lost interest in his TIME MACHINE, that was about as close as he could hope to come to old-fashioned time travel.) Even his refrigerator could give him an illusion of productivity if it was chilling something—a can of pop, a tray of not-yet ice cubes—rather than merely keeping it cold.

Dank liked doing laundry so much that now and then he offered to do mine. I always refused—partly because it appalled me to picture my author demeaning himself, and partly because Dank saw laundry as science in action, and whenever he ran out of All or Fab, he'd seize the opportunity to perform what were in effect chemistry experiments with various unsatisfactory substitutes—dishwashing detergent, Pine Sol, Murphy's Oil Soap, Mr. Bubble, Lava, Comet, Head & Shoulders, oven cleaner, and once even toothpaste. Another of his experiments involved drying a washload of whites with a full box worth of fabric-softening sheets, twenty-four in all, to see just how wonderfully soft he could make his underwear.

His favorite part of laundry, though, was emptying the lint screen, peeling away that pelt of gray fuzz with the same frivolous care he took to remove the rind of a tangerine in one piece. Back in the bad old days of laundromats (days that in my case are here again, since this tiny rented house doesn't come with a washer and dryer), he'd sometimes open all the dryers not in use, and clean out *all* their lint screens. Dank always liked to empty things, especially things that hadn't been emptied in a while, that had been slowly and furtively filling, as if they'd been getting away with something until he came along to put an end to the abuse. Although he had a housekeeper who came in once a week, she was forbidden to empty the receptacle of the paper shredder in his study because Dank liked to do it himself. Geniuses are strange, and Dank's idea of fun could be every bit as baffling as some of his other ideas. In seventh grade, the semester he studied trombone, he'd had a game of waiting as long as possible to drain the spit from his instrument through the valve in its slide. Even as a child he had loved to empty the steel reservoir of the old-fashioned suction-mounted pencil sharpener now in his study. Even now he sometimes sharpened every pencil in the house, just to have a bigger clump of pencil shavings to purge.

A B C D E F
G H I J K L
M N O P Q R
S T U V W X
Y Z

Jablonsky, Jock: Our next-door neighbor at 109 Empedocles Street. He and Dank got off on the wrong foot back in 1983, when Dank moved to Hemlock to be close to Hirt: Dank had barely finished unpacking when he decided that two doors down was too far off, and tried to get Jablonsky to swap houses. Dank even drew up an elaborate list comparing the two houses on a dozen different points, and finding his own—the one he was big-heartedly offering to trade away—superior on every count. The list offended Jablonsky so much that at last he started yelling, chased Dank off his property, and warned him never to set foot on it again. All that, though, was before I arrived. By the time I came to Hemlock, Dank and Jablonsky had resigned themselves to a grudging co-existence. But Dank still saw his neighbor as an ogre—as the angry man who'd started bellowing that day and whipped off his muscle shirt as if preparing for a fight (though why a muscle shirt would impair his fighting was unclear).

That first impression may have been to blame for Dank's other basic grievance against Jablonsky: that he was "just like Stan," Dank's hated brother-in-law. I didn't see the resemblance, except that both were big men, fond of sports, domestic beer, and classic rock. Which reminds me that I too got off on the wrong foot with Jablonsky: One afternoon, soon after moving in next door, I asked him politely to turn down his car stereo (which he liked to blare while working in the yard), and he responded by turning it *up*. So I hated him too for a while, but over the years I decided he wasn't as bad as he seemed. And now, of course, I positively miss him, like everything else about Hemlock, even the rain (which, unlike the rain here in Clackamas—the horrible Portland suburb I wasn't going to name, but to hell with old-fashioned discretion—somehow never depressed me), even my petty, scheming, self-important colleagues in the English department. And I may be seeing them again before too long: Yesterday, October 23, 2006—I learned that Dank left me his house. I could be back there right now if I chose, and to hell with the two sections of freshman composition I've been teaching here in Portland at a junior college. But I've deemed it wiser to wait a little longer for the dust to settle. I think I can hold on for a few more months in Clackamas, now that I have something to live for.

When Dank was murdered, the police spoke to Jablonsky, but of course Jablonsky had nothing to do with it. Someone so ready to raise his voice, and if need be his hand, never has a chance to store up the kind of resentment that could drive a man to sneak into another's house in the middle of the night and club him to death in his sleep. No, murders like that are committed—when not by perfect strangers—by the civilized and craven, by people too meek to stand up for themselves except once or twice in a lifetime, in spasms of unpracticed and unbridled self-assertion.

Jensen, Molly, née O'Toole (1931–2001): Dank's second wife. He met her—in 1979, when he was twenty-six—at a Trekkie convention or comic-book show or action-figure swap-meet or Dr. Who symposium or some other nerdorama for the same sad demographic. Never one for long engagements (probably because all women, even women desperate enough to settle for Dank, de-

veloped in his presence a sudden disapproval of premarital sex),
Dank married her a few weeks later. He'd recently misdiagnosed
himself with an incurable disease, and when he popped the question he thought he'd soon be dead. In the meantime, what he
wanted most was mothering, and the bossy, loud, chain-smoking,
game-show-watching Molly was more than old enough to be his
mother. She even looked a little like his mother, though more like
a prehistoric fertility goddess—squat, wide-hipped, and stupefy-
ingly big-breasted. Better yet, she'd once been married to a science fiction writer Dank admired, German Jensen, and for Dank
that gave her an aura of sorts.

After half a year they split up, with hard feelings on both sides.
Molly's aura hadn't lasted long once she revealed (on the honeymoon) that she'd been married to Jensen for less than a week, and
hadn't heard from him in more than a decade. Another factor in the
marriage's collapse had been Dank's failure to die within six months,
as scheduled. By continuing to live, he protracted a marriage that
neither of these—face it—frankly unappealing people would have
rushed into so rashly, perhaps, if they'd known it would drag on like
that. Still another factor was old-fashioned lust, or maybe *Wanderlust*: Dank blamed Molly for putting an end to the swinging single
life that he came to see, in the course of their brief marriage, as a
paradise lost. That paradise, of course, was an illusion, a mirage in
Dank's defective rearview mirror, one frequently steamed up by
heavy breathing. In the two years between his first divorce and
second wedding, Dank in fact had been unable to talk anybody into
having sex with him. Singledom was wasted on poor Dank, who
never figured out—to use a crude but colorful expression—how to
get the milk *without* buying the cow. (OH)

Juvenilia: Though she didn't foresee her son's potential as a
writer, Mrs. Dank at least had sense enough to save his school-
work, his drawings, and some extracurricular jottings, just as

she did for his twin sister, Jane. By the time I came along, those documents were jumbled in a cardboard box of the same vintage as its contents, and no effort had been made to segregate the early works of a major American author from the scrawls of his remarkably ungifted sister. If anything, their mother had discerned more promise in her *daughter's* work than in her son's, according to him, as judged by the allotment of coveted display space on the front of the refrigerator (a place of honor in that family of big eaters). I've been through that box, and sure enough, the papers signed "Jane D" are much more likely to have brittle pieces of Scotch tape adhering to their corners, or at least discolored trapezoids of dried adhesive.

Dank himself, as a child, never thought of writing as anything more than a rainy-day activity, something to do when he got sick of playing checkers, drawing race cars, or watching cartoons. Nonetheless, enough of his apprentice work survives to enable us to chart his development—to plot his trajectory as a young writer by connecting the dots. Here are four specimens at five-year intervals:

At two (I traced this from an early drawing):

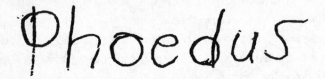

At seven:

One time there was this Marshin thats name was Zok. He had a famly. Suddely, a lazur beam shot out of a UFO at Zok! Therefor, he died. Exsept then anoHter UFO came that there was a bigger lazur on it. Sudnely, the lazur shot a deth ray out of it at the other UFO that killed Zok and blew it up! TO BE CONTD.

At twelve:

Back in the Olden days of Space travel, they didn't have that good of rocket ships. Don't get me wrong, they still worked! However they had unexpected tragedies that happened. To name one example, seven crack Astronauts sadly lost their life in the tragical Explosion that happened when the rocket they were in exploded, surprisingly, right before it was getting ready to Blast Off, due to a tragical Malfunction that occurred. After that famous Tragedy happened they started to be more careful about the different precautions there were and Safety, naturally. It was "high time" to stop "cutting corners": so to speak. They even ran Computer stimulations of all the various different Problems that might sadly go wrong to see what would occur in case they tragically happened.

At seventeen (in his first published story, BARRETT'S BARGAIN, by which point Dank's adult style was pretty fully formed):

<u>Just my luck if the Venusians got there first,</u> thought Barrett grimly, as he piloted the USS Extrovert through the Centaurian meteor shower. He'd been sent to stake a claim for Terra on the big plutonium deposit they'd just discovered on planet X-19, but someone couldn't keep his mouth shut, typically, and the news of the incredible discovery had spread through the entire galaxy. The Venusians knew about it too, for example, who used plutonium in their religion and therefore would savagely kill for it, especially an earthling. <u>Wonder what kind of "welcoming committee" they've arranged for</u>

<u>me</u>, Barrett wondered with a chuckle, as he patted the trusty plasma gun in his holster. X-19 loomed in the distance. Grimly, he stared out the window of the flight deck. It being darker outside than in the well-lit spaceship, he could see his own reflection: an athletic, handsome, square-jawed man with two day's stubble and a confident, ruthless expression in his cold blue eyes that women found irresistible. As he gazed, he lost sight of the view beyond the window, and therefore he was taken by surprise when suddenly a laser beam . . .

ABCDEF
GHIJKL
MNOPQR
STUVWX
YZ

A Knock on the Head: This astounding novel, which started as a fantasy about Dank's hated neighbor Jock JABLONSKY, is written as the journal of a man named Bruiser. From one day to the next, Bruiser develops a nervous disorder that makes him increasingly—and by the end unbearably—sensitive to noises, odors, flavors, eyesores, itches, aches, and so on. The first chapter shows us Bruiser before the onset of his disorder, so thick-skinned that, like a bird rolling on an ant hill for the fun of being bitten, he seeks out strong sensations just to feel *something*: the hottest hot sauce, the loudest music, the goriest movies, the roughest companions. His transformation starts with a knock on the head suffered in a routine brawl. By the end of the book, Bruiser can barely handle easy listening, finds Cream of Wheat too highly-flavored for his palate, and considers it a major trauma if he stubs his toe or (since his morbid sensitivity is emotional as well as physical) his next-door neighbor frowns at him.

The change is ingeniously reflected by the prose style, just as if there were a strict correlation between sensitivity and intelligence. Bruiser starts out sounding like this:

> So I'm fuckin' washing my Camaro in the driveway, crankin' Skynyrd on the tape deck, when this fuckin' four-eyed fat-ass writer prick next door sticks his big ugly head out the window

and asks me *right in the middle of "Freebird"* to turn down the music. *Bad move*, fatso . . .

He ends up sounding like this:

A further irony of the whole *debacle* is the failure—I might almost say refusal—of my former "drinking buddies" quite to grasp the nature of my new condition; they persist in the delusion that a hearty "clap" on the back is still a suitable manner of salutation for one in my state, is indeed *de rigueur* as of yore, and not in fact—what it so plainly and all indisputably *is* now—as gauche, as inappropriate, as altogether *not* "the ticket," as that unspeakable Camaro still, alas, parked in my *soi-disant* driveway, though I daresay my "driving" days are over . . .

(Dank had been reading, or knitting his brow at, my copy of James's *The Art of the Novel*, having by then already devoured all the other how-to-be-a-writer books.) It is in chapter six of eleven, or midway through *A Knock on the Head*, that Bruiser's prose sounds most like Dank's—which the novel thus proposes as a golden mean between Neanderthal insensitivity and overbred hyperesthesia. Even in the early chapters, though, the prose is more tuneful and carefully wrought than in any of its author's *published* volumes—and I trust that readers will share my disgust that the novel, one of Dank's most brilliant, is *un*published. As a rule, the unpublished novels are distinctly better written than the published, presumably because their author had more time to polish them. A sad irony: The few books by Dank that can be savored sentence for sentence are available, for the time being, *only* as synopses.

A B C D E F
G H I J K **L**
M N O P Q R
S T U V W X
Y Z

Landor, Pandora (b. 1978): The last great unrequited passion of Dank's life was for a woman a quarter-century his junior: He was forty-five and she twenty when they met, in April 1998, at the Zeitgeist, an arty coffee house half a mile from our house. For several years in his mid-forties, for reasons he couldn't or wouldn't explain, Dank did a lot of his writing at the Zeitgeist, where a demitasse of bad espresso cost three bucks, and where the plump and unpretentious author with his sweatpants and his seven-dollar haircut stuck out like a Milk Dud in a box of fancy chocolates. He met Pandora at one of the weekly open-mike evenings he used to attend (sometimes with me in tow), and even to read at, now and then, in hopes of meeting group-ies, though until Pandora came along he never did meet any-one that way. If your audience has its heart set on sow's ears, you can't fool it with silk purses, and Dank's visionary fiction was denied the applause granted even the lamest Bukowski imitations.

On the fateful evening, we came in just in time to hear a man with a shaved head say: "Fuck, yeah. My first poem is called 'A Thought.'" A pause, and then, "O'Malley said it best: 'In the same way that many yaks—'"

But Dank—who doubted perhaps that O'Malley, whoever he was, had said *anything* best, and who surely knew that there could be no thought worth thinking whose best expression featured an analogy to many yaks—wasn't really listening. No, he was staring at two other patrons, a boy and girl sitting on the tête-à-tête or "conversation chair" that had spooked Dank so much the first time he saw it. (Ever since the NEWEL POST catastrophe, his first glance on entering an unfamiliar room was for things whose names he didn't know. If he saw one, he would either leave the room or, if that wasn't feasible, stay as far as possible from the mystery object, as from a truculent stranger who might pick a fight.) Both looked to be about twenty. The boy's most salient feature was a fedora; the girl, or young woman (neither one seems right, so I'll just alternate two wrongs, though I can think of *other* words that fit her perfectly), had bright blue hair, a nose ring, and a Betty Boop tattoo, but so do lots of people. What really set her apart from any member of her gender Dank had ever seen was that she was *reading one of his books.* Or at least she had the book—THE REVOLT OF THE UNSUNG—on the tabletop in front of her, and drummed her fingers on it, as on a lover's familiar haunch.

Dank's first impulse (as he told me later) was to flee the premises. His second, which he heeded, was to bolt into the men's room. Romantic opportunities and quasi-opportunities often had gastric repercussions for Dank. To him it made perfect sense that one leading seller of gags and novelties marketed the same versatile substance—an all-purpose mixture of licorice powder and glucose—as both Love Potion and Belching Powder.

Dank spent so long in the rest room (maybe trying to wake up—see REALITY DETECTOR) that he almost missed his turn to read. When he did get to the microphone, he repeated his name to make sure his fan would hear it, then mentioned a few of the books he had written, including, of course, THE REVOLT OF THE UNSUNG. During this preamble, I saw the boy in the fedora whispering excitedly to the blue-headed girl, and pointing at the book, with the result that she was listening to Dank and not the music in her head by the time he started reading a short story—never published and no longer extant—of which I remember only the first sentence: "*'Watch it, pal—that used to be my leg!'* bellowed Jenkins irritably."

When he finished, the loudest, most raucous applause—almost the only, aside from my own—came from the young woman Dank was already in love with. As he'd hoped, she and her friend approached him afterward and introduced themselves as Aaron and Pandora. And though it wasn't Pandora but Aaron who asked Dank to autograph the book (which Pandora, it turned out, had never even opened—there were few books she *had* opened, and until that evening she had never heard of Dank), she seemed impressed that her friend was so impressed. It was she who invited our author Dank to hear their rock band, Safety Flush, caterwauling that same evening at a nearby bar. What with my aversions to live music and secondhand smoke, I didn't attend the show myself, but when Dank got home around two AM, he was more exhilarated than I'd ever seen him. He said he'd smoked a joint with the musicians after the show, and when he left Pandora had given him a hug.

Though I am not a big fan of Ms. Landor, it's conceivable she meant no harm by that first hug. She was one of those annoying extroverts who go around hugging everybody (though she never ventured to hug *me*—she must have detected my lucid dislike). In Dank's case, though, a hug was all it took to ignite a lust that it would take a lot of pain, some of it physical, to snuff. Even if Pandora hadn't decided the moment she met him to use him, she soon had that inspiration. Dank was pleased to learn that Aaron wasn't her lover, but Pandora had a crush on another bandmate, a tall blond rock god named Travis. Travis was also a fan of Dank's fiction, to which he'd been the one to introduce Aaron, in fact. Even before they met Dank, they had been planning a pilgrimage to 107 Empedocles Street, such as several other readers—usually students of mine, and (as Dank always lamented) always male—had made over the years. Their admiration elevated Dank in Pandora's opinion, but never above the station of someone she could use to make Travis jealous, or at least to make him notice her. And Dank either failed to see this or accepted it as a price he was willing to pay for her company, though in that case he should have had more sense than to fall in love.

Dank's first "Pandora phase," in the spring of 1998, consisted of six weeks of tagging along wherever she went, whenever she let him, and hanging out at her house (the aptly nicknamed Hell House) as much as possible, with Pandora and her housemates, pretending to enjoy the kind of music they enjoyed.

He also did a lot of drugs. Not counting the correction-fluid binge of 1993 (see THE REVELATION), Dank hadn't subjected his system to anything stronger or stranger than fortified wine since 1981. Now, though, in a doomed attempt to "pass" for a member of his young friend's Dionysian subculture, Dank overrode his middle-aged good sense (to say nothing of his lifelong fear of brain damage) long enough to swallow, snort, or sniff whatever substances Pandora and her substance-loving friends were resorting to any given evening to ward off the terrors of unaltered consciousness.

Among the evils to fly out of Pandora's box were psilocybin mushrooms, and Dank had them to thank for the hallucination—"a vision of pure evil," he insisted—that would terrify him, off and on, for the rest of his life. Walking home alone from Hell House, late one afternoon, with pupils mushrooms had dilated to the size of dimes, Dank looked up at the heavens and saw a giant yellow disk. It wasn't, however, the sun.

No, it was "a smiley face," he said, like the one he'd seen so often on lapel buttons and elsewhere in the 1970s, when it had served as a sort of nonverbal injunction to Have a Nice Day. Except that there was something wrong about *this* face— something unspeakably malevolent about the smile. Never again, it seemed to decree, would *Dank* have a nice day. Once he tried to draw the face, but he failed to convey its horror, though by then he'd seen the smile several times—it had a way of reappearing (though only to Dank) when he was upset. One day when we were grilling burgers and the coals wouldn't burn right, Dank grabbed my shoulder and demanded "Don't you see it too!?" and pointed with his free hand to the clear blue sky. These apparitions grew more common toward the end of his life. They exacerbated his AGORAPHOBIA. And they were Pandora's fault.

It was also thanks to her that Dank landed in the hospital twice in one year (1998). Well, modern science, which no longer recognizes simple heartbreak as a cause of heart attack, might just let her off the hook for the first of those disasters, though even more directly than his other heart attack (in 1993—see THE MAN I KILLED), this one seems to have been triggered by sexual rejection.

Whatever the connection, Pandora was the heartbreak that preceded Dank's second heart attack. He followed her to the Alibi Tavern one evening in the fond belief that she was his "date," lost track of her while buying their third round of Pabst (it didn't help that the bartender made him wait ten minutes before acknowledging his presence at the crowded bar), and finally found her in the men's room, of all places, making out with Travis by the condom-vending machine.

On his release from the hospital, Dank called Pandora (who'd visited him only once, in the company of Travis) with an elaborate speech he had written to read to her answering machine. When she herself answered, he hung up, then called her back a minute later and asked *her* to hang up and let her machine get the next call, on the grounds that he was psyched to talk to it and not to her. What he then told the machine, to pass on to Pandora (who probably erased the message without listening to it), was that they simply weren't "right for each other," and that he was sorry, but it was time for him to "move along." Pandora had never officially dumped him because she'd never seen him as her boyfriend in the first place, so Dank dumped *her*. That should have been the end of it, and I wish I could quarantine Pandora in this single entry, but she infected too much of Dank's life for one entry to cover.

Laughing Matter: When a long relationship ends painfully, some people bounce into a rebound relationship. Dank wasn't like that—not where wives were concerned—but as every artist knows, there are also rebound *projects*: rebound poems, rebound paintings, rebound sonatas, possibly even rebound cathedrals. And there are rebound novels. In July 2001, on the very day he finally closed the books for good on the ill-fated *Space Tundra* (see EVERYBODY DIES), Dank rebounded by embarking on another novel, *Laughing Matter*.

Norma is a "typical suburban mom" whose only singularity is her lack of humor: Nothing has ever struck her as funny. She tenses up when someone tells a joke because she never knows when to laugh, and even when she does determine that the time has come (from the teller's cues, or from the reactions of other listeners), she is still obliged, in the words of a catty acquaintance, to "fake the laughter orgasm."

One afternoon, though, while cheering on her daughter's team, Norma is brained by an errant soccer ball—one of those life-changing knocks on the head that occur in several stories dating from 2001, the year Dank's fear of brain damage caused him to glue foam-rubber strips to the edges of coffee tables, the corners of bookcases, and anything else that he might trip and hit his head on. Within hours, Norma develops a bizarre disorder: She starts finding other people's misfortunes terribly funny—the more unfortunate, the funnier. She can contain herself when someone slips and falls in a puddle or dents a car in a low-speed collision, but the news of a cancer or a suicide is more than she can bear, and causes her to burst out in irrepressible laughter. At first it's only strangers whose tragedies she finds so comical: Her condition announces itself as she's reading the evening paper (a few hours after the fateful soccer game), comes across an article about a toxic spill in some third-world country, and realizes that she's laughing. "So this is what it feels like," she tells herself, more thrilled at first to have achieved a laugh than appalled by the occasion. Gradually her newfound sense of humor finds targets closer to home—acquaintances, relatives, neighbors and friends, and finally her husband and children. In a few weeks she goes from an all-too-well-adjusted soccer mom to a pariah. The novel leaves her in a mental institution laughing uncontrollably, because by then she's come to find her *own* misfortunes funny.

Norma is another of the smug and self-righteously average moms for whom Dank reserved his most sadistic destinies. Our author had some issues with his own mother, Dolores, who sent him to psychiatrists throughout his adolescence, for problems ranging from timidity to moodiness to hypochondria. When he was thirteen, she threatened to commit him to a mental institution if she ever caught him masturbating again. (Later she would say that it had been an idle threat, and so perhaps it had, but what mattered was that Dank believed her at the time, and he never forgave her.) The following year, in the middle of summer, his mother grounded him for an entire month in an attempt to cure his probably-incurable agoraphobia with reverse psychology, or rather homeopathy. Far from developing a wholesome, Huckleberry-Finnish yearning for the great outdoors, Dank grew so accustomed to his cell, as convicts sometimes do, that when his mother finally told him he could go outside again, he said no thanks. And when, a few days later, she forced him to go out and play, he suffered the first of his panic attacks.

To the day he died, Dank nursed these grievances and others, some going back to before he was born. At family reunions he avoided his mother as much as possible, though when they did come face to face, he was so well behaved that I wondered if she knew how much he hated her. But maybe so, since in 1991 he'd threatened to sue her for custody of all her photographs of him—demanding even to be cropped out of group portraits—insisting that his image was his property. Not that Dank wanted to look at himself: He just didn't want his mom to look at him, with the disapproving scowl he considered her default expression. (To be fair, *I* never saw Delores scowling at her son: The two times I met her, she struck me as friendly enough.) All his life, Dank thought of mothers as the real arbiters of normality, and the ones really to blame for the atrocities committed in its name. The bully who tormented Dank in junior high tormented him not because that bully's father was a drunk who finally went to jail for domestic violence, but because his mother read *Good Housekeeping* and *Better Homes and Gardens*.

This theory struck me as a bit unfair to moms in general, and especially to Dank's, who had raised the twins singlehandedly from 1958, when they were five and their father vamoosed, to 1971, when they were eighteen and father Edmund reappeared and married their mother again (which explains why Edmund, in photos of that era, looks so much younger than Delores, so much better rested). It still puzzles me that Dank was so much harder on his well-intentioned mother than on his absentee (and, by all accounts, thoroughly worthless) father. I guess it's easier to hate the people you see every day.

"La Vie en Rose": Okay, this one's even stupider than average. In a gloomy future where "Man's tragic air pollution" has led to ever-gray skies, a totalitarian state boosts the morale of its citizens by making them all wear rose-colored contact lenses. The lenses are implanted surgically, soon after birth, and stretch implausibly to accommodate the growth of the eye. What else? Oh yes—they last forever. At the time of the story, some eighty years after the widespread implementation of Operation Sunrise, few people can remember what the world really looks like, and of course nobody listens to those tedious old-timers.

But then one day a plucky young ophthalmic surgeon has the curiosity to remove his lenses—and is appalled by what he sees (the only sane reaction for *any* character who finds himself inhabiting one of Dank's absurd and spottily imagined worlds—virtual realities with more dead pixels than live ones). But he isn't called Dr. Seymour for nothing (though it's never clear if "Seymour" is a surname or—as would befit the story's *Romper Room* mentality—a forename), and instead of reattaching the lenses as he had planned, the doctor joins an underground of other clear-eyed renegades and anti-pollution crusaders determined to do something about the gray itself, and until then to see the world as it is. So "La Vie en Rose" points a timely moral, and one as courageous and original as most of Dank's opinions: Pollution is Bad.

Like so many of Dank's stories, "La Vie en Rose" opens with a red (or rosy) herring, a minor character with no part in the actual plot—in this case, the guy who services the doctors' hovercars:

Bronc Strong was a mechanic for over ten years now, a well-built, tall man who commanded respect any place that he went. The telltale grease from fixing motors on his rosy, calloused palms, showed he was an honest, working man; not some "intellectual" with a head full of "book learning" but no common sense or know-how. Some of the Physicians couldn't even fuel their own hovercars, thought Bronc with a disgusted snort!

The story might have been less ludicrous (though still ludicrous enough to proclaim it one of Dank's) if the state attempted to keep workers focused on their work by fitting everybody with *gray*-tinted lenses because the skies are always a lollygagging blue, as they always seem to be here on the coast of Spain, at least in the vicinity of _____. And that blank is blank not because I'm "on the lam"—what lawman would cross the Atlantic to nab the person who euthanized Dank?—but because the town in question hasn't been ruined by tourists yet, and it *would* be criminal to contribute to its ruin. The air is scented with orange blossoms, the beaches bespangled with big unbroken seashells, and the climate warm enough for sandals even in November.

Since I'm paid by the word, I may as well mention that Dank had a pair of rose-tinted glasses, and sometimes wore them indoors. He didn't wear them for the illusion of rosiness, though, but rather for the thrill of whisking them off and—like the fearless Dr. Seymour Seymour—suddenly seeing the Truth. As for prescription lenses, the myopic author settled for thick ugly horn-rims, and was never without them except when publicly impersonating an author (since they didn't fit the rough-and-ready PUBLIC IMAGE he affected) or in the frequent intervals between sitting on his current pair and getting a replacement. (In *The Born Loser*—fittingly, Dank's favorite comic strip—a pair of broken eyeglasses is one of the four emblems of futility on the Thornapple's coat-of-arms, along with a straitjacket, an IRS 1040 form, and a losing poker hand.) Just once, during one of his ridiculous pursuits of a much younger woman, Dank tried contact lenses, but they were not a success. The very first evening, after attempting for at least ten minutes to remove the lens from his right eye as he'd been shown that morning at the clinic, pulling back the eyelid with his left forefinger and gingerly whisking away the flimsy lens with the tip of his right, he realized that it had popped out onto his cheek earlier, at the onset probably, so that for the past ten minutes his fingertip had been abrading his bare eyeball. Dank spent a sleepless night and returned to the clinic first thing in the morning to have the other lens removed by a professional, and that was the last time he ever wore contacts. (OH)

"La-Z-Boy": A story presented as the diary of a pathologically lazy man, one whose condition (caused by a "new virus" that sounds a bit like plain old-fashioned mono) worsens daily. As with some of Dank's other downward-spiraling narrators, the writing changes to reflect the ravages of the disease: The entries, sentences, and words all become shorter and shorter. The final entry—our last snapshot of this tailspin—consists entirely of an ominous "etc.", which we know to have cost the hero superhuman effort.

The tale—only eighteen pages long, though first imagined as a novel—is less interesting, perhaps, than the circumstances of its composition. In the autumn of 2000, Dank really did develop a debilitating weariness—one his doctor wrongly diagnosed as Chronic Fatigue—and grew progressively more lazy. His decline was more gradual than his character's, taking about a year a half to reach its nadir, and then several months for him to recover, to the degree that he ever did recover.

Dank's incapacitating laziness was, I'm convinced, imaginary—psychosomatic—in origin, but no less debilitating for that. (After all, imagination was what made him tick.) Whatever its cause, his new condition didn't make him sleepy, and indeed exacerbated his insomnia—so much as to revive his fears of FFI, though I'd venture to say his sleepless nights were due to his listless days: It must hard to get a good night's sleep when you've lain in bed all day just staring at the ceiling.

Even before he abandoned the upright stance, and the daily war with gravity ("my least favorite of the fundamental forces," he once told me), Dank hadn't been getting much exercise, since by that point he was too phobic to leave the house for no good reason. (I no longer leave the house myself, when I can help it, but I'm in Clackamas and not in Hemlock, after all. And on a chilly gray November day like this one, on the ugly, noisy, pedestrian-unfriendly thoroughfare I call my street, with the air full of diesel exhaust and sidewalks strewn with fast-food containers and cigarette butts, there's no reason to subject yourself to any more sensory data than absolutely necessary.)

The onset of Dank's malaise was so insidious that afterward we couldn't agree about when it had started, though we did agree that its cause had been MacDougal's savage attack on Dank in print. As mentioned in the entry I've reluctantly allotted that attack (see Peter Pan in Outer Space), MacDougal's stink bomb of a book set off a series of events of which the little critic's death was certainly the least regrettable. The real tragedy was that, at the beginning of a new millennium, which ought to be a thrilling time for SF writers everywhere, MacDougal's book made Dank unhappy—so unhappy as not just to sap his will to live, but, worse, his will to *write*. And, like so many of Dank's moods, this unhappiness assumed a freakish form, the form of what I call his La-Z-Boy phase.

Dank wrote "La-Z-Boy" in October 2000, though at that point he didn't know how far his life would go in imitating art. He got the title from the brand name of his favorite chair. Dank bought a new La-Z-Boy every other year and put it in the living room, in front of the TV set and beside the water fountain (a white porcelain wall-mounted bubbler like the ones he'd drunk from as a schoolboy, and which he'd had installed in 1988 in fulfillment of a boyhood dream). The old chair he demoted to his study, and the chair *it* replaced to his basement workshop, so he could rest between inventions. By the end of his life, there were half a dozen La-Z-Boys down there—it was too much trouble to lug the retired ones back upstairs and out to the curb.

Even in his most energetic periods, Dank sometimes got stuck in his latest La-Z-Boy ("stretched on the rack of a too easy chair," like Sir Paridel in the *Dunciad*), channel-surfing hour after hour, wanting to get up and go to bed but nightmarishly unable to jump some neural gap between deciding to rise and implementing that decision. In the past, though, he had always managed finally to escape the chair with the same spasm of the will he used to wrench himself awake from a long and tedious dream. On the night of September 15–16, he was trapped all night long (until I came down at 8:00 AM and lent him a hand), by his inability to muster the willpower needed to launch his three hundred and fifty pounds out of the chair. He had soiled himself. If not for me he'd be sitting there still.

Afterward he dated the onset of his odd disorder to that fateful night, but I put it a month earlier, around mid-September. Dank and I had planned to spend the second half of that month in Maui, since I was on sabbatical that term, and a recent windfall (he'd finally been paid for the film rights to PLUS SEVEN) had enabled Dank to take such daydream vacations. Less than a week before our scheduled departure, however, MacDougal's book appeared and left Dank too depressed to travel. And so we stayed home, even though our tickets were non-refundable, and some of Dank's other arrangements were almost as hard to cancel, especially the ones he forgot about until they came into effect. He forgot, for instance, that he'd paid a catsitter one hundred and fifty dollars to stop by once a day and check on Dookie, refill the food and water bowls, and use the slotted spoon to scoop the turds out of the litter box and into the big Chock Full o' Nuts can Dank had reserved for the purpose. When the teenage sitter showed up the first day and found Dank watching *Jeopardy* in his pajamas, she refused to give back the hundred and fifty, claiming she had turned down other jobs to take this one. In that case, Dank insisted, she would need to stop by every day to feed the cat and pan for paydirt, even though the cat's owner was home. And that's what happened—though Dank hated intrusions while he was writing, and couldn't concentrate until the kid had come, performed her duties (with him sternly looking on), and gone for the day. Then again, he hadn't done much writing lately anyway. He was too busy watching TV.

By the end of our phantom vacation, Dank was no longer on speaking terms with that first catsitter, but he'd already hired another, a neighborhood boy who would look after Dookie until the cat vanished the following year. (I'd reluctantly offered to take care of Dookie myself, but Dank must have sensed that my relations with the cat were already strained, and he didn't want to strain them further. I'd told him once that Dr. Johnson made a point of heading out each morning to buy oysters for Hodge, lest his servants resent the extra chore and take out their resentment on the cat.)

Dank's treatment of the girl had struck me as uncharacteristically petty, but I later came to see it as something more worrisome than pettiness: a heady realization that, as long as he had money, he could pay people to do all the things he didn't want to do himself—things he had always done in the past, but of which the very prospect filled him with exhaustion now. I date Dank's paralyzing weariness to that epiphany. It never would have happened if he hadn't known he could get other people to do all the things that would leave *him* too weary to do.

Soon he was paying people to cook his meals, answer his mail, and even do his laundry, a chore he'd once enjoyed. For the next eighteen months, in fact, the house was aswarm with strangers whose livelihood depended on Dank's laziness, though for a few more months he resisted yielding in more glaring ways to that laziness. In February 2001, though, he decided he was too tired to climb the stairs any more. Luckily—or unluckily, if you share my theory that his weariness was, if not exactly voluntary, at least opportunistic (lost in the wilderness, Dank would have made every effort to survive)—he already had a means of avoiding that chore. Like those prudent, forward-looking shoppers who stock up on cut-rate Christmas decorations in mid-January, when no one else wants to think about Christmas, Dank had started laying in geriatric paraphernalia back in his thirties, whenever he found a good deal on something he might otherwise someday regret that he hadn't snapped up: canes, aluminum walkers, big boxes of adult diapers, a shower safety bar, a motorized stairway lift, even semi-perishables like denture fixatives and effervescent cleaners. The too-good-to-pass-up deal on the stairway lift included installation, and so he'd had a lift running up the left side of the master stairway since 1984 (already certain by then that he'd spend the rest of his life in that house). Prudently, however, he'd refrained from using it for the next seventeen years, not wanting to wear it out before his dotage, when he would surely be too enfeebled to climb.

But now, though only forty-six, he started riding upstairs whenever he was too weary to walk. At that point he still had good days and bad days, and for a month or so he resisted the lure of the lift except when dead tired. If he did give in to the temptation on a "good" day, a day when he could easily have gotten upstairs unassisted, Dank appeared rather sheepish about it: When I happened to descend the stairs on foot as he was slowly riding up in his magic escalator, he reminded me of Dookie pretending not to notice me when I rudely watched him using his litter box. (Later, he—the cat—took to turning his rear end to me on those occasions, which meant he often missed his aim while urinating, making a puddle on the floor outside the box even as he stood inside convinced he was being a good boy.) After about a month, though, Dank stopped asking himself if he was really too tired to climb, and no longer looked embarrassed but contemplative when he met me on the stairway.

Once he made that concession to his illness, it was all downhill for Dank. Thanks to PLUS SEVEN, he had enough money in those days to hire assistants to do things for him that nowadays even the rich generally do for themselves. At one point, he not only had a cook to prepare his food—only purees and puddings, since it was too much work to chew—but a nurse to feed him.

By September 2001, Dank no longer left his bed at all, most days, except to use the toilet. (He never quite worked up the nerve to use a bedpan or to hire somebody to wipe him after stools, but those were becoming more and more infrequent anyway. Dank had pioneered a new kind of constipation: Too *lazy* to empty his bowels, he put it off like any other chore.) He hadn't left the house in months. On days when he felt peppier than usual, he'd have assistants lace him into his supportive corset and hoist him into his electric wheelchair for a few turns around the ground floor of his house, whence he'd moved his bed—or paid big men to move it—midway through his illness. (If that's what it was, an illness.) In any case, it lasted from the fall of 2000 to spring of 2002.

For how it changed his writing habits, see PRODUCTION LINE.

Legitimacy: Elsewhere (though unfortunately in the person of my rabid fellow commentator—see INFLUENCES) this guide discusses Dank's lifelong addiction to the sort of unpretentious science fiction that kept him sane throughout a troubled adolescence. Part of his secret, I think, as a writer, was that he never lost touch, as a reader, with the pleasure principle. He never forgot what it feels like to read for sheer enjoyment, with no thought for self-improvement or cultural adornment. Most writers spend so many hours in their teens and twenties straining to love the right books, and—like self-repressing perverts—*not* to love the wrong ones, that by thirty they no longer even know what it means to love a book, and so of course their own are anything but lovable.

Only once did Dank forget that books are supposed to be fun. For a few years in his early forties, in a misguided effort to win back Wife Number Three (see FEBRERO, GABRIELA) by "going legit," he swore off science fiction not only as a writer but even as a reader (a renunciation he referred to cryptically as "gafiating"). In the effort to purge his imagination of Martians, he didn't go so far as reading Homer or Virgil or Goethe, but he bought the ten most recent Pulitzer Prize-winning novels, books he'd avoided till then because their plaudits made them sound like chores to read, just as he avoided foods recommended for their nutritional value. (He later told me that he hadn't gotten more than a few chapters into any of those ten high-fiber novels.)

As for writing, at first his idea of going legit had been to give up genre fiction altogether, as ex-alcoholics are supposed to give up alcohol, but Dank had sense enough to know that Gabriella wouldn't be scanning the pages of *Analog* month after month to make sure he'd really gotten over his first, adolescent love. No, if he was going to win her back, he reasoned, it wouldn't be by swearing off SF, but by *also* writing so-called literary fiction—by making a big enough splash with a non-genre novel. And though for the rest of his life he kept bellyflopping into the mainstream in an attempt to make that splash, he continued writing science fiction too.

Still, he was serious enough about being a Serious writer not just to buy and read a book called *Get Some Respect: The Disgruntled Scribbler's Guide to Writing Serious Fiction*, but to highlight *every single word*, saturating its two hundred pages of dubious advice with so much fluorescent yellow ink that the book felt palpably heavier—with the weight of emphasis— than a book of its size should. This book assumed that its reader had already mastered the "craft" of fiction, or mastered it enough to satisfy the fans of romance novels about spunky nurses, say, but wanted now to write books that would also satisfy snooty reviewers and professors. The chapters had titles like "Pumping Irony," "Putting in the Symbols," "Are Your Characters Hard Enough to Understand?," "Make the Reader Reach for the Dictionary," "Put that High-School French to Use," and "The Six Big Themes No Book Reviewer Can Resist."

But to return to science fiction—as Dank himself returned, after a couple of years—I used to wonder why he'd chosen *that* as his means of escape. I understood why he continued to read the stuff as a grown-up: Think of all the grown-ups whose taste in popular music was formed in junior high. And for Dank, moreover, life had continued in some ways to feel like junior high—a muddle of anxiety, bewilderment, frustration, and embarrassment from which no one could be blamed for wanting to escape. But why science *fiction* and not, say, science fact, since he could have escaped with either to the farthest reaches of time and space? The answer I finally arrived at was that fiction is a better way of forgetting recent ordeals. Dank read—as some drink—to forget. Science fiction helped him to endure the traumas first of junior high and then of later life by interposing artificial memories—the more vivid and lurid the better—between him and the painful events of everyday existence. All those bug-eyed monsters sped up the process of sedimentation by which time buries whatever it can't heal.

The Life Penalty: In 1998, our world-weary hack imagined a future where felons are punished not by truncation but *extension* of their lifespans. "Top scientists" have found out how to prolong life indefinitely, but the quality of life is so poor (thanks to the usual suspects—pollution, global warming—but also, one feels, to the ineptitude with which this brave new world is evoked) that no one *wants* to live forever. No one wants to live at all, and no one would without Big Brother to coerce them. To make matters worse, World War III has left 99.9 percent of the men it didn't kill completely impotent. It's up to the remaining few—of whom one, the narrator, bears a sickening resemblance to the book's much-married author—to inseminate the women. But not even lucky studs like them especially want to live forever, so bitter is life in 2098—so bitter that (our fatuous narrator solemnly explains) police have confiscated all the belts and razor blades, as if the earth were one big prison, and all its inmates on suicide watch. Because of the alarmingly shrinking population, suicide is deemed the greatest crime of all—if you try and fail, the penalty is endless life in a real prison, a high-surveillance hell where suicide is not an option. (Law-abiding folk, however, are allowed though not required on their hundredth birthday to stop receiving the longevity injections that make death impossible.)

The Life Penalty is Dank's most pornographic book[*] and vies with twenty others for the title of most absurd. The four-hundred-page abomination consists for the most part of stomach-turningly explicit play-by-play accounts of the narrator (again, a stand-in for Dank) bonking one beautiful woman after another, and all in the high-minded cause of propagating the race. Now and then a giant mutant beetle or a solar-powered hovercraft goes by for benefit of any adolescent boys (as always, Dank's core readership) who might be ashamed to read flat-out pornography without the ennobling pretext of sci-fi, but otherwise the book is like an extremely long and unlikely letter to *Penthouse* ("Now, I never dreamed that an average guy like me would ever have a chance with a hot babe like Dot Matrix . . ."), if not quite as literate. (OH)

Lips, Leopold (b. 1951): A con man who "befriended" Dank in 1995. They met in Tacoma at an SF convention where Dank had agreed to deliver the keynote address, though he hated public speaking and only ever did it in hopes of meeting worshipful young groupies. He never did succeed in meeting one that way: After the speech, inevitably, he'd find himself either ignored altogether, or buttonholed by a pimply teenage boy with literary aspirations, or at best by an old lady who had en-

---

[*] While I agree that *The Life Penalty* isn't one of Dank's unqualified triumphs, I disagree with Hirt about the reason. If the book is flawed, that's because it is one of the few in Dank's oeuvre that betrays a cynical miscalculation as to what would sell (he was strapped for money at the time) instead of by the irrepressible storytelling drive of a great spellbinder. Dank reasoned that adults, almost by definition, are people who like to think about sex—all the time, if his own mind was any indication. Books that asked them to think about anything else, as most of his others had done, were bound to be unpopular, since not many people like to think about two things at once. (BB)

joyed the large-type edition of Come, Sweet Death—never a worshipful young groupie. (Not to suggest that Dank had no interest in people *except* as prospective sex partners, but after all, when nobody is having sex with you, life does sometimes seem like a videotape of an R-rated movie whose moving story, timely message, and Oscar-worthy repartee you're unable to appreciate because you're too busy fast-forwarding through all that to get to the sex.) So our author was neither pleased nor surprised when a middle-aged man with some kind of accent (Flemish, as it proved) cornered him after his talk—heading off any groupies who might have been headed his way—and started praising The Demolition of Phineas Duck. Dank perked up, though, when the man claimed to be an inventor with a dozen patents to his name. Dank perked up even further when Lips proposed that they collaborate on the ambitious project they wound up calling PALs (q.v.).

Such as it was, their friendship was based on mutual admiration: Dank was Lips's favorite writer (if Lips didn't use that line on every writer he met) and Lips was the only real inventor Dank had ever known (if Lips *was* a real inventor). Dank, I gathered, was the more admiring: Apparently the awe of the unpublished for the published is nothing to the awe of the unpatented for patents, though in Lips's case those patents proved to be for disappointingly drab and un-Tom-Swiftian "inventions"—minor improvements on existing computer components.

Speaking of inventions, Lips claimed to be related to the man who developed speedwalking. (Though Dank prized his walks less for their physical than for their mental benefits— clarity, perspective, calm—in 1991 he experimented briefly with speedwalking himself, to see if he couldn't reap those benefits faster, and get back to his desk.) But if in fact he was, and if such "inventions" make any money for their thinkers-up and jotters-down, none of that money went to Cousin Leopold, who was always broke, and always borrowing. In the course of their infuriating friendship, he bilked our author of thousands in loans and thousands more in "investments." His only virtue was that Hirt too hated him—possibly sensing a rival for Dank's reverence—and stayed away from the house when Lips was around. See also: PRAISE THE BIG BOTTLE.

Listening to Decaf: For the last twenty years of his life, Dank needed six cups of coffee every morning just to get up to the baseline he'd awakened to as a matter of course in his pre-caffeinated youth. (In THE PLAGUE OF CANDOR, he imagines "waking pills" to be taken first thing in the morning—the mirror image of the sleeping pills he needed by that point to lose consciousness at bedtime, just because his system was aswim in caffeine.) At his peak in the late 1980s, he drank twelve or fourteen cups a day. When he got sick of coffee, he'd drink tea instead, or swallow No-Doz. He was also fond of Sgt. Popp, a caffeinated, carbonated, caramel-colored soft drink that did its best to taste—as I somehow knew without ever deigning to taste it, and without a household name (à la "root beer" or "ginger ale") for the genre of soda pop in question—like certain other, more successful soft drinks sold, like Sgt. Popp, in prune-colored cans.

Unlike his periodic AMPHETAMINE abuse, Dank's coffee habit wasn't one that he could live without. Many times he tried to break the habit, and more than once he made it past the throbbing headache to the lobotomized repose beyond, but he always relapsed in a matter of weeks because he needed coffee to write. By his account, he had written just two things without the aid of caffeine since acquiring the habit as a teenager. One was an unpublished tale about a costumed "superhero," C-Man, whose civilian alter ego is an invalid, bedridden by lethargy. Only by ingesting a blackish secret potion is C-Man transformed, briefly, into his crimefighting alter ego—just an ordinary able-bodied man, however, with no special powers.

The other work, which dated from our author's last attempt to kick the habit, in 1993, the year a psychiatrist published a surprise bestseller called *Listening to Prozac*—was *Listening to Decaf.* Unlike *Prozac, Decaf* is a book of aphorisms, a hefty collection of thoughts of which their author was especially proud. He once told me that *Listening to Decaf* was "the wisest and most serenely insightful thing" he'd ever written. Here are a few samples of that wisdom, insight, and serenity:

> *Everybody wants to accomplish something big. What are they trying to prove? That's what I want to know. Do they think they'll live forever if they build great monuments? Look at Ozymandias. It's high time people started trying to accomplish something small. What's better—a boulder or a pearl?*

> *Isn't it about time we all started being nice to each other? I hear a lot about big abstractions like Justice, Freedom, and Truth, but how often do you hear anybody singing the praises of plain old-fashioned Niceness? Try being nice for change—you'll like it!*

> *Seems like everybody's in a hurry. What's the big rush? That's what I'd like to know. Maybe it's time we all learned the gentle art of sitting in a chair and doing nothing. Not eating, not reading, not writing, not thinking, not talking, not surfing the World Wide Web. Not even watching the TV shows. Just sitting in a chair.*

And he published, at his own expense, a whole book of such reflections. And a *big* book, too, more than eight hundred pages—which, when I add that those pages were the product of not quite two months, might seem to suggest that Dank was *more* productive without coffee. But no, he was just less picky about which of his thoughts to preserve. It was as if he lacked the energy to smother in the cradle the more sickly of his brainchildren. You'd think that once he resumed his coffee habit, Dank would have noticed that he'd rated his decaffeinated thoughts a bit too highly, but not even the greatest writers are always able to recognize the relative merits of their own books. Dank never gave up the conviction that in *Listening to Decaf* he'd fathomed more abysses of profundity than most mortals ever manage to fathom with just one life's air supply.

"Long-Distance Relationship": In 1995, a Sunday inventor and science fiction writer invents a time machine (as Dank himself would later: see TIME MACHINE) and, after a few visits to the future—the overheated, overcrowded one Dank envisioned in so many other stories—travels into the past for a change, on his fortieth birthday, and falls wildly in love with Lucy, a beautiful twenty-year-old science fiction fan he meets at a convention in 1955. And *she* falls wildly in love with *him*.[*] For the next year they rendezvous once a week, always "at her place"—that is, in 1955—because although she has a self in 1995, there she's sixty years old. As to why they don't split the difference and meet in 1975, when she too is forty, and has her own apartment, the narrator assures us[†] that *Lucy* is the one who insists on meeting way back in 1955: already madly in love with him at twenty, she can't bear to wait two decades to see him again.

---

[*] Which demands at least as *massive* a suspension of disbelief, on the part of the beleaguered reader, as the initial time-travel premise, since the lucky forty-year-old is a dead ringer for Dank. (OH)

[†] Anxiously, repeatedly. (OH)

One week the inventor goes back even further—back to 1950. Here again the older Lucy—old enough to give consent, as it were in retrospect, on behalf of her fifteen-year-old self—is the one to insist on a 1950 rendezvous: She's an aspiring writer and decides she'd be further along with her art if she'd met her mentor sooner. They've neglected, though, to take into account that at fifteen she won't *remember* the arrangement, or even recognize her future lover. He winds up terrifying her, is mistaken for a rapist, and barely makes it back to the present in one piece, his time machine belching black smoke and riddled with bullet holes.

The ominous story was written on the day of Dank's decision, in September 1998, to marry the deplorable Pandora LANDOR, who'd renewed contact with him just two weeks earlier, or four months after breaking his heart so violently as to land him in the hospital.

Before discussing poor Dank's last and saddest marriage, though, I need to say a few words about my eviction.

Pandora and I had always hated each other, and it was strictly her idea to get rid of me—to insist that I move out before she moved in. Dank had handed on her verdict with profuse apologies, but I still left in a huff, refusing his offer to pay for a hotel in town and to store my bulkier belongings till I got settled elsewhere. No, I sullenly hauled them to U-Store-It and then drove to San Diego to visit my brother. I was on leave that semester and kept telling myself I was happy to get out of Hemlock. Maybe I was, but my main emotions were fury at Pandora and a painful—even tearful—sense of betrayal by Dank. The first week he sent me a few mollifying e-mails, messages I read a dozen times but didn't answer. After that, there was no word from him for almost a month, and then I got a message that read in its entirety: "Marriage didn't work out. You can move back in now. D."

Though by then I was already homesick for Hemlock (so imagine how I feel *now*), and eager for the story of Dank's most recent heartbreak, I waited a week to answer the summons, both because I still resented my eviction and because I hate to be taken for granted. I didn't like the way he seemed to think he could just put me out of the house like a bad dog—and whistle me back like a good one—whenever he wanted, even if it was true. But when I finally did reply, by telephone, to say I'd be back the following evening, Dank sounded less delighted than embarrassed. The call left me very uneasy, and I kept telling myself, on the long drive back to Hemlock, that I'd overestimated his fear of solitude.

Actually, I'd *under*estimated it, and forgotten the uncanny way that Dank's post-separation loneliness always seemed to draw freeloaders to his house. When I arrived, the night after my phone call, the place was dark. I let myself in and lugged one of my cartons up to my room, only to find a male stranger snoring in my bed. I didn't stick around long enough to confirm my hunch that the usurper was Lips, but retreated to the local Comfort Inn and waited till morning to retake my room.

Dank apologized when I saw him the next day, and Lips relinquished my room without a fight, moving to the one below, though it would take me several weeks to get rid of the complicated stink he left behind—a stink whose components included pipe tobacco, aftershave, foot powder, feet, and sweat. Not till I was fully reinstalled in my old habitat did I get around to asking Dank about his marriage. He still seemed a bit crestfallen that it hadn't worked, though even Helen Keller could have seen that catastrophe coming. After all, Pandora hadn't done much to encourage Dank's delusion that his passion was reciprocated. Even after moving in with him and ousting me, she'd kept her room in Hell House.

And admittedly it was a nice one, as I remember thinking the time Dank pointed it out from the street: a glassed-in veranda on the second story that must have gotten lots of sun. But that didn't explain why Pandora went over there almost every evening, sometimes for hours and always alone, claiming she needed to "work" in her "garden." Pandora was hardly the gardening type, and (as even Dank ultimately noticed) was apt to head over to Hell House rouged and perfumed, in a skimpy black sheath and high heels. It's safe to say that any time she spent there on her hands and knees was passed not in the garden but with Travis, in his bedroom or in hers, on which her husband was paying the rent though he'd only once set foot in it.

It seems that Pandora, when she suggested the farcical marriage, had just found out she was pregnant. She'd insisted on keeping the baby, but even Travis had more sense than to marry her (more sense than Dank, in other words), and in any case Travis had no money. Pandora's plan seems to have been to walk out on Dank the minute the baby was born and to live happily ever after on alimony and child support, which she knew he'd pay out of the goodness of his heart. As Raymond Chandler wrote about another *femme fatale*, "she was the kind of girl who'd eat all your cashews and leave you with nothing but peanuts and filberts." When the pregnancy miscarried (and lucky for the fetus—in a better world people like Pandora would be sterilized), soon after she discovered that Dank, too, had no money, Pandora moved out and agreed to a no-fault divorce, since the alternative would have been permitting him to consummate their marriage. Needless to say, she never returned the much-too-expensive diamond ring that Dank bought her in a manic moment of prenuptial happiness. (Where other manic types need therapy for anger management, Dank needed *happiness* management.)

But enough, for now, about Pandora. Perhaps someday she'll realize that her sordid, ugly, greedy, meaningless existence was once irradiated with significance because a great man happened to take an (unaccountable) interest in her. Who'd have heard of Leda if it weren't for Zeus?

A B C D E F
G H I J K L
M N O P Q R
S T U V W X
Y Z

MacDougal, Ewan (1945–2000): American critic and college professor, as well as a colleague of mine at Hemlock College, where he taught the eighteenth century and liked to say that nothing worth reading had been written since the death of Dr. Johnson. He hated me for picking a *living* author as my area of expertise. And yet he and Dank had been friends in the mid-1980s (after Hirt, who taught at the college himself in those days, introduced them). Not for long, but long enough for Dank to add a flattering portrait of MacDougal to Sight Unseen, and for MacDougal to mention Fastland in an article on the legacy of Swift, praising the book as "a latter-day *Gulliver's Travels*, a work Swift himself would be proud to have penned." Dank cherished that praise to the end of his days, even after his quarrel with its author, and even though he'd never read a word of *Gulliver's Travels* until MacDougal piqued his curiosity by telling him he'd written a latter-day equivalent. (And even then Dank made it only to Brobdingnag.) He was flattered by the attention of the first professor to take an interest in his works (this was years before I came along), and MacDougal, despite his disdain for the age in which he found himself and the books that age produced, seems to have liked the idea of instructing a living author in the virtue of Augustan wit.

In 1985, though, they had a falling out, and the next time MacDougal referred to Dank in print, in a review of some other curmudgeon's cantankerous book about Swift, he disparaged FASTLAND as "a sad example of how low the satiric tradition has sunk in our degraded age." As far as Dank could tell, this volte-face was due to his well-meaning but extremely ill-received remarks on the novel MacDougal himself had been toiling away at for almost a decade and had just asked Dank to read in manuscript. MacDougal's novel was a pseudo-historical romance about a love affair between the stunning Lady Mary Wortley Montague and a surprisingly large-penised Alexander Pope (wishful thinking on MacDougal's part—as I happen to know—insofar as Pope is modeled on MacDougal). *Tiny Giant* (an allusion to Pope's 4'6" stature) has never been published, and never will be, but on the strength of Dank's description I don't hesitate to call it a disaster. I'm sure Dank was kinder to it than a candid critic would have been, but that wasn't good enough for little MacDougal. Maybe Dank made a joke about short men with something to prove—MacDougal stood just 5'1". Maybe he mistook a zeugma for a syllepsis, or even a chiasmus. MacDougal himself may not have known the reason for his sudden change of opinion with regard to FASTLAND, and to Dank in general. ("The work of criticism is rooted in the unconscious of the critic," wrote Randall Jarrell, a good poet and an even better critic, "just as the poem is rooted in the unconscious of the poet.") In any case, Dank's comments enraged the would-be novelist, not only ending their friendship, but creating a resentment that festered for seventeen years before finally issuing in MacDougal's purulent attack on Dank's own fiction, PETER PAN IN OUTER SPACE. (Not that MacDougal had never expressed his hatred of Dank in the intervening years: One of his first moves on becoming the chair of my department back in 1998 was to restrict me to just one Dank-related course per year.)

But MacDougal was as good at making enemies as his eighteenth-century role model. Students said he scraped his fingernails on the blackboard several times a term, in a never-more-than-momentarily-successful attempt to compete for the class's attention with the clock above the door. As a chairman he was just as irritating. When he died abruptly, in his bathtub, on the day his book was published, the police interrogated not just Dank and me but also half a dozen of my colleagues. (I think it would have been funny, and fitting, if we'd *all* pitched in to kill him, as in the Agatha Christie novel whose title I withhold in case the reader hasn't read it yet. Which reminds me of another of the many books Dank never got around to writing, a whodunit—or rather a whodidn't—to be called *Et Tu?* Since in summary a nonexistent book can be as satisfying as the other kind, the time- and paper-wasting kind, let me summarize *Et Tu?*: A man is murdered, on a dark and foggy evening, in his dining room, at a dinner party, by all but one of seven guests, each with good reasons to want the victim dead. We know *one* guest is innocent because neighbors saw somebody leaving well before the time of death fixed by the coroner. But they didn't see *who*. Naturally each suspect claims to have been the early departure, and the detective must determine which of the seven is actually telling the truth or all seven will go free.)

Now that MacDougal is dead and his books are out of print, the only monument to his malevolence still standing is the house he had custom-built for himself in 1999, several miles out of town, in the middle of a thicket, at the end of a long winding gravel driveway not easy to spot from the highway, at least after dark. At his request, the architects designed a midget bungalow in which anyone much taller than 5'1"would need to stoop to stand erect, and go outdoors to jump for joy. Let me mention one more time that MacDougal stood 5'1":

Whether he was designing a house, bawling me out for assigning *Ulysses* ("This isn't Harvard, in case you haven't noticed"), or urging the air-traffic controllers of the literary world to ground Dank's flights of fancy, MacDougal's shortness—or at least his hatred of the tall, his wish to incommode all but his fellow Lilliputians—was always the key to his resentful, low-ceilinged esthetic.

"Mama's Boy": Ugh. A baby boy is born with a "tragic heart defect" diagnosed just before birth: If the umbilicus is cut, he'll die. And so the improbable mother persuades the unlikely obstetrician not to cut the cord, and then manages to keep the thing intact, and her son alive and well, until her own death thirty-eight years later.

"Mama's Boy" is narrated by the fat asthmatic science-fiction-writing son, as he and mother lie on their twin deathbeds, side by side. The preposterous story relates the would-be-poignant highlights and low points of his implausible life: persecution by classmates (before the mother wisely opted for home schooling), puberty, wedding night, several near-snappings or near-shearings (one intentional—a suicide attempt) of the vital cord, a modestly successful effort to lengthen it ("like those Savages they have in *National Geographic*, who stretch their necks, or maybe their lips"), and even an attempt to "run away" whose record-setting silliness is almost lost in that of the piece as a whole. The story manages to be both painfully embarrassing and profoundly boring, making it a minor summit in Dank's lifelong conquest of things unattempted yet in prose or rhyme. (OH)

The Man I Killed: In 1993, while speeding from one bar to another at the height of his worst-ever binge of drinking—a weeklong effort to forget his recently-absconded third wife, Gabriella—Dank hit a sixteen-year-old boy. The kid had been even drunker than Dank, and witnesses agreed that he'd been jaywalking, though also that Dank had been going too fast. One speeding, one jaywalking, both drunk—one driving drunk, one walking drunk. Luckily for both, the boy suffered nothing worse than a broken leg. (Our author, on the other hand, incurred the first of his two heart attacks.) But it was Dank's second arrest for drunk driving, and at the time his license was still suspended for the first arrest, a few weeks earlier and also wife-related. And so the famous author went to jail for a month, and lost his license too. He was so traumatized, in any case, that he vowed never again either to drink *or* to drive. (He soon broke the first half of the vow, but kept the second, just about, with a little help from the DMV.)

When one learns that that boy already had a history of vandalism, car theft, and assault, and would next come to the law's attention for attempted rape, it is hard not to feel that, if anything, Dank did society a favor by sidelining him for a month or two. It's almost as hard to share our author's horror at the thought that, had his Honda reached the intersection just a moment later, or the kid a moment sooner, the former would have run over the latter. As I've been reminded far too often lately, there's no dearth of budding thugs. I'd like to run over one or two myself. Clackamas produces more than its share, and in these parts their natural prey—teacher's pets and mama's boys and members of the Chess Team (and the Science Fiction Club!)—have been hunted to extinction. As a result, our up-and-coming felons are forced to pick on *grown-ups*, on *former* teacher's pets, who may have imagined, the day we turned eighteen—or twenty-one, or thirty—that at last we had attained lifelong immunity from adolescent bullies. Think again. Just yesterday, as I was lugging home a bag of groceries, I passed a group of loitering illiterates in front of Dunkin' Donuts, and one of them threw an éclair at me, getting custard all over my leg. Sometimes you can almost taste your karma, and lately mine has tasted like that stuff they add to antifreeze to keep pets from drinking it.

In Dank's mind, though, the near death of a juvenile delinquent got mixed up with the stillbirth of a blameless baby (see Dank, Phoebus K., Jr.), and if one product of that confusion was inordinate guilt, another was the fascinating novel he wrote in the months after the accident. In *The Man I Killed*, a world-famous writer runs over an eight-year-old boy (Dank seems to have split the difference between his blameless stillborn son and the young rapist), not because the driver was drunk, but because he is a sociopath, and running people over happens to be his idea of fun. When arrested, he feels no remorse, but he doesn't want to die. And death looks pretty likely, since his latest victim's father is the governor of the state where the story is set. But the governor grants him a stay of execution long enough to write a book about the child, one that starts as straight biography but turns into a novel, extending the boy's lifetime to age seventy. The killer's book is excellent, the phantom future he imagines for his victim wonderfully persuasive—but necessarily perfunctory, with all the years it has to cover. And so the governor, realizing that he has a major author at his mercy, strikes a ghoulish bargain with him: Like Scheherazade, the author can extend his life indefinitely, purchasing one stay of execution after another by writing a series of novels about the governor's son—one per year, each chronicling another year of the life that might have been.[*]

---

[*] The sheer tastelessness of the novel's preposterous plot may divert the reader, briefly, from the moldiness of the "metafictional" structure, one that subjects us to long stretches of the fictive writer's novel without ever making up its mind to relegate the writer's own life to a mere frame story. *The Man I Killed*, in other words, fails to make up its mind as to what it's *about*—above and beyond mere "aboutness," that flinty quarter-acre already so de-

Dank considered *The Man I Killed* his masterpiece, and when it sank without a trace (and at the point in his career when he was most obsessed with fame—see THINK OF ME), Dank did everything he could to generate a "buzz" about the book: making a point of pretending to read it in parks, in restaurants, in coffeehouses, and bursting once or twice a page into stagy, booming laughter; going into bookstores throughout northern California to ask if they had that new book everybody was talking about; placing a personal ad in which he billed himself as a brilliant, beautiful, and "uninhibited" young lady seeking a man who didn't need to be handsome, wealthy, young, employed, or even able-bodied, but did need to share her fervor for her favorite book (Dank saved all 184 replies, and though it was clear to me that few of his suitors had taken the trouble of buying and reading that book, many claimed to have done so and loved it); logging into chat rooms and getting himself flamed by repeatedly turning the talk to his novel whether the official topic of discussion was bondage, Dianetics, or Jack Russell terriers ("Speaking of dogs, there's a great one in that super new novel everyone's reading . . ."); sending a form letter urging the adoption of his book to every professor of English listed in the MLA directory, but not always the *same* form letter, since the reasons why a medievalist, for instance, should add it to the syllabus were not the reasons recommending it, for instance, to a specialist in

---

pleted by imprudent overplanting in the 1960s that no book can thrive there now. Not even one fertilized by the bottomless heap of manure that Dank always had at his disposal. As for that éclair, Bill, its owner never would have thrown it if he hadn't seen that deep down you *remain* a fellow adolescent. They have teenage hoodlums in Vienna too, and pastries (I just ate a Sacher torte, superbly rich and moist and dense, here in this world-class café on the Ringstrasse), but no one would dream of flinging a pastry at *me*. (OH)

African-American literature ("Not only is the hero's cellmate African-American, but two other characters, including the unforgettable Duane . . .").

For more about Dank's time in prison, see THE PUNISHMENT.

The Man in the Black Box: Philbert is a lowly sanitation worker who drives a big street-cleaning vehicle. One day he bumps his head in a low-speed collision and becomes aware of the interconnectedness of all things. His understanding of causation is suddenly so advanced that in order to assure his bowling team a victory, or to thwart the shadowy government's thugs who make a point in stories of this sort of harassing telepathic children, lovable extraterrestrials, and anybody else with psionic talents, Philbert is apt to do something as seemingly random as throwing his wife's freshly baked lasagna out the window or purposely stepping in a steaming heap of dogdirt. He also spends an awful lot of time in the Black Box, the windowless cinder-block bunker that the former owner of his house (a celebrated SF writer) built in the backyard for reasons of his own. For some reason, Philbert's superhuman understanding of causation (a metaphor, of course, for the novelist's ability to make connections among the most disparate parts of reality) works only in the bunker.

There really was (and is) a bunker in Dank's yard. He built it to protect his manuscripts, though he soon took to writing in there too. In August 1995 somebody burglarized his study. The thief or thieves took nothing but Dank's ailing laptop computer—which he'd been planning to replace soon anyway—and some financial records from a locked file cabinet, using Dank's own crowbar to pry open the top drawer. Because of the computer, though, and because the file drawer had been mislabeled MANUSCRIPTS—UNPUBLISHED,

Dank became convinced that someone was after his writing. At least, that was *one* of his theories. Some others:

—Militant survivalists had done it in retaliation for his scornful depiction of right-wing extremists in THE PLAGUE OF CANDOR.

—Sinister government operatives had done it because one or another of the wild speculations in his fiction had hit on a sensitive classified truth (see AUTOMOBILES), and they wanted to make sure his work in progress wasn't about to disclose further secrets.

—His next-door neighbor, Jock JABLONSKY, had done it, just to be mean.

—One of his ex-wives had done it.

—I had done it, for reasons known only to me.

—No one had done it because it hadn't happened—it was all a dream from which he hadn't yet awakened.

That last theory sounds a little less absurd when you learn that Dank was dozing in his study when the robbery occurred, in the La-Z-Boy that stood beside the file cabinet, with the laptop in his lap, and a few feet from the crowbar he kept on hand for home defense. And Dank was a light sleeper. It's hard to see how anyone could have entered his study, pried open that drawer, and taken his laptop without his noticing.

The day before the break-in, Dank had had a premonition that someone was about to burglarize his house. He had called the cops to tell them so, but even if they hadn't stopped taking him seriously by then, there was nothing they could do until the crime occurred. When a policewoman finally showed up several hours after the break-in (that they had "only sent a woman" struck Dank as proof that the police *still* weren't taking the incident seriously), she waved off his reproachful told-you-sos and implied that he himself had committed the "crime" he'd reported. By that time I'd reached the same conclusion: Just a few days earlier, Dank had been fretting about his income tax (he hadn't filed in three years because he couldn't bring himself to face the paperwork) and had said he wished his file cabinet would catch fire, since the loss of his financial records would give him an excuse for his continued delinquency.

If Dank did break into his own file cabinet, though, and steal his own laptop, he must have done it in some kind of fugue state: He was sincerely indignant at the policewoman's verdict, and for the rest of his life he continued spinning theories as to what had really happened that black afternoon. His favorite theory, though, remained the first—that some rival author was out to steal his intellectual property. The day after the break-in, Dank bought a wheelbarrow, a ton or so of cinder blocks, and several big bags of cement, and in less than a week he erected the Black Box, as he referred ever after to the odd structure that still stands in his backyard, and will stand through Armageddon. Dank had planned it as a perfect cube, six feet to a side (though partly buried), with its floor as well as its ceiling and walls composed of cinder blocks, to prevent intrusion by tunneling; but he was not a skilled mason, and the actual edifice—oozing mortar from its joints like tuna salad from a sloppy sandwich—is not as edifying a Euclidean solid as its Platonic conception. Worse, he forgot to allow for the difference between outer and inner dimensions—a negligible difference in the construction-paper mock-up he'd built beforehand, but a big difference when the faces of your cube are composed of cinder blocks. Inside, his writer's haven measured only 4'8" to a side—not even big enough for Dank to recline full-tilt in the bunker's La-Z-Boy, much less to stand upright. He'd also neglected to provide for ventilation. The only opening to the outer world was a crawlway on one side with a hinged metal door, like the door of an oven. Since that door had to be shut while he wrote, Dank had to leave it wide open for an hour before every session, to air out the bunker so he wouldn't suffocate mid-novel.

But that defeated the purpose of an impregnable bunker, especially since a busy man like Dank couldn't squander an hour a day sitting and guarding the entrance to his bunker while it "breathed" as slowly as a newly opened bottle of wine. So that became one of my duties: sitting outside and guarding the bunker during its airings, armed with a BB gun that I had orders to discharge at any rival author who tried to get in. And in fact there *was* sometimes a rival loitering in the vicinity, though I never found a pretext to "pop a cap in his ass" (as my students would say): Often, in the warmer months, I'd see Hirt in *his* backyard, sitting with a glass of whiskey in his Adirondack chair, pointedly ignoring me, no doubt waiting for a poem to occur to him. (Jarrell again: "To have written one good poem . . . it's like sitting out in the yard in the evening and having a meteorite fall in one's lap.") At that point I hadn't come to hate him as much as I would, or I might have been more trigger-happy.

But it wasn't just for selfish reasons that I suggested to Dank that he go back to doing his actual writing in the house, maybe by a window opening on birdsong and the scent of lilacs borne in on a gentle breeze, and use the airless bunker as a big strongbox to store the results. He seemed so hurt by my suggestion that I realized I didn't understand just what the bunker meant to him. And in any case my vigil at its entrance was a picnic compared to his eight- or ten-hour ordeals inside, with the steel door shut tight and bolted even at the height of summer, since the security of a sealed bunker soon became a precondition of writing at all. He had no other light or company within those walls than his laptop, the reclining chair he'd built the bunker around (having at least foreseen that it wouldn't fit through the crawlway), and a chamber pot, since he himself fit through the crawlway only with effort, and preferred his stinks to the nuisance of squeezing through every time the call of nature diverted his attention from the call of art. But it would have stunk in there in any case, since his chair had gotten rained on at least once before Dank finished bricking up the ceiling, and was rotting. Nonetheless, he insisted on doing all his writing in the bunker for about a year there before gradually phasing it out.

The main product of that era was *The Man in the Black Box*, a scrumptious trail mix of crunchy action sequences, nutty Eastern wisdom, and fruity paranormal speculation, all inspired—and, Dank claimed, enabled—by the claustrophobic conditions in which it was written. The book was one of his best selling and most lauded, garnering enthusiastic notices even from mainstream reviewers. It did so well, in fact, that Dank began a sequel, *The Man in the Black Box is Back*, but abandoned it because he couldn't face the prospect of another prison term in *his* Black Box.

The Man Who Knew Enough: So we've been reduced to culinary metaphors. Okay, here's a recipe for *The Man Who Knew Enough*: Take the tripe of one Spillane, an ounce of overripe Camus, the pickled gizzard of one Raymond (Chandler and Carver work equally well), an amply marbled slice from the paunch of Alfred Hitchcock, a bunch of hothouse Dreiser with the dirt still clinging to its roots, a small can of spiced Hammett "best when used" decades ago, the steroid-shrunken oysters of one Hemingway, a plop of Poe, a thick and fibrous slab sawn off the tawny liver of an aged Bukowski. Hack everything into bits. Cram everything into blender. Hit REHASH and hold out for a heavy brownish sludge that looks like it's already been through a digestive tract once or twice. Now fold in a cup of high-fructose corn syrup. While you're at it, why not add a handful of that tar-black fungus you found growing on the float ball in the toilet tank? Add a dash of Danielle Steel, a pinch of *The Prophet*, a hint of McKuen, and some little flavor pillows of Confucius from the drawer with the take-out menus and the plastic forks. Pour into loaf pan. Put in oven till half-baked. Dump on silver platter plainly meant for something better. Garnish with Pop Rocks and breath mints.

As for the *plot* of the novel, never mind. Suffice it to say that *The Man Who Knew Enough* (a lot more than its author knew) is the kind of yawn-a-minute mystery that pathologically thrillable reviewers describe as a "paranoid thriller." Is it thrilling? No. But it *is* mysterious. How the hell did it end up in print? (OH)

"The Man Who Sued Himself and Settled Out of Court": This story is unique among Dank's works (surprisingly, considering his lifelong recklessness) in being written from a hospital bed. Elsewhere I discuss Leopold LIPS (the sponger who moved in with us after Pandora left), my efforts to get rid of him, and, finally, his overdue departure. An unforeseen effect of that departure was that Dank became obsessed with Pandora again, three months after their divorce.

In the meantime, he'd persuaded himself that Pandora didn't "go for" him because he wasn't sufficiently "hardcore": He didn't ride a motorcycle, he hadn't been arrested for any violent crime, and he'd never even worked up the nerve for something called "stage-diving." I'm not a member of the subculture in question, but I have made inquiries, and it seems that stage-diving involves climbing up onto the stage while a show is progress and flinging yourself into the throng of fans in the pit, trusting them to catch you, or at least to break your fall. More fun than it sounds, no doubt, or people wouldn't do it—as presumably they do, or would there be a name for it?

Dank took to haunting the clubs where Pandora hung out, and when he finally spotted her, he made his first and final dive in a bid to win her back. Well, some are wise and some are otherwise. As for how that dive went wrong—for starters, Dank was bigger than the average diver. Punks his size are usually employed as bouncers at those shows, and so have no chance to dive except perhaps on breaks. What's more, the crowd that night was thinner than average, and the fans up front less densely packed. And poor Dank couldn't even dive into the thickest part of the crowd, where the bigger punks were clustered, because one of those punks was an ex-lover of Pandora's who seemed not to like him. So our author belly-flopped into an isolated group of four or five young women, Pandora among them, and we'll never know if it was heartless-ness or just self-preservation that caused them all to leap out of the way, each perhaps trusting the others to catch him or, failing the others, the floor. All we know for sure is that it was in fact the floor that finally intercepted Dank.

The stage from which he dove was a good six feet up, and Dank, at his most recent checkup (just a month before his dive), weighed 333 pounds. It doesn't take a physicist to see how hard he must have hit. Had he been attempting, once again, to kill himself? Such a fall might well have proven fatal to someone his size, though Dank was the Rasputin of suicide attempts.

This time he spent *two* weeks in the hospital, with his head bandaged, his left arm in a sling, and his right leg in a cast. His mental state was even more pathetic: Throwing off all reti-cence and stage-diving into the arms of an unknown posterity (and I trust *posterity* will handle him more gently than those moshers did!), Dank told me the sad facts of his last marriage.

He'd already told me that once, just once, he'd been in Pandora's Hell House bedroom. He'd told me several times, in fact, and always with a knowing look that of course I took to mean that once at least during their courtship he had succeeded in sleeping with her, as he hadn't during their marriage. Now, though, he admitted that she'd led him up to her bedroom because he'd started crying one day in her kitchen, as they sat around smoking pot with her housemates and she and Travis started making out in front of Dank.

Dank cried again as he told me all this, and now, as I remember that appalling conversation, with our author bruised and bandaged head to toe, I find Hirt's ongoing malice even more outrageous. Dank suffered so much, and so unfairly, in his lifetime. How could anybody want to kick his corpse around? I'm seriously tempted to hit "block sender" again and finish writing this encyclopedia all by myself.

Pandora hadn't led Dank to her bedroom to give *him* a turn, as he'd tearfully hoped at the time, but just to give him a "time out," a chance to simmer down. When he did, he noticed that her hothouse of a bedroom—a glassed-in veranda—was teeming with cannabis plants. Pandora had a garden after all. As soon as he mentioned the pot plants, Dank looked remorseful and swore me to secrecy, as Pandora had sworn him. I took the oath with fingers crossed and then, the moment I got home, called the Hemlock police. Back then they still saw me as a law-abiding citizen (this was before the nightmarish muddle concerning MacDougal and me), and they acted promptly on my tip.

In a perfect world, Pandora would have gone to jail, to a women's prison of the sort you see in trashy films—sleazy guards, sadistic warden, a hulking bull-dyke cellmate—and would have stayed there a long time, at least till menopause. This is not a perfect world, though, and somehow Pandora got wind of the raid (I think a phone call from a friendly neighbor tipped her off at work) in time to skip town with only the clothes on her back (or hardly any, if she'd dressed as usual that morning), confirming her guilt in the eyes of the law, and ensuring that she could never return. It was galling that she hadn't suffered more for all the suffering she'd caused, but at least she was out of the picture.

Before the news of her departure caused him to pause his writing for a month of misdirected mourning, Dank found time to write "The Man Who Sued Himself and Settled Out of Court," the tale of a society where the laws that govern how people treat one another also apply to—and are *enforced* with regard to—the treatment of the self. "After all," demands the title character, "if suicide is such a crime, then why not self-assault? Reckless self-endangerment? Self-harassment, self-defamation, self-intimidation? Self-delusion? Self-abuse?" This enlightened culture's corollary to the Golden Rule is: *Do unto yourself as you would have others do unto you.* (And as the narrator points out, that *doesn't* go with saying: Most of us treat ourselves *worse*, on occasion, than we would want other people to treat us.) In one scene, the title character, an author, commits a shocking self-hate crime and promptly makes a self-arrest. In another scene he sues himself for libel because his new novel features a scurrilous depiction of an author clearly based on him.

"March": For twenty years now, a composer—a sort of cross between John Philip Sousa and John Cage—has written, rehearsed, and conducted a march every March, to greet the spring. This year, though, he can't come up with a new tune. At last he gives up and snaps his baton like Prospero's wand. He resigns himself, in the final paragraph, to being "no longer a real creator, but just an embittered and malicious musicologist." People who write about the creations of others, the story implies—unfairly and a bit offensively, I'd add—are always blinded (or in this case deafened) by the envy of the sterile for the fertile. An ancient theme, already old when Robert Burns denounced a critic as a "murderous *accoucheur* of infant learning," the tune is one that unreflective authors have a bad habit of humming when anyone tries to speak frankly to them about their work.

Like February, Embers, and August and April, "March" is a relic of Dank's abandoned project to write a book of stories concerning the months of the year. According to his original plan, each story would be written in the month for which it was named and during which it was set. He wrote "March," as I recall, on the first day of 1999 that really felt like spring. He'd never liked that celebrated season, which made it so hard to stay at his desk (or which, to say it *auf Deutsch*, tickled and tormented his monolithic *Sitzfleisch* with distracting *Wanderlust*). But he enjoyed a special surge of inspiration *any* time the season changed. Predictably, he got to wondering if there was any way to produce that surge more than four times a year. For a while in the late 1990s he experimented with creating microseasons in his house. With the help of a snowmaker and an institutional refrigerating unit from a restaurant-supply store, he turned a basement storage room into a walk-in cooler where it was winter year-round. In the dog days of August I'd find him down there in a parka, snow pants, and mittens, sitting at a little desk scrawling in a spiral notebook (he was afraid his computer would freeze) and sipping hot cocoa that steamed in the cold air. Then, when it really *was* winter, I'd find him, in his Speedos, on a padded lawn chair in the extra bedroom, which he'd enhanced with two portable heaters, a humidifier, sundry tanning lamps and Gro-Lites, and all kinds of outdoorsy plants—there was even a tub of hydrangeas—creating a climate so tropically sultry that I'm tempted to believe Dank's claim that once or twice he even got it to rain in there.

Me: The story of a bachelor who lives alone, reads science fiction, finds and loses love, and writes a novel. What makes this fascinating masterwork unique* is that its incidents derive entirely from Dank's day-to-day experience during the months of its writing: He worked on it only at bedtime, incorporating all the highlights of his day, confining himself to the faithful transcription of real events in the order they occurred, and forbidding himself to invent a single incident that didn't happen or to leave out any notable event that did. (How notable? He could omit a stubbed toe, but not a sprained ankle.)

But how, without fibbing or fudging, was Dank supposed to turn his ordinary plotless life into a satisfying novel? His solution was to transfigure that life, not in the *telling*, but sooner, in the *living*—to lead his life in such a way that it would make for a good read. For a few months in the spring of 1986, he made his diary into a novel by making his days novelistic, doing his best to lead the vivid, eventful, and readable life of a fictional character, even when that meant provoking events he would normally try to prevent. If, for example, he wanted his hero to expose himself in public, Dank himself would have to drop his pants. (He had sense enough to do so in front of ancient Mrs. Fleisch, so nearsighted that she either didn't see what he was attempting to show her or didn't recognize its owner as her next-door neighbor.) Conversely, if he *didn't* want to write a root canal into his novel, he'd have

---

* *Fascinating? Masterpiece? Unique?* Well, as a famous art historian once wrote about an infamously overrated painter, "No degree of dullness can safeguard a work against the determination of critics to find it fascinating." (OH)

to cancel his dental appointment—and more than once he invoked the exigencies of art as an excuse to do what he wanted, and not do what he didn't.

That, in fact, turned out to be the real interest of the project for its author—not the results, enthralling as they are, but the way the process of writing the book briefly and magically transformed his real life. Though Dank was thirty-three when he wrote *Me*, he had never had sex out of wedlock (meaning he'd had sex with just two women, since at that point he'd been married only twice), and he'd developed a fatalistic conviction that something he wanted so much could never come to pass. He might have gone to his grave without a single fling to his name if he hadn't decided that his slice-of-life narrative needed a little love interest. What had always seemed impossible till then, as if forbidden by a witch's spell, was easy as long as Dank viewed his actions as no more than the drafting of a novel. (Not as easy, though, as getting that first lover—the varicose lady who heated and touted free samples on weekends at Food Planet—to dump him a week later, when the time came for his hero to know heartbreak.)

But the most intriguing byproduct of Dank's experiment—of his effort to lead the life of a fictional character—was not his fifty-something lover but THE PLAGUE OF CANDOR, the novel he composed concurrently with *Me*, since the plot of *Me* included the writing of a novel. To judge by the real-life reception of that novel, its author, Rebus Blank, was a better writer than Dank.

"The Meanest Genie": Now and then, Dank returned his spaceship to its hangar and his ray gun to its holster and took a break from his official genre to spend a wild weekend with its dubious bachelor uncle, Fantasy. "The Meanest Genie" was the result of one such spree.

Written in a single drug-befuddled afternoon—an afternoon its author might have been spent more fruitfully talking to his plants or alphabetizing his socks—the laughably fatuous story features a tight-fisted genie named Gugg who grants just one wish instead of the usual three. And even that one wish is offered with the caveat that if wishers get too greedy and ask for too much, they get nothing. Gugg refuses, though, to give examples of what is or isn't too much: You make your wish, he vanishes, and your request is either granted or not. Some go for broke and ask for superpowers like invisibility (Dank's own idiotic, onanistic heart's desire), others for pitifully little—a new muffler for the family car, say. The hero of "The Meanest Genie" asks the title character for just enough money to pay for his child's urgent "operation." Dank asks the reader to care about a child who is never introduced or named or even sexed, and whose malady is never specified. Both requests are refused.

Written in a snit in 1981, the mercifully short story expresses (incoherently) its author's bitter disappointment with the Guggenheim Foundation, which had just refused his plea for $168.39, the amount he needed to get his phone turned on again after the long-distance hijinks of some freeloader got it turned off. I prefer to read the story, though, as an allegory for poor Dank's career: He asked his muse for next to nothing, in the way of artistic distinction, and was denied even that. (OH)

The Melville Brotherhood: A local writers' group Dank joined in 1987. Membership was open to obscure and unsuccessful writers of every stamp, though members were not just supposed to be unknown, but unjustly and, if possible, outrageously neglected. It is a measure of Dank's obscurity that, notwithstanding all his books, his fellow Melvilleans tolerated him,*

---

* They were right to recognize him as a Brother. I met Dank before his lack

since it was understood that if any member ever did get famous, he'd be drummed out of the club as a traitor. Dank may have had that bylaw in mind the day he got the idea for a directory of the obscure and undistinguished to be called *Who's Nobody*. In this volume, one of the many of which his death deprived us, the nobodies would be selected at random and screened for nondescriptness—and dropped from subsequent editions if they killed the president or found a cure for cancer or otherwise distinguished themselves from the crowd.

Dank and his brothers in neglect met every Tuesday afternoon at Coffee Town. The Melvilleans were pariahs not just in the literary world but even in the smaller world of Coffee Town, where their lowly status was the fault, I think, of a certain member, Eberhart Wagenknecht, a handsome, well-dressed, clean-cut German who, however, never bathed. If you shared a crowded elevator with him, you'd never suspect that *he* was the one to blame for the stink, and the employees at Coffee Town still hadn't figured it out. Some of them seemed to think it was Dank, as if there were a proven correlation between body size and body odor. (Actually, considering the many hard-to-get-at folds and crannies that obesity brings into being, he didn't smell nearly as bad, or as much, as you'd expect.) Other employees seemed to assume that the stink was collective—that that's just the way it smells when a group of unsuccessful writers get together to complain about a world that lacks the courage to listen to them. That's what I myself had vaguely been assuming till the day I found myself alone

---

of talent had entirely declared itself, and afterward, though as a rule I have no time for mediocrities, I "grandfathered" him in, as they say. As for Dank's other "literary" friendships, they were erected on the same foundation as all friendships between bad but self-deluded writers: that of unearned mutual respect, of a readiness to humor each other's delusions. (OH)

with Wagenknecht outside the men's room, awaiting our turns, and realized that, notwithstanding his old-world manners, his knowledge of Bach, or his *feuilletons* reviling American pop culture as only a German émigré can, *he* was the source of the stink. And he never missed a meeting.

Like a mental institution where each inmate thinks "*I* don't belong here—all the *other* patients are *crazy*," the Melville Brotherhood consisted of some dozen writers each of whom cursed Fate, or cursed the Publishing Establishment, for forcing him (there were no women in the Brotherhood except for one old biddy who seldom attended) to associate with such a bunch of crackpots, hacks, and losers. The composition of the group changed from week to week, but there were regulars I came to know only too well, since as Dank's biographer I felt obliged to tag along. Along with Wagenknecht, for instance, there was Pock, who was less interested in getting published than in getting into *Guinness*, and to that end was writing the world's longest autobiography. (The last I heard, he'd passed the seven-thousand-page mark and was closing in on age eighteen.)

There was Dawson, who described himself as an "outsider physicist" and attributed his failure to get his papers published in any of the "so-called 'reputable' journals" to the fact that his ideas were too bold and new for the hidebound physics establishment. He'd given Dank a copy of his *magnum opus*, a fat and patently self-published volume expounding the new science of Dawsonomy, and boasting on its cover the following Publisher's Note:

The foremost thinker of the Modern period, Dawson has completely revolutionized the type of Thoughts that educated Men now think. Compared to Dawson, so-called "famous scientists" like Einstein are as little children playing with Chemistry Sets. Buy this famous Book—you won't regret it!

There was Plinkett, a burly former weathercaster who now wrote amusingly inept detective novels about a dashing weatherman named Plunkett, who solved crimes in his spare time with the aid of knowledge that no one but a weatherman would have ("It's simple, Lieutenant: With the barometer 31 and falling, there's no way Pirelli could have . . ."). By the time I came along, Plinkett and Dank no longer spoke: once, at some long-ago meeting, Plinkett had made a scornful remark about science fiction and Dank had retorted that weathercasting was itself a form of science fiction—a bunch of semi-educated guesses, almost always wrong, about the future. Plinkett had lobbied for years to have Dank expelled from the Brotherhood on the grounds that he was insufficiently Neglected, and yet in 2001, when Dank quit of his own accord, Plinkett acted as insulted as if he'd been jilted. I understand that he was questioned in connection with Dank's murder.

There was Ed Elbow, a forty-four-year-old who'd just received his PhD in creative writing from one of the few schools to offer such a degree. He'd already earned MFAs in creative writing from not one but three different programs, and before that a BA in creative writing from his undergraduate school. Not that he'd been in school uninterruptedly since kindergarten: He'd taken a whole year off once to roll up his sleeves and work for a living, first as a bartender, then as a short-order cook, then in a homeless shelter, then on a fishing boat—and all strictly for the life experience so vital (he'd been told in workshops) to a writer, since he was independently wealthy and didn't need to work at all, much less to sell a book. And he'd yet to write a book. By now he should have been the greatest writer of all time, since according to Dank, Continuing Ed (as they called him) had, in fact, had talent to begin with. That talent had disintegrated, though, as a result of decades of "constructive criticism," the way the facial bones and cartilage of a plastic surgery addict finally disintegrate from the strain of too many surgeries.

There was Schreiber, the group's founder, who had written half a dozen novels but never shown them to a soul—least of all his fellow writers—because he was afraid that someone would steal his material. The others called him "paranoid," which in his case at least was surely more accurate than "neglected." For that matter, they *all* seemed a little paranoid. Once I bought a day-old sticky bun and, hoping to refresh it, stuck it in the seldom-used microwave oven (which, as luck would have it, was in the only room with a table big enough to accommodate the writers), whereupon the entire Brotherhood jumped up as one man and rushed out of the room, led by Dawson (cupping his hands over his testicles), or maybe by Dawsonomy, which for all I know may disapprove of microwaves. Once the oven stopped, the writers returned, one by one, but warily, and not right away (they seemed to think the deadly radiation needed time to dissipate, like smoke), casting reproachful looks in my direction.

Last and least was Blount, who didn't blush to call himself an author though the whole of his life's work consisted of *a single word*, a distillation into a syllable or so of the feelings and the findings of a lifetime. The magic word was to be published when Blount died, and remained a secret while he lived: He kept it, all by itself, on a floppy disk in a safe deposit box. Whenever he "revised" the word—i.e., replaced it with another, as he sometimes did several times a day, when his writing was going well—he drove over to the bank with his laptop and updated the diskette. When his turn came to show his work to his fellow Melvilleans, all Blount could show were superseded drafts of his immortal word—other words (in other words) that had each once been enshrined on that diskette, for an hour or a month, till Blount became convinced that some better word said it all even more eloquently. Dank once showed me a list of these earlier drafts, and among the mantras that at one time or another Blount had seen as summing up his life were "tragicomedy," "nevertheless," "until," "again," "of," "as," "if," "and," and, inscrutably, "artichoke."

Though members were forbidden by the bylaws of the Brotherhood to ridicule one another's work, it was clear that most of them refused to take Blount's project seriously. The exception was Dank, who had published so many millions of words, and saw Blount as a well-deserved reproach to his verbosity. With the misplaced reverence of a Casanova for a celibate, Dank was all too ready to see the unprecedented slightness of Blount's output as evidence of greater seriousness, and to denigrate himself as a mere chatterbox, rather than an inexhaustible artist with an irrepressible talent. Blount encouraged him in this delusion, maintaining that even the briefest books are needlessly wordy, and that in essence every book—every work of art, in fact—is either a sigh, a sob, a moan, a groan, a gasp, or a yawn. (When I pressed him to say more about this "theory," Blount cited examples from Dank's *oeuvre*, explaining that NEVER MIND ME is best heard as "a world-weary yawn," THE SADIATORS as "a muffled sob," and THE CONSEQUENCES as "an educated gasp.") Dank once wasted a month trying think of a word that would say it all for *him*, and finally settled on "furthermore." Quoth the maven, "furthermore." Luckily for us, though, finding his *mot juste* didn't stop Dank from writing whole books.

Though I myself refused to join the Brotherhood, I was a de facto member, since for several years I escorted Dank to every meeting (both as his biographer and as his bodyguard, since, like Hansen forty years before—see HOBSON'S CHOICE— Plinkett was forever threatening to "kick" his "ass"). Aside from Dank, I was the only writer at that table who could truthfully complain of "neglect" as opposed to thoroughly deserved oblivion. That's not a boast, just a reflection on the caliber of our fellow Melvilleans—of the spitballs, BB guns, and peashooters with which they hoped to bag the big game of literary glory.

Melville Prize: A literary prize invented by Dank in 1996. The prize was supposed to be awarded annually, by the MELVILLE BROTHERHOOD, to some unjustly neglected living writer, to give him a foretaste of the glory that would surely be his once he died. At Dank's insistence, the first winner was the present commentator, in token recognition of my unpublished novels (though in all the years I knew him, Dank himself read only one of them). My prize came with—or, to be precise, consisted of—a hundred dollars donated by Dank and a plaster bust of some unidentified luminary he had found at a garage sale. Dank thought the bust looked a bit like Herman Melville. I couldn't see the resemblance, but I was touched by my friend's good intentions, and graciously went through with the charade.

The second and last Melville Prize was conferred, in 1997, on that neglected writer Owen Hirt, who refused to attend the award ceremony (at Coffee Town, of course), as if to tell the Brotherhood what A. E. Housman once told *his* admirers: "You would be welcome to praise me if you did not praise one another." And yet Hirt made sure to list the plaudit in his author's note when *Final Notice*, his last book of poems, was published the following year. He must have known there wouldn't be any more plaudits coming his way

Soon after *Final Notice* appeared and disappeared and the poet found himself no less neglected than before (though even less unjustly, as its seven readers can attest), Hirt officially, and rather self-importantly, swore off the literary life forever. No doubt he thought he was punishing the world for its failure to recognize his genius. Like Dank with his telephone (see THE MEANEST GENIE), the world, if it wanted its service reinstated after disregarding that strident final notice, would first have to pay the whole of its outstanding balance—and pay interest on the lion's share of homage and attention that Hirt considered long overdue. Too bad there aren't collection agencies for debts like that.

Memoirs of a Science Fiction Writer: A brief (140 pages) but still exhausting trudge through the bogs and barrens of Dank's past. The book is basically a list of the regrettable events that, as far as Dank could tell, had made him the writer he was. Highlights of the list include such archetypal moments as learning to read, learning to write, the onset of puberty, the thrill of model rocketry, the hell of junior high, the destruction of his brand-new *Stranger in a Strange Land* lunchbox ("by Mike Daley, Brad Werther, Lee Hansen, and Mark Perrier—the same kid that wrecked my *other* lunchbox!"), his first encounter with the fiction of Theodore Sturgeon, his first and only meeting with the man himself, his first published story, his "crucial" decision to "live" for his "art." (Maybe "read" and "write," above, should also be in quotes.)

The book's only claim to fame is that *every single word is in italics*. Dank, evidently, felt that each and every thing that had ever happened to him, as of 1991, was worthy as such of special emphasis.

Publishing a book about your life has always struck me as a really greedy act: not just a bid for fame and fortune, but for shelf space in the minds of perfect strangers, often crowding some of their own memories off the shelves, or at least making those memories harder to find, like anything that makes a storage room more cluttered. And for such a vacuous life! In a perfect world, the length of a biography would be a function of the interest of the life in question—and the whole of Dank's *Memoirs* would fit, with room to spare, inside a fortune cookie. (OH)

Mental Exercises: On learning that the author who'd stolen his third wife belonged to Mensa, Dank hastened to apply for membership himself. In perhaps the worst humiliation of his life—and one I hesitate to mention, lest posterity put as much faith in standardized testing as my credulous era does—he flunked the qualifying IQ test. Dank himself put too much credence in the test (in my opinion, to take it at all is to take it too seriously), as if it proved him unworthy, once and for all, of the lady Mensans he had hoped to meet. As if, no matter how many books he had written, he were less of a genius than all those lucky test-takers who happened to be better at deciding what comes next when confronted with a series like 1, 1, 2, 3, 5, 8, 13. Never mind that Dank was his era's leading writer of "day-after-tomorrow" fiction, and knew more about "what comes next" than a whole cruise ship, or Love Boat, of Mensans.

I will refrain from specifying Dank's IQ as measured by the test, since I can't imagine any more distracting biographical item, any fact (or "fact") more likely to obtrude itself between his reader and his books—and of course the books themselves are the only intelligence tests that ought to concern us. I will, say, though, that contrary to a malicious rumor circulated by MacDougal, Dank's IQ was in fact above one hundred.

But it wasn't high enough for Dank. He decided that the lady at the HEIRLOOM CLINIC had been right after all: He wasn't worthy "yet" to donate his seed to an elite sperm bank. And so he became obsessed with raising his IQ. For a while there nothing else mattered. He even seemed to think a higher IQ would help him lose weight. I once heard him speculate that Einstein probably burnt off more calories in five minutes of "thinking about math and stuff" than the average jogger did in half an hour of mindless huffing and puffing.

He bought a book of practice IQ tests and with their help he did succeed in raising his average score by nine points in one month. And of course Dank took for granted that those higher scores reflected a surge in sheer brainpower, not just the acquisition of a meaningless skill. Well, we are all guilty of such self-deceptions, and writers guiltiest of all: At least they are notorious for scheming and schmoozing their way to the top and then conveniently forgetting how they got there, convincing themselves that their fame is a pure by-product and proof of their talent. Of *that* kind of self-deception Dank was innocent: One reason for his lifelong neglect is that he had no flair for self-promotion. "In the saturnalia of ignoble personal passions, of which the struggle for literary success, in old and crowded communities, offers so sad a spectacle, he never mingled," as Matthew Arnold said about another underrated writer.

In the interests of improving his IQ, anyhow, Dank also went on a special diet of so-called smart foods, drinks, and drugs, and devised a strenuous regime of mental exercises whose only visible manifestation—if I happened to enter his study during one of his "sets"—was an inscrutable jumble of letters and figures on the chalkboard he'd bought for the purpose. He sounded almost mystical when describing his mental workouts, but insisted that his exercises were the "intellectual equivalents" of such physical exertions as preliminary stretches, jumping jacks, deep-knee bends, one-armed push-ups, uphill sit-ups, isometrics, power lifting, rope-skipping, and wind sprints.

By that point, Dank was convinced that many everyday activities and substances cause brain damage—so many that he'd had to supplement his theories on the subject with another theory to explain why we aren't all profoundly retarded by now. According to Dank, we all tend to grow more and more intelligent as years go by, but this growth is almost always offset by the wear and tear of everyday life, with its millions of insults to the intellect. So in theory he didn't need smart drugs or *How to Ace Your IQ Test* in order to become a genius. All he needed was to avoid, religiously (and for Dank as for so many SF types, intelligence *was* a religion), every possible source of brain damage. He used the analogy of the guy in *Guinness* with the fifty-five-inch fingernails, whose secret was not some magic Jell-O diet or unique metabolism, but just a life devoted to pampering his nails.

A Midwinter Night's Dream: This fanciful novel begins with everybody in the world waking up one morning from exactly the same dream—one about an empty house, a supermarket, an arrest, a station wagon, and a mob of protestors in scuba gear. Different theories are proposed to account for the impossible event—as a message from God, say, or maybe one from aliens in UFOs. Even atheists tend to treat the dream as a sort of sacred text, and rival schools of dream interpretation vie ferociously—to the point of bloodshed—to assert their different exegeses.

The dream features actual people, the same for every dreamer. One is an ordinary housewife from Nebraska, a woman known only to her family, friends, and neighbors until the night of the dream. Afterwards her image is televised around the world, billions of strangers recognize her with a shudder, and she becomes a worldwide celebrity, even a sacred figure and destination for pilgrimages, as well as a sudden source of pride for her hometown, which till then had barely noticed her. Celebrity also descends on people who remember and record the dream especially vividly—though as with differing interpretations, differing transcripts are also hotly contested, as hotly as accounts of the same historic event by rival historians. As for the scattered few who didn't have the dream at all and make the mistake of admitting it, they are treated as heretics in some parts of the world—ostracized, persecuted, sometimes even put to death.

In a minor oversight that for me only adds to the charm of the book, Dank forgot all about time zones and started his tale with an eight-page montage of people all over the world— a nomad in the Gobi desert, a little Japanese boy in a rice hut, a pastry chef who sleeps above his bakery in Paris, an Eskimo family in its igloo, a science fiction writer somewhere in California—all waking "at the same instant." Dank often forgot about time zones, even when jet-lagged. One weekend while attending a Worldcon in Baltimore, he called me twice at seven AM Eastern time, forgetting that in Hemlock not even the birds were awake yet. And once in 1998, while dieting in penance for his second heart attack, Dank lamented at dinnertime: "All over the world, people are sitting down right now to big hearty Norman Rockwell dinners, and all *I* get is half a grapefruit." For someone whose fiction ranges around so recklessly in time and space, he could be surprisingly provincial.

When I interviewed him for my dissertation in 1991— almost a decade after *Midwinter* was published—and asked about what I'd assumed was his poetic license in regard to that opening montage, Dank looked confused. When he finally understood the question, he was so aghast that he tried to get the novel's publisher (which hadn't caught the error either, after all) to destroy all unsold copies. When that didn't work, Dank spoke of buying up and burning the 2,883 copies remaining (from a print run of five thousand), but even with his author's discount, he couldn't afford to. What he ended up doing instead—taking at face value the publisher's surely-sarcastic suggestion—was to fly to LaGuardia, get a cab to the warehouse in New Jersey where the unsold copies of his book were biding their time, and paste into each and every one a homemade errata slip advising buyers not to read the eight pages in question.

"Midwinter Day," my dictionary says, is an archaic name for Christmas, so Midwinter Night should be Christmas night, but it's clear that Dank was thinking of the winter solstice: Several times he tells us that everybody in the world has the dream on "the longest night of the year" (here forgetting not about time zones but about hemispheres). Well, it's just a few days' difference, and might be even closer if our pagan forebears had been a little better at pinpointing the solstice. Isn't that the reason Christmas happens in December, in the depths of winter—as a way of whistling in the dark, brandishing our puny torches in the face of a night that threatens to settle in for good? I've always hated winter. I was honestly convinced I wouldn't make it through this latest until the reading of Dank's will in October 2006.

Dank's last will and testament—the same document that designated Hirt to write this reader's guide—left the house to me. When he drew up the will in August 1998, Dank and I had been sharing the place for almost four years, and he must have felt it would be cruel to turn me out into the rain when he died. His sister, though, had no such qualms, and even threatened to contest the will in court. It was her husband's prurience, ironically, that spared me that ordeal: Stan was stupidly convinced, and convinced his stupid wife, that Dank and I had been lovers, which gave me at least as good a title to Dank Manor as she had.

Before I could return, though, I had to overcome the fears that had led me to flee Hemlock in the first place—the fear of meeting an end as sudden as Dank's, for one, and a fear that the police thought *I'd* had something to do with his death, just because I'd had so much to do with his life. There'd already been one ugly brush with the law, years back, though not in Hemlock. But I won't go into that, not in this entry. Maybe later. (But I try to bear in mind that encyclopedias are seldom read cover-to-cover like novels, that for the reader's purposes it makes no sense to speak of "earlier" and "later" entries.) What finally got me to return to Hemlock was the reflection that nothing that might happen to me there could be worse than what was happening in Clackamas.

And so, just last week—on Friday, December 15, 2006 (the last day of the semester at the junior college where I'd been marking time)—I moved back to California, back into a house that feels palatial after my six-month ordeal in that Clackamas suicide hut. As much as I miss Dank, I'm feeling more festive, and less self-destructive, than I expected to feel on Christmas Eve. I've started to archive the reams of loose paper—handwritten, typewritten, dot-matrixed, laser printed, Magic Markered—in our author's study, truly an Augean task (it even *smells* a little like a stable in there). Yesterday I bought and trimmed a Christmas tree and hung some holly in my bedroom—the same room I had before. The master bedroom is bigger and probably brighter, but I can't even bring myself to set foot in there—the room where Dank was murdered— much less to *sleep* in there. Besides, the room smells even more insistently of its last tenant than the study does. Thomas Moore: "You may break, you may shatter the vase, if you will/ But the scent of the roses will hang round it still."

"The Mind Reader's Just Desserts": We are in "a classy coffee house" in *fin-de-siècle* Zurich. A clairvoyant ne'er-do-well named Jurgen is using his "unrivalled psychic powers" to beat everyone at poker. Like a cartoon villain, Jurgen has a handlebar moustache.

We know he's mean because we see him kick a nosy poodle. As the dog scurries back to its horrified owner, a "majestic and indignant Senior Citizen at the table in the corner over by the pastry cart, with a heaving bosom," you can just hear the short-order cook in the all-nite kitchen of Dank's imagination (a diner where the smoke alarm is always going off, the pickle wedges garnishing the burgers look recycled, and the walls are papered with full-color posters illustrating the Heimlich maneuver): "One comeuppance, coming right up!"

Comeuppance arrives in the unlikely form of a graduate student. He looks like an easy mark, the vague and disheveled young man who joins the card game after Jurgen gleefully ruins "the Baron of Basel." When the poodle-kicking psychic tries to read *his* mind, though, he (the psychic, not the student) is "instantly" driven insane. Turns out the student is none other than young Albert Einstein, and he'd been "multitasking, as geniuses will"—not just playing cards but also "thinking about Relativity."

This mercifully atypical foray into historical fiction is all too typical of Dank in other ways. Everything, in fact, proclaims it Dank's: the fear of difficult ideas and of modern physics in particular, the inability to think of any more interesting use of clairvoyance than gambling, the failure to picture an unfamiliar setting instead of borrowing a room at Coffee Town—the one where Dank's neglected-writers circle met—and calling it "the card room of the Café Zurich." At least he managed not to mention the microwave oven.

Back in our Oakland days, Dank bought a book called *Teach Yourself Telepathy*, as if it were a skill he could attain by simple diligence. I told Dank that even if he did teach himself to read my mind, he wouldn't understand it. As for Dank's mind, reading *it* would surely be like reading an especially fuzzy xerox of a xerox, or the faded printout of an old dot-matrix printer running low on ink. (OH)

The Mystery: One night a middle-aged bachelor's bedtime routine is disrupted by the baffling absence of his toothbrush from
the toothbrush glass. Did it fall behind the toilet? No. Did he
drop it in the wastebasket by accident? He didn't. Where the
hell did it go, then? He'd been meaning to replace that toothbrush anyway, yet he finds that he can't let the mystery rest—
and his failure to solve it gradually drives him insane. He quits
his job in order to devote all his time to the problem, briefly
engages a private detective, reduces his elderly mother to tears
with an unprecedented burst of savagery, stops bathing, and
by the end has become one of those foul-smelling men who
haunt the reading rooms of public libraries in their quest for
enlightenment.

Before he's that far gone, though, our hero wonders if perhaps he got rid of the toothbrush somehow in the middle of
the night in an instantly forgotten—if not somnambulistic—
attempt to force himself to buy a new one the next day, as for
several weeks before the disappearance he'd been resolving to
do, every evening, in his daily planner. By the time I knew him,
Dank himself no longer used appointment books or planners,
possibly because—to judge by those he let me see for the biography—they had only led him to procrastinate. It had always
given him a dangerous illusion of efficacy to draw up lists of
things to do tomorrow, even if yesterday he had vowed, as he
usually had, to do them today. Even "plans" as simple as "buy
toothbrush" tended to recur day after day for weeks, because
as easy as it is to buy a toothbrush, it's always easier, on any
given day, to write "buy toothbrush" yet again on tomorrow's
page of plans, and forget about it till tomorrow.

The Mystery was composed in 1995 in response to the still-
unexplained loss of Dank's own toothbrush. Though he didn't
get quite as obsessed as his fictive counterpart, he did get obsessed, interrupting his writing for several days to search for the

missing item, tearing open and meticulously sifting through the contents of three big garbage bags (after lugging them back from the curb to the kitchen), and even suspecting *me* of foul play. Several times I looked up from a book (in the living room, where we read in the evenings) and found him watching me narrowly. More than once he "accidentally" burst into the bathroom just as I was brushing my teeth ("Oops—didn't hear you in there"). He even got a roll of quarters from the bank and placed them temptingly all over the house, to see (as he later confessed) if I'd take the bait and confirm his worst suspicions as to my thievery. It amuses me to recall that, far from stealing his quarters, I guessed their purpose and set out several more. By that point, after all, I'd made it my vocation to understand my landlord, and not just his printed fiction but his private theories, neuroses, and delusions. And I knew that when he made the rounds of his money-traps, he'd forget where some of the quarters were placed and conclude that I'd taken the ones he couldn't find.

Life is full of minor mysteries, especially life *chez* Dank. Like his oeuvre, his house was a minefield of surprises, some of them unpleasant—less akin to finding a shiny new quarter than to springing a forgotten mousetrap (as I did once) while groping around on the top shelf of a high cupboard. One of the basement rooms, for instance, had its door barred by a two-by-four. One day I made the mistake of opening that door and was almost buried alive by an avalanche of dirt that took me a good hour to clean up enough that I could close the door again. Dank was in Reno that weekend at a "relax-a-con" (more easygoing, as SF conventions go, than a World-con, a pro-con, or a ser-con), and I had to wait two days to find out *why* the room was full of dirt.

It turned out that back in 1985, or soon after he moved into the house, he'd gotten the idea of digging a tunnel connecting his basement to Hirt's. Hirt was the whole reason Dank had moved to Hemlock in the first place, and bought the house he'd bought, just two doors down from his old roommate. (Hirt had moved to Hemlock the year before to teach at the same college, in the same building and department, where I now teach, though by the time I came aboard in 1994, the contentious and mistrustful poet-professor had lost his teaching job.)

Still wearing his convention T-shirt and a RENO IS FOR LOVERS cap, Dank led me back down to the basement and removed a sheet of drywall from the north wall of the laundry room. Behind it was the entrance to his secret tunnel, an unlit crawlway three feet square in cross-section, shored up with plywood, and draped with cobwebs attesting to its decade of disuse. But not even he could explain why he'd been so set on digging a tunnel—a chore to which he'd devoted the better part of a summer, neglecting his writing outrageously—or what purpose it served, aside from a subterranean assertion of his friendship with Hirt. And though Hirt had grudgingly consented to the tunnel, he hadn't lifted a finger to help his friend dig, or dispose of the dirt. It was in the course of that Herculean task, by the way, that Dank not only filled and thus effaced his former tool room, but also accidentally buried all his basement windows: Once the room was full, he'd hauled the rest of his diggings upstairs and outdoors, and spread them evenly around his grounds, causing his yard to rise some three feet above the lots on either side, and his basement windows to vanish, making it look as if the house were sinking. (There'd been a lot of digging, and a lot of dirt, because of course Dank hadn't been able to run the tunnel through the intervening basement—JABLONSKY's—so he'd had to burrow *under* it instead.) After three months of backbreaking labor, Dank finally struck the concrete of Hirt's foundation—but just as he prepared to punch a hole through to the basement, Hirt changed his mind and revoked his consent. Not for another two years, and only in exchange for a large and never-repaid "loan," did Hirt finally let Dank finish the tunnel.

As for that toothbrush, we never did find out where it was hiding, but about a year later Dank entered the bathroom one morning and found the old brush back in its old place, and its successor in the wastebasket.

A B C D E F
G H I J K L
M N O P Q R
S T U V W X
Y Z

Never Mind Me: In his fictional debut, Agent Bronson Harder pursues a psychopath who, without malice or hope of advantage, kills his parents, siblings, colleagues, former lovers, friends, and others who "know too much" about him—although, till the first murder, there was nothing much to know. Unlike the self-effacing hero of THE ERASURES, the killer seeks obscurity rather than minimum impact. He wants to be forgotten, right away, by everyone, and will stop at nothing to get rid of anybody who might remember him, might think or speak or dream about him. At one point there is even talk of placing his remaining friends and relatives in a witness-protection program, as if they were hiding from the Mafia and not just from a madman whose life they've had the misfortune to witness.

Dank began writing about serial killers during the last innings of his second marriage. It can't be a coincidence that the killer's second wife and second victim—the fat lady who is lured to the roof of a tall building and pushed off, and who when she hits the pavement is described as "popping like a water balloon"—bears a strong resemblance to Molly JENSEN, Dank's own second wife. He told me, years later, that Molly had interfered with his personal growth.* She'd closed off op-

---

* In other words, she wouldn't let him sleep with other women. Every time he got an erection, Dank mistook it for "personal growth." (OH)

portunities for him, he said. He compared her to a Scrabble
player who keeps squandering prime spots on dinky words like
"dog" that don't afford good outcroppings for further words.
But he and I were playing Scrabble at the time, and I had just
spelled "cat" with the "t" on a triple-letter square, for a grand
total of five points, so maybe Dank was actually (if "tactfully")
complaining about my pennywise approach to the game and
not—or not only—about his second wife.

Probably because of the ambiguity of his own position as
a cult author neglected by the larger literary world, Dank was
intrigued throughout his career by scenarios in which a prominent person becomes obscure or an obscure one prominent.
In 1995, soon after I embarked on DANK!, he proposed to
write a reciprocal biography of *me*: We would dine together
every evening (as we did most evenings anyway), talk about
our lives, and then adjourn to our word processors to process
each other's more notable, quotable words. I was thrilled and
flattered by this proposition—at least until Dank told me his
intended title, *A Biography of My Biographer*, and at my prod-
ding confessed his longtime ambition of writing a biography
of "a nobody." Still, I was disappointed when he abandoned
the project, but since he later made me the protagonist of one
of his best novels, PLANET FOOD, I guess I can't complain.

Newel Post: "The principal post at the foot of a stairway," if
Webster's is to be believed. See NOMENCLATURE PROJECT.

Nomenclature Project: Dank's own name for one of many stabs
at self-improvement—one of his (all plainly unsuccessful) Get-
Smart-Quick schemes. Granted that he had more room for improvement than most, Dank was no good at self-help. He'd long
since torn off his bootstraps in his efforts pull himself up. Elsewhere, Boswell has discussed a few of Dank's efforts to raise his
IQ—to push his number up into the triple digits. There were many

efforts. Dank tried biofeedback. He tried brain food, smart drinks, smart drugs. He tried Transcendental Meditation. Though an agnostic, he even tried prayer. But he didn't *have* a prayer.

In 1995, Dank became obsessed with building his Word Power, convinced that everything would be different—that beautiful women would fight for his favors, and high-powered editors for his manuscripts—if only he knew the name for the vestigial claws on Dookie's forelegs, the name for the knurled metal collar that fastened an eraser to a pencil, the name for the concavity on the underside of a wine bottle. (Dank was strictly a Budweiser man, upgrading on special occasions to Corona, but now and then Boswell threw caution to the winds and splurged on a bottle of Paul Masson or Gallo.)

This mania—this compulsion to discover, as Dank said, "what all the different stuff is called"—originated in a *contretemps* I happened to witness. It was at a party I reluctantly attended in Dank's company, in 1995, some two years after Gabriella, his third wife, wised up and ran off with another, smarter, better, better-selling, and more highly decorated writer, one she'd hooked up with at another party. But I'd better back up: In February 1993, Dank had made the big mistake of flying Gabriella with him all the way to New York City for some kind of anniversary party thrown by the publisher that had just released *S.P.U.D.* under one of its less reputable imprints. No one at the party had ever heard of Dank, and the few guests to whom he introduced himself seemed even more indifferent to his existence when they found out he was nothing but a science fiction writer. Long before they left, Gabriella must have realized how little Dank's celebrity among the sci-fi writers of northern California counted in the larger world of letters. Clearly, all the other men at the party outranked hers—even the waiters, perhaps, and certainly the only guest who'd shown an interest in talking to them, a novelist from Santa Cruz. He'd taken advantage of one of Dank's trips to the men's room, evidently, to get Gabriella's number. Three months later, she too moved to Santa Cruz, and Dank had a brand-new king-sized bed all to himself.

You'd think that that debacle would have taught him to steer clear of literary parties, or at least of parties thrown by that specific publisher, but—like most writers—Dank grew sadder without growing wiser. Each night a malicious cleaning lady wiped the blackboard where he'd been chalking things up to experience. At his publisher's next party, or at least the next to which Dank was invited, two years later, in March 1995—a come-one-come-all gala at a private art museum rented for the evening to *fête* the publication of his editor's own novel—our lovelorn hack ran into Gabriella and the man who'd stolen her.

In the spirit of a rider remounting the horse that had thrown him, Dank had once again flown to New York (though this time alone) for the event. Since I happened to be in the city myself that weekend, I let him persuade me to join him. By the time we got there, the crowd had splintered into half a dozen conversations. Naturally, Dank failed to butt his way in anywhere; a misguided loyalty prevented me from ditching my embarrassing companion and adding my luster to one of the more illustrious huddles—thank God I haven't had that albatross around my neck at the *soirées* I've attended lately in Rome and Madrid! We were on our way out when we ran into Gabriella and her current author in the front hall by the staircase. They'd just come in with my agent, Tom Wainwright, who as well as being my agent,[*] and Dank's, was Dank's replacement's agent too.

Dank flushed bright red when Gabriella hugged him. He took off the coat he'd just put on, as if overheated by the hug, or the

---

[*] (October 2007) As he was mine from October 1993, when Dank put us in touch, till January 2007, when Tom said some odd, disturbing, unforgivable things. At that point I not only fired him but severed his connection with the Dank estate, of which I am executor. I'm now looking for another agent to represent Dank's seven great unpublished novels. Qualified parties interested in this once-in-a-lifetime opportunity are urged to contact me through my publisher. (BB)

better to feel the next, if another was forthcoming. There followed a bit of awkward chitchat, made all the more awkward for Dank by Gabriella's pretense that it *wasn't* an awkward situation, and by the geniality of Dank's replacement, whom he hadn't seen since that fateful other party, and who behaved exactly as he had back then, as if he hadn't stolen Dank's wife in the meantime. Dank was no match for those two, and stood through several minutes of *politesse* on their part, almost mute, and with an anxious and apologetic smile, like a deaf man who suspects that a joke is being told.

Finally a raising of voices ("Well! It's so good to see you again!"), like the swelling at the end of a symphony, told him he could go. But then he couldn't find his coat. Where had he put his coat?

"It's hanging on the newel post," said his usurper.

Dank looked puzzled, then looked panicked. Alone with me, he didn't try to hide the yawning gaps in his vocabulary. If I used a word he didn't know—and there were many—he would simply say "the what?" In front of Gabriella and the man for whom she'd dumped him, though, Dank couldn't very well admit his ignorance of newel posts.

The look of panic gave way to another blush. Deciding finally to take a chance, Dank timidly approached the coat rack.

"No," said Dank's replacement, "the *newel post.*"

At that point Tom took pity on the fattest of his authors and fetched the coat himself. To my regret, I have to say: Dank's chagrin was easily the highlight of the party, and I would have liked to see him squirm a little longer. But since he was one of the (lesser) cash cows who enabled Tom to focus most of his energies—more or less pro bono—on *serious* authors, it was in everyone's interest for Dank to feel indebted to Tom.

"Oh," he said, "the *newel* post." But it was too late to save face, and his was beet-red. All he could do was vow never again to be outclassed like that.

And so began his Nomenclature Project—a kind of second childhood that came all too readily to Dank, who, with his over-sized head, fat torso, and short chubby limbs, had retained, or rather regained, the bodily proportions of a very well-fed baby. I still see him toddling down Empedocles Street, one hot August day, wearing nothing but a pair of diaperlike white shorts and pointing a fat forefinger at anything to which he hadn't yet been in-troduced: "What's *that*?" After a weeks of pestering me with the question—a simple walk around the block became a minefield of widgets and whatsits, gizmos and gadgets, split-level gilhoolies and flowering thingamajigs—he started hiring consultants: a land-scape gardener to take my place on walks and identify the flora, an architect to drive him around town and point out different types of roofs, an auto mechanic to acquaint him with the all greasy odds and ends under the hood of Boswell's El Camino.

Dank also blazed through *Twenty Days to Greater Word Power* in an astounding eighteen, and I suppose his word-hoard did in-crease a bit, though mainly with regard to concrete objects, things like newel posts—things he could point at like a two-year-old and demand to know the name of. And once he knew—or thought he knew—the names of everything, he became still more annoying: Now, instead of interrupting me on walks to ask what this or that was called, he'd interrupt to say "Wow, get a load of the lenticels on that deciduous cherry tree!" or "Gee, I never noticed the cop-ing on that stepped retaining wall!"

But even that obnoxious habit had its entertaining aspects, as did all Dank's efforts to sound intelligent. I made a point, throughout the Nomenclature phase, of inventing names for things whose real names I didn't know or (more often) didn't feel like telling him, and soon my prank was paying dividends: At least once a walk, Dank would point at something like a locust on an oak gall and—with patent pride in his misinformation, and almost touching faith in his informant—say, "Boy, check out the stippled porlock on that laputa!" (OH)

A B C D E F
G H I J K L
M N O P Q R
S T U V W X
Y Z

"Oops": A family of four takes refuge in its private fallout shelter, at the onset of WWIII, with a month's supply of canned goods . . . but no opener.*

---

* If—God forbid—they ever make an audiobook version of this reader's guide, here would be a perfect spot for three descending blats on the trombone: *wah wah wahhhhh*. (OH)

A B C D E F

G H I J K L

M N O P Q R

S T U V W X

Y Z

The Pageant: Not so much a novel (though packaged as a novel) as a long and tedious set of variations on a dinky and limited theme. A rich ugly man named Dieter sets out to diversify society's notions of beauty through a series of alternative pageants. Arguing that beauty contests, like IQ tests, always privilege certain forms or facets of the quality they measure, our hero (who, like his author, has almost as much to fear from IQ tests as from existing norms of beauty) organizes contests designed to overturn the standard heartless hierarchies.

His first innovation is a dorsal beauty contest, with swimsuit, nightgown, and even talent segments, but always with contestants seen from behind. Needless to say (and when did Dank say anything that wasn't?), the winner proves a whole lot less attractive from the front. (Dank himself was equally unsightly coming and going. Even in the DOG HOUSE days, there were few sights more repulsive than Dank lumbering upstairs for his after-breakfast nap.)

Spurred on by the improbable success of that event, Dieter stages next a bird's-eye beauty contest: Who is most beautiful when seen from overhead? That too makes a hit, and other competitions follow:

—A long-distance beauty contest: Who is most beautiful seen from a hundred yards away?

—A "glimpsed beauty" contest: Who is most beautiful when seen for a tenth of a second, by a flash of light in a darkened auditorium?

—A beauty endurance contest: Who is fairest of them all when gazed at for hours?

—A "remembered beauty" contest: Who wins when judges wait a week, a year, a decade, before casting their votes? (I cast mine for Dank's third wife, who, though nothing special, grew more ravishing in his imagination with every passing year, so that it must have been a shock to him see a photo of her and be reminded of what she really looked like.)

—An "ugly duckling" contest: Whose beauty quotient rises the most between ages ten and fifteen, or fifteen and twenty-five?

And so on—and on, and on, for several hundred pages. To get through this one, the reader must be as patient as Dieter himself when he inaugurates a "lifelong beauty" pageant: Contestants enter at age five, then return for follow-up viewings every five years until age seventy, at which point a queen is crowned with what amounts to a lifetime achievement award. Dieter doesn't live to see the first one crowned, but the omniscient narrator does, and makes us sit through the crowning too.

Dank got the name "Dieter" from the credits of *Das Boot*, which he had on videotape, and watched (not the movie, just the credits) whenever he needed a name for one of his more visionary characters. Despite a semester of high-school German, he pronounced "Dieter" as if he meant "one who diets," and in light of Dank's own mania for dieting, I'll venture to suggest that the rich, ugly Dieter is a stand-in for Dank, though of course Dank wasn't rich. (When you sell your soul in a buyer's market, it doesn't fetch that much.) Whether or not he was as ugly as he sometimes thought, Dank was no Adonis. Someone skilled in trick photography might perhaps have made him look no worse, or not much worse, than average; but true beauty doesn't need a good photographer. Beauty shows itself no matter what the angle, backdrop, lens, or lighting, and whether its possessor be in swimsuit or in nightgown, juggling nectarines or playing *Kitten on the Keys*.

It was a lifelong source of tension between us that as well as being taller, more intelligent, more literate, more talented, and more socially adroit than Dank, I was also notably more handsome—*so* much more handsome that we must have formed a jarring pair when seen in public. I, of course, played down the difference, but Dank knew, and knew *I* knew, that with a simple wink I could have had my pick of the women he panted after in hopeless pursuit. It put me in an awkward position when he moaned and groaned about his unrequited passions—and he did so all the time, as obsessed with sex as a starving man with food. Where *I* thought of sex as an all-too-obtainable rest from the rigors of art, art for Dank was a consolation prize, a way of trying not to think of all the sex he couldn't have. When he complained to me of Gabriella's cruelty or Pandora's shallowness, I felt like a billionaire with a friend too poor to buy a loaf of bread. But at least a rich man can always treat a poor friend to a good dinner. There was no way for me to share my good looks[*] (and the sex they entitled me to) with poor Dank.

Somewhere or other, though, he got the idea that whatever the rest of him might look like, his *hands* were unusually hand-

---

[*] A personal asset—one of many—that Hirt overrates, unless I underrate my own "good looks": More than once I was mistaken for Hirt, at least until he decided to sport the beard that made him look more like Abraham Lincoln. And even then people mistook us from behind, so I certainly could have held my own against Hirt in one of Dieter's dorsal beauty contests. (BB)

some. In 1990, after seeing something on TV about body-part models who earn a good living by brandishing their hands in Palmolive ads and such, Dank flew to Los Angeles and tried to interest talent agencies in his. The only agent to show any interest, the only one who didn't laugh Dank off the premises or call security, proved to have a lot in common with the dodgy literary agents to whom Dank had fallen prey as a young writer, in his desperation to place his more "serious" efforts. You know, the sort of agents who place ads in writers' magazines, and turn down no author willing to shell out a hefty "reading fee." Dank paid one swindler several hundred dollars to take a bunch of photos of those golden hands and (supposedly) to circulate this sad "portfolio" in high places. Needless to say, nothing came of that investment, though Dank did get copies of the photos. It's safe to say his hands are better documented than those of any other minor writer. (OH)

"Pals": Another nod to *1984*. This one takes place in a totalitarian society where friendship is outlawed, along with wives and privately owned children (there are state brothels and nurseries instead). The official line is that such bonds are selfish—detrimental to the tepid and undifferentiated fellow-feeling that the state enforces as the greatest good. But even though friends are forbidden, sociability is compulsory. At quitting time on Saturday, each worker calls a service reminiscent of our carpool information lines, and depending on how drunk he wants to get, how much he likes to think about spectator sports, how much he wants to boast about his visits to the brothels, and one or two other indices of permitted variation, he is matched with three other like-minded strangers. Those strangers serve as "the boys" for a night on the town, and the big computer at the Ministry of Fun makes sure that he'll never cross paths with them again.

The horror with which Dank evokes the prohibition on friendship is exceeded only by the relish with which he imagines a world where women function strictly as prostitutes, broodmares, and nursemaids. And if that makes sense when you consider that Dank, when he wrote "Pals," was on the brink of his second divorce, it makes less sense when you consider that in those days his best friend was Hirt. Even harder to explain is that Dank and Hirt were still friends fourteen years later when I came along. Hirt was hard to compete with, in fact, because he'd known Dank so much longer than I had. Luckily, he'd always been a bit of a recluse, and didn't seem to have much time for Dank (though if this encyclopedia can be said to have benefited in any way from Hirt's dyspeptic input, that is because he happened to witness some key moments in Dank's life that I myself happened to miss). But his very inaccessibility raised his value in Dank's eyes, so that on the rare occasions when Hirt did find time for him, Dank was painfully eager for whatever scraps Hirt might toss his way—though of course Dank took *my* company for granted. Sometimes I felt like a bedraggled hausfrau vying with a sexy mistress for her husband's love.

Whenever he invited Dank over for dinner, Hirt made a point of not inviting me. When he ate at our house, I felt even more excluded. True, I was suffered to sit at the same table and partake of the same food and wine (and though Dank and I were happier with beer, Dank made a point of buying wine when Hirt came over because *he* preferred wine, when those were the only options; I always pictured him sipping something vile and pretentious like Campari). But I was never welcomed into their conversations, which consisted of in-jokes, allusions, and memories that meant nothing to me. If I tried to chip in with a quip or a question, I was usually ignored—unconsciously by Dank (too intently focused on the guest of honor to remember me), but scornfully, it always seemed, by Hirt. His treatment of me was harder to pardon than Dank's, because Hirt didn't have the excuse of rapt preoccupation. His friendliness toward Dank seemed more dutiful than heartfelt—it didn't prevent him from noticing Dookie, for instance; but he didn't stoop to notice me.

So I sat and listened, like a child allowed to be seen but not heard. (And in fact my youth was part of the problem: They each had fourteen years on me, and even Dank, who treated me as an equal the rest of the time, seemed to remember my juniority, my whippersnappage, whenever Hirt was around.) I listened and hated, and they reminisced, though their memories seemed to be numbered, or anyhow named, so that often a "reminiscence" consisted of no more than the *title* of the memory in question: "This reminds me of The Graduation Brainstorm." "Some day you'll have to write about The Lobster Incident." "Watch out, or I'll tell *him* [now and then Hirt did deign to acknowledge me, with a "he" or a "him" and a jerk of the head, but never more than momentarily, and seldom with a glance in my direction] about The Avocado." And the same titles kept recurring: The Death Ray, The Avocado, The Reluctant Vulcan, The Lobster Incident, The Transdermal Patch. Naturally, these shorthand reminiscences excluded me, the more so as Dank and Hirt never took the trouble to explain the allusions. (And I was too proud to ask about them afterward—too proud to show how avidly I'd followed conversations into which I hadn't been welcomed.) Over the years I pieced together the stories behind most of those intriguing titles, but in some cases I was—and still am—forced to use my imagination.

In August 1998, the three of us went camping. This might have been a three-way bonding ritual, but all it did was re-affirm the bond between Dank and Hirt, and my exclusion from their longstanding intimacy. I was accustomed to being ignored when Hirt was around, and had hesitated when Dank proposed the trip. He promised that this time I *wouldn't* feel excluded, though it seemed that somebody would have to, since there were three of us but just two tents. One was a bit wider than the other, and given the widths of the campers, the best arrangement might have been to put Dank in the smaller tent and let his future commentators share the larger. Even after four years of unwavering contempt from Hirt, I was willing to forget the past and start anew with him, and I still wanted his friendship for no better reason than that he had always withheld it. With a naïveté I blush now to recall, I'd looked forward to our camping trip as the weekend when everything would change, but Hirt made a big point of ignoring me throughout the three-hour drive to the campground, an ordeal for which I was wedged in the back seat of his Lexus (we had to go in his car, since of course an El Camino *has* no back seat) with his cooler, lantern, camp stove, laptop, and all sorts of other high-tech gadgets Hirt found indispensable for roughing it. And then we quarreled on our hike about which way to go when we came to a fork in the trail: down a prickly path to the shores of Mirror Lake or up a gentle rise to the top of Lookout Bluff? Dank played the peacemaker at first, insisting that it made no difference to him, but wound up siding with Hirt, who wanted the lake. In my anger—less at not getting my way, or at letting Hirt get his, than at what I took to be a snub from Dank (forgetting in my misery his penchant for the downward path)—I fell silent, fell into a sulk, and fell behind the other two.

By the time we got back to our campsite, my self-pity had assumed a life of its own, like a chemical reaction that has to run its course: Once the baking soda and the vinegar unite, there's nothing you can do but sit and watch your pet volcano foam and fizz. By that point, moreover, Dank had given up his efforts to include me, so I was left alone with my bad mood. Sitting on the ground with my back against a fir tree, thirty feet or so from my companions, I felt myself sneering with envy as I watched those flannel-shirted would-be-woodsy literati butch it up. They built and lit a sorry little campfire—no merit badge for *them*. At some point I closed my eyes, but I couldn't close my ears to their infuriating chit-chat. I still hoped some magic reconciliation would occur around the fire over pork and beans, but they didn't even summon me to dinner. At some point I opened my eyes and saw them sitting, with their backs to me and bowls in their laps, on two stumps beside the larger tent, far from any other seating, as if to emphasize that three would be a crowd. There was nothing to do but go over to the camp-fire, serve myself some pork and beans (yesterday, 1/12/07, my now-former agent had the nerve to call this guide—of which I'd sent him "A" through "N" to get his thoughts—"self-serving," but sometimes you either have to serve yourself or starve), and retreat to the base of my tree. At the time it struck me as pro-foundly right—and misery can be an altered state as mind-expanding as any acid trip—that *I* had chosen a towering fir while *they* had reflexively headed for stumps.

So when bedtime finally arrived, it went without saying that Dank and Hirt would share one tent and I would get the other. I pretended I was glad to have one to myself, but when they resumed their giggly reminiscing in their tent—unless of course they were laughing at *me*—I felt a jealousy so strong I thought I'd lose my mind. I wanted a rabid or misanthropic grizzly to burst into our clearing and tear them both to pieces. If it killed me too, so much the better.

At last, though, they fell silent, and I drifted off myself—only to wake with a start to the thunder of Dank snoring. I'd heard the sound before, of course, but not at such close range, and by the end of the night I was glad after all that we hadn't shared a tent. Especially as Dank's repertoire of night sounds included not only snores, and smacking of lips, and clacking of teeth, but apneac snorts—snorts so loud they almost scared me as I lay there, eyes wide open, in my sleeping bag, or rather insomnia sack. I hadn't thought to bring earplugs—and neither, I gather, had Hirt, who spent part of the night in the back seat of his car, after staggering a mile through the pine woods with his computerized bedroll and his solar-powered pillow, to the parking lot. On the drive back to Hemlock in the morning, he was even crankier than I was, and though I ceded the shotgun seat to Dank as I had the day before (come to think of it, *that's* when my big attack of self-pity began: riding in the back seat to the campsite and failing to gain entrée to the conversation going on up front), he and Hirt barely spoke. Somehow that made me feel like I had won. Nonetheless, the outing left me hating Hirt more fervently than ever, and even now it makes me doubt afresh the sanity of this collaboration. Why on earth should I collaborate with someone who wouldn't deign to speak to me even in the wild?

PALs: Not a book (and not to be confused with the story discussed in the previous entry), PALs is nonetheless a form of fiction, a line of "virtual friends" that Dank developed in collaboration with Leopold Lips, in the late 1990s, as a money-making venture. In 1996, Lips proposed that they pool their talents, and Dank's savings, to develop virtual pen pals for people so bashful or socially inept as to have trouble making and keeping friends even online, or for people who want to practice their people skills in solitude, or just to expand their circle of acquaintances. Lips, who claimed to be a computer programmer as well as an inventor, said he could write the code for these cyberfriends (which he and Dank planned to market on interactive CD-ROMs), but needed a novelist to develop the characters, giving each a backstory, a psychology, a set of interests and opinions, and a voice, thereby establishing the parameters for his or her cyber-behavior. Dank was fascinated by the challenge. In a 1998 interview, he claimed that several of his PALs—Smart-Alec Andy, Cheerful Chuck, Oliver the Optimist, Sympathetic Sue, Easy-Going Ed, Easily-Impressed Eileen, Raunchy Rebecca (and, yes, there were X-rated PALs, "adult" friends for cybersex), Larry the Liar, Prima Donna Polly—ranked among his proudest achievements in character-ization.

As a rule, these cyberpeople were more tolerant than "conventional" people (Polly was an exception—touchy and temperamental, quick to take offense, slow to forgive, and un-willing to forget, she was designed for advanced players only), though for the sake of verisimilitude even the most under-standing cyberfriends would have their limits. If you crossed the line and said something too insulting, your friend would fall silent for a day, a week, a month—what Dank dubbed a "cybersulk." If you *really* crossed the line, the password-pro-tected disk would disable itself, meaning that the cyberfriend in question would never speak to you again. The amazing thing is that Lips and Dank never had such a definitive quar-rel themselves. Even Easy-Going Ed was less forgiving than Dank, who refused to listen to my warnings about Lips, and continued to believe in him, and to fund their joint venture, even after Dank discovered that Lips had spent several thou-sand dollars of Dank's capital on hair-replacement operations. But before they could perfect and market PALs (an acronym, according to Dank, though he'd forgotten what it stood for), Lips dropped out of sight.

Pants on Fire: This amazing novel—its author's masterpiece, in my opinion—remains unpublished for the same depressing reason that so many masterpieces have to wait so long for a chance to show their stuff: the outrageous cowardice and conservatism of publishers, booksellers, and bookbuyers—readers—in the face of the truly new. Readers who feel unfairly included in that blanket condemnation can prove their difference by demanding—for as long as it takes, at the top of your lungs, and in whatever forums you have access to—that Dank's unpublished novels be published at once!

Pants on Fire is presented as a letter from death row to an appellate court by a pathological liar named Larry (who started life not as a literary character but as an interactive CD-ROM—see PALs), a convicted killer wired to a lie detector and typing on a modified computer hooked up to the lie detector too. The detector, we are told, samples his sincerity after every word, then gives an average truth value for every sentence—either "T" for true or one of four degrees of falsehood, F_1 to F_4, depending on how big a needle-jump the lie occasions. (Though the protagonist was recycled from another of Dank's projects, the brilliant premise—probably Dank's most ingenious—had its origin in my account of the ridiculous and inconclusive polygraph test to which I was subjected, in September 2000, in connection with MacDougal's death). The lie detector doesn't always disambiguate his statements; if, for instance, Larry tells us "Dick killed Jane" and the polygraph says he's lying shamelessly (F_4), we still don't know if *Larry* killed Jane, or if someone else did, or if Jane killed herself, or if she's still alive and well. But by examining enough of Larry's truth-valued assertions—a whole novel's worth—the reader is gradually able to close in on the truth. An editorial foreword (ostensibly penned by a legal scholar) tells us that, though

Larry is undoubtedly a liar, there is still reason to doubt that he's guilty of the murders for which he is sentenced to die. Readers must decide for themselves whether Larry is guilty or not guilty.

I admit that in synopsis Dank's unpublished literary novels don't sound much like the ones for which he is known. To judge by the reaction of his former agent (now my former agent too), they must seem even more dissimilar in their full form. Two weeks ago, in what will certainly remain our final conversation, Tom insisted that in *none* of the seven manuscripts I sent him last June, the day after Dank was murdered, does he recognize "the voice, the mind, or the imagination" of his oldest client. As if our author had been one of those dutiful hacks whose consumers count on a perfectly uniform product, like that scotch whose major claim to fame, to judge by the ads, is not its age or taste but simply that it "never varies."

Agent Wainwright added that in any case the books are "too odd" for him to sell "in today's marketplace," even as he wondered why Dank himself had never shown him those seven manuscripts, "if in fact they really are his work." I won't dignify the bizarre insinuation of that last clause with an answer. Instead, let me point out the irony of Tom dismissing the works in question as unsalable even as he wonders why Dank never bothered to show them to him. Maybe, Tom, the reason is that Dank knew you and your limits a lot better than you ever knew him or his.

"Parallel Bars": Frank is a sexually frustrated bachelor, like Dank himself. Unlike Dank, who knew he had no chance, Frank frequents singles bars, though most nights he goes home alone. One night, as he's burrowing around in his bedroom closet looking for his "love doll" (a surrogate he bought once at a sex shop "in the depths of loneliness," and re-inflates like a flotation device any time he sinks back to those depths), Frank finds a magic portal to another world. "His eyes widened at the unexpected surprise he discovered, and he felt a sense of wonder," Dank informs us, probing the innermost recesses of his two-dimensional character's psychology.

In many ways, the world is a lot like ours, insofar as Dank could paint a likeness of our world with his rudimentary palette of kindergarten colors, his broad coarse-bristled brush, his shaky hand, and his reluctance to focus on anything farther away than the tip of his thumb. There are, however, minor differences: Dinner comes *after* dessert, for example. And Phoebus K. Dank, in this topsy-turvy world, is a celebrated author, one whom Frank consults at one point as an expert on parallel worlds. Almost as implausible, the women are more sexually assertive than the men. Any male can get laid, even one as fat, ill-dressed, and socially inept as Frank, a spitting image of his author. Any man who steps into a singles bar near closing time finds himself mobbed by beautiful women vying for his favors.

Nothing need be said, I think, about the daydream basis of this pitiable story, except that it dates from the summer (1990) of Dank's highly unrequited crush on TAMMI, and that he'd been doing lots of fantasizing about a universe where he'd be irresistible—rather than repulsive—to the other sex. Like GRAY EMINENCE (another exercise in cosmic wishful thinking written that same summer), "Parallel Bars" expresses as well its author's adolescent (although lifelong) fascination with the idea of parallel worlds. More than once he spent a sleepless night endeavoring to get his little mind around that big idea, or around the slightly more respectable, less metaphysical, but no less adolescent* thought of life on other

---

* Why "adolescent?" According to astronomers, there may be millions of planets right here in our own galaxy that could sustain intelligent life, and our galaxy is only one of billions. The surprising thing would be if there

planets—of creatures "as intelligent as us" *("us"? "us"?)* right here in our own universe. Considering what a wide berth he gave to intelligent life here on Earth, you wonder why Dank was so eager to imagine it in distant galaxies. But then he liked everything better when it was farther away. Like all science fiction fans, Dank was addicted to the Rapture of the Far. When he trained his telescope on anything terrestrial (not counting what's-her-name, the "inspiration" of this embarrassing story—see BOSWELL THE BURGLAR), he always made a point of looking through the wrong end, to pretend the object of his scrutiny was nowhere near. (OH)

Pass the Brains: The Table Talk of Phoebus Dank: On January 1, 1999, I made a resolution to start jotting down Dank's sayings for posterity, as I was already jotting down his doings. We always had dinner together when he wasn't too busy on a book to eat a proper meal, and now I asked permission to bring a tiny spiral notebook to the table and jot down his talk when it would bear repeating.

At first he resisted the idea, arguing with typical humility that he was "a writer, not a talker." And it is true that, unlike

---

weren't other planets out there where our counterparts are eating, drinking, watching sitcoms, writing novels, driving nails, having sex, and so on. Dank told me once, however, that any time he thought about those "other" planets, he lapsed into a kind of pigheaded Earth chauvinism unworthy of a writer of his world-bestriding, galaxy-hopping, faster-than-light imagination. No matter how many other planets out there had "the same stuff of us," surely (he couldn't help telling himself, with a surge of earthling pride) none had ever come up with a soft drink as good as Sgt. Popp, or a TV show as awesome as *The X-Files*, or a pet as lovable as Dookie, or a creature as bewitching as his third wife, or for that matter one as irritating as his second. It is typical of Dank's humility that he didn't see *himself* as one of the flowers of Terran evolution. (BB)

Samuel Johnson or Samuel Taylor Coleridge, say, Dank was not a dazzling conversationalist. It could not be said of him, as it has been said of them, that he squandered his talent on talk. So efficiently did he channel his energies into his writing that he had little left for the art of living, let alone the art of conversation. But the words of a great man are surely worth preserving, no matter how unpolished.

And finally Dank consented, though I had the misfortune of embarking on the project the year *his* New Year's resolution was to swear off dietary fiber and subsist as much as possible on organ meats—on the stuff Food Planet sold as "variety meats" and priced almost apologetically low, as if it were understood that a scrupulous butcher would have tossed those lobed and glossy brown and purple things to the dogs. He had always had a baffling taste for organ meat, and soon after I met him (but before we started sharing meals, luckily), had attempted to boost his IQ by eating a brain every day (see AMNESIA). In my efforts to choke down, and keep down, the meals of that era, I may have missed some memorable comments: Dank prided himself on his cooking, and a fear of hurting his feelings made it impossible for me to refuse the results. A few selections from the book (in which, like that other Boswell in his *Life of Johnson*, I tried to specify the context of every remark) will suggest what I suffered for its sake:

—"I like it when the plot and the subplot climax simultaneously," he declared, passing the sweetbreads.

—"I mean, I know I'm no John Updock [*sic*] or Norman Mailer," Dank conceded, spreading a dab of homemade stomach pâté on a Triscuit. "But remember what Zog 23 [one of several 'Yoda' figures in Dank's later fiction] always says: *The warp drive of imagination will outstrip the ramjets of mere craftsmanship.*"

—"Have some more heart," he urged, holding out the serving dish. "Come to think of it, that would be good advice for writers: 'Have some more heart.' In other words, they should be more compassionate."

—One evening when we were feasting on lamb tongue: "I guess some people don't like tongue because it tastes you back."

—"If you have to comment on another writer's story, always use the 'poison sandwich' method," he advised one day at lunch, holding up his hefty kidney-on-rye sandwich by way of illustration. "First say something nice, then say what you really think, then say something nice again. Works like a charm!"

—"If you're writing a searing indictment, you better make damn sure that it's a good read, too," Dank counseled, helping himself to a hefty third serving of his special spaghetti and eyeballs. "Make sure that it's a—a—a—what's that thing they always say? You know, in book reviews? Oh yeah: make sure it's *a rattling good yarn*."

—"I could've written it [THE ACADEMICIAN] even faster, but when I rush the final product always seems a little undercooked. By the way, I think I undercooked these prairie oysters."

—"I set my fiction in the future so it won't go out of date so fast. Like when your mom buys you clothes that are big enough to grow into. Since the world keeps on changing but the book just stays the same. So it keeps on getting less and less true. Like a sign that says 'WET PAINT.' More lungs?"

After a few months of that, thank God, even Dank got sick of organ meats (or at least his colon did—see CONSTIPATION). But he still enjoyed a can of pig brains now and then (never cow brains: see AMNESIA), and still reverted to his theory that they made him smarter. More than once I found him at his computer typing one-handed and eating brains straight from the can with a spoon or melon baller or, one time, with his fingers. Once I glanced at the nutritional data on the label—which did say "fully cooked"—and learned that though a six-ounce helping of brains provides no dietary fiber, and no vitamins to speak of, it does contain a lot of cholesterol: 1,150 percent of your RDA, in fact.

Speaking of sickening meals, I don't think I mentioned my pitiful excitement the one and only time—in April 1999, or less than a year after the camping fiasco—that Hirt invited me to tag along with Dank for dinner at his house. By that point I hated Hirt, but my hatred was partly defensive, or rather retaliatory—an attempt to scorn him back. And the irrational awe he still inspired in Dank naturally colored my attitude too, so that I wanted his respect if not his friendship. Neither, alas, was forthcoming. The dinner (overdone meat in an oversalted sauce—an attempt at stroganoff, I think) was even more of an ordeal than the ones I'd suffered through when Hirt ate at our house, not just because he couldn't cook but because his scorn, which up to then had always taken the form of ignoring me, that evening seemed more conscious and active. He still didn't deign to answer my questions, laugh at my quips, or follow up on any of my conversation starters, but when I spoke he paused to look at me before turning back to Dank. The effect was especially insulting because I sensed that those brief acknowledgments of my existence were his dutiful concessions to hospitality.

But then Dank excused himself to use the toilet. "So, Bill—tell me all about yourself," said Hirt, even turning his chair to face me. And as if to show that I hadn't learned the lesson of the past two hours—hadn't learned the folly of my wishful thinking—I eagerly complied, telling myself "Finally! I passed the test and from now on he's going to be nice!" I'd have two good friends in town instead of one, and the second only two doors down from the house where I lived with the first. So I told him all about my childhood, my hopes, my dreams. Dank was still suffering from the aftermath (again, see CONSTIPATION) of his zero-fiber diet, so I had lots of time to talk about myself. Not counting the ill-fated series of interviews I conducted in his kitchen in the first few months of 2006, it was the closest thing to a sustained conversation I ever had with Hirt, and it wasn't very close. He did seem to listen to my babble, but he didn't volunteer anything about himself, or laugh at any of my jokes, or so much as acknowledge my thrice-repeated suggestion that "we should hang out more often." No, it was more like talking to an especially cryptic shrink than a potential friend, and I left his house not knowing *where* I stood with Hirt.

I found out soon enough: On our brief walk home, Dank mentioned that one of the characters in Hirt's latest book, of all things a novel, was modeled on me. Evidently—and with Dank's complicity—Hirt had endured my presence at his table only in the name of research. Although as it happened he never finished that book, or any other book, and in fact quit writing altogether soon after our dinner, the episode left me more keenly resentful than ever of Hirt and his ridiculous "friendship" with Dank.

Payload Pete, Boy Rocketeer: A lonely, brilliant seventh-grader builds a rocket ship in his backyard and—ignoring the skeptics and scoffers—flies it all the way to Ganymede (one of the moons of Jupiter, if memory serves). Ganymede proves to have breathable air, potable water, and edible fungi—luckily for Pete, who in his impatience to see the universe forgets about fuel for the return trip, and whose only provisions are a bologna sandwich and a juice box. In the end he is rescued by NASA and returns to Earth to find himself a hero.

The germ of this "young-adult" novel, with its tacked-on happy ending (Dank had wanted to leave Pete on Ganymede, but the publisher objected), was Dank's nostalgia for the summer of his thirteenth year—the summer he devoted to model rocketry. What seems to have interested him was not the science of ballistics—the possibility of making a rocket go a bit higher by redesigning the fins, say—but the idea of sending living beings further from the surface of our planet than they would ever go on their own. Live payloads are forbidden by the code of model rocketeers, but Dank, who several decades later would microwave a lightning bug (bearing it no malice, merely curious), couldn't rest until he'd sent a few earthworms—or Earth worms—into space, or as far in that direction as his rockets were able to take them. He also sent a bee up, once, and afterward it thanked him for the trip by stinging his thumb. The eggs he sent up, though—Grade A extra large—were unfertilized, so no one could object to them. In any case, he wasn't the only boy rocketeer whose idea of fun was sending egg after egg where eggs were never meant to go. So many eggs are used in model rocketry, in fact, to judge by magazines devoted to the hobby, that I suspect it was invented by the egg cartel, like Secretary's Day by the greeting-card cabal. (There is, to be sure, a whole subgenre of SF in which mankind overcomes the distances of interstellar space by sending eggs—human, though, and fertilized, and cryogenically frozen—to destinations that no living, aging human could reach in a lifetime, and then hatching them on arrival.)

Needless to say, all those eggs and bugs and worms—and even, once, a goldfish in a tiny cylindrical tank—were fill-ins for the rocketeer himself. Like Payload Pete, Dank would have liked to send himself to outer space, to a habitable planet he'd share with wise and sympathetic aliens who, never having seen an earthling before, would have no way of knowing that this one, with his acne, his flab, and his glasses, his high-water pants and his panic attacks, was by human standards a defective specimen and not an Adonis.

But that wasn't possible. After a summer, Dank abandoned

model rocketry as too expensive: Every cent he squandered at the hobby shop was one less he had to work with at the bookstore. When forced to choose between actually launching dinky little cardboard rockets and reading about giant interplanetary rockets, Dank opted (as so often) for the imaginary, the larger-than-life, not the small and merely real. As far as he was concerned, the rockets in his favorite science fiction *were* the real ones—their cost and size and thrust more than offset their nonexistence.

Careful students of our author's oeuvre will notice that Pete's father drives one of those big street-cleaning vehicles with the enormous rotary brushes, just like Timmy's father in THE MAN IN THE BLACK BOX and Henrietta's brother in HENRIETTA'S PERFORMANCE. As a child Dank had dreamed of driving one himself, convinced that there could be no better life than operating that big and civic-minded Dr. Seuss contraption. Every now and then his boyhood dream revived, but on the five or six occasions when Dank presented himself at city hall to apply for the job, there were no openings. See also QUITTING TIME.

Personal Power Plant: After his first heart attack (1993), Dank bought a bicycle to get in shape, but he biked so slowly that he never broke a sweat. I can see him even now, in the screening room of memory, biking up Empedocles in such a comically low gear that his pedals made several revolutions for each one the wheels made. Except when going downhill—often he asked me to drive him and his Huffy to the highest point in Hemlock so that he could coast back to our house without pedaling at all—Dank went so slowly that he had trouble maintaining his balance. After a wipeout in 1995, he gave the bike to me and turned a big west-facing room on the third floor into a gym. But he seldom broke a sweat there either. His "workouts" consisted of languidly curling his none-too-massive dumbbells, or going nowhere on his stationary bike, or lying belly-up on his foam-rubber mat (a mat he used less for stretching than for resting between exercises, and on which he often fell asleep mid-workout), or jogging briefly on his treadmill, which faced a window and, beyond, two blocks away, the graveyard where Dank now rests in peace, having finally, suddenly arrived after years of jogging toward it without ever seeming to get any closer. Actually, he didn't jog, he walked, and none too briskly, and his biking too was more like walking than like jogging. It wasn't even always clear, when I saw him on the treadmill, if he thought he was working out or just stretching his legs, since sometimes he found it hard to sit still while writing. He'd even rigged up a lectern with a laptop computer in front of the treadmill, so he could type as he walked. Sometimes I urged him—echoing his doctor's orders—to exercise more energetically, though the one time he took my advice and did some jumping jacks up there, I thought a wrecking ball had gotten the wrong address.

For the most part, though, his efforts to get fit relied on wishful thinking. At some yard sale he'd found an old-fashioned fitness device of a sort I'd seen only in cartoons, a device suggesting that back in the days when such machines were mass-produced, other people must have had theories of fitness as crazy as Dank's. The thing consisted of a wide canvas belt that encircled the user's belly and attached to a motor, mounted on a steel post, that caused the belt to vibrate either gently or frenetically, depending on which setting the user opted for. Not even Dank could explain how such a contraption was supposed to help him lose weight—I guess the idea was that the vibrations would somehow jiggle the unwanted pounds away—but for several months, till the thing shorted out, he put in at least half an hour a day looped into his motorized fat massager.

In 1998, though, Dank had another heart attack, and had to face the fact that his home workouts were a washout. Finally, reluctantly, he joined a public gym, in hopes that the gazes of strangers would shame him into actual exertion. He might even lose a little weight, since the calorie is a unit of heat, after all, and when he did exert himself Dank produced a lot of heat. We once spent a weekend on nearby Mt. Whitney, and though Dank didn't try to climb that famous mountain, he did insist on digging out my El Camino on the morning of our departure, after a snowfall buried it overnight in the parking lot of the Sierra Lodge. Overinsulated by the bright-orange snowsuit he called his "exosuit," Dank worked up so much heat that when he finally set aside the borrowed shovel, took off the oven mitts he wore in lieu of mittens, and joined me in the frigid car, steam rose from his hands as well as from his mouth and nostrils.

And the gym—though not as much fun as shoveling snow, for a chronic Californian—did force Dank to exercise for a few months, or until his trial membership ran out. Then he quit, and not just due to laziness, but also to the sense of Sisyphean absurdity that comes with so much wasted effort. It was no good to remind himself that insofar as it helped his heart, the workout wasn't wasted at all: He couldn't stop thinking that he was walking or biking or jumping without *getting* any-where, lifting weights without rearranging his world.

By the time he quit the gym, Dank was hard at work on a scheme to harness the kinetic energy expended in a workout, to convert it to electricity by means of little dynamos attached to every treadmill, exercycle, and so on. At a public gym, each patron would bring along his or her own battery, about as big as a lunchbox, and would lug it from machine to machine, plugging it into the dynamo on each, and thereby storing the energy of the workout for his or her own use, to be tapped at his or her convenience. Imagine the satisfaction of putting in a strenuous workout, then going home and plugging your laptop into your gym battery, to let your workout fuel your writing session. Dank even built a prototype and used it in his home gym for a week or two (until it overheated and emitted what to him smelled like an about-to-blow-up odor). I recall my squeamishness when Dank announced at dinner that he'd run the toaster oven off that battery, long enough at least to make our tuna melts: It was like eating something salted with his sweat (a seasoning I wouldn't have put it past him to try, incidentally—see THE SALT FACTORY).

Personal Worst: Recently I heard some tedious novel described as a "lie-in-the-bath-with-a-glass-of-wine" kind of book. Well, *Personal Worst* is a sit-on-the-couch-in-your-underwear-eating-cold-Pop-Tarts-straight-from-the-box sort of book. It features a bunch of barbaric fraternity boys—those favorite easy targets of vindictive nerds, and favorite focus of their efforts to convince themselves, if not the rest of us, that the personal computer is more deadly than the dodgeball.

The lads of Kappa Kappa Kappa have become obsessed with surpassing one another's worst-ever acts, and when one ups the ante by killing an innocent stranger (with a penlight laser of the sort we'll all be carrying by 2011, if Dank's crystal ball was right), the other brothers follow suit, each trying to set a new high-water mark of heinousness. Can Agent Harder stop them? Do we give a shit?

Though for Dank the book is only averagely unreadable (for any *other* writer, it would be an absolute nadir), the title sums up perfectly what seems to have been Dank's ambition as a writer all along: With each book he lowered the bar another notch and still managed to limbo beneath it, achieving one personal worst after another.

Even its author saw that the premise of *Personal Worst* was too skimpy by itself to yield a novel, so he gave Harder a side-kick, a genetically engineered cross between a housecat and a

St. Bernard. When they aren't roughing up frat boys or sniffing for "clues," Harder and Hooky—as the would-be-lovable neopet is named—have all sorts of nauseating, would-be-rib-tickling, would-be-heartwarming interactions straight out of *Turner and Hooch*. These moments (that feel like ages) of Comic Relief, or Innocent Mirth, alternate mechanically with gruesome homicides; the result is not so much an emotional rollercoaster as an emotional merry-go-round, or at best a Tilt-a-Whirl.

And as if that weren't enough, Agent Harder has a girlfriend as well now, one with the platinum tresses and porn-star proportions of a life-size Barbie doll. Just the sort of woman I would fantasize about myself, if I got laid as seldom as Dank. I'd like to tell his shade that—if it's any consolation—I've been having sex enough for both of us. And sex enough for Boswell too, since he too seems never to have got the hang of sex. If he were sexually fulfilled, he'd never have developed such an all-consuming schoolboy crush on Dank. Hard to say who's more pathetic. At least Dank had some testosterone in his veins, though all it ever did was make him miserable. Boswell, on the other hand—*(OH)

Peter Pan in Outer Space: Reflections on the Poverty of Science Fiction in General and Phoebus K. Dank in Particular: An embittered critic's attempt to hitch his Porta-Potty to Dank's rising star. The critic was of course the malignant dwarf MacDougal, and his

---

* All right, I think we've heard enough from Owen Hirt—and given his still-legendary policy, as a professor, of flunking any paper that contained a sentence fragment, it seems only fitting that he be cut off mid-libel. "The Poison of the Honey Bee/Is the Artist's Jealousy," says William Blake, but an anti-social bee like Hirt, who gathers all his nectar from the sour grape, doesn't produce enough honey to justify the poison. Or the hum. As of today—January 17, 2007—the only voice you'll hear in this encyclopedia is mine. (BB)

inane, preposterous, forgotten book was nonetheless histori-
cally important because of the tragic turn it gave to Dank's
career, and to his life (though by now it should be clear that
there can be no neat distinction between Dank's literary and
extraliterary lives).

I'll never forget the day the book was published—or at least
the day (September 8, 2000) it hit the shelves of Hemlock's
only bookstore. It happened to be the day of our weekly trip
to the store, a trip we made by car that day, though Hemlock
Books-n-Such was just around the block, next door to Coffee
Town. Dank's agoraphobia, though nowhere near as bad as
it was to become, sometimes flared up enough to make even
the shortest walk unbearable. Once or twice, before the two
stopped talking, I'd even conveyed him to Hirt's.

There was nowhere to park on Democritus Street, so I
dropped our author at the bookstore, rounded the corner,
and found a barely-legal spot on Redwood, partly blocking
someone's driveway. Then I walked back to Hemlock Books-
n-Such, pausing to gaze in the window of the mirror-resil-
vering service. On reaching the bookstore, I made my way
through the maze of tables piled high with thrillers and the
latest in self-help and all that kitschy "human interest" fiction
about moms with kids with cancer or with mental retardation
or shaken baby syndrome. Maybe because I always try to tune
out my surroundings as I pass through the inferno of Current
Bestsellers, I didn't notice anything amiss until I walked into
the middle of the crime scene: There, in a circle of horrified
browsers, Dank was squatting on his massive hams, grimacing
and—even as I watched—extruding a coil of feces on a book I
later identified as *Peter Pan in Outer Space*. I rushed forward,
grabbed his shoulder, and urged him to stand and pull up
his pants. He ignored me. Evidently he'd been grimacing and
squatting for a while, because a moment later the two big-

gest, dumbest members of Hemlock's police force barged in and dragged poor Dank out to the car with his corduroys still around his ankles. He wound up spending the night in jail, which did nothing to weaken his growing conviction that the world was a minefield of mishaps waiting to mishappen, and that any time he left the house, disaster was bound to result.

Though nothing I say about MacDougal's book can suit it as perfectly as Dank's instinctive non-verbal response, a few words are in order. MacDougal singles out for demolition several dozen of Dank's novels, though to anyone who has read all those books it is obvious that MacDougal hasn't. In his preface, he does his best to impersonate a reasonable scholar, claiming he just wants to take "a closer look" at the leading SF authors of his day, but soon you realize that what he really wants is not to inspect them but—like a boy burning bugs—to *annihilate* those authors with his magnifying glass. And because of a childish grudge, he focuses his hatred most fixedly on Dank. Unlike Hirt's bloodthirsty comments in the present volume (and Hirt and MacDougal were friends, by the way), MacDougal's book confines itself to the sort of bloodless snideness permitted in civilized academic writing. One thinks of the critics derided by his darling Alexander Pope: "So well-bred spaniels civilly delight/In mumbling of the game they dare not bite," but in *my* book that makes him even more hateful. Here are some typical verdicts:

—On HAPPY PILLS: "In this book Dank's false cheerfulness goes beyond mere insincerity, to harden into something like an involuntary rictus."

—On LISTENING TO DECAF: "Here, as in all his more reflective, introspective, navel-gazing efforts, Dank reminds one of a loner playing solitaire so incompetently that he keeps getting stuck with most of the cards still face-down."

—On the metafictional bloodbath at the end of Everybody Dies: "Like so many other would-be-shocking 'innovations,' it delivers no more 'shock of the new' than the average joy buzzer."

—On F for Fatal, the second Agent Harder book: "Less a sequel than an afterbirth."

—On The Consequences, one of Dank's few ventures into Magic Realism: "[T]he narrative equivalent of a clumsy child's inability to stay within the lines of his coloring book."

—Retracting the praise he had tendered years before—before their falling-out—in his review of Fastland: "As to how I reconcile my claim that Dank is an abominably bad writer with my earlier claim that he had gotten steadily better throughout his career, it's simple: He was *such* a terrible writer to begin with that he was able to improve year after year without ever ceasing to be terrible."

By now, moreover, Dank no was longer even improving, according to MacDougal, who divides our author's oeuvre into three epochs: Juvenilia, Prime, and Senilia. Those academic categories may be valid for some authors, but not for one who was already eighteen when his first story appeared, and only forty-seven when *Peter Pan in Outer Space* came out. The frivolity and malice of MacDougal's book is manifest in the way it classifies as "juvenilia" everything Dank wrote before the age of thirty-five, and as "senilia" everything he wrote after forty.

Nowhere does MacDougal mention that he *knew* Dank, or that the two had been enemies for years. Come to think of it, a full disclosure would have had to mention MacDougal's height, 5'1", as well, since his malevolence was that of an embittered dwarf in an old fairy tale. "As small tyrants are always found to be the most severe, so are all little critics the most unmerciful," to quote the earlier and wittier (and taller?) of the two great Samuel Butlers.

So it's no wonder Dank was angry. No wonder he was moved to defile a book that had shit all over him. And I was even angrier. I'd already hated MacDougal, though he had long since learned not to air his anti-Dank sentiments in my vicinity, since it was well known that I got fighting mad when anyone impugned my author. I had enough self-restraint, and liked my job enough, not to let his slanders goad me into open violence of the kind that can get even a tenured academic canned (and we're almost as hard to fire as civil servants). But that wouldn't stop me from snapping off his windshield wipers when no one was looking, or smearing Vaseline on his office doorknob, or calling the campus bookstore, disguising my voice, and canceling MacDougal's orders for next semester.

And now he'd published a whole book attacking Dank. It didn't take a psychic to see that the book would disrupt its subject's life for the worse, though at the time I didn't foresee what a Pandora's box of disaster *Peter Pan in Outer Space* would be for its subject—didn't foresee that the book would prove to be the single worst thing that ever happened to Dank. At the time, I confess, I couldn't shake the crazy feeling that MacDougal's book had been written for no other reason than to offset *mine* (see FASTEST PEN IN THE GALAXY), to cancel it out, and that Dank himself was just a hapless casualty of MacDougal's effort to annihilate *me*. MacDougal was attacking me, in fact, whether he'd intended to or not, since my whole career depended on the axiom that Dank's books were worth reading, studying, and celebrating—and here was a whole book insisting that they weren't. And hostile critics always sound so *sure* of themselves. Even when you know they're idiots or creeps, it's hard to get their verdicts out of your head long enough to enjoy the books—or films, or restaurants—they've trashed. (In 1987, after reading a hostile review of a favorite science fiction author, Dank spoke of suing the reviewer for hedonic loss, as wives sue reckless drivers who have left their husbands impotent: Never again would Dank be able to take the same unalloyed enjoyment in that favorite author's books.)

So I won't pretend to regret what happened to MacDougal so soon after his book appeared, though I've come to think that the main motive for his sneering wasn't malice after all. In the 1890s, there was a French music-hall performer with the stage name of Le Petomane who outgrossed Sarah Bernhardt. His act consisted of making all kinds of remarkable noises with his anus. Probably he had some ennobling rationale for his craft or sullen art (maybe something, anticipating Cage, about the arbitrariness of conventional distinctions between noise and music), but it's hard not to think that, whatever his top end might claim, Le Petomane did what he did mostly because he could, and could get attention that way. And it's almost as hard not to think that MacDougal had the same motive for making his own indigestions so sonorous.

"The Plagiarists": Three unrelated vignettes about "precogs" who for different motives mimic other people's *future* doings: a serial-killing copycat who borrows his distinctive M.O. (planting bombs in computers and then detonating them, via the Internet, while flirting online with the victim) from another, much more celebrated serial killer of the twenty-second century; an untalented but prescient poet who plagiarizes a future Nobel-winning author's not-yet-written poem; a standup comedian who does a brilliant—though at the time inscrutable—impersonation of a future American president who hasn't yet been born.

The alert reader will recognize the piece as yet another manifestation of its author's obsession with *doubles*. Dank's fiction teems with doppelgangers, lookalikes, understudies, identical twins, alter egos, split personalities, mimics, impostors, precursors, and proxies. Of the many nonexistent novels he attributes to his fictive double, Philip K. DICK, my favorite involves a narc named Fred living undercover as a drug dealer named Bob—so undercover that not even Fred's superiors are aware that he is also Bob. When they assign him to spy via closed-circuit cameras on Bob and his housemates (riffraff modeled on the freeloaders who'd taken advantage of Dank over the years), Fred appreciates the irony at first. But not for long: In order to pass for a dealer, he has to sample his own wares, of which the bestselling, Substance D, slowly severs the connection between the two hemispheres of his brain, so the left lobe doesn't know what the right is doing—and soon Fred himself no longer knows that he is also Bob. Dank was fascinated by the idea that a self could split into factions unaware of one another's doings. The split-personality theme not only runs throughout his oeuvre—from throwaways like THE TIRESIAS FORMULA to profound meditations like THE WILSON TWINS—but overflowed his fiction to flood his extraliterary life: He never shook the suspicion, for example, that he himself had been the one to steal his own toothbrush and to burglarize his study.

The Plague of Candor: In what may be the greatest of Dank's published novels, the world is swept by an epidemic of Tourette's syndrome, or at least by a widespread compulsion to blurt out forbidden thoughts. The epidemic is caused by a manmade neurotoxic virus developed by Defense Department scientists as a sort of truth serum for use on spies and prisoners of war. The book begins with the "liberation" of that virus from a government laboratory, in the name of universal candor, by well-meaning terrorists. Then, wearing gas masks (in the conviction that their cause entitles them alone to continue dissembling), they burst into a seminar on business etiquette—which the terrorists consider the epitome of forked-tongue hypocrisy—and release the pathogen, touching off a global change in human behavior. The virus is transmitted by word of mouth: The air currents generated by ordinary conversation, or at least by the raised voice of a compulsive truth teller, are enough to waft it from person to person.

Though not fatal, the illness is incurable, and so contagious as eventually to infect and transform our whole species. Dank, however, is less interested in the epidemic's aftermath, the *fait accompli* (when, since *everybody* suffers from the same disorder, everybody grows accustomed to other people's tactless and—by our standards—antisocial blurts), than in the transitional period while some people are still able to contain their thoughts and some are not. That difference divides the species more profoundly than differences of race, religion, generation, class, or gender. The yet-uninfected shun the infected as not only contagious but also insufferably rude—or more exactly, the horror of infection and the hatred of rudeness become inextricably conflated and confused. As for the sick, they see the healthy as not only smug but suspiciously self-possessed, as if their immunity from the blurting disorder were due not to sheer dumb epidemiological luck, but to secrets so unspeakable as to resist and defeat even the promptings of the virus. And in fact some of the healthy seek out infection or—if they prove to be immune—*pretend* to be infected, in order to enjoy a jester's license to speak the truth.

Though the terrorists are shady foreigners of some unspecified stripe, the plague begins, as only fitting, in America. Some of the most amusing passages in the book concern the measures taken by other nations in their belated and futile efforts to prevent us from infecting them. England, for example, not only closes its ports and airport to Yanks, but mandates immediate quarantine and testing of anyone saying anything inappropriate or even just uncharacteristically frank. If infection is confirmed, the subject is deported to Australia.

None of Dank's books has a stranger history than this one. The novel was written in 1986, concurrently with ME, and ostensibly by Rebus Blank, the author figure in that book. As I said in the relevant entry, ME was strictly modeled on the events of Dank's day-to-day life during the months of its writing, so that if he wanted Blank to eat a bug or pick a fight or take a casual lover or write an SF novel called *The Plague of Candor*, Dank was forced to do so too. By a paradox that he would never succeed in explaining or repeating, Blank's book was by critical consensus the best thing that Dank ever wrote. Never mind that he'd conceived of that novel as existing only in the fictive world of the *real* novel, ME. Never mind that *Candor* languished, in Dank's big green file cabinet, for several years because he thought its publication would amount to plagiarism. In the end he couldn't resist the temptation to yank the book out of its parallel universe and publish it as his own work.

The Plague of Candor not only netted Dank a nomination for the 1992 SFANC award, but the love, however short-lived, of his third wife, Gabriella FEBRERO, whom he met at the award ceremony. One of the sad ironies of their relationship is that—though poor Dank himself bore no resemblance to the suave and dashing Rebus Blank—Dank's successor in his third wife's affections, yet another author, was a dead ringer for Blank as described in ME, a book his third wife hadn't even read. Afterward, Dank never shook the feeling that he'd been punished for appropriating his character's novel—that Blank had avenged himself by coming to life under a pseudonym and stealing away the ill-gotten wife that the success of Blank's book had garnered Dank.

"Planet Adam": Our old friend ADAM ABLE, ASTRONAUT, is hired to transport a cargo of beautiful, submissive brides-to-be to a frontier planet where a "critical shortage of women" is "hurting the morale of the space colonists." Morale drops even lower, one assumes, when those colonists find out that Adam's ship has just crash-landed on another planet (one with "a perfect South California climate"), and that the same "electro-gravitational anomaly" that caused the mishap makes a rescue mission impossible. That leaves Adam all alone with his adoring cargo, since the rest of the crew died in the crash—meaning all the other men aboard and also Adam's quasi-lesbian First Officer, Lt. Gabriella, the only woman on the ship ever to scowl at him:

> Though her manner was brusque and official, her womanly breasts stood up pertly beneath the sheer fabric of her synthetic gingham jumpsuit, that being what all female astronauts wore. *A little too pertly*, Adam thought wanly, reflecting with a yawn that once again his steel-gray eyes, tallness, square jaw, and muscular, fit physique had caused a telltale reaction to happen to yet another woman.

In addition to its "many fruit trees laden with delicious fruits," this Eden is replete with all sorts of edible creatures, since Dank could not imagine a meatless paradise. Neither can Adam. "Now, *that's* the kind of meal that sticks to the ribs," he says to one of his versatile space concubines, after eating a roast sirloin of smeerp. But *what* ribs? Wouldn't God have needed all twenty-four, and then some, to make all those Eves? (OH)

Planet Food: This brilliant but (therefore?) unpublished novel is set entirely inside a supermarket, where we join a man named Billy as he spends an hour pushing an old shopping cart with a wayward wheel up and down the aisles. Dank had a theory that supermarkets rig their carts to tug the shopper to the left or right, making it a little harder to cruise down an aisle without buying anything. In Billy's case, however, the wandering cart represents the peripheral tugs of nostalgia and desire that can turn a routine shopping trip into a profound and sometimes harrowing contemplation of his life. As he shops, he reflects on the memories the various groceries evoke—so many associations that by the time he reaches the checkout line, we know his whole life story. Each chapter is devoted to a single aisle (Produce, Baking Needs, and so on). The book ends with our hero leaving the store by the same electric doors that let him in two hundred pages earlier, the cashier's automatic "Have a nice day" still ringing in his ears. And though, from everything we've learned by then about Billy, his mind, and his misfortunes, it seems unlikely that he *will* have a nice day, then or ever, at least he's had a nice, calm, meditative, air-conditioned life-enhancing hour.

I have a special reason to regret that *Planet Food* has yet to be published: Billy is modeled on me, just as the supermarket he describes so lovingly is modeled on the one across the street. The book is a fulfillment, in the key of fiction, of Dank's longstanding wish to write a biography of his biographer. By 2001 he knew me well enough, both as a human being and as a fellow shopper, to know which foods I liked to pause at when I shopped, what memories those foods evoked, and what emotions tinged those memories. In case I'm ever so famous as to merit a conventional biography, I assure my future chronicler that both in its fidelity to my actual past and in its grasp of my psychology, *Planet Food* is as accurate as if I'd written it myself.

Like this commentator, for example, Billy grew up in St. Louis and then moved to the West Coast. Like me, he makes a living teaching undergraduates, trying vainly to instruct them in the proper use of "lie" and "lay," the difference between "its" and "it's," and the inexcusability of "utilize." Like me—like every professor of English—Billy is a closet novelist, and one thing he thinks about, at several points (peanut butter, instant coffee, fabric softener), is his stunted career as a writer, a career that corresponds at every point to mine. Like him, I started writing in the eleventh grade, at the urging of a dumb but well-intentioned teacher, Mr. Fenwick ("Mr. Funwick" in *Planet Food*). An unsuccessful novelist in his own right, Mr. Fenwick was a true believer in creative-writing programs. Just as a would-be welder goes to welding school (and Mr. Fenwick favored heavyset blue-collar similes for the "craft of fiction"—itself a dead blue-collar metaphor), so should aspiring writers hasten to obtain vocational training for their own manly trade.

So I opted for a college with a major in creative writing. Like Billy, I spent four years "crafting" laconic, hard-hitting, and pompously solemn little stories, usually set in a laundromat or diner, and always featuring the carcinomas, jumper cables, drinking habits, simple pleasures, money problems, twelve-step programs, go-go-dancing single mothers, brimming ashtrays, housecoats, slippers, pregnancies, felonies, epiphanies, adulteries, and plain-spoken wisdom of salt-of-the-earth types whose like I'd never met in real life and didn't want to, though I knew them well from other published stories, the ones my teachers kept upholding as exemplars. I never understood why people liked to read that stuff, assuming people really did, or how my teachers had reached a consensus with so many editors, reviewers, and anthologists that *that* was what fiction should be. Still, I went about learning the drill as doggedly as I had learned the Pledge of Allegiance and recited it day after day for years, taking my teachers' word for it that it meant something worth meaning.

I might still be pledging my allegiance to laundromat fiction if not for an incident in my final semester (and Billy's, since in relating my past I'm also summarizing *Planet Food*—despite appearances, this isn't a digression). That term, the foreman of our fiction workshop was a semi-famous visiting writer, a sort of cornbelt Chekhov who seemed to have it in for me, or at least to sense that my heart wasn't in the game he wanted us to play. The last time I was "workshopped" (a suitably ugly, unnatural verb for an ugly, unnatural process), I shared the spotlight with a freshman who had taken a year off before college to work in a slaughterhouse (and whose A+ workshop stories now appear in all the highest-paying magazines). After damning my submission with ten minutes of faint praise, the teacher went on to sing the praises of the freshman's gritty, realistic, cattle-stunning story for an hour and a half.

Another young writer might have responded by giving up altogether, or by redoubling his efforts to write the stories his teachers were after. I, though, vowed to figure out what kind of fiction I actually *liked*, and to try my hand at that. I vowed, in other words (in this one province—not in general, I'm afraid; see TEACHER'S PET) to give up on pleasing other people and to please myself instead. If I'd been so lucky as to like bestsellers, I might have made a fortune pleasing myself, but most of us are fated to please ourselves in private and find another way to make a living. Or to abandon all hope of pleasing ourselves, and give the reading public what it wants, or what its keepers think it wants. Or to convince ourselves that we too like the kind of fiction that gets published. That's the compromise most writers settle for, of course. Nine out of ten would probably write strange ill-selling stuff like mine, if they could just forget about the marketplace and follow their own noses. I admit, though, that there may be a trace of willfulness in my case: It's as if a music teacher had torpedoed my ambitions as a concert violinist, so in a huff I bought a bass guitar and formed a punk rock group (the way Dank did in 1998—see PUNK ROCK). Among other things, my books are a way of saying "fuck you" to the Gritty Realist and his ilk.

Not surprisingly, his ilk has said the same to me. My novels, as I say, remain unpublished, though I've gotten shorter work in lots of little magazines, including *Spunk, Thud, Putsch, Pulp, Misfit, Mayfly, Stinkhorn, Synapse, Penny Whistle, Palinode, Mutter, Moist,* and *Mallomar: The Journal of Experimental Writing*. Dank, by the way, was never an experimental writer. His most inspired formal fireworks and structural shenanigans were suggested—inspired—by me. At dinner, in the midst of random conversation, I'd say "You know, somebody really ought to write a novel in the form of story problems," then excuse myself to use the bathroom and discover, on returning, that in my absence Dank had dashed off THE BIG BOOK OF PROBLEMS. I'm exaggerating, but you get the picture. And that may be why he made so little effort to publish his more formally ambitious novels in his lifetime: a sense that they weren't "really" his, though God knows I never begrudged him my ideas. As for why his own approach to fiction wasn't more "experimental," he must have known that his perception of reality was already so anomalous that even if he aimed for the safest, drabbest realism, he'd still wind up writing novels like nobody else's.

But if, in his art, he opted for the tried and true, with the real world he experimented constantly. Relentlessly. Not even the plumbing was safe. Once he modified the toilet in the downstairs bathroom so it would flush with hot water. After a few days, thank God, and several scalding backsplashes, Dank undid *that* modification (though without renouncing the private sanitary theory that had prompted it), and the toilet bowl no longer steamed like a hot spring.

Dank was always asking "What would happen if . . .?" What would happen if he took No-Doz and Unisom at the same time? Immodium and Ex-Lax? *Unisom* and Ex-Lax? Would he defecate in his sleep? If you drink a bottleful of blue food color, does your sweat turn blue? How blue? How soon? And does your urine too? Will the supermarket let you buy a single filbert from the bulk-food bins? Will they let you buy it with a credit card? A check? If you lift a sneaker by its lace and swing it overhead in circles for an hour—until it's really "used to" that trajectory—will it continue to circle when you release it? Will your computer explode if you Google for "e"?

Plus Seven: In the third Agent Harder novel, Harder matches wits with a cryptographer who doesn't dare to murder the people he wants to because he has made the mistake of publicizing his grudges. He knows the FBI would quickly zero in on him if his enemies all started dying, especially dying the elaborate deaths he's got his heart set on inflicting. And so, instead of killing the people he hates, he kills the seventh person listed in the phone book *after* each of the people he hates. (A misanthrope as well as a psychopath, he reasons that *all* men are evil, and that these strangers about whom he knows nothing no doubt deserve to be killed just as much as the hateful people who happen to have crossed his path.)

This arbitrary substitution of strangers for enemies makes

it impossible for Harder to establish a common link among the victims, or to profile the killer by his choice of targets. Although the killer's real enemies all turn out to be middle-aged white male employees of the same Orwellian government bureau where the killer works, the Ministry of Clarity, their surrogates—men and women, black and white, old and young, rich and poor—have nothing in common but bad luck. The maniac, moreover, uses a completely different method for each victim. Harder knows he's dealing with a serial killer and not just a bunch of unrelated crimes only because the villain, like so many fictive killers, has a weakness for needlessly elaborate means of murder, means that in this case seem specially tailored to specific people—but not to the people they're used on. A retarded janitor who shares a surname with the killer's glibbest and most fancy-talking colleague (and also, incidentally, with the newel-post enthusiast who'd recently made off with Dank's third wife—see NOMENCLATURE PROJECT) is killed by an unabridged dictionary dropped on his head from a high window. On examining the murder weapon, detectives find eight words highlighted: "cranium," "crush," "know-it-all," "logorrhea," "newel-namer" (a near-future synonym for "know-it-all"), "pretentious," "showoff," and "verbose." Such incongruities suggest to Harder that the victims may be proxies, and with a lot of luck he finally nabs the killer (and, the epilogue assures us, sends him straight to the Eradicator, the near-future's fully-automated means of executing felons) just as the latter is about to kill *himself* because he's listed seventh in the phone book after a certain hated cousin.

The title, *Plus Seven*, has a special significance to me, since the pinnacle of Dank's achievement is—or rather the pinnacles are—his seven great unpublished novels. Though only three of those novels had been written when *Plus Seven* appeared in 1996, I still like to think of that title as an allusion to their author's hidden masterpieces—to the math one must perform to come to a true reckoning of Dank's total genius. I don't know if any such allusion was intended, though, because he never talked about the books in question. Only once did we discuss one—PLANET FOOD—and Dank was so unfair to that brilliant *tour de force* that I found myself getting indignant on its behalf. Dank, I should say, was one of those authors who care only about their latest book, the one in progress. His previous books seemed as alien to him as if someone else had written them. And that was fine, I guess, in the case of those in print—once a book is published, it does take on a life of its own—but it meant he couldn't be bothered to send out, or even to *like*, anything that hadn't been sold while it was still fresh in his affections. I came to see it as *my* job to advocate for Dank's unpublished (and—says Tom the Gutless—unpublishable) novels. Even before his death, I knew that those books were unlikely to be published in his lifetime. If anything, Dank's continued existence made them harder to publish, since I couldn't push them as aggressively as they deserved while their author was alive and refusing to say a good word for them himself, to Tom or to anyone else.

Plus Seven: The Motion Picture: The only feature film made from Dank's fiction in his lifetime, though I wasn't too surprised when Boswell told me that some other films are in the works.* It was

---

* Indeed: Adaptations of THE PLAGUE OF CANDOR, VIRTUALLY IMMORTAL, and THE COLLABORATION are all in development, so maybe Dank will finally get his due.

In honor of Dank's stated wish, in his last will and testament, that Hirt should write the reader's guide, I've reluctantly decided, after lots of soul-searching, to reinstate him as my fellow commentator. Almost as reluctantly as I'd have complied if Dank's will had stipulated that he be

only a matter of time, after all, before some schlockmeister in Hollywood recognized Dank's special brand of adolescent fabulation as a filmable and bankable commodity. I wouldn't even be surprised, just sickened, if—thanks to the purchasing power of the thirteen-year-old American male—Dank's shade enjoys the type of posthumous fame that he and his fellow neglectees in the MELVILLE BROTHERHOOD liked so much to fantasize about, when they got bored of wanting the pre-posthumous kind. Or when their eyes got bleary from scanning the horizon, watching impatiently for their ships to come in. And maybe the reason his garbage barge didn't arrive in his lifetime is that Dank did everything he could to ward it away from the harbor. His behavior on the set *Plus Seven* is a case in point.

In a move they soon regretted, the movie's producers, on buying the rights to the book, agreed to a clause in the contract that entitled Dank to watch the filming of his novel. When shooting began in December 1999, Dank was on hand. His only previous experience with Hollywood had been a period in the mid-1980s when he moonlit, pseudonymously, as a writer of "novelizations" (usually of trashy science fiction movies), and now Dank showed up at the studio with unrealistic expectations. He wanted his book to be filmed scene for scene, just as written. He wanted a garrulous voiceover (*his* voice, of course) to salvage all the parts that didn't lend themselves to filming—his introspective interludes and kindergarten wordplay and would-be-philosophical digressions, all the crap that gives print a bad reputation. He insisted that his idiotic "symbols"—a certain house, a certain couch, a

---

buried in some meadow later rezoned as a toxic-waste dump. (Though Hirt was *always* more a toxic-waste dump than meadow.) Of all Dank's writings, none was left in more dire need of revision than his last will and testament. You really should revise your will at least as often as you replace your toothbrush. (BB)

surly lady coroner, a foot-thick dictionary, a malfunctioning micro-wave oven—all be painted or upholstered or clad and shod or bound or housed in day-glo orange.

Dank had problems with the casting too. He made a big stink when he saw the actress they cast to play Brandi, the sultry young widow who furnishes the "love interest" (*"That's* not what Brandi looks like!"), though he was unable to point to any passage in the book that contradicted the casting assistant. Somehow Dank had gone three hundred pages without specifying any more about Brandi's appearance than that she was "redheaded" and "big-breasted"—and certainly the actress they had chosen fit the bill on all three counts. Evidently Dank, when he wrote the book, had envisioned some other kind of big-breasted redhead.

Dank had also objected to her casting because she'd been in other movies, and those other movies—those rival narratives—were the last thing he wanted the audience thinking about while enjoying *his* movie (as he always spoke of it, even to the director—not *"our* movie" but "my movie"). He had tried in vain to get the casting lady to consider only first-time actors. Actually, Dank went further than that, demanding in a long, impassioned letter that the leads, at least, be not only first-timers but *last*-timers: Dank wanted them all to sign contracts promising never again to appear in a movie—or on television, or on stage, or even as models on billboards or magazine covers—to ensure that they would always be identified with their (preposterous) *Plus Seven* characters. (For supporting actors, the stipulation was a little less extreme: No other movies for the next five years, just as workers who leave certain high-tech jobs are contractually forbidden, for a stated pe-riod, to do the same kind of work for a competitor.) Needless to say . . .

Undaunted, Dank bounced back with a still dumber idea. The screenwriters hadn't found room for all the novel's minor characters, but at Dank's insistence they'd worked in *mentions* of a few who hadn't made the cut ("You look like my cousin's accountant, the one that was busted for embezzlement"). Dank decided that these offstage characters too should be cast—should be associated in the ads and in the credits with specific actors, the more familiar the better (consistency was never one of *Dank's* hobgoblins), even though those actors would not be seen or heard. Their purpose was to let the viewers put a face and voice to the phantom characters.

After a week of Dank's interference, the actors threatened to walk off the set unless he butted out—and, with the usual "I know when *I'm* not wanted" (though Dank in fact had *no idea* when he wasn't wanted), he agreed to go home. I'm amazed they didn't eject him even sooner. I've run into several movie people here in Mallorca—where I've spent the better part of January— and I've even gotten some amusing if martini-powered offers to act in upcoming films. I find it hard enough to imagine Dank on the same *island* with these people (whose names, if I stooped to name-dropping, you'd surely recognize), much less on the same set. In any case, with Dank no longer breathing down his neck, the director wound up making so many changes (all of them improvements, though none enough to turn a tenth-rate novel into better than a ninth-rate movie) that when the film premiered in August 2000, our author, who'd flown to LA for the occasion, stormed out of the theater before it was over. (OH)

Pornography: Whatever a great author reads is of interest to his own readers, and I see no reason to be coy about Dank's penchant for pornography. Normally he looked at it in the privacy of his bedroom or bathroom or study, but when depressed— too depressed to care about what posterity would think—he brought his men's magazines into the common areas of what was, after all, his house. (I don't flatter myself that Dank cared what I personally thought of him, but since I was his emissary to posterity, he mostly hid from me his more shameful secrets except when drunk or depressed—as, however, he frequently was.) More than once I found him sitting in the living room, or at the kitchen table, paging gloomily through an antique *Playboy*. Once, when the phone rang while Dank was perusing a centerfold, he put his index finger on the model's haunch as if to mark his place before lifting the receiver, and he kept his finger there throughout the conversation, though the caller was his mother.

As a rule, the magazines were old enough to qualify as collector's items. In the basement room where he hid all his hideable secrets (see TEACHER'S PET), Dank kept an ancient cardboard box that had once held smaller boxes of Puffa Puffa Rice but now contained his adolescent porno hoard, spanning the ages from twelve to twenty-one. (Science fiction writers tend to have long adolescences.) It was clear that the images in that box had once lain in orderly strata, with the oldest at the bottom, and though later upheavals of lust or nostalgia had disrupted the geological record, it was still possible to reconstruct the eras of Dank's newly formed and very slowly cooling sexuality, since most of the images belonged to magazines with dated pages.

Dank had come of age, of course, before the epoch of Internet porn. His earliest surviving smut consisted of the sort of low-grade ore with which the randy adolescents of his generation had to satisfy themselves: mail-order undies catalogs, glossy pages torn from books (*library* books?) about breastfeeding, racy ads from *Cosmopolitan*. These gave way to "tasteful" magazines like *Penthouse*, and those to crasser ones with harsher lighting, less airbrushing, and—for me, anyhow—more of a gynecological interest than an erotic one. Sometimes Dank had saved just a single page of a given magazine. When he'd kept the whole issue, there were always paper clips marking favorite images. This gave me some intriguing insights into his pubescent id, insights I'm not sure that I should pass on to posterity.

I will, however, mention one: From twelve to fourteen, Dank was attracted almost exclusively to a certain facial expression. He hadn't wasted a single paper clip on any of the badly faked orgasmic grimaces, and he had no use for other standard porno faces—for the scowl that signifies no-nonsense sexual intent, for instance, or the sneer that perfectly expresses the contempt the model feels for the sad men who will drool all over her image. Dank, however, as a sad young man—or rather as a randy seventh-grader—had had a *smile fetish*. Or maybe a friendliness fetish: He'd liked naked ladies who looked like they might let him have his way with them out of sheer kindness. And their smiles—their compassion—had to look authentic. Comparing the few models he had flagged to the many he hadn't, I realized how very rare a real, unforced smile is in porn—almost as uncommon as in family photographs.

Dank told me once that as a little kid, back before he started noticing breasts or smelling like a grown-up, his understanding of sex was "two people taking off their clothes and being extra nice to each other." Judging by his oldest porn, that was still his understanding well into his teens—maybe because he encountered so little kindness in that era that it seemed the only thing worth wanting, at least as fervently as everyone around him wanted the thing they called sex.

"Postcard to the Future": Not a story but an open letter to posterity, scribbled in a panic in 1999, and sent with insufficient postage. Dank had just watched a lurid shockumentary on imminent disasters—global warming, radiation, drug-resistant pathogens, killer asteroids, and killer bees, to name a few. The show (on Fox, of course) had left our forward-looking hack envisioning a not-too-distant future when the human race will be reduced to a scatter of surly, semi-literate, ill-groomed, and isolated troglodytes: science fiction fans, in other words. "Postcard to the Future," addressed to those scruffy survivors, is Dank's attempt to keep the torch of culture burning through the long dark age ahead.

At seven pages, the thing is hardly a "postcard," though it *is* mercifully brief, either because Dank didn't want to tax posterity's attention span, or because he had only seven pages' worth of information about the past and present to share with the future. That information included the Pythagorean theorem, the number of feet in a mile, the formula for finding the volume of a cylinder (the first thing *I'll* want to know if I'm ever bombed back to the Stone Age), and, of course, "$E = MC^2$," though Dank doesn't say what that equation means, or even what the variables stand for (probably because he himself had no idea), only that it's "Einstein's world-famous math equation." Nor are the arts neglected, though our correspondent fears that not a single statue, canvas, or recording will survive. But he does his level best to describe "the powerful esthetical enjoyment" that a luckier era derived from "a famous symphony by Beethoven, or a giant painting by Picasso, or a major novel by Zelazny" (not the last time Dank would mention those three titans in a single sentence). He also does his level best to advise the budding writers of the future, trotting out the usual nonsense about process versus product, about showing versus telling, about "exercising" your "demons." Dank almost always did his best—it's just that his best was so bad. He's on firmer ground when it comes to the state capitals, and ends with a list of all fifty. Whatever else the people of the future might be left to puzzle out for themselves, Dank was determined that at any rate they'd know why the Russians bombed—or the bees stung—Sacramento. Something tells me, though, that, as Voltaire rightly foretold of Rousseau's *Ode to Posterity*, "Postcard to the Future" will not reach its destination. (OH)

"Praise the Big Bottle": In this fantasy smacking of *Raise the Red Lantern* (a video he must have rented half a dozen times), Dank imagines a world just like ours except that bigamy is legal. Hilarity ensues when the lucky narrator carries Bride Number Two across the threshold of the house he shares with Number One. From then on, he indicates which wife he wants to sleep with, on any given night, by leaving a bottle of champagne standing phallically in a special ice bucket ("like it had to be kept chilled or else it would blow its top prematurely") outside her bedroom door.

I try not to wonder what it means that Dank wrote this story in February 1999, the month Lips moved in with us the better to swindle him at close range, and to sponge off of him in the meantime. He might be there still (be *here*, that is, since I'm there now) if not for a stroke of luck. For a few months, though, the intruder ate his meals at our table, hogged all the hot water (since the ancient water heater needed hours to recover from a single long and songful shower, of the sort the *Lieder*-loving Lips indulged in daily), and also monopolized the living room. He'd spend hours channel-surfing, with the volume turned way up (he was half-deaf), from the sacred La-Z-Boy that *I* had never dared to sit in even when its owner was away. Dank was so thrilled to have a bona fide Inventor in his house that he ignored these nuisances, but they drove me to distraction. And except for his after-dinner walk—as predictable in its timetable and itinerary as Kant's—Lips never left the house at all, as far as I could tell. When he wasn't in the shower or the living room, he was usually in "his" room, directly below mine, sedulously teaching himself to play the tuba he bought the day he moved in—probably with Dank's own money, and probably because he knew that no other instrument was as certain to annoy me. After a month of tuneless oompahs (which sounded at all hours, though as sporadically as the installments of a Chinese water torture), I'd become convinced that Lips was trying to get rid of me so that he could prey on Dank unhindered by my wary chaperonage. After another month, he'd almost succeeded: It was clear that *one* of us would have to go. Earplugs are useless, or even worse than useless, when it comes to the rumble of a tuba: They're so much more effective at dampening high frequencies that they seem positively to amplify the low ones, giving them a salience more irritating than the more random original noise. Not for the first time in my life, but for the first since moving into Dank's normally quiet and studious house, I came to think of consciousness as a disease of which hearing is the most distressing symptom.

I would have handed Dank an ultimatum, except that I had recently complained about Hirt, and I was afraid Dank would think I was jealous of his friends and wanted him all to myself. So instead I started a covert campaign against Lips. Whenever he was in the shower, I used the downstairs bathroom, or at least I flushed its toilet—sometimes more than once—to divert all the cold water long enough to scald him. One day, while he was showering and I was sick with a bad cold, I snuck into his room and sneezed twice on the mouthpiece of his tuba, but to no effect. A few days later I barely resisted an impulse to demolish the tuba with a wrecking bar while Lips was watching *Guiding Light* and Dank was in the basement trying to invent a microwave refrigerator. (He himself seemed not to mind the oompahs, and even spoke of digging out and dusting off his junior-high trombone in order to jam with his houseguest.) At the last moment, though, I set down the wrecking bar, found some Krazy Glue instead, and glued the tuba's spit valve shut—a form of vandalism subtle enough that as far as I could tell Lips never suspected foul play. But neither did he discontinue his own foul playing, though his oompahs soon developed a slight gurgle, unless I just imagined one.

My imagination ran away with me that summer, so that I suffered more than Lips from my campaign against him, because I convinced myself that he was retaliating furtively for my furtive attacks, when in fact he probably never even noticed them. At least, I see no evidence in retrospect for my conviction that Lips was poisoning me (back then my only evidence was that as soon as poisoning occurred to me as something one of us might try, my stomach started hurting), and I'm not proud of my efforts to poison him back, especially since they didn't work. Forget what you've read about rhubarb leaves, potato eyes, and peach pits: They may be "poisonous" in some abstruse biochemical sense, but they're useless on people like Lips. Not that I'd wanted to kill him, of course, but I *had* hoped to enfeeble him, to dial him down a few notches, shorten the length of his showers and dampen the blats from his tuba.

What to do? I could neither drive away my enemy nor drive a wedge between him and his host, for if Lips had the resilience of Rasputin, Dank had the patience of Buddha. I took to scanning the classifieds at breakfast, hoping Dank would notice and ask why I was suddenly circling ads for apartments and rentals. I toyed with the idea of really moving out, ceding the house and its owner to Lips, but I knew that if I did, my hatred of him would continue to fester till it ate away my brain. At that point, though, luckily for my sanity, Lips inherited a fortune from some uncle—not the one who'd invented a new way to walk, but a factory owner who, according to his nephew, had cornered the market for "a small domestic object" Lips refused to specify. His vagueness on that point made me wonder if this uncle had been wished into being by the sheer intensity of his nephew's dream of easy money.

The money itself, though, was real enough for Lips to move out and on—back to Europe, I think—since he'd been living with us only for monetary reasons. He left his tuba (which I amused myself by filling with cement; it stands to this day—I can see it from my study window as I type these words—in the backyard, by the bunker, on its bell, as if the Earth were just a cosmic tuba blast), but he took some other things. A dozen of Dank's rarest science fiction paperbacks—the ones in the special glass-fronted display case, including a signed first edition of *Dune*—disappeared at the same time as Lips. I felt sorry for Dank, but that's what you get for letting creeps into your house. And at least the stolen books assured that Lips would never move *back* in. That was the main thing.

The Pray-o-Matic: What if somebody invented a machine to pray for him—a motorized prayer wheel—and it *worked*? Would he optimize it, making the wheel spin faster so that he could pray for better stuff? Would he mass-produce it, so that others too could finally get some answers to their prayers? Given that the prototype, like other prototypes (and like the book in which he stars), is cumbersome and bulky, could he design a compact bedside model to kneel in front of at bedtime? Could there be an even smaller handheld version—no bigger than a cell phone, say—enabling busy people to phone in a prayer any time they have a moment?

But would powerful interests oppose the invention? What interests? The Catholic church? The drug cartels? The sex industry? Pretty much anyone selling goods and services that people would pray for rather than pay for, if prayers got results? And what happens if two people rev up mutually exclusive prayers at the same time? What happens when the two machines go head to head, or rather tug in opposite directions like a tractor pull? Do they overheat and start to smoke? Does the Pray-o-Matic tend to malfunction now and then, and give some other output than the one requested? Does it sometimes grant the letter of a prayer and not the spirit? And are such malfunctions deadly? Or is that not a problem, not at first, because the machine (once again, like the novel) is so inefficient that a sofa-sized and megawatt-squandering model is barely able to ward off a mosquito or pray into existence a single stick of gum, and in order to do something major, like influencing the outcome of a big football game, you need a Pray-o-Matic bigger than an ocean liner? Do the defense departments of all the major nations nonetheless pour billions into prayer-based weapons? Does the novel, and incidentally the world, end with a World Prayer War?

For answers to these and other questions, read *The Pray-o-Matic*. For an answer to the question of why the book was written, God only knows.

Dank's third wife was a practicing Catholic, and he was so enamored of her that he followed her to church on Sundays, though he'd always thought religion incompatible with his Scientific Worldview. *The Pray-o-Matic* dates from their brief marriage and may be seen as Dank's attempt to marry high technology and age-old theology. It wasn't the first time his adolescent skepticism (lifted straight from Bertrand Russell) gave way to his adolescent penchant for extending the frontiers of mechanization. In the DOG HOUSE era, though he styled himself an agnostic (or, in more pretentious moods, a *gnostic*), Dank frequently consulted Dial-a-Prayer when depressed or uncertain or afraid, just as he'd later cast the *I Ching*. He'd memorized the numbers of *several* Dial-a-Prayers, some in other area codes, and if he didn't like the first prayer he heard, he'd keep dialing till he got a prayer he did. (OH)

"A Presentimental Journey": Written the same day as THE FUTURE TENSE OF "OUCH," this is the story of a psychic whose powers are genuine but limited: She can foresee only her own future, and can't actually foresee even that; she can only *forefeel* it—feel the emotions appropriate to upcoming events. At first this is a skill she can turn off and on (by shutting her eyes and squeezing the bridge of her nose), but later she is afflicted with these presentiments all the time, and they tend to drown out her responses to what's happening at the moment, especially because she's already responded to *that*. At any given moment, she feels what a normal person would feel twenty-four hours later, so that if she's destined to win the lottery on Tuesday at 4:37 PM, she feels a burst of elation at 4:37 on Monday, though she has no idea why (sometimes she tries to infer the events her emotions foretell, but she seldom guesses right). By the time she finds out, she'll be busy responding to whatever will happen at 4:37 on *Wednesday*.

Production Line: Dank's name for the elaborate and expensive committee approach to writing that he inaugurated in December 2000, during his bizarre and never diagnosed year-and-a-half attack of incapacitating laziness. No matter how enfeebled, he never stopped producing the novels that he considered his reason for living. Even when he was too weak to open a carton of milk, the flow of weird and wonderful fiction from his workshop continued undiminished. He was more prolific than ever, in fact, cranking out a dozen novels in the space of sixteen months. But only one of those novels (PERSONAL WORST) has been honored with an entry in this guide to the Dank canon, because Dank's participation in their actual production dwindled to an extensionless point as he discovered how far he could go in delegating the "inessential" parts of the job to assistants. He was already paying helpers, after all, to shave and bathe him; it was only natural for Dank to wonder if he couldn't also hire out some of the more onerous parts of the writing process. Since, as far as I could tell, his fatigue was due to MacDougal's savage attack and Dank's subsequent crisis of faith in himself as a writer, it made sense, in a way, for Dank to phase himself out of the process that produced his fiction.

At first he farmed out only the descriptive passages. He told me at the time that he'd always found descriptions hard to write, maybe because he'd always skipped them as a reader. He suspected that all readers skip descriptions, but feared that some might feel cheated if descriptions were omitted. So he didn't dare omit them, but he had no qualms about subcontracting them. In reply to my suggestion that he *should* leave out the parts he had no interest in writing—that that's what authenticity means for a writer—Dank said: "Once I started leaving out, I'd never stop. It would be like those cartoons where the guy pulls a loose thread and it unravels the entire sweater."

But such an unraveling had already begun—not of Dank's fiction itself, but of his writing regimen. By April 2000, he had also farmed out dialogue, to an unsuccessful screenwriter. (No shortage of those.) Next came sex scenes, which he was able to buy for a song from Amanda Pennyworth—the only woman in the MELVILLE BROTHERHOOD and, at sixty-eight, its oldest member—who wrote children's books and was impatient with the limits the genre put on her libidinous imagination. Next to go were dream sequences, which like descriptions Dank had taken to skipping long ago in his own reading (on the grounds that they "didn't really happen"—not even in the world of the novel—and so didn't "count"). Next, epiphanies. By September, Dank was writing only "key sentences," which for a novel might amount to ten or fifteen pages. By the summer of 2001, he wasn't writing even those—wasn't writing at all, in fact, merely supplying the premise and coordinating his assistants' contributions into a coherent whole. He held weekly meetings in which his helpers stood around his bed discussing any problems they were having in obeying his instructions—in building on his premises, writing the stories he'd imagined.

It might seem that at this point Dank had rolled back his duties as far as they could go, but his ever-worsening fatigue, and his penchant, too, for taking things to their logical extremes (a penchant reflected in so many of his stories), led him to go one step further: In December 2001, he delegated the job of overseeing the assembly line to a foreman, me. For the next four months—until labor problems shut down our fiction factory forever—it was my job to assign specific passages and then piece them together, making sure the seams weren't too conspicuous, and especially looking out for jarring shifts in tone from one assistant's passage to another's, so that the book (unlike this guide, alas) would read as the work of a single author.

As for Dank, his main contribution at that point was the plot or premise—fifty or a hundred words laboriously uttered in the face of overwhelming drowsiness. I could tell that his brain was still working feverishly, possibly producing his best ideas ever, but it was too much work for him to write down or even to dictate those ideas except in the stingiest of paraphrases. For a few weeks there, even such dictation was too much for Dank: He'd lie in bed with tears in his eyes, visibly conceiving and consigning to oblivion one good idea after another.

As a result of all this, there are a dozen novels to which our author signed his name without having written a word, and in fact without having bothered to *read* them (though he always glanced at them before authorizing me to send them to his agent). Though I oversaw their assembly, I've forgotten half of them. The ones I can think of, offhand, are *The Backache That Got Into Mensa* (a first-person narrative by a chronic pain that isn't merely sentient but more articulate, intelligent, and civilized than its gym-teaching host); *Chrono Craig's Perpetual Present* (in which the hapless title character is trapped in a runaway time machine traveling backward at a rate of exactly one hour per hour); *Following Yonder Star* (a Yuletide space opera with a heroine named Gaia Peril and an extraterrestrial take on the Santa Claus myth); *Half-Truths* (in a totalitarian future that prosecutes subversive thoughts, a rebel scientist infiltrates the big truth-serum factory and dilutes a batch so that it elicits half-truths rather than whole ones); *The Return of Payload Pete* (thirty years after his trip to Ganymede, the now-balding hero has a midlife crisis, builds another spaceship, and escapes a loveless marriage and a boring job by flying to Titan); and *Elizabeth*, whose title character was an average or composite of all the Lizzes, Betsys, Beths, and out-and-out Elizabeths that Dank had ever known (or so he claimed; it's hard to see how Dank's short, fat, loud, rude, obnoxious cousin Betsy, say, could form any part of her toothachingly sweet, inaudibly soft-spoken namesake's genotype, unless it was the part played in fancy perfumes by foul-smelling substances like ambergris and civet).

Only one of the assembly-line novels, PERSONAL WORST, is good enough to merit its own entry in this guide to all things Dankian, despite the fact that Dank had no more to do with it than with the other eleven. To be sure, we'd started from his premise and had relied on the crimefighting smarts of his proprietary Agent Harder. Still, it amuses me that Tom—who knew nothing of the Production Line, as he knows nothing of so many things—never doubted that Dank himself had written PERSONAL WORST. And yet for some reason Tom balked at FOOD PLANET, which I sent him at the same time (February 2002), in the same mailing carton, admittedly without Dank's knowledge or permission.

Public Image: Although my fellow commentator won't shut up about the continuity between Dank's life and art, there was in fact a glaring *dis*continuity. Dank had built a sort of firewall between his public and his private selves, lest the raging curiosity sparked off by his books and by his public duties as an author—readings, signings, interviews, and so on—also consume his "inner life," such as it was. Being Dank, however, he'd relied less on sober calculation than on blind chance in picking a public image—that is, picking the kind of person to impersonate during interviews and readings, at lectures and conventions, and even while posing for infrequent paparazzi.

Two days before he sat for his first jacket photo in November 1994 (for THE MAN I KILLED, his forty-second book—until then no publisher had deemed his face a selling point), Dank tagged along with me to a Halloween party. I dressed as a priest and Dank as an explorer, in jodhpurs, pith helmet, and a khaki-colored many-pocketed safari vest (all rented from the costume shop on Main Street), and brandishing a genuine machete that our host made him leave on the bed with the coats. Normally he would have dressed up as an astronaut, as he had every time he'd dressed up at all since 1985, when he blew the better part of his advance for PAYLOAD PETE, BOY ROCKETEER on a supposedly authentic NASA space suit he'd seen advertised in the back of a photocopied fanzine. On October 31, 1994, though, he was eager to impress a dark-haired girl he had glimpsed once in the host's apartment, a girl of whom he knew only that she hated science fiction (according to the host, a friend of mine and fellow writer), favored gruff outdoorsy men, and was planning to attend the party. In fact she never showed, but Dank had so much fun in his safari outfit that he decided to wear it again—since he hadn't yet returned it—for the cover photo. And when, a few months later, an interviewer from the *Hemlock Herald* asked about that photo, Dank was ready with a long account of his recent hunting trip to Kenya. "You can't just spend your whole life cooped up indoors," he concluded. "That's what's wrong with our society. I mean, you gotta get *out* there, roll up your sleeves and get your feet wet."

And from then on, that would be his shtick: He was an adventurer like Hemingway, a no-bullshit man of action who somehow found the time to write a novel now and then, when he wasn't hunting sharks or wrestling pumas or rappelling down the insides of volcanoes. He even spoke of buying the explorer costume, but was persuaded (by our agent, who helped Dank perfect his rugged public image) that that might be seen as protesting too much. Whenever Dank attended a convention, though, or had a photo op, or met the press, he made a point of appearing, minus his eyeglasses, in a heavy red lumberjack shirt, blue jeans, and hiking boots, with a Swiss army knife clipped to his belt. He looked a little like the guy on the Brawny paper-towels package.

If Dank hadn't been such a marginal and vanishingly minor writer, someone might have bothered to investigate his pose and expose him: Not only had he never shot big game in Africa, he'd never even ventured out of the United States* (though he had a passport he'd applied for long ago, vaguely planning to attend the Nobel ceremony with a view to "networking"). And his neighbors knew of course that the flannel-shirted man of action was a lie: They'd all seen Dank padding over to Food Planet in the baby-blue bathrobe his mother had sent him and a pair of fluffy slippers left behind by one of the wives. Among the consolation prizes of deserved obscurity, however, is that even if you do have enemies, nobody is interested in what they say about you.

---

* One reason Dank never left the country was that he was too busy. And one reason people like Hirt make such a brouhaha about their travels is that, like certain other forms of connoisseurship, travel is—and always was—a consolation prize for arty dilettantes, poets *maudits*, and writers *manqués*. Real artists see and feel more on their imaginary travels than tourists like Hirt do on their "real" ones. I'm not ashamed to say I've never left the country either, and yet I'm convinced that I experience the Côte D'Azur (for instance) as vividly in poring over travel magazines as Hirt experiences it *in situ*. (BB)

There's no need to dwell on Dank's ridiculous hypocrisy, except to say that he himself was unaware of it, as he was of almost everything the rest of us find unignorable. He had no sensation of duplicity when he whisked off his glasses, put on a burly shirt, and prepared to fib to some reporter about his latest death-defying exploits. It didn't even occur to him to make those feats of derring-do less strenuous as he got fatter. He'd always assumed that part of the job of being a writer—whether you are Hemingway or Henry James, Walt Whitman or Paul Valéry—is to erect a façade, to project a persona much larger than life and make it bellow, any time some nosy reader tries to figure out what kind of person *really* wrote your books, PAY NO ATTENTION TO THAT MAN BEHIND THE CURTAIN! (OH)

Punk Rock: Dank's attempt to start a punk-rock band might seem like just one of his vanity projects, but for once vanity had nothing to do with it. He was inspired not by any delusions of musical talent, but by the sadder delusion that belonging to a punk-rock band would earn him the love of the ridiculously-named Pandora LANDOR. As an attempt to conquer another artistic domain, Dank's foray into music was less grandiose than most of his ventures outside the mildly remunerative genre of oddly premised, badly written science fiction (the one art for which he had an undisputed knack). The whole point of punk rock, after all, is that you don't *need* to be a musician. But you need to be more of one than Dank, I guess, since even after he dropped six hundred dollars on a bass guitar (that instrument of choice for would-be rockers too untalented to play a true guitar but too arrhythmic to play drums), and almost as much on a fancy leather jacket with the words PUNK ROCK picked out in sequins on the back, nobody would play with him. Finally he was reduced to paying session musicians to impersonate his bandmates, though not even for better-than-union wages would they acknowledge him offstage, not even between sets. Neither would they wear the T-shirts he'd had custom-made for them, the ones emblazoned with the band's name, IDLE THREAT, above a larger-than-life image of Dank's head. In addition to plunking his guitar, Dank wrote all the "songs," set them to "music" (assorted two- or three-chord combinations of the four he knew), and screamed them at the few who cared to listen. Ms. Landor, though, was not among those few.

Readers interested in Dank the lyricist will be disappointed to learn that just one Idle Threat song has survived in manuscript. (As for the country-music song—"Illegally Parked in the Handicapped Zone of Your Heart"—that he wrote years earlier, while wooing his line-dancing second wife, all but the title is lost.) It might be possible for a truly zealous fan to transcribe the others from repeated listens to the caterwauling on the cassette recordings of his band's three shows, but the anthem already on paper, "Punk Rock," probably conveys all you need to know about Dank's songwriting skills:

I don't gotta follow no rule
I don't gotta go to no school
I don't gotta obey your fascist laws
I don't gotta show just cause
Too bad, that's the way it goes
And if you don't like it I'll sock
You in the nose
Sorry my wild lifestyle gives you a shock
I can't help it I'm PUNK ROCK!

(OH)

"The Punishment": Written during Dank's brief prison term for drunken driving, and reflecting his anguished awareness, during the month in question, that that month could never be restored to him, this is the story of a near-future dystopia that finds a new way to empty jails, punish malefactors, and deter potential malefactors. Instead of killing or incarcerating felons, the state calculates each convict's life expectancy and then, depending on the crime, medically subtracts so many years from that expectancy by injecting lethal time-bomb viruses set to go off when triggered by specific metabolic changes due in so many years. To boost the deterrent effect of this punishment—since many felons are shortsighted and unlikely to fret very much, at age twenty, about dying at sixty instead of seventy—the penal system also seeks to *age* them, both inside and out, by as many years as it is subtracting from their life expectancy. Special doctors age them both cosmetically (dewlap implants, facial *drops*, complete or partial balding via electrolysis, surgical wrinkling, liver-spot tattoos, simulated crow's feet and character lines) and with regard to general wellness, vigor, zest, and the like. As much as possible, the system seeks to fast-forward the convicts, to simulate the effects of a ten-year sentence, say, in the space of a few weeks of medical tampering, so that after a few weeks the convict is released looking and feeling ten years older, and society is spared the cost of incarcerating him for a decade.

Dank, as I say, spent a month in jail himself, an ordeal he later described as "almost as bad as junior high." He spent most of his time in the prison library, where the pickings were so slim that he resolved to read his way through an old set of *World Book* encyclopedias, and was up to F by the time they turned him loose. Even years later he was distinctly more knowledgeable on subjects beginning with the first six letters of the alphabet.

A B C D E F
G H I J K L
M N O P Q R
S T U V W X
Y Z

"Quitting Time": A mental institution in a bleak no-nonsense future employs a special triage nurse to decide which inmates should be allowed to kill themselves—which have no good reason to remain alive, and are suffering so much, with so little chance of improvement, that preventing them (even non-forcibly, with pep talks) from committing suicide is not just pointless but cruel.

Though not officially required or even encouraged to kill themselves, those granted the right are informed of the specialist's decision and assisted with means and advice. Our protagonist—the nurse in charge of recommending suicide—is initially appalled by her duties and reluctant to give up on anyone. Soon, however, she gets the hang of the job and even begins, as she grows more and more depressed herself (exposed, as she is day after day, to near-toxic levels of despair), to suggest to certain *non*-suicidal inmates that, as she likes say, "It's quitting time"—that they're more unhappy than they realize, have much less to live for than they think, and might just be better off dead. The climax comes when she is called before the institution's board of directors, who demand that she answer allegations about overstepping her directive. Instead of denying the charges, she roundly states that most of the directors—and addresses them by name, giving excellent reasons for each—would also be better off dead.

Dank made several attempts on his own life over the years, especially in 1993 after his third wife left him. The night he acknowledged (after a month of denial) that she was gone for good, he walked over to the Red Herring—the nearest thing in Hemlock to a singles bar—and did his best to interest a woman, any woman, in a suicide tryst (something he later said he'd "always been meaning to try"), but found no takers, not even when he dropped his demand for sex beforehand. So he went home alone, as usual, and swallowed a handful of sleeping pills but then immediately changed his mind and chased them with a handful of No-Doz. The results were ugly but non-fatal. He also changed his mind a few nights later when he tried to hang himself from a low bough of the tallest tree in his front yard—changed it the moment he kicked away the chair, and luckily for him the rope stretched just enough so that instead of twisting in the wind he found himself standing on tiptoe, unable to untie his slipknot, and stuck like that till the police showed up to cut him down.

The day after failing to hang himself, Dank stole a street-cleaning vehicle he'd found idling irresistibly in front of City Hall. When he refused a policeman's shouted order to end his ten-mile-per-hour joyride and pull over, a low-speed chase ensued. Dank eventually led his pursuers to his house, where he was unable to give the arresting officer any better explanation for his misbehavior than that he'd been "sick of walking." At his arraignment, Dank requested clemency on the grounds that after boarding the street cleaner, he had activated its sweeping mechanism (though he later told me he'd done that by accident, while trying to get the vehicle in gear), and that in consequence his crime (for which in the end he was fined) had done some good, in fact some community service: He'd swept the streets of his getaway route.

I myself have never attempted suicide, though I thought about it constantly during my six months in Clackamas (see ABRUPTOPHOBIA, THE ACADEMICIAN, THE ARCHITECT, THE COLLABORATION, HENRIETTA'S PERFORMANCE, and A MIDWINTER NIGHT'S DREAM). Since moving back to Hemlock about two months ago (it is February 21, 2007, as I write this), I've been less depressed but also much more anxious. I'm even beginning to wonder if it was such a good idea, coming back. In another entry I think I mentioned that, about a week after Dank's murder, I received an unexpected e-mail from Hirt (the one that led to our collaboration on this guide) and duly forwarded it to the Hemlock police. I soon regretted that law-abiding gesture: To my surprise, the police seemed less interested in Hirt and his involvement with the victim than in me and mine. Their suspicions were especially absurd because I'd moved out of Dank's house several weeks *before* his death. By the time of that tragic event, I no longer called Hemlock home, and in my reply to their menacing e-mail I calmly told the police that on the night Dank was killed I'd been in Portland—six hundred miles away.

I thought that that would be the end of it, but then I got *another* message from the police—while the ping of the first was still ringing in my ears—repeating their request, or demand, for my telephone number, my current address, and my availability to speak to them in person, i.e. in Hemlock. They also asked if I could "prove" I'd been in Portland on the night that Dank was killed. I've always wondered what police are thinking when they ask somebody not just to remember but to *document* his movements after a week has elapsed. Did they expect me to produce a convenience-store clerk with a calendric memory who could tell them, "Ah yes, I distinctly remember customer Boswell purchasing a package of Fig Newtons and a quart of chocolate milk from the Burnside Superette on the night in question"? I also marveled at their hubris, their autocratic manner with a man no longer living in their jurisdiction. So I didn't bother answering, but just used the "block sender" option to ensure that no more day-blighting e-summonses from the Keystone Kops would show up in my inbox. And in fact I never heard from them again.

But once they learn I'm back in town, I'll have some explaining to do.

A B C D E F
G H I J K L
M N O P Q R
S T U V W X
Y Z

"The Realists": In what may be Dank's single dumbest story—and I know how stiff the competition is—"hard-working scientists" make the astounding discovery that some physical objects are *more real* than others. Two peas in a pod may look alike and taste alike, but that doesn't mean they're equally real. The scientists develop "a special Geiger counter" that gauges the reality of a given pea—or pet, or person, or planet. Wealthy connoisseurs (or "Realists") cough up outrageous sums for the realest things they can find. A plastic ukulele with a sky-high Reality reading fetches more at Sotheby's than a rare but "only moderately real" Stradivarius. As for our lucky narrator, he goes from a starving fat man to a multi-millionaire when it turns out that everything in his house, from the mousetraps in the attic to the fuse box in the basement, is "unusually real."

It may be worth mentioning—insofar as anything can be where Dank is concerned—that "The Realists" was written during his infatuation with a TV show called *Antiques Roadshow*, in which a prissy expert glances at two ancient and equally hideous writing desks, say, and pronounces that one is worthless and one worth a trillion dollars. As for that Geiger counter, Dank himself would later try to invent such a gadget—see REALITY DETECTOR—but that doesn't make the story any less unlikely: If such a gadget did exist, its needle would remain at zero in the vicinity of "The Realists" or any of Dank's other works of fiction.

Needless to say where Dank is to blame, "The Realists" is an amorphous mess. As he himself once pointed out, at the onset of our brief abortive attempt at a COLLABORATION, Dank was no more than a content provider; *I* was the form imposer—the only time he ever said anything witty enough to bring home the truth of Chamfort's observation that "a fool who has a flash of wit is both astonishing and shocking, like a cab horse at a gallop." In the brilliant crowd I run with nowadays, among Chamfort's compatriots and modern counterparts, wit is so common that anyone who utters a *less*-than-witty string of words looks like a racehorse with a limp. I, of course, enjoy the chance to stretch my legs, effortlessly clearing any hurdles placed in my path by the trickier verbs. I try not to imagine what kind of figure poor Dank would've cut among my new *compagnons*. (OH)

Reality Detector: Sometimes, in the course of an ordinary day, some anomaly would give Dank a sudden hunch that he was dreaming, and he would try to wake up, closing his eyes, clenching his fists, squinching his face, and in general tensing every voluntary muscle. If he was trying to escape from a seated position—i.e., a dream, if in fact it *was* a dream, in which he happened to be sitting—he looked exactly like a man struggling mightily to move his bowels. Needless to say, this always caused a stir when it happened in public, as it did once at a Chinese restaurant when he saw a typo on the menu: "Human Stir-Fry." On that occasion, our waitress summoned the manager, who spoke even less English than she did, and I had my work cut out explaining just what Dank was and wasn't attempting to do.

After a few of these false alarms, Dank had the prudence, when the sense of unreality afflicted him in public, to seek out a rest room and try to wake himself up in one of the stalls, thus avoiding a scene just in case he *wasn't* dreaming. One afternoon I got a phone call from the Hemlock Public Library, whose employees had come to think of me as our eccentric author's keeper. The head librarian said that Dank had been in the men's room, in the handicapped stall, for more than an hour, grunting and groaning, and that a *real* paraplegic needed to use the toilet. I drove over—parking where a doctor would, in the no-parking zone out front—and after fifteen minutes managed to talk Dank out, without a flush because he hadn't gone in there to defecate. (Not that he never "multitasked" on such occasions, straining to wake up and defecating too—getting the chore out of the way—if he hadn't moved his bowels yet that day.) Later he told me that he'd been browsing in the reference section when he saw a box of pasta shelved between two dictionaries: That had done it.

In the spring of 1997, after an especially realistic nightmare, Dank became obsessed with developing a surefire way to distinguish reality from dreams, and vowed not to sleep again until he'd solved the problem. It took him eight days, and many hours in the basement, hammering and soldering. I want to stress that although as a boy he'd gone through an "Edison" phase, Dank as an adult reverted to Edison mode only when he'd been without sleep for several nights, and for that reason any discussion of his inventions is bound to give a misleading picture of his mental health. I'm willing to grant that he went briefly and harmlessly insane every time he'd been awake for more than forty-eight hours or so, but once he finally got to sleep, he always woke up sane.

Before he could go to sleep this time, though, he had to drag a mattress down to the basement, since his solution was too big to lug upstairs. According to its inventor, the Reality Detector enabled him to determine with better than ninety-nine percent certainty, just by twisting a few knobs, whether he had in fact awakened or was only dreaming he'd awakened.

The prototype of the device—crammed with vacuum tubes—was about the size of a refrigerator, but Dank also made plans for a compact bedside model that would rest on top of any sturdy nightstand, enabling the sleeper to determine his status before rashly getting out of bed.

Late one night the year before, at the height of yet another insomniac psychosis, Dank had "realized" that certain everyday objects—of the long list he recited, all I remember is pinochle decks, cuticle scissors, articulated buses, and the Barcelona chair—are "impossible to dream about." He'd gone to bed in triumph . . . only to have his theory exploded when, in the space of one horrendous nightmare, he dreamed of no fewer than seven of the items on his impossibles list. The Reality Detector, though was based on a more subtle version of that theory. It was possible (he now conceded) to dream of *anything*, even the Reality Detector—but that machine had been designed to behave in ways that a dream-replica could never convincingly mimic. The visible "behavior" of the machine was confined to seven needle gauges like those on a gas meter, calibrated in decimal fractions and multiples (from milli- to kilo-) of a *dank* (as, with atypical immodesty, he'd named the basic unit of reality). Below the seven gauges was a row of seven knobs, each affecting the reading on the dial above it. Dank claimed that in most cases he needed to consult only the milli- gauge to determine whether the machine was operating in a lifelike or in a dreamlike fashion. The indicator on the next dial over, the centi-, seldom moved any faster than the hour hand on a clock, and in a week of nightly use, the kilo- indicator (corresponding to what would be the epoch hand on a clock) budged only once, in what Dank recognized at once as a nightmare.

This madness lasted a week, and then one morning Dank woke up as sane as ever. Claiming he was sick of sleeping in the basement—since he couldn't very well come out and say he'd finally realized his machine was *in*sane—Dank enlisted my help in dragging his mattress back upstairs. He left the Reality Detector down in the dark to gather dust alongside the TIME MACHINE he'd built two years earlier, in the course of yet another long insomnia.

The Revelation: Far and away the longest thing Dank ever wrote, this four-thousand-page undertaking was inspired—dictated verbatim, according to Dank—by a mystical experience. That experience occurred on the night of July 17, 1993, or more probably the morning of July 18. Dank had been under unbearable stress: His third wife had left him, his bank account had bottomed out, and he'd just spent a month in jail for drunk driving (see THE MAN I KILLED). As if all that weren't bad enough, a mysterious skin condition, possibly psychosomatic, had been causing him to itch all over so insistently that he was scratching himself until he bled. The itch had baffled three different dermatologists since it first declared itself a few weeks earlier, just as Dank was putting the finishing touches on a novel about an intelligent though microscopic fungus from outer space, a fungus that enslaves humanity by afflicting us all with just such a skin condition. Soon, just like the earthlings in *The Seven-Light-Year Itch* (which by that point he'd destroyed, notes and all, lest his imagination infect the human race with terminal itchiness), Dank was unable to sleep at night unless he drugged himself to the point of general anesthesia. On the night in question, he'd run out of Unisom. There wasn't even any beer in the refrigerator—and since he was naked and coated from head to toe with Vapo-Rub, he couldn't very well walk over to Food Planet.

Dank was in his study when it happened. He'd gone in to rifle the bottom drawer of his desk, where he kept the little bottle of booze they'd given him the one time he flew first-class—kept as a reminder that he *had*, once, flown first class. Instead he found a little bottle of correction fluid, a substance that till then he had used only as instructed, though he'd heard of its bewitchments from the solvent-huffing cyberpunks he met at conventions. But he hesitated to abuse the stuff himself (feeling, perhaps, that for a writer it would be mixing business with pleasure). So he continued digging in the bottom drawer, but his ounce of airline scotch was gone.

He looked at the white plastic bottle again. On the back was a boxed warning:

INTENTIONAL MISUSE BY
DELIBERATELY CONCENTRATING
AND INHALING THE CONTENTS
CAN BE HARMFUL OR FATAL

He wondered how you went about "concentrating" White-Away with a view to getting high. Not by evaporation, surely, since it was the vapors themselves that did the trick. Maybe they meant not to concentrate your *thoughts*—he liked the idea that a psychotropic drug could be fatal if taken in the wrong frame of mind. He unscrewed the cap and held the bottle to his nose: The thick white liquid smelled like turpentine. Maybe it would cheer him up, if it couldn't knock him out. Maybe it would make him feel funny for a minute. That people tended, unless otherwise instructed, to inhale the stuff, on purpose, suggested that it must do *something*. That was good enough for Dank.

As he switched the bottle from his left to his right nostril, wondering exactly how posterity would judge a writer who committed suicide because he itched (and also wondering if his correction fluid would still be usable as such when he was done with this intentional misuse), his itch abruptly stopped. On his knees before the open drawer, he froze: Any motion might reawaken the itch. He forgot about the itch a moment later, though, when his study was suffused with a blue glow whose source Dank never would determine—maybe outer space, although his blinds were closed—and his mind suffused with words. Well, I guess his mind was always full of words, but now it was painfully crowded. The Light (as Dank refers to it in *The Revelation*, with a capital letter befitting a sentient being) flickered and vanished, and Dank grabbed a pencil. A full day later he was still transcribing, though after forty-seven pages a bad cramp had forced him to put down the pencil, or rather its successor, and boot up his computer. And still he hadn't eased the pressure of words wanting out (it was, he later told me, like one of those dreams where you stand at the toilet and keep pissing without ever easing your bladder). He was exhilarated but also terrified, fearing that the itch had migrated to his brain the better to drive him mad. And yet one of the first things the Light had told him—or one of the first he'd transcribed, of the millions it had told him simultaneously—was that the itch had been a test, and that he, Dank, had passed.

He was less relieved than disappointed the following day when the pressure finally did let up and, after a few more pages dribbled out, the flow stopped altogether. Disappointed, because he knew he'd released only a small fraction of the Light's disclosures. For the next month, Dank tried everything he could think of to lure it back—to repeat the vision MacDougal would later describe as "a cut-rate epiphany, a Blue-Light Special"—by reproducing the circumstances as closely as possible. In addition to huffing his way through several dozen little bottles of correction fluid, Dank went so far as to camp out in his study and to rub himself, every night at bedtime, first with poison ivy and then with Vapo-Rub. He never did succeed in rekindling the Light—which is probably just as well, from a psychiatric standpoint—but for the rest of his life, off and on, he struggled to recall its message. *The Revelation* is the paper trail of that struggle.

Needless to say, I was eager to see it, but Dank, though always glad to show me other works in progress, refused to let me read *The Revelation*. He even kept it locked up in a big safe in his study—not to protect it from me, he insisted, but to protect *me* from *it*: Like *The Seven-Light-Year Itch*, the book was potentially lethal, a virus of truth that could wipe out our whole species. When the safe was finally opened by a locksmith a few days ago—on February 21, 2007—the manuscript inside, almost three feet high when put in one stack, proved to be written in a code that so far I haven't cracked. The epigraph, a common misquotation from *The Tempest*—"We are such stuff as dreams are made of"—is uncoded, but the rest all sounds like this (to quote just the first line): "sdf90 34qmc n%4aa cy80r env40 t9gn4 guj58 nnm@d 490vn 33d#z dg0n0." Judging by that epigraph and by Dank's bizarre conviction, late in life, that he was not a real person (see WHAT NEXT?), my hunch is that the truth encoded in those several thousand pages probably concerned illusion and reality. Or not. Dank refused to tell me even that, though once when pressed he did say that *The Revelation* wasn't like a virus so much as a wonder drug: If taken as directed, it "could make everybody feel better," but it had a dangerous potential for abuse. If so, the encryption is like a child-proof cap: Only when humanity is advanced enough to crack the code can it be trusted with the contents.

The Revolt of the Unsung*:* Ghostwriters, speechwriters, understudies, body doubles, bodyguards bigger and badder than the boxers they protect, teaching assistants for famous professors, canny wives of cloddish statesmen, nameless and faceless but gifted musicians backing and boosting flamboyant but talent-less frontmen—in this early novel they all band together and rebel. Some of them already belong to unions, but they decide that those unions (Musicians, Actors, and so on) don't ad-equately represent their interests—that, predictably, the exist-ing unions are in complicity with the existing distribution of glory. And so, led by a heroic young ghostwriter, they form a new cross-professional union for the unsung talent support-ing the so-often-overrated—or at any rate complacent, flabby, laurel-propped, no-longer-hungry—stars. They strike for more money, of course, but also for more recognition. And the strike is a success. Special lawyers and courts emerge to determine who is the *real* talent behind a given performance or production and award top billing accordingly. The radical edge of Dank's fable is blunted at the end, however, by the ironic—and prophetic—"twenty years later" epilogue: The former understudies and assistants, now famous themselves, have taken to hiring their own unsung lackeys to do the real work. Like so many other successful revolutionaries, they rep-licate the abuses they set out to overturn.

The book has an interesting history. Written in 1981, while Dank was making ends meet by working as a typist for an-other, slightly more successful science fiction writer who must be nameless here (as he was in my entry for THE HEAD PRO-TECTOR, which he also inspired), *Revolt* reflects Dank's theory, in those days, that literary success has less to do with talent or hard work than with careerism, connections, clubbability, photogenicity, dumb luck, and so on. Although he'd ostensibly been hired for his speed as a typist (eighty wpm, with surpris-ingly few typos for someone so erratic in everyday life), Dank soon realized, as so many typists have, that he was expected to do more than type. He let me listen once to a recording of his employer's "dictation," a recording he'd held onto as especially damning evidence, and it sounded less like a book on tape than a notebook on tape:

> Um, so the spaceship lands right on the White House lawn, and when the door opens, of the spaceship I mean, you know, it's one of those doors like on *Get Smart* that automatically raise up, and, um, this little, um, like, gangplank extends out and the aliens, there's like fifty of them, at *least*, and they go down the gangplank, they look like giant ants, and, uhh, they're all waving these weird things that kinda look like guns, but from another galaxy, and then the Secret Service guys . . .

Dank had effectively been hired, and for not much more than he'd have earned flipping burgers, to ghostwrite books that somehow sold better than his own, and yet he was forced to maintain the pretense—not only publicly, but even one-on-one with his self-satisfied employer—that he, Dank, was no more than a typist.

He had his revenge in *The Revolt of the Unsung*, where the odious arch-villain—a flagrantly overrated hack who leads the fight against the understudies—is modeled on Dank's employer. At the time, it must have seemed to Dank that he himself would always be on the side of the underdogs, those with more merit than acclaim. Twenty years later, though, he realized that he'd joined the exploiters, or at least might be perceived as having done so. That was during the attack of incapacitating laziness that led Dank to farm out the writing of his books to salaried underlings. Financially there was no question of exploitation—none of the books of that strange era came close to recouping the salaries of his assistants—but Dank still knew he'd laid himself open to charges of hypocrisy.

Right around the time he started his PRODUCTION LINE, he also contemplated tracking down, buying up, and destroying every last copy of *The Revolt of the Unsung* in private hands. What dissuaded him from this quixotic plan was not my argument that it would surely backfire, calling *more* attention to the compromising book, but his laziness: At the time he was too weak even to get out of bed.

Rocket Roy: In this hermit's variation on the "Cozy Catastrophe" genre, Roy, a "leading astronaut," is chosen for a one-way trip to outer space—a solo flight, with no hope of landfall and no means of keeping in touch with the rest of his species but a radio that becomes less and less useful as the growing distance between Roy and Houston makes for gaps of months and finally years between his words and theirs. On the other hand, Roy's giant rocket has a life's supply of all his favorite foods (barbecue potato chips, lime Jell-O, Nutter Butters, Sgt. Popp); a full run of *Playboy*s (and no doubt a life's supply of Vaseline and Kleenex); every episode of *Star Trek*, *Lost in Space*, and *Dr. Who* (on bulky videocassettes—Dank's "astonishing" imagination failed to envision DVDs); and "the thousand greatest Science Fiction novels of all time," though you'd think that even Roy, after years in outer space, might get a little sick of all those flying saucers, Martians, clones, and bug-eyed monsters—might wish he'd spared a little shelf space in his rocket's library for "mundanes" like Dickens, or at least for fiction set back in the world he'll never see again.

Rocket Roy is nothing but a daydream dating from its author's early boyhood, though the *Playboy*s were inserted later. To those of us who love our lives and love our unrestricted access to the surface of the Earth—who love to snorkel in the clear blue waters of a coral reef, then lie on the beach at the side of an actual flesh-and-blood woman, as I did yesterday—Roy's rocket sounds like an especially cramped and lonely hell. To an agoraphobic onanist like Dank, of course, that rocket was a vision of Valhalla. (OH)

Ruefle, Billy Ray (1959–2006): The last of the nomads who over the years rushed into Dank's life and under his roof to fill the vacuum left by a departing wife or, in this case, old friend, insofar as Hirt had ever been Dank's friend. Whatever he had been, he'd been it for twenty-eight years by the spring of 1999, when the two stopped speaking forever (see next entry), so their quarrel left a real void. Moved as much by pity as by fear of another perpetual houseguest like LIPS, I did my best to fill that void myself, or at least to keep my lonely-hearted landlord entertained with quips and quotes until he got accustomed to the void. (And if Robert Frost could be acquainted with the night, surely Dank could be accustomed to the void.) I even canceled classes for a week so I could spend more time with him (and screen out phone calls from potential spongers).

A few weeks after his quarrel with Hirt—an episode that left him painfully self-conscious about his public image—Dank learned that someone was impersonating him at SF conventions. This impersonator was using Dank's prestige with fans—as Dank himself had never successfully used it—to seduce the ones with two X chromosomes. I was furious and wanted Dank to sue, but he was too pleased by the impression the impostor had made on his behalf. The fanzine that first alerted our author to the existence of his doppelgänger spoke of how Dank—looking fitter, even taller, than ever before—had been the wittiest and most well-spoken panelist at the Decatur convention.

Dank, in those days, was finding the burden of Dankhood too heavy to bear by himself. Like the twins in THE COLLABORATION, who decide it's too much trouble each to perform all the functions of a separate individual, Dank now found it too much trouble to perform both the private and the public functions of a writer. At that point he still enjoyed the private part, the writing per se, but he could no longer face the rest of the job. The interviews, the readings, the schmoozing at conventions, talking to reporters, scowling for photographers, answering his fan mail—it was all too much for Dank. He needed a proxy. Rather than sending Ruefle an order to cease and desist, Dank sent him a ticket to Hemlock, though Ruefle chose instead to ride here on his Harley-Davidson instead. For the next three months he lived with us.

Ruefle did look like Dank—a rather more attractive Dank, and a slimmer one as well, just eighty pounds overweight instead of a hundred and eighty. He was also a much better dresser, and much more at ease in the limelight, which Dank gladly ceded since he'd always found it blinding, even at the shamefully low wattage with which it shone on him in his lifetime. Anyone who knew Dank from cover photos only, though, or who hadn't seen him for a decade in the flesh, would have had no trouble shrugging off the differences between the two, on being presented with Ruefle and told it was Dank on a diet. Even I was fooled the first time I saw Ruefle on his motorcycle: For a moment of sheer terror that now strikes me as prophetic, I thought it was actually Dank on that hog, though Dank could barely stay astride his ride-on mower.

Ruefle not only resembled our author, but had a talent for impersonations, and at least once tricked me by answering the phone as Dank. That soon became part of his job: answering the phone for Dank, *as* Dank. If *I* answered and the caller asked for Dank, my instructions were to give the phone to Ruefle. Even if it was Dank's mother.

Unlike his predecessor LIPS (whose room he inherited), Ruefle was good company—so fond of impersonations, and so good at them, that he could make a tête-à-tête feel like a dinner party. Sometimes he'd go for hours without ever lapsing into the lazy Southern drawl that as far as I could tell was the real voice of his real self, insofar as he still had a real voice or self. Though I'd dreaded his arrival, I soon found myself gravitating toward him, now that Dank was less available than ever: It had become depressingly clear that *part* of the public life our author no longer enjoyed was his meals with me. He was my best friend but, but that's not how he thought of me. He still saw me as the scholar who'd portray—*be*tray?—him to posterity. When we ate together, it obliged him to put on a public face in his own house.

So I sometimes went for days without a glimpse of Dank. I ate my dinners with Ruefle instead, and he seemed to like my company as much as I did his. (Later I discovered, I admit, that his companionship, the time he spent with me, had been part of Ruefle's job—one of the things expected of him in exchange for room and board. But I still flatter myself that he *enjoyed* that part of the job.) I hoped he would stick around. I even found myself concerned about his safety. Dank liked the idea of appearing to the world as a free-wheeling, fun-loving, hard-living biker, but I fretted every time that biker thundered off into the night with a pint of bourbon in his bloodstream. Maybe it was for the best (though at the time it drove me to tears of self-pity) that after a few months, Ruefle moved across the bay to play house with a "dancer" he had met in a topless bar. He continued, though, for two more years, to impersonate Dank on public occasions, allowing our author to grow ever stranger in private.

A B C D E F
G H I J K L
M N O P Q R
S T U V W X
Y Z

The Sadiators: In a polluted, overheated, overcrowded future where life is so grim that the average person's will to live is dangerously feeble, mortal combat is the favorite form of public entertainment. Combatants kill, though, not with "real" weapons but with words. Premised on the notion that it is just as possible to talk people *into* suicide as talk them out of it, this disturbing novel envisions a society where mortal enemies settle their disputes with verbal "suicide duels"—legal, rule-governed conversations that continue until one contestant persuades the other to end the contest by committing suicide.

Often the opponents know each other well and have decided after years of embittered coexistence that the world simply isn't big enough for both of them. (Dank imagines a population crisis that helps explain the popularity of this highbrow blood sport.) Some of the combatants, though—the Sadiators*—are professionals: cruel, ruthless, thick-skinned, sharp-tongued critics of their fellow men, quick to spot a weakness, a sore point, a raw nerve, no matter how skillfully concealed.

The plot of the novel involves a greenhorn hero who takes on a famous Sadiator—the victor of his twenty-seven previous

---

* So called, presumably, because they kill by saddening, as if gladiators killed by *gladdening*. In other words, the title is as stupid as the story to which it's attached. (OH)

bouts—in revenge for the death of the hero's two older brothers in earlier duels. I won't spoil the book by saying who wins, but some of the details of the institution Dank imagines are worth mentioning. Professional duels serve as a form of legalized barbarity, sanctioned as entertainment, but there are still rules, as in a formal debate: Duelists take turns speaking for set periods, and while one is speaking the other must suffer in silence. Opponents face each other in electric chairs, and each has only to punch in a three-digit code on a keypad to turn on the juice, so that even a moment or so of despair can be lethal. A duel has no time limit and doesn't end until one contestant surrenders and electrocutes himself. The longest duel, we are told, dragged on for nearly seven months (though with adjournments for sleep), while the all-time fastest win was sixteen seconds. Bouts are divided into hour-long rounds with five-minute breathers in between. Most duelists have "cheerer uppers," seconds whose function is akin to that of corner men in boxing—dressing cuts, toweling off blood and sweat, giving pep talks and tips ("Probe his second marriage more—that's his real weak spot").

It is considered unwise for professionals to duel more than once a year, or amateurs more than once in a lifetime. Even a quick and lopsided win leaves the winner wounded. Sometimes, indeed, the fights kill *both* combatants: The apparent victor also commits suicide, days or years or decades after the duel proper, as the opponent's words finally find their mark, like an ultimately fatal sword or gunshot wound incurred by the official victor in an ordinary duel.

Dank wrote *The Sadiators* after an atrocious argument with Hirt. The argument ended their friendship forever, and really did leave Dank with thoughts of suicide, so I'd better explain how it happened.

Elsewhere I've alluded to my efforts at befriending Hirt, my failure, my disappointment, and the dinner at his house where my frustrations came to a head. The next few times he came to *our* house for dinner, as he did all too often in that era, I made a point of boycotting the meal and holing up in my room on the pretext of a stomachache. You'd assume, or I assumed, that sooner or later Dank would ask me why I always had a stomachache when Hirt came over. The question would have given me an opening to air my grievances against his unspeakable friend, but as I've said elsewhere, Dank was not a noticer, and I doubt he ever detected a pattern to my absences.

Sometimes when I heard laughter I'd leave my room and tiptoe back down to the landing to eavesdrop. I never caught them talking about me, but more than once I heard Hirt saying something rude about Dank or his books—books that I too had a stake in, after all, as the world's foremost Dankian. "So, would you number AMNESIA among your twenty worst books?" Hirt would ask, or "So, which of your novels are you least ashamed of?" or (when Dank said he'd never considered writing until he met Hirt) "Took you that long to figure out you were even worse at everything else, huh?" I told myself they were old friends, with a tradition of persiflage dating back to senior high, but the teasing was oddly one-sided: I never once heard Dank make fun of Hirt, either to his face or behind his back. And though Dank always laughed off Hirt's disparagements—as if that were the price of friendship with a fellow writer less successful but more vain and self-important than himself—*I* found it harder to laugh. It was as if some guest kept insulting my spouse.

At the same time, I almost envied Hirt his freedom to criticize Dank's writing. I don't mean that Dank let Hirt say things he wouldn't have taken from me. I mean that I was muzzled by personality. My compulsively ingratiating manner wouldn't let me vent the occasional impatient and ungrateful sentiments that anyone is bound to feel for any person, place, or thing he spends his life inspecting, contemplating, and discussing.

Hirt, anyhow—to get back to the origins of *The Sadiators*—was making me an outcast in my own house. It was intolerable. Luckily, a few months after the dinner that sealed my hatred of him (see PASS THE BRAINS and see what I put up with), a murderous review of COME, SWEET DEATH, the brand-new Agent Harder novel, was published in the *Hemlock Herald* under Hirt's name. ("The newspaper is the natural enemy of the book, as the whore is of the decent woman," say the Goncourts.) The minute I saw the review, I hastened to show it to Dank, who of course had had his share of bad reviews, but few so malicious as this one. And as far as he knew, it was the first time *Hirt* had ever attacked him in print. In conversation, as I say, Dank's oldest "friend" made little effort to conceal his low opinion of Dank's talents and the uses to which they'd been put.

Until now, though, Hirt had never felt the need to holler his opinions from the rooftops. A bad review for everyone to read—that was crossing a line. Dank fumed about Hirt's treachery for days, but didn't mention it to Hirt until the latter finally called as if nothing had happened. (One of the tacit rules of their friendship was that Hirt called Dank and not vice versa, since it was understood that Dank had time for Hirt whenever Hirt could fit him in.) When Dank brought up the review, Hirt had the audacity to say he hadn't written it. He hadn't even *read* the novel in question, he said, and *that* much may be true, but since when do reviewers need to read the books they ravage? MACDOUGAL devoted a page and a half, in his murderous book about Dank, to a nonexistent novel called *What If the Nazis Won the Civil War?*, a title that some prankster at the house that published ROCKET ROY had added to that volume's list of Books by the Same Author, and that had been routinely carried over to subsequent lists.

Hirt's refusal to admit to writing the *Herald* review was especially galling to Dank because the piece was clearly an "insider" job, getting personal in a way that none of Dank's other detractors could have gotten, not even MacDougal. And the prose also pointed to Hirt: It was the same blend of vanity and venom ("the same old sausage, fizzing and sputtering in its own grease," as Henry James described Carlyle) with which readers of this guide must by now be only too familiar, the blend Hirt plainly favors for invective. His attack focused on what he called Dank's "split personality . . . the chasm between his mousy private self and manly public pose":

> *"Pay no attention to that man behind the curtain!"* bellows Dank's brawny authorial persona, implying in every ponderous sentence that his hypermasculine protagonists—square-jawed, hard-assed, hairy-chested thugs like Agent Harder, who routinely pummels muggers, picks fistfights with strangers, and smacks his wife for asking him to fetch some Tampax on the way home from the gun show—are based on the author himself. In point of fact, the author is a bespectacled fat man who flinches whenever a stranger approaches, gets trapped indoors for weeks on end by sheer agoraphobia, and once or twice, while having sex with his (much older) second wife, blurted out his mother's name . . .

And Hirt insisted that he hadn't written that! To my delight, a bitter argument ensued between the two "old friends." They hung up friends no more, with Dank saying, in effect, "You're envious," and Hirt, "Whoever did write that review was right—you *are* a terrible writer." I'm pleased to say he never again came over for dinner.

Dank, though, was so traumatized by their last conversation (especially devastating because he hadn't yet recovered from Pandora and the blow *she'd* dealt his self-esteem) that after hanging up he tried to kill himself. I was at school that day, meeting with Chairman MacDougal to discuss my student evals (theirs of me, that is), or rather to let him berate me while I hung my head and thought of better times, like the time MacDougal slipped and hit his head on the icy pavement of the teachers' parking lot, or the time he got so ill at our department's yearly potluck dinner. I had walked to campus, and Dank seized the opportunity to use my car. He tried to kill himself in the garage, behind the wheel, with the engine running, windows open, and garage door closed, but—luckily for him and for posterity, or as much of it as still likes a good read—he ran out of gas.

Dank could never bring himself to repeat the words that had made him want to die, just as I can barely stand to copy out my students' more obnoxious allegations ("Dr. Boswell acts all nice at first, but if you piss him off he's like the Incredable Hulk"; "It was *supposed* to be a class on Virginia Woolf, but he kept changing the subject to some stupid sci-fi writer"; "This [Masters of the Modern Novel] is the worst class of all time. BOOZE-well made us buy a stupid Xerox of his own retarded novel and we wasted four whole classes on it even though it isn't even published"). Dank did tell me, though, that Hirt had announced his own decision to stop writing—to stop casting his pearls before swine. Almost the last thing Hirt ever said to Dank, in fact, was that writing is a waste of time—a selfish, private, solipsistic, and unwholesome vice, like masturbation, only pretentious. Hirt, for one, had better things to do. *He* preferred Life to Art.[*]

---

[*] (October 2007) As far as I know, he went on preferring Life right up to the day of his suicide in the summer of 2007. See—in due time—Yours Truly.

Dank recovered from his enemy's near-fatal words, though for the rest of his life he kept reliving their fatal conversation, giving himself the good lines for a change, and remembering (as he'd forgotten at the time) to ask Hirt for the treasured first edition of *The Moon Is a Harsh Mistress* Dank had lent him ("I know you don't like science fiction, but *this* one is different") not long before they stopped speaking forever.

Dank never did make another attempt on his life. What he did instead was vacate a big part of it, the public part, as a man with two houses might abandon the one plagued by vandals, or a man who can no longer afford to heat his whole house might close off half of it. Except that Dank didn't so much abandon his public self as let someone else inhabit it rent-free—see Ruefle, Billy Ray.

The Salt Factory: In April 1993, following a heart attack that Dank himself attributed to a broken heart, his doctor placed him on a low-sodium diet—a real deprivation for Dank, who even as a child had favored salty snacks and had always spent his allowance, on his weekly trips to the candy store, on a little bag of chips and not a candy bar. In May 1993, our salt-deprived author embarked on a novel about a visionary entrepreneur named Sal who sells a line of table salts extracted from human tears. Sal employs a crew of Weepers to sit around all day eating saltines, drinking water, and reading tearjerkers or listening to tearful music or watching tear-provoking movies in his screening room, all while wearing special goggles designed to intercept the Weepers' tears and conduct them to the dehydrating apparatus. Even though Sal pays these workers only minimum wage for their undemanding and cathartic work, the salt itself is expensive—not as expensive as saffron, but almost—and meant to be used only for very special, festive, delicately seasoned dishes. The tiny packets come in numerous

varieties, classified either by the tear-provoking stimulus—
Ordinary People, Chopin's *Preludes*, Death of Little Nell—or
by the demographics of the weepers: orphans, adolescent girls,
lovelorn poets, homeless men with chronic depression, elderly
women. (Connoisseurs agree that the tears of elderly women
make for the most subtle and thought-provoking salt.) Sal
also thinks of selling Rich Man's Tears in little vials, but can't
because—not one himself—he is unable to find a rich man
willing to weep for an hourly wage.

Sal's products do well enough to inspire a competitor, Sol,
who undersells the hero by offering a distinctly inferior product—derived from tears, all right, but tears evoked by onions,
which of course produce a much more copious and depend-
able flow than even the saddest works of art. (*Sal's* employees
are forbidden even to eat onions, or garlic, or any of a dozen
other pungent foods for which he subjects them to periodic uri-
nanalytical spot checks.) The resulting salt is harsher and less
interesting, and tainted, too, with a faint onion overtone, as if
compelled to tell the world that it was elicited by a crude physi-
ological reflex in which human feelings, hopes and disappoint-
ments, memories, sympathies, rages and fears, played no part.

Though the withdrawal pangs that came with his new low-
salt diet may have suggested the plot of the novel, Dank had
always been intrigued by the idea of somehow *harnessing sorrow*, since it's such a cheap and inexhaustible resource. He said
once that the man or woman who finally found gainful employment for sorrow would be as big a benefactor to humanity as Lips would if he ever perfected a cheap, efficient way
to make salt water potable (one of the many get-rich-quick
schemes in which Lips had enlisted Dank as an investor). And
nothing is more plentiful than salt water. I replied that a machine for harnessing sorrow had already been invented, that
art itself is just such a contraption (though a versatile one that

does other things as well, or almost as well), and that Dank's own art, so busy with psychic and physical pain, was a perfect case in point. He'd harnessed his own sorrow so efficiently that it not only paid the bills, and gave his readers countless hours of enjoyment, but left hardly any residue of unprocessed misery. That's why Dank's life must be adjudged a happy one, though crowded with misfortunes: He couldn't even stub a toe without converting his tears into art (see THE TOE)—into a special name-brand seasoning to make his readers' otherwise-insipid lives more savory. And how could the proprietor of such a thriving saltworks *not* be happy?

Second Thoughts: A whole book of short stories about strange *revisions*: a chef at a fancy restaurant recalling a patron's meal several minutes after it's been served because he's had a brilliant afterthought involving tarragon; an architect remodeling one of his houses without the owners' permission (he waits until they're on vacation and returns with a construction crew); a skywriter climbing back into his plane to publicly retract a message, after finally tasting the soft drink he's been touting and deciding that it isn't as delicious as he made the heavens claim; a middle-aged neurotic, with all sorts of "issues" regarding his dead parents, who rewrites the text on their gravestone several times a year—though each time it means buying a new stone—following each "breakthrough" in his never-ending therapy; a surgical perfectionist re-anesthetizing and reopening an unsuspecting patient (during what's supposed to be a simple follow-up exam) in order to clear away some of the unacceptably ugly scar tissue the surgeon knows to be lurking in there; a writer recalling a thousand-page novel—buying up and burning every copy in existence—because of a single belatedly-seen error, a dangling modifier, that he can't bear to let stand.

The Selected Poem of Phoebus K. Dank: A privately printed chapbook, less selective than it sounds because Dank was not a poet, or very seldom a poet: He published just three poems in his lifetime, which works out to roughly one every seventeen years. The one that made the cut was occasioned by his learning that his third ex-wife, who a few years earlier had left him for a better novelist, had just left *him* for a poet. Good for her. The untitled piece consists of 256 lines of blank verse. It begins:

> One day when I was walking slowly down
> The street I had a thought that almost made
> Me faint . . .

and ends:

> Or so at least it struck me on that dark
> Day when I, Dank, was walking down the street.

At one point, the speaker passes an old friend's house and thinks of telling *him* about the thought, but the old friend isn't home. I was less lucky on countless occasions when Dank and I both lived—too close for comfort—on Empedocles. He especially liked to drop by in the evening, when I sat in my living room trying to read. Otherwise he seldom left his house and had forgotten how to knock on doors—especially a problem since he'd once received a shock from a defective doorbell and no longer rang them. One night while reading a biography of Nollekins, I heard a scratching sound, or rather realized that I'd been hearing one for several minutes. I traced the noise to my front door and yanked it open to discover Dank (indignant about the delay). Another night he made me jump, and hurt his hand, by slamming a fat fist against that door—not in anger but to test a new and more efficient knock that had just occurred to him: one mighty thump instead of a series of diffident raps. His extraliterary innovations were as clueless as his literary ones.

But back to the selected poem. Readers curious about the rather adolescent "thought" that almost made its thinker faint (in a nutshell: You can never know another person since everybody has a public persona that hides the True Self), or in Dank's two other poems (a sonnet and a limerick), will find them, some day soon, in the posthumous vanity volume of uncollected scribblings stipulated by their author's will. Those poems, in fact, are three of the best reasons to avoid that needless volume when it appears, since, as the lines above make all too clear, Dank was even more inept as a versifier than as a novelist. (OH)

Serial Killers: MacDougal, in his rabid and libelous book, makes a fuss about the fact that Dank's works include "no fewer than" four novels involving serial killers. (MacDougal didn't live to see the fifth.) He infers that Dank himself is "a latent sociopath," whom "only cowardice and sloth prevent . . . from acting out his lethal fantasies." But if Dank did in fact have "an unhealthy obsession," it was one he shared with the wider reading public. Even I, a mild-mannered academic, knew as much as he did about serial killers, especially as of September 2000, when I did a little research on the subject in connection with a course on serial-murder mysteries. I've done a bit more research in the six and a half years since then (it is March 2007, and the crocuses in Hemlock seem as surprised by their reactivation as I am by mine). I've done enough to see myself as something of an expert, and certainly enough to have amassed a store of trivia. I know, for example, that serial killers tend to be white males. Another blemish on our transcript. I know they differ from mass murderers as much as serial monogamists differ from orgiasts. I know that to qualify as an official serial killer, you must take at least three lives (just as, to be a saint, you must perform three miracles), and on three separate occasions. I can imagine a felon hesitating before murder #3: Does he really want to cross that line and go from just an ordinary man who got indignant on a couple of "occasions" to that ultimate pariah and box-office favorite, the full-blown serial killer?

Sight Unseen: Now out of print, and surely out to stay, this novel was published pseudonymously as the opus of an author blind from birth. *Sight Unseen*, in other words, is a crass and shameless effort to redeem a half-assed premise, and exalt its slipshod execution, by ascribing them (with the collusion of the seedy other agent Dank retained for his more shady dealings on Grub Street) to a disadvantaged Other for whom any book at all would be a brave accomplishment. Long before the ugly truth about its authorship leaked out, the book—ostensibly the true confessions of a blind Lothario—was roundly denounced: With no humorous intent, Dank makes his persona a latter-day Mr. Magoo, bumping into buildings, falling into manholes, picking up and speaking into hair dryers instead of telephones, and so on. Even worse, the guy is absurdly unable to tell his six lovers apart, whether by voice or feel or scent, and so must take their word for it that each is who she claims to be. Midway through the book, when he decides to settle down and gets engaged to the lover named Lucy, the other five all start *impersonating* Lucy.[*] (OH)

---

[*] Once again, Hirt misinterprets a book by failing to hear its sonorous personal resonance. Dank himself was a bit of a Mr. Magoo, and if he never walked into an open manhole, that's only because chance—more merciful than in cartoons—never placed one in his path.

After decades of rubbing elbows with writers and teachers (since I have one tweedy, suede-patched elbow in each camp), I'm convinced that absent-minded novelists are just as common as absent-minded professors.

"Sleight of Hand": In this story (whose title was "Hand Job" until I told Dank what that phrase ordinarily means), a flaky New Ager named Maya undergoes surgery on her palms so that the lines will foretell a longer life, a happy marriage, and so on. Her disreputable surgeon botches the job, though, and so botches Maya's fate.

According to his notebook, Dank got the idea for the story while doing the dishes (the only time he really noticed his own hands—and, according to Agatha Christie, "the best time for planning a book"), way back in 1980, but it wasn't written till July 2001, and not by Dank, who wasn't writing his own stories at that point. And as long as I'm discussing sleight of hand, I invite the reader to pause and marvel at the conjuring trick that Dank's career had become as of July 2001. By then, "Phoebus K. Dank," the noted science fiction writer, was as fictional a figure as Aunt Jemima, Ronald McDonald, or Franklin W. Dixon—no longer a man but a brand name. It might have seemed, to his brand-loyal readers, that the same old hatchet was hacking its way through the forest of symbols, but in fact he had replaced both the handle and the blade, delegating the public part of the job to RUEFLE and the private to the crew of sullen fictioneers who made up the PRODUCTION LINE.

We think of novelists as more alert and more observant, but that's just because they're better at PR. Dank himself—the greatest writer of his time— was the *least* observant person ever. During the Pandora muddle, he tore through a pot of lipstick-red impatiens playing "loves me, loves me not," hoping in vain for just one favorable verdict, cursing Fate with every ravished flower, and never noticing that all impatiens have four petals. But just as there are excellent astronomers who never look through telescopes, there are remarkable writers—think of Borges—who never look up from their books to inspect the real world, but instead perform all kinds of thrilling calculations with the data amassed by other observers. (BB)

And speaking of Ruefle: One wet November night he crashed his motorcycle, landed on his head, and (though he'd been wearing a helmet for once) lost the use of all four limbs. It will give some idea of how far things had gone by November 2001 that neither I nor Dank saw any reason why quadriplegia should disqualify Ruefle from impersonating Dank as he'd been doing for the past two years. Even without the use of his limbs, Ruefle still came across as more active, manly, and outdoorsy than his employer (who by then was bedridden by simple indolence). Ruefle, however, wanted now to focus on the task of being Ruefle.

S.P.U.D.: A book of linked short stories, set in 2027, about people with unlikely handicaps. It's implied but never stated that their problems are due to the same polluted atmosphere—thick with mutagens, carcinogens, teratogens, and even a new threat called psychopathogens—that beclouds so much of Dank's near-future science fiction. The title is an acronym for the support group to which they belong, and whose weekly meetings frame the stories: the Society for People with Uncommon Disabilities. Each week a different member expounds, to the best of his or her abilities, on some outlandish disability, and each account takes the form of a story:

Adam is unable to descend stairways, though perfectly able to climb them.

Bess is unable to process data from more than one sense at a time, which means she can't make sense of television because either the sound or the picture is missing.

Chuck can't remember his plans from one moment to the next: He goes into the kitchen for a sandwich, forgets what he's there for, and returns to his study empty-handed.

Dawn's mood is affected only by misfortunes: She wakes up cheerful but gets more and more depressed as the day wears on, since as long as she's awake, her state of mind can only worsen. By bedtime she is almost always contemplating suicide, and often she has to call it a day by mid-afternoon, go upstairs, draw the blinds, and crawl under the covers before anything can happen to depress her even further.

Eric, Frieda, Greg, and Helen find it impossible to multitask while walking—to walk and chew gum, say, or walk and talk, or walk and whistle—and fall over if they try.

Ivan, a construction worker, can't control the volume of his voice when he's upset. We see him frantically mumbling inaudible warnings to a buddy about to be squashed by a falling girder . . . and then a few days later bellowing condolences to the victim's widow at the funeral.

Janet is unable to distinguish retrospectively between dreams and memories of actual events: Those who don't consider her psychotic call her a compulsive liar.

Kent is unable to bend at the waist.

Lydia can't seem to speak a declarative sentence (not even one as inoffensive as "It's beginning to rain") without instantly, compulsively, retracting her assertion, as if compelled to remain noncommittal even on the least controversial subjects.

Other tales concern inabilities to spit, to belch, to sneeze, to yawn, to blink, and the surprisingly dire repercussions of each deficit. Dank himself had some unheard-of disabilities, though most his were not innate but acquired, just as the corresponding skills had been. He had simply gotten out of practice and forgotten how to do the thing in question. (The final tragic worsening of his agoraphobia was partly due to his long bout of hypochondriac fatigue, during which he got out of practice at going outside.) Thus, after an especially singleminded writing binge in 1990—when, in his determination to finish TESLA'S REVENGE, he'd gone for weeks without leaving the house or even getting dressed—he found he'd forgotten how to tie his shoes. He still remembered how to do *something* with the laces that looked a little like the knot he'd learned in nursery school, but unlike that one, this one never stayed knotted for more than a minute. Instead of relearning the skill, he gave up on it, gave all his shoes to Goodwill, and bought a bunch of loafers.

Dank sometimes worried that his disabilities, if they got any worse, would reduce him to a basket case before his time, "barely able" (in his colorful expression) "to wipe [his] own ass." In 1991, he drew up a checklist of skills to practice daily: sharpening a pencil, peeling an orange, making a sandwich, microwaving something (often the sandwich), and speaking to a stranger (though most days he settled for dialing someone picked at random from the slender Hemlock phone book, asking for me, and then apologizing for getting the wrong number—a practice that must slowly have been making me famous in the local calling area).

"The Stray": In addition to the five Agent Harder novels, Dank also wrote a short story in which the special agent matches wits with a serial-killing *dog*, a rabid pit bull given to savaging people who remind him of the ones who abused him in the past.

Elsewhere (see INSOMNIA) I've mentioned FFI, the rare and lethal disease that ran in Dank's family. Though a blood test had established that Dank himself was free of the fatal gene, he had his own theories about diseases, doctors, genes, and blood tests, and he probably fretted as much about dying of insomnia as some of his relatives who'd tested positive. In the spring of 2005, his long-simmering anxiety about the disease boiled over messily, along with his agoraphobia. The incident responsible for both developments, and for "The Stray," oc-

curred on Democritus Street, on April 28, during what began
as a walk around the block. For the past three years, in fact,
Dank's walks had all been walks around the block, ever since
the rainy day in the spring of 2002 when, still out of practice
after sixteen months of sedentary hypochondria (see LA-Z-
BOY), he tried to cross Empedocles Street and was knocked
back onto the sidewalk by a passing moped. He never set foot
into the street again, as if it were a shark-infested ocean and he
a swimmer who had nearly lost a limb. For three more years,
though, he continued, on his good days, to range freely on the
island of his own block, an island bounded by Empedocles to
the north, Sycamore to the east, Democritus to the south, and
Redwood to the west. In addition to our house, and Hirt's,
and dozens of others, the island on which he was stranded had
a coffee house and Hemlock's only bookstore, not to mention
a locksmith, an H&R Block, a beauty school, a chiropractor,
and a pedicure salon. Not the precise assortment of shops that
Dank would have chosen for his desert island, but Robinson
Crusoe got by with even less.

And so—in the end—did Dank. On April 28, 2005, as I
was saying, an untethered pit bull (according to the victim,
though Cynthia, my editor, whose apartment overlooks Democritus, saw the incident and insists the dog was just a chocolate Lab) came sprinting out of an alley and headed straight for
our author, singling him out from a dozen pedestrians. The
dog knocked him down, jumped on his chest, and was on the
point of ripping open his throat (or, in Cynthia's account, of
licking his face) when the sound of a siren caused the assailant
to flee.

Somehow or other Dank made it back to the house, where he
collapsed on the living-room sofa. He was so upset by the incident that he couldn't sleep for several nights, though part of what
kept him awake was his very terror of insomnia—his terror of de-

veloping a lethal disease from one day to the next. And that was when it would happen, from one day to the next, except that that elementary distinction would be blurred by the collapse of what Wordsworth calls the "blessed barrier between day and day."

When he finally did nod off he slept for thirteen hours, and when he awoke he came up—or came out—with a theory that FFI, like schizophrenia according to some experts, requires both a genetic predisposition and a precipitating event. He might or might not have the gene, but he could try to avoid the event. It's no secret, after all, that an upsetting event can cause anyone to lose sleep. For those with the lethal gene, Dank reasoned, an upsetting event could cause them to lose a *lot* of sleep, lose forever the *ability* to sleep—a loss that isn't just regrettable but deadly. And so he vowed never to leave the house again, since it was easier to avoid events at home. Although he got over his aversion to events per se, Dank's agoraphobia remained on red alert for what remained of his odd life. At length I did persuade him to leave the house once more, but it was not a success.

Strike of 2002: A wildcat strike, by all but one of Dank's employees, ending the era when the ailing author subcontracted some of the more mechanical parts of his job, as great painters did routinely in the Renaissance (letting their apprentices paint the boring background and the dreary drapery while the master focused on the famous patron's face), and as big-name animators do today. The only one who dared to cross the picket line, who braved the raucous mob outside Dank's house to help the stricken genius download some of the immortal stories teeming in his brain—the only loyal employee, I'm sorry to say, was the author of this note.

The troubles were provoked, ironically, by one of Dank's own books—by 1981's REVOLT OF THE UNSUNG, in which

Dank envisioned a worldwide uprising of talented assistants demanding their fair share of glory and money. As mentioned in my entry on that book, Dank came to see it, some twenty years later, as a reproach to him and to his fiction factory, and he often spoke of buying up and burning every copy. Idle talk, but an assistant overheard it, one dull February day. He told his fellow hacks about "the novel the boss doesn't want us to read," and so they all made a point of reading it, though till then they'd made a point of never reading Dank.

I still marvel at the greed of those assistants. Some had MFAs, but not one had (or has) succeeded single-handedly in writing a salable novel for grown-ups. Dank, of course, had written several dozen. Until his book radicalized them by articulating their own (unearned) grievances better than any of them could have, they had joked nonstop, when they thought I couldn't hear them, about the poor nutcase who paid them to write books that nobody read.

Then, from one day to the next, they started grumbling about "exploitation," though in fact Dank paid them so well that he *lost* money on the books they helped with. Nonetheless, his hired ingrates kept insisting that those books were "really" theirs, though the premises—to which the works in question owe what merit they possess—were Dank's. And even at his laziest, he always took at least a hasty look at every manuscript, and had a hasty talk with Agent Tom about it, as I learned when—strictly as a prank, of course—I sent Tom one of *my* unpublished novels, claiming it was Dank's. (Tom spotted the imposture right away, which wasn't hard to do, since the book—*Lost in the Supermarket*, still unpublished—was much better than the hasty, non-canonical, assistant-written reading matter Dank was sending Tom in that strange era.)

Anyway, his assistants demanded more cash. If he'd *had* more cash, Dank would have humored them, no doubt, but his movie money from PLUS SEVEN—the seemingly inexhaustible sum that had made it possible to pay assistants in the first place—now was almost gone.

So they walked off the job, one afternoon in the middle of THE TOE (which I finally finished single-handedly), and returned an hour later with big picket signs: "WE WRITE THE BOOKS—HE GETS THE GLORY"; "YOUR NEIGHBOR IS A FRAUD"; "PAY NO ATTENTION TO THE MEN BEHIND THE CURTAIN." For the next few weeks, at least two bellyachers could be found out there from dawn to dusk, pacing in front of the house or lounging, in Dank's lawn chairs, on Dank's lawn, harassing passersby with the particulars of their dimwitted "protest."

Me, too, they harassed, when I came or went. Though till then they'd called me Bill, Dank's assistants now found other names for me, like "scab," "lickspittle," "suck-up," "kiss-ass," and "brownnose." Especially "brownnose." I heard that ugly word so often that at last I looked it up—not of course to check its meaning or its only-too-transparent etymology, but to see how *Webster's* would do justice to that etymology, how they'd reconcile the claims of decency and clarity. In this case, I'm pleased to say, they opted for the latter: "*brown + nose*; from the implication that servility is tantamount to having one's nose in the anus of the person from whom advancement is sought." But of course I never sought "advancement" from Dank. No, I prefer another word on same page, *brownie*: "a good-natured goblin believed to perform helpful services (as threshing, churning, and sweeping) during the night."

Within a week things had gotten so ugly that there was no question of the strikers ever going back to work, with or without their famous raise, yet they persisted in harassing me and Dank. I remember the day when a striker lay down in the path of my car, as I pulled into the driveway, and the superhuman self-denial that it cost me not to run him over. (Luckily for both of us, I'm a black belt in full-contact self-denial.) One evening as I returned from the college on foot, all four assistants were waiting for me, and somebody spit in my face. That night I decided on armed retaliation—only fear of prison had restrained me up to then. (An ugly incident before I came to Hemlock, and another here in town after MacDougal's death, had left me almost pathologically lawful, or at least pathologically anxious not to provoke the police.) When I kicked open our front door that morning, though, and strode out with a Louisville Slugger, like an old-time union buster, there was nobody left to clobber: The picketers had given up.

Stuck in the Middle with You: There are many books of bests and quite a few of worsts, but the *middle* range of human accomplishment, the "eh"-inspiring performances of life's perennial C students (an army of billions, after all) has been notably neglected. Enter Phoebus K. Dank with this impeccably tepid "celebration of all things adequate," as he calls it—and while only the most generous could apply that adjective to some of Dank's productions, he undeniably comes closer than usual, in this Big Book of Mediocrity, to writing what he knows. And for once his rambling, shambling, flat-footed, toe-stubbing prose seems almost suitable.

So if I say that all I could manage by way of response was a heartfelt yawn, that isn't as much of a put-down as it would be with some books. "Highlights" of this one include a chapter on middle children, a chapter on middle age, and a chapter on the middle class. There's even a chapter on Wednesday, the day the Germans call *Mittwoch*. There's a brief anthology of damningly faint praise from lukewarm reviews of famous books. (Like all third-rate authors, Dank was an avid collector of inspirational anecdotes about indignities suffered by great writers of the past.)

There's a list of baseball players with the most consistently average batting averages, and another of famous people with college
GPAs in the C range (like Dank's—I myself was an A student).
There are pompous sidebars on the statistical concepts of mean,
mode, and median, on Aristotle's theory of the golden mean, on
the bell curve, and so on. There's an undistinguished chapter on
the undistinguished children of great musicians, politicians, poets,
painters, actors, athletes, scientists, and so on, with a sidebar on
regression to the mean. For someone whose own father was,
if possible, even more of an unmitigated washout than the son,
Dank shows a surprising compassion for the likes of Frank Sinatra
Jr., Julian Lennon, Hartley Coleridge, Brandon Lee, and a mob of
other disappointing aftertastes and epigones (to say nothing of
such tragicomic *siblings* as Billy Carter, Alice James, and Branwell
Brontë). Perhaps because he always saw *me* as his father in art
(though in fact I was just a few days older than he), Dank found
it all too easy to empathize with other also-rans and wannabes
dwarfed and made ridiculous by their more gifted sires.

The book appeared, to hoots and hisses, in 1991. Dank was
always indefatigable when it came to answering hostile reviewers and insisting, humbly but doggedly and often at great length,
in Letters columns everywhere, that the books they'd dismissed
as stupid, shallow, and unfunny were in fact much smarter, much
deeper, and much funnier than the overworked reviewer had noticed. Dank's replies to bad reviews of *Stuck in the Middle* were
especially amusing because he was still sold on its sappy "I'm
OK, You're OK" rhetoric of tolerance:

> After all, nobody's perfect. I don't claim to be another Shake-
> speare, just to write an honest book for folks who work an hon-
> est job and want their money's worth when they go to Barnes
> & Noble. Granted, it may not be Roquefort, but who wants
> Roquefort every single day? [This was shortly after the TAMMI

debacle, when Dank did in fact eat Roquefort every day.] Sometimes nothing hits the spot like a good slice of American cheese.*
(OH)

"The Suicide Man": The story of an actuary working for a
company that sells suicide insurance. Mort used to work for
a suicide hotline but got sick of telling strangers not to kill
themselves, no longer certain he was doing them a favor,
much less adding to the sum of human happiness, since the
sad are not much fun to be around. (For a similarly unsenti-
mental view of suicide, see QUITTING TIME.) Mort is now paid
to assess the present and future suicide risk of current and
prospective policy-holders. Just as events like radiation poisoning shorten their victim's life expectancy, so (explains Dank)
there are events that forever decrease your *will* to live—events
that, without causing you to kill yourself, abridge by days or
months or years the period in which you'll find it worth your
while to grin and bear it. Mort's job is to keep track of such
events—death of a loved one, public disgrace, even balding
or graying—and to calculate their impact on Voluntary Life
Expectancy. If something terrible happens, your premiums go
up and stay there as long as you live.

If *I* were one of Mort's insurees and he knew my state of
mind, my premiums would have gone through the roof last
night. Yesterday, after months of working up my nerve, I finally
called the Hemlock police to tell them I was back in town and

---

* The year he wrote the book, Dank also started (but soon quit) a compi-
lation of trivia he planned to call *Dank's More Often than Not*, a series of
fun facts a la *Ripley's*, but favoring *norms* instead of anomalies: "According
to the Department of Agriculture, some 2,000,000 one-headed calves are
born every year." (BB)

eager to be of any help I could in apprehending Hirt. I figured it was better to go to them than have them come for me—in the middle of a class or at the height of a faculty meeting, as likely as not—and agreed to report to the station house on Main Street first thing in the morning. Last night was rough. Not for a good nine months now had I had so much trouble mastering the urge to end my life. Not since those first terrified and desperate weeks after Dank was clubbed to death (and I'm afraid that some of that desperation and terror found its way into my early entries, since the embarrassing truth is that this encyclopedia began less as a simple reader's guide than as an elaborate suicide note).

But somehow or other I made it through the night, and at eight AM presented myself to the Hemlock police, wishing I had a cyanide capsule stowed in my cheek to bite on if things got too ugly. It didn't help that, as I say, I'd been in trouble with the law before—and here I was in a police station again, sweating and trembling again. But again I survived. It wasn't fun, but wasn't half as bad as I'd expected. Mostly they just yelled at me for dropping out of sight the year before, and for disregarding (or actually blocking—see QUITTING TIME) their e-mails, when they wanted to talk to me. Turns out that that in itself was a crime, but not one they plan to prosecute. It doesn't hurt that I'm a VIP in Hemlock now, since, by the terms of Dank's will, the college stands to come into a lot of money—including every cent that accrues to his estate from the several lucrative Hollywood deals now in the works—but only on condition that *I* administer the new Dank Studies program, which might be hard to do from jail. Come to think of it, that farsighted condition may have been a factor in my rehiring too—and at the rank of Full Professor now—though my department had already filled the spot I'd vacated.

I left the station feeling relieved, chastened, and sheepish—

sheepish because I'd stayed away so long, and lain so low, and it turned out they'd never suspected me of the murder, as I'd absurdly worried, but at worst of being in cahoots with Hirt somehow, or at least of knowing more about his whereabouts than I let on. But no, I truly have no idea where he's hiding, or no more of one than I've gleaned from certain digressions in his entries. If I did, the cops would be the first to know. And of course I'm hardly "in cahoots" with him, except insofar as our collaboration may be seen as a cahoot.

A B C D E F
G H I J K L
M N O P Q R
S T U V W X
Y Z

Tammi: Yet another of Dank's creepy unrequited crushes. Creepy but legal: Just as law-abiding youngsters wait until they turn eighteen, in states where that's the legal age, before they first get drunk, Dank patiently awaited his thirty-sixth birthday in order lawfully to undergo another rite of passage: falling in love, or in lust, with a girl half his age. Tammi was an annoyingly cheerful and bubbly Food Planet employee (not the harpy in charge of free samples—old enough to be her granny—but a teenaged cashier), and the most ardent of Dank's many hopeless passions in the dozen years between wives two and three. He met her on his birthday, December 16, at Register 11, while purchasing a HAPPY BIRTHDAY cake, and when Tammi asked who the cake was for and then echoed its sentiment in tones as cloyingly sweet as its icing, poor Dank was smitten. He liked her smile, he told me. He clearly liked her chest. He liked—and insisted on hearing a sexual invitation in—the way she said "Have a nice day." For the better part of 1989 he made a point of paying for his purchases at Tammi's register. Like anyone who drinks too much coffee, Dank hated waiting in line (Balzac on the beverage: "One wants everything to proceed with the speed of ideas"), yet he waited patiently in Tammi's. Spurning the express lane, he'd join the queue that led to her, no matter how many shoppers were already in it, how many housewives with cartloads of groceries and grannies with fistfuls of coupons, and no matter if he himself was buying just one item (and even that was often a mere pretext to talk to her).

Now and then I joined him on a shopping trip, so I'm in a position to say that Tammi felt nothing for Dank. (I know this because she was clearly attracted to *me*, and there was such a difference between the timid smiles and lingering glances with which she rang up my groceries and the bland have-a-nice-dailiness with which she rang up Dank's that I almost felt sorry for him, though he was too blissfully oblivious to social cues to see that Tammi had as little interest in him as I had in her.) It was amusing to study Dank's preadolescent flirtation techniques. Aside from always addressing Tammi by name—by the name on her plastic badge—his main tactic was to praise Food Planet's wares, as if she herself would find that flattering: "Your guys' store-brand oven cleaner is *at least as good as* Easy-Off. If anything, it's *better.*"

Another of his tactics was to choose his groceries with a view to impressing his favorite cashier, especially after she exclaimed one afternoon, in her flat midwestern accent, as she scanned my wedge of Roquefort: "Wow—classy!" For the next few weeks, Dank ate an awful lot of Roquefort, and *pâté de fois gras*, and supermarket caviar, and washed it down with wine instead of beer, though he never understood the first thing about wine (i.e., why people drink it). Once, to look poetic, he even bought a little plastic bag of blossoms—purple, yellow, pink, and blue—labeled EDIBLE FLOWERS, though he had no idea if the flowers tasted any good, or if, rather, simple edibility was all they had to recommend them. Soon his refrigerator was bursting with dainties chosen to dazzle a ditzy eighteen-year-old who read Kahlil Gibran and dreamed of one day opening her own beauty parlor.

But things really got out of hand after what I later dubbed the Lobster Incident. One afternoon, at Dank's insistence, we were standing in Lane 8—I with a lime and a bottle of tonic water, Romeo with a big classy lobster he'd refused to let the fish guy wrap—when another, older checker, Doris, opened an express line in Lane 9 and beckoned us over.

I was happy to comply, but Dank said, "No thanks."

"Sir, why wait for her to ring up all those groceries? I'm open over here."

After one last anguished glance up 8, at busy Tammi, who wouldn't see his lobster after all, Dank joined me in Lane 9. A minute later, though, outside, he shouted, "Stupid goddamn bull-crap!" and flung his living, twitching purchase into the big dumpster by the loading dock.

After that, he always made a point of buying at least eleven items, so no one could coerce him into an express lane. And since some days he felt impelled to make *two* visits to Food Planet during Tammi's shift, the groceries piled up faster than he could eat them.

Finally Dank worked up his nerve to ask her out for coffee. To my amazement, Tammi said yes—out of simple pity, one assumes. Afterward, predictably, she said she wasn't interested in seeing anybody. Dank was devastated—and convinced that somehow he had blown the "date." For the next week he replayed their outing frame by frame, trying to figure out what he'd done wrong. Said something tactless? Belched or broken wind? Leered at the sexy *barista* who'd made their espressos? In any case, he never got another chance with her. (OH)

"Teacher's Pet": A new student with the retrospectively suspicious last name of "Perfecto" appears in Mr. Mahlman's eighth-grade physics class at Central Junior High. Perfecto soon antagonizes classmates with his all-round apple-polishing—his A-plus exams, his endless quest for extra credit, his hair-trigger hand-raising whenever a question is asked and the robotic correctitude of his replies. Not a class goes by without Mr. Mahlman singling out Perfecto (as even Mahlman calls him—

no one seems to know his forename) as a model to the rest of them, a Gallant to their Goofus. Even the smart kids begin to detest him, and when his classmates finally lose patience, one day after lunch, and jump Perfecto in the boys' room, it is Marty Nussbaum, until recently the teacher's pet, who discovers, when he tries to rip his rival's face off, that the new kid is really a robot. Mr. Mahlman, it turns out, is an inventor, but instead of building a robotic sex slave, as mad scientists have done since the dawn of science fiction, Mahlman built himself a model student—the kind that teachers dream of, Dank implies, as ardently as adolescent boys dream of big-breasted sexbots.

Most of the time, Dank roots for the wimps and geeks and gimps and not the bullies in his fiction, but "Teacher's Pet" is a striking exception. It's clear that Dank himself despises Perfecto—despises him so much that I was a bit offended when he showed me the story, since I'd told him recently that *I* had been a teacher's pet. Dank had not, and that should come as no surprise: Academic excellence (like Hirt's 3.8 GPA in high school—Dank's was 2.6) is so far from being evidence of genius as almost to betoken mediocrity. Or to indicate, at best, a deep conformability, an eagerness to please, that would smother any native genius in the cradle.

Or almost any. I myself did very well in school—better than classmates who may have been smart and hard-working, but lacked my sense of what the teacher wanted to hear. Even as a child, whoever I was with, I was all too good at guessing who they wanted me to be and impersonating him. On a bus trip to Seattle when I was seventeen, I sat next to a muscle-bound survivalist who flaunted his swastika tattoos and regaled me, from Des Moines to Coeur d'Alene, with rants against taxation, gun control, and blacks. On the way home, I sat beside a hippie whose talk was of composting toilets, animal rights, and universal love. And without any sense of imposture, without especially wanting the friendship or approval of either seatmate (beyond ensuring that neither elected to hate me or hurt me), I convinced each one that I was on his side. There was nothing odd or wrong about my pliability, I told myself: It was an extension of the same good manners that prompt us to say "pleased to meet you" whether we are pleased or not, and to nod encouragement in conversation with people struggling to express their thoughts, whether or not we approve of those thoughts. These harmless microfictions give the real self *more* freedom (so I told myself) by enabling it to think and feel with impunity. I agreed and still agree with Schopenhauer (even if that famously ill-mannered thinker didn't practice what he preached): "Courtesy is a counterfeit coin. To be stingy with it shows a lack of intelligence."

By the time I headed off to college, though, my true self was doing all its thinking and emoting in a vacuum—it wasn't free to *act* because my unassertive, diplomatic (not to say chameleonic) public self had taken over and wouldn't let the other get a word in edgewise. I'd lost the knack of saying what I thought—to an annoying roommate, for example, or a graduate advisor steering me onto a path I knew I didn't want to take. My "real" self, in other words, had become a *virtual*, a strictly hypothetical self—the one that *would* have called the shots if I had somehow ceased to care what other people thought. One sign of its increasing unreality was the increasing murderousness of my daydreams. Like an embittered quadriplegic, I could afford to wallow in anti-social feeling and sociopathic fantasies because there was no longer a connection between what I did and what I felt like doing.

I try not to imagine where it might have ended if I hadn't found a way to bridge the gap between my inner and my outer selves by finding a job for the outer that the inner could—

sincerely if not always unreservedly—approve of. My vow to consecrate my life to the study of Dank (see THE ILL-ADVISED AND THE INADVISABLE) was the most important choice of my life, since it amounted to a refusal to let my true self atrophy altogether.

I'm convinced, by the way, that Dank himself underwent a similar split between his public and private selves. His obsession with SF began in junior high, at a time when he was tormented by bullies and so was naturally attracted to the fantasies of power furnished by all genre fiction catering to males. The implicit author of his own SF is always much more macho than the real Dank—especially in his early pseudonymous novels, but in his other books as well. Writers run a special risk, I think, of developing the sort of schism I'm describing: Literature, after all, is the original virtual "chat room," where—as on the Internet—the temptation to misrepresent yourself is irresistible. And it's dangerously easy to prefer your pseudoself, and even, finally, to think of it—the larger and luckier self that lives only on paper or in pixels—as your *true* self, just as a puffer fish might think its true self is the puffed-up version. Off the page, in the flesh, Dank went no further than most male American writers in impersonating his rugged and stoic authorial persona. For interviews and jacket photos and the like, he did take off his glasses, muss his hair, and (once even during a heat wave) put on a brawny woolen lumberjack shirt, the better to live up to his would-be-manly readers' image of their would-be-manly author.

Dank was very touchy, incidentally, about insinuations that there were really two of him, and that the public one was an imposture. Hirt's lampoon to that effect put a welcome period to the long loose run-on sentence of their friendship. When I got around to reading *Get Some Respect* (see LEGITIMACY) on the off-chance that someday I'd want some too, I saw that I'd been wrong in thinking Dank had highlighted every word in the book. In the chapter called "Plato's Fun Factory: How to Write Sure-Fire Philosophical Digressions," I found one sentence *un*emphasized, an island of white in that ocean of yellow: "Science fiction writers and readers tend to be meek and timorous souls like Nietzsche, who love nothing better than to fantasize about the feats of bold, assertive figures as *un*like themselves as possible." I smiled at the vision of Dank grimly highlighting all the *other* words in a self-defeating effort to de-emphasize that one unacceptable assertion. It seemed like something he would do. But then I noticed that in fact the sentence *had* been highlighted, only in a different, fainter, paler yellow, maybe older (since the yellow of highlighting tends to fade even if the book stays shut), and maybe by a different hand. Yes, that's what must have happened, I decided: Dank had bought the book at a used bookstore, had found those few words highlighted, and had hastened to hide the embarrassing sentence by highlighting all the other sentences too.

He hid the book itself in his usual hiding place, the little basement storage room with the irresistible black-and-orange KEEP OUT sign on the door, and the unresisting padlock—fearing he would lose the key, he kept it *in* the lock. In that room he also hid the bulk of his PORNOGRAPHY and, during his crush on Pandora, his easy listening records, on the off-chance, or off-off-chance, that he persuaded her to come home with him some night, since the sight of all that Perry Como might convince her that he wasn't, after all, the hard-bitten punk she'd been about to give her body to. As for his other secrets—*Get Some Respect*, for one—it wasn't clear whom he thought he was hiding them from, or if he knew I knew about his hiding place, which I thought of as Dank's Subconscious.

But back to me and the windowless basement of *my* true self. Could that self approve wholeheartedly, and round the clock, of Dank and all his works, or would it still need an assist now and then from my false self? Well, perfect enthusiasm is as rare as any other form of perfection. (And whatever Dank may have thought, I'm *not* another Perfecto.) Valéry: "Every enthusiast contains a false enthusiast, every lover a false lover, every man of genius a false man of genius. . . . This is necessary in order to understand oneself, count upon oneself, think of oneself; in order, in short, to *be* oneself." But a large enough majority of my true self sincerely did admire Dank that I was able to go public with that admiration, and to make it a career, without the nauseating sense of fraudulence that I imagine haunting them downstairs in Culture Studies, those theory-maddened academics who, when clever, young, and clueless, made the mistake of devoting their lives to bumper stickers, soda cans, or singing commercials. (I'm typing this at school, in the cushy corner office that came with my reappointment.)

As for the dissenting opinion, the small part of me that sneers at Dank, it may *think* it speaks for my true self as a whole—and may sometimes even, briefly, make me think so too—but most of the time I know it's just a sourpuss, and that Dank is the best thing that ever happened to me. It's no exaggeration to say he saved my life, or at least my sanity.

Teller, Jessica (b. 1954): Dank's first wife. They met as freshmen in college and married four years later, probably because she was the only female in the Science Fiction Club (whose meetings Dank continued to attend long after dropping out of Berkeley), and so by default an object of desire to the dozen desperate male virgins in Dank's reference group. It may have been the sale of BOOST— his dismal, instantly forgotten debut novel—that enabled Dank to bear off such a hotly contested prize. What with her short hair, baggy sweater, and big glasses, Jessica reminded me of a character on *Scooby Doo*, the brainy coed Velma—the only character not to have rated a chewable vitamin shaped like herself, I recall, in the era of Scooby-Doo vitamins. Like Velma, she was rumored to be a lesbian—rumors her marriage to Dank never really laid to rest, or not to my satisfaction, even if he did manage somehow to sire a child of sorts upon her. She never liked me, and it was clear she envied the awe I inspired in Dank.*

As far as I know, both bride and groom had been virgins till their wedding night, and not since his prenatal days had Dank lived in such close quarters with the opposite sex. And even though—or just because—he'd shared a womb with his twin sister, he never slept well with anyone else in the room. Even an ant farm on the nightstand could keep him awake—or so he boasted, proud of what he fancied his poetic nature, his hypersensitivity, like the princess and the pea, when in actuality he had the thickest hide[†] of any writer I've ever encountered. One reason (of many) that he didn't make the grade at college was that he was obliged to share

---

* I think it's clear by now who envies whom. Hirt and I are both nobodies, though *he* hasn't faced it yet. Fate linked us to the same somebody like twin experiments in admiration and envy—in the different balance of those two emotions that different people will arrive at when obliged by circumstance to obsess about their betters. Hirt served me as a useful guide to what to avoid in my attitude toward Dank: If I were ever tempted (not that I ever really was) by the ugly passions that drove the poet insane, I just told myself, "Watch out—that's the sort of emotion that *he* would emote." (BB)

† Not true. Dank was anything but thick-skinned, least of all literally: Some days he wore his sweatsocks and sweatpants inside out because the nap of the fabric tickled his ankles and legs. As for his insomnia when sharing a bedroom with other sentient beings, that was no boast but an honest lament. Sometimes when he dozed off in his study, in his later years, the things in his aquarium somehow combined forces to startle him awake, though at that point the tank contained only a few placid sponges, a sprig of crimson coral, and one or two slowly undulating sea anemones. (BB)

a room—a trauma that reverberated, in his fiction, for the rest of his life, as the smallest traumas will for those with the emptiest lives. As for his first marriage, he was able to fall asleep only after Jessica did, and awakened whenever she awoke, though somehow he slept through his own snorts and snores, which were often what woke *her*. Within a few months, he took to sleeping on the couch, and from some stray comments he made at the time, I gathered that by that point Jessica had phased out sex. She was clearly the model for the frigid and humorless housewife in LAUGH-ING MATTER (though it was written long after their divorce), who finds sex with her—pudgy, four-eyed, literary—husband so nauseating that she routinely applies a transdermal motion-sickness patch beforehand. (OH)

***Tesla's Alternative*:** An alternative-history tale starring Nikola Tesla, inventor of the alternating-current generator. The biography I glanced at says that Tesla worked for Thomas Edison at first, but later feuded with him because Edison was waging a campaign (back in the days when AC and DC vied for market share like VHS and BetaMax) for *direct* current. In Dank's version, Tesla electrocutes his mentor, making it look like a mishap, and goes on to become our nation's greatest inventor. Since in real life Tesla was insane, in an endearing Howard Hughesy way (refusing to shake hands, refusing hotel rooms with numbers divisible by three, terrified of spherical objects like billiard balls or marbles, obsessed with inventing a camera to photograph thoughts), the alternative world he does so much to shape is a bizarre one.

The novel was written in 1982. Twenty years later it came back to haunt its author after the non-accidental electrocution of someone Dank had every reason to want dead. I forget if I've mentioned the night in September 2000 when MacDougal was killed in his bathtub just hours after his appalling book about Dank—Peter Pan in Outer Space—hit the shelves of Hemlock's only bookstore. As police reconstructed the event, the "killer" must have arrived around eleven at MacDougal's house, a tiny bungalow on the outskirts of town, beyond Heidegger Street, in a thicket of dwarf pine planted by the victim a decade earlier (after paying bigger men to cut down the bigger trees that had stood there until then). Perhaps the caller had been planning to bludgeon or strangle MacDougal, or to spy on him, or just to lay eyes on the deck the little man had been building in back of his house—and bragging about in his weekly mass e-mails to the rest of us—all summer long.

After mounting the famous and still-unfinished deck and silently picking his way among what looked like the entire line of Black and Decker tools for the home handyman (one symptom of MacDougal's short-man complex was a rugged love of power tools), the caller peered in through the unfrosted bathroom window that faced the woods beyond the deck, and found the little man splashing around in the tub. On a whim, his visitor grabbed a portable circular saw (connected to an outdoor outlet by an orange extension cord), hit the switch, and heaved it through the window and into the tub with Mac-Dougal.

But if the cause of death was easy to deduce, the "murderer" remains a mystery. (Quotation marks because we can't assume he intended to murder MacDougal, though murder too can be a form of literary criticism, when provoked by an inexcusable book. Maybe the angry reader to thank for that well-aimed projectile just wanted to give the unshockable critic a jolt.) All that's known for sure is that it wasn't Dank, who'd been in custody at the time due to his arrest for public defecation. So pat was his alibi that the police suspected him of getting arrested on purpose, after enlisting someone else to do his dirty work. But I assure the reader, as Dank himself succeeded in assuring the police, that there was no premeditation in the act that led to his spending the fateful night in lockup. And MacDougal, after all, had other enemies.

Readers may wonder how *we*, by the way—Dank's most rabid critic and Dank's most fanatic fan—managed to co-exist for so long in the confines of the same department. Hemlock College, though, was such a steaming heap of envies, insecurities, maneuverings, antipathies, ambitions, pretensions, delusions, self-deceptions, and resentments that MacDougal's personality, uniquely horrible though it was, most often got lost in the crowd—or lost in the fray, in the *battle royale* of academic self-advancement—just as his person got lost in any crowd whose average height was more than 5'1".

Like a dim dank cellar where nothing grows but fungus, or like one of Dank's own post-apocalyptic futures where the only fauna still standing are roaches and rats, Hemlock College favored the survival of the foulest. The school was infested with jackals and weasels, vipers and toads, circus bears happy to put on a tutu and dance in exchange for a pat on the head, yappy little lapdogs who mistook themselves for watchdogs, amorous spaniels who asked nothing more than to lick the hand, to hump the leg, to snuffle the rump of their owner. My department was no exception. I used to wish MacDougal dead, or never born, or never tenured, but if I'd never known him, I'd never have suspected that things might have been even worse.

As it is, I can't decide whom to hate most, now that MacDougal is gone. The tenured existentialist—a walking PDR of diagnoses and prescriptions for the Plight of Modern Man and the Sickness of Our Times—who teaches the creative-writing workshops? The anorexic composition teacher, a permanent adjunct and certified Wiccan high priestess who runs her own coven—and who, behind my back, calls *me* a "weirdo"? (I've reluctantly taken to thinking of her—and all the others—in the present tense again, since it looks like I may soon be back at Hemlock College.) The poets, those more-evolved beings (Meredith: "As we to the brutes, the poets are to us") who, with their souls uncorrupted by lucre, can channel into networking, logrolling, grant applications, and academic intrigue the energies that lesser writers channel into marketing? The young deconstructionist with his silly shaven head and silly leather jacket and silly wishful blather about the Death of the Author? (I say the police should haul *him* in for questioning!) The joker who teaches creative nonfiction (always the zaniest member of any department that has one, the poets being too solicitous of their careers for all but the most calculated zaniness), and who warns advisees to avoid my courses on the grounds that I'm "psychotic"? (This from a man arrested once for driving not just drunk but *nude*.) Bah! Too bad they weren't *all* in that tub with MacDougal.

Thermotard: Dank's backyard writing bunker (see THE MAN IN THE BLACK BOX) had no heat, and even Hemlock gets cold in the winter. To cope with the weather, Dank paid a tailor to make him three special one-piece body suits of heavy wool, each an amazing combination of footie pajama, turtleneck sweater, ski mask, and gloves. Aside from a buttoned flap in back—which he used to enter (head first) and exit the suit as well as for potty breaks—there were no other openings, no other breaches in this second skin, except the mouth- and eyeholes in the ski-mask and the missing fingertip-holes of the gloves. At Dank's request, each "thermotard," as he dubbed the suits, was a different color (bright red, bright blue, bright yellow) and in the winter of 1995–96 he wore one or another of the suits night and day. Out in his bunker he also wore sweatpants, a sweatshirt, and boots. Back in the relative warmth of our house, he'd take those off but not his thermotard, leaving it on for days on end, since (like the bunker itself) the thing was a hassle to enter and exit. At that point in his life, Dank's basic mood tended to change no more than once every few days, and—though he denied it—he clearly favored different suits in different moods. Specifically, he favored the red suit when he was manic, to the point where I came to think of it as his Happy Suit. As for the yellow one, that was his Anxious Suit, and when he was feeling yellow he'd sometimes make me stand guard outside the bunker even while he was inside with the door bolted. The blue suit, his Sad Suit, was for dumps and doldrums, and at one point he went for several weeks without removing it even to bathe, so that for me his melancholy came to have a color and, increasingly, an odor.

"These Are Not My Children": After being brained by an errant soccer ball while cheering on her daughter's team, a "typical suburban mother" starts insisting that her children *aren't* her children, disregarding all evidence to the contrary—their tearful testimony ("Don't you recognize me, Mommy?"), her husband's reassurances ("Honey, let's be rational"), her photo album, and of course her memories, spotty as those have become since her head injury. The family doctor diagnoses amnesia "complicated by the patient's refusal to accept her role as housewife." The truth is even grimmer: Josh and Jenny aren't her children after all, but orphans implanted—like the heroine—with phony memories, as part of a top-secret Pentagon experiment. Only the husband—in reality a government psychiatrist—is in on the secret.

The story dates from June 2001, when for several days and nights Dank kept insisting that he hadn't written his own books. He no longer recognized himself in their rugged, stolid, stoic, manly narrators, to say nothing of their tough, assertive, self-assured, two-fisted heroes. Neither did he recognize himself in any of his published interviews, which also presented a much more self-assured and virile author than the real one. Like most (though not all—see WHAT NEXT) of his other delusions, this one soon passed, and may be dismissed as a figment of exhaustion, since a flaring-up of Dank's ongoing, self-fulfilling terror of insomnia had been causing him to lose a lot of sleep. But it's still worth asking why, on that occasion, his derangement took the form it did.

Dank, at the time, had been delegating his public persona to somebody else for two years, so it was only natural that he didn't see himself in any of the snapshots or hear himself in any of the soundbites of *that* era. His policy of paying RUEFLE to impersonate him, though, was a symptom of a preexisting problem. The schism between private self and public self had widened catastrophically for Dank in 1999, but by then it had already existed for decades, hidden like the flaw in the golden bowl, and predisposing if not dooming him to an appalling fracture of the psyche.

When did it begin, the hairline crack that spread unnoticed and ultimately tore my friend in two? We can only speculate, but my guess (as I suggested in my note on TEACHER'S PET) is puberty. The problem began when Phoebus opted for the most disastrous way to cope with routine adolescent feelings of inadequacy. Rather than working to make himself more adequate in the eyes of the world (exercising, losing weight, learning how to talk to girls), or even in his own eyes (acing his report card, improving his chess), Dank took to thinking no more than necessary about his real life, and as much as possible about the visions of power and glory supplied by the rocket-fueled fiction he was reading. For the last four decades of his life, all he really wanted—aside from sex of course—was to be left in peace to read and write his science fiction.

He wanted to retreat so far inside himself that nothing the outer world did to him would even reach the inner Dank. He wanted to forget about the real world altogether, and as for the real Phoebus, he didn't want his readers ever to lay eyes on *him*. The man behind the curtain had been hiding there so long he'd forgotten his relation to the famous Wizard.

"Think of Me": A divorcée in her forties develops the delusion that her mood at any moment depends on what other people are thinking. If people, present or absent, known or unknown, are liking her, wishing her well, remembering her fondly, then her mood enjoys an invisible lift. If people are hating her, resenting her, despising her, her mood declines. Often the various feelings directed at her cancel out, or cause her mood to vibrate busily without elevating or depressing it—but she much prefers that agitation to the emptiness she feels when no one is thinking about her at all, not even in dreams. Phoebe (for that is her name) prefers even *bad* moods to the deathly stillness that ensues when the whole human race happens to direct its attention elsewhere. Phoebe invents this delusional system, in fact, to make sense of "the Stillness," as she calls her devastating bouts of depression. In the end, in a desperate bid for attention, she murders a Hollywood actress who has never known the pain of being neglected, unthought-of, undreamed-of.

As her name suggests, poor Phoebe is Phoebus in drag, and her desperate hunger for attention—her need to feel that people are thinking about her, one way or another—reflects the need *he* felt, in 1993, when his third wife left him for a much less gifted but more celebrated author. Fame was never Dank's reason for writing, but for a few months it became an obsession. He took out a full-page ad for himself in the local paper, like the ads that run at election time, except that he wasn't running for office, just pleading for attention. He hired a skywriter to write his name in the heavens. He spent a furtive week at the Hemlock Public Library writing it himself—together with his claims to fame—in *Who's Who*, *The Timetables of History*, the *World Book Encyclopedia*, the *Oxford Companion to English Literature*, and all sorts of other reference works, always in the spot where, alphabetically, he belonged. (Not until he'd already defaced every book that might plausibly—or even implausibly—feature an entry on Phoebus K. Dank did it occur to him that he could have typed that entry on addendum slips and *pasted* them into the books.)

Toward the end of this summer-long folly, Dank went door-to-door, like one of those earnest save-the-redwoods canvassers, to tell everyone about himself. Once he got beyond his own neighborhood, he had many doors slammed in his face, though he always started his spiel by assuring strangers that he wasn't there to sell them anything, or to ask for money or to use the toilet, that he just wanted to tell them about this incredible writer he knew. (With strangers, he fared better if he spoke of himself in the third person, not letting on that he himself was Phoebus K. Dank.)

Things I Gotta Do: A few months ago, while sorting through the papers in Dank's study, I found a special memo pad. At the top of each 3" x 5" sheet, in a jocular font, are the words *Dumb Things I Gotta Do*. According to the yellow sticker on the gray cardboard back of the pad, Dank bought it at Food Planet for fifty-nine cents. According to the cover, the pad once contained one hundred sheets, bound at one edge by a strip of rubbery adhesive. When I found it there were only ninety-nine, each covered with Dank's cursive and bearing an idea for a book he never got around to writing. (He was such rapid writer that he never bothered jotting down ideas for mere *stories*, any more than you jot down a memo when the phone rings to remind yourself to answer.)

One of the unwritten books, *Extrapolation*, was to feature a painter of age-progressed portraits, life-sized predictions or projections of how children will look as adults. The painter's customers are mostly doting parents who want to see their sons and daughters in the prime of life, but one envious woman pays the painter to portray her "luscious fourteen-year-old stepdaughter" as a withered crone. Gazing at the memo pad, I pictured Dank himself as a geezer, Dank as a not-yet-dead ringer of old Father William, the backflipping, headstanding codger in *Alice in Wonderland*—Dank in a parallel world where nobody clubbed him to death. It was a simple problem of distance, rate, and time, like the ones I wrote for pay in 1991 to test the algebraic skills of young mathematicians: If Phoebus writes three books per year and wants another ninety-nine, how long will he have to live?

A few days ago I found the missing hundredth sheet in a battered copy of *The Martian Chronicles*. It featured a synopsis of VIRTUALLY IMMORTAL, Dank's last novel, leaving me to wonder if he'd planned to write those hundred books in the same order they'd occurred to him. We'll never know, just as we'll never know exactly what Dank would have done with any of the ninety-nine unrealized ideas. But since he was one author who could truthfully have said, with Cyril Connolly, "The books I haven't written are better than the books that other people have," I hereby summarize an armload of Dank's phantom novels just as if they were real:

The Boy Who Cried "Martian": "A retelling of the world-famous cautionary tale." What was wrong with the original version? Nothing—but Dank thought it was due for updating: "Nowadays, with all the UFOs out there, you're

in more danger of being abducted by a Martian than devoured by a wolf."

The Exacerbator: Agent Harder pursues a psychopath whose
specialty is kicking people when they're down—robbing
beggars, assaulting battered wives, disarming one-armed
men, blinding the one-eyed, maiming the maimed, disf-
iguring the ugly, egging on the suicidal, sneaking into
hospitals to kill the injured, even setting houses on fire
again as soon as the firemen leave. The psychopath turns
out to be a hellfire-and-brimstone preacher who believes
that suffering is always deserved and divinely ordained,
and "just a *hint* of what God would *really* do to us if His
sissy son didn't make Him pull His punches."

Mike Mulligan and His Manual Typewriter: A century from
now, when all books are written by computers, one plucky
throwback—"a middle-aged lovable fat man" with a fat
lovable cat—resolves to write a novel the old-fashioned
way. But publishing, too, is controlled by computers,
and in order to get his novel published, Mike has to use
a pseudonym—CyberMike 2101—so that when (computerized) critics vote it the Book of the Decade, a computer
gets all the credit. In the end Mike proves his authorship, however, and proves an inspiration to other human
writers.

Never Again: A dystopian novel set in a police state where
repetition is the greatest crime: People are only permitted to read any given book—watch any movie, see any
painting, hear any piece of music, visit any tourist destination—once.

Prequels: A book of stories about the childhoods of famous
literary characters: Holden Caulfield as a fussy baby fond
of biting his mother while feeding; Mersault as a sadistic
three-year-old whose early *actes gratuits* feature frogs and

firecrackers, bugs and magnifying glasses; Lady Macbeth as a sullen adolescent ("sort of like that creepy Goth that works at Coffee Town") . . .

A Specialist in Chaos: Agent Harder on the case of a new kind of serial killer: a "top chaos theorist" who, driven insane by his area of expertise ("by his lifelong contemplation of sheer Chance") settles a grudge against the cosmos by choosing his victims entirely at random.

The Taster: A recovering alcoholic is doing his best to stay off the bottle but finding it hard because he earns his living as a wine taster.

The Therapist: The clinical adventures of a psychoanalyst who believes in reincarnation. Not content to track his patients' problems back to early childhood like other analysts, this one pursues the origins of specific phobias, fixations, and hysterias back to the patient's previous life. According to the analyst, neuroses are not caused by any specific event, but by the patient's last life as a whole.

"Think Tank": Due to a zany bureaucratic mix-up, a mentally retarded man is awarded a job in a think tank. Hilarity ensues when he tries to keep up with the other pundits—to "pass" not just for normal but for brilliant.

When I first read this story, I took it for a bit of oddly heartless fun at the expense of a beleaguered population. Later, though, I learned that Dank had written it during his stint as a college instructor and had based the mentally retarded hero on himself—a projection of his own sense of inadequacy at faculty meetings and cocktail parties where everyone knew, or pretended to know, much more about something or other than Dank, a college dropout, officially knew about anything. (Actually, Dank knew more about books—how they work, how they come to be written—than any of my colleagues in the Lit Department.) For his sake I'm glad he didn't stay in academia, but I can't help wishing that Dank had spent a term or so in my department, with its agonizing weekly meetings and its mandatory yearly potluck (where through the years I tested, with encouraging results, some of the dainties I would later try to no effect at all on the cast-iron-stomached LIPS)—and had written a novel about it.

This may be the place to say a word about Dank's tendency to underrate himself, his outrageous but sincere humility. He had so little of the celebrity's aura about him that once, when he was guest of honor at a big convention whose organizers had flown him all the way to San Diego to discuss The Changing Face of Science Fiction,[*] Dank failed to persuade the gatekeepers that he wasn't just a kook *impersonating* the Guest of Honor. He showed up without his badge or any other identification, and fifteen minutes later headed straight back to the airport after failing to gain entry to the convention hall—an experience he would describe for the rest of his life as "positively Kafkaesque," though a year before his death he told me that he'd never read a word of Kafka.

Three-Way Bulb: Few readers finish every book they open before opening another. Some of us keep a harem, and seldom get into bed with the same favorite two nights in a row. *Three-Way Bulb* is designed to make a virtue of the habit of reading a book in haphazard installments—in nonconsecutive terms of attention. The novel consists of three disparate parts: a picture book for children with drawings by me, of all people, and just a line or two of easy reading at the bottom

---

[*] Part of the problem was that his own—large, puffy, pallid—face seldom appeared on his books because none of his publishers considered it a selling point. (OH)

of each page; a so-called young-adult novel for junior-high readers, addressing their concerns (schoolyard bullies, teenage crushes, puberty, etc.); and a demanding literary novel aimed at full-grown, well-read high-brows. All three sections have the same protagonist, Bob Buswell, seen first as a clever kindergartner, then a bright but lonely seventh-grader, and then a maverick graduate student. I'm proud to add that Dank got the idea, and the title, from the three-way light bulb in my reading lamp (the tall one by the platform rocker in the living room, opposite his La-Z-Boy), which afforded three different levels of brightness.

Who would buy a book like that? No one, according to Tom (for whom that question—rather than "How *good* is it?"—appears to be the only one that matters). But I'd club *myself* to death if I thought all readers were as narrow-minded as Tom. I think many readers would cherish the book like no other. Even at its dimmest setting, *Three-Way Bulb* is one of Dank's most brilliant novels. So it pains me to relate that the book remains unpublished due to the refusal of Book Cartel—from the highest of high-powered New York agents to the mousiest of librarians in the sleepiest of small-town libraries—to touch a book that can't be pigeonholed by the age of its intended readers. When *Three-Way Bulb* is finally published (*when*, not *if*), it should be shelved in the small-children's section of libraries and bookstores, though only part of it, Part One, is aimed at small children. Parts Two and Three concern the repercussions of things done and undergone earlier in the book, but Dank saw to it that no young child would make headway in Part Two (even including a masturbation reference, à la Judy Blume, in the second paragraph of that second section to ensure that any parent reading aloud would stop at that point). He also saw to it that no Young Adult (in the publishing world's misleading sense of the term) would make it more than a page or two into

Part Three, which corresponds to a seventeen-year jump in the age of the first-person narrator and begins with an eight-page discussion of PhD programs. And yet Dank was confident that the first part would make such a lasting impression on young children, and the second part on Young Adults, that they'd never forget the book they'd had snatched away from them as kindergarteners, or had flung aside in disgust as adolescents. They wouldn't think about the book for years, but when ripe for the next section they would pick it up again, and with more interest than they felt for any other book, because *this* one had such a special connection to earlier chapters of their own lives.

In the year 2000, during an attack of writer's block so bad it made him fear he'd never write again, Dank started to think about wringing money out of his existing oeuvre by merchandising. I just found a copy of a letter to his agent, dated 10/13/2000 that suggests how *much* he'd thought about it. Why, he wondered, shouldn't his books be "turned into" Saturday morning cartoons, say, or video games, or even breakfast cereals? He went on to suggest the best books for each medium. Those he envisioned as cartoons included AMNESIA and PAYLOAD PETE, BOY ROCKETEER. Books he thought might lend their premises or settings to video games were THE ERASURES, BARRETT'S BARGAIN, and—unaccountably—THE SADIATORS. As for breakfast cereals, Dank had high hopes for AUGUST AND APRIL, which he pictured as a multicolored cereal with little marshmallow Aprils and Augusts, and for HAPPY PILLS (with special "flavor capsules" and marshmallow pills). And, in the same vein, it occurs to me that *Three-Way Bulb* could be the basis of not one but three linked cereals (cf. Frankenberry, Booberry, and Count Chocula): one a Technicolor nightmare on the lines of Lucky Charms, one a less-infantile but still presweetened cereal à la Frosted Mini-Wheats, and one a grim no-nonsense adult penance à la Grape Nuts. Each box would show an artist's conception of Bob Buswell at the appropriate age.

Today is April 12, the three-month anniversary of the traumatic phone call that spelled the end of my twelve-year connection with Tom Wainwright, literary agent and foe of innovation. Among other unforgivable things, Tom said that *Three-Way Bulb* reminded him "alarmingly" of a novel by *me*, the one I sent him back in 1994, when he became my agent and found a publisher for my first book on Dank. It's true that back before I knew of Tom's hostility to bold new works of fiction by unfamiliar writers, I did send him my first novel, *Three-Point Perspective*, but the resemblance Tom imagines between that book and *Three-Way Bulb* is strictly a trick of the light. After all, it's been thirteen years since I showed the book to Tom. I didn't bother showing him the ones I went on to write after moving to Hemlock (except, as a prank, *Lost in the Supermarket*—see Strike of 2002), since he'd made it clear that he had no interest in my fiction, only in my books on Dank. I'm amazed that he remembers it at all, after so many years, especially since his comments back in 1994 made it clear he hadn't read it very closely—hadn't given it a chance. Tom seems almost anxious to ensure that books like mine *don't* get a chance. But I have more confidence in the venerable guild of literary agents than to think that Tom speaks for them all. Surely there are some who really do seek bold new voices, rather than just claiming to. Maybe there is even such a seeker among the readers of this reader's guide. If so, he or she has probably been wondering how to get in touch with me, so here's my address: Dr. William Boswell, PhD, Dodder Professor of Contemporary Letters, 207 Peacock Hall, Hemlock College, Hemlock, CA 95529.

Time Machine: Elsewhere I've discussed the episodes of sleep-deprived derangement that enliven Dank's biography. During one such episode, in February 1996, Dank convinced himself that he had built a working time machine. It was the year of the Black Box, and I remember my relief the day Dank came in from his bunker in the sad blue THERMOTARD he'd been wearing for almost a month, headed upstairs, and reappeared a little later, freshly showered, in the red one, asking if I thought he was too old to be an astronaut. Yes, I answered truthfully, and thus set Dank to brooding on the cruel march of time. He spent the next week in the basement—building his own spaceship, I assumed, since NASA wouldn't give him a seat on one of theirs.

It turned out he'd been building another kind of vehicle—a time machine, a timeship. In defense, however, of Dank's basic sanity, or semi-sanity, even at his most deranged, I emphasize that this was an extremely modest time machine: It transported its passenger only *one minute* into the past or the future.

This vehicle was temperamental, too, as prone to malfunctions as a photocopier. One evening Dank emerged from the basement, after a day of time travel whose soundtrack had included an insistent buzzing and occasional shouted profanities (it was the only time I ever heard him say "fuck"), convinced that he was trapped in the future—only one minute ahead of the rest of us, but still. He spent the whole night trying to return to his own time, but with no success. When I came down for breakfast the following morning, I found him seated at the kitchen table, looking more haggard than I'd ever seen him, and claiming now to be trapped *two* minutes ahead of the rest of us. You'd think that that would be as good a place as any for a science fiction writer with a flair for coming-soon and coming-next scenarios, but Dank didn't see it that way. He was so distressed at being stranded in the future that I volunteered to join him there, and be his Friday.

With tears of gratitude he accepted my offer and led me straight down to the basement. The chassis of his time machine turned out to be a La-Z-Boy, one he'd banished to the basement sooner than normal because its all-important reclining mechanism had broken—all-important for the purposes of routine time-wasting relaxation, though evidently not for time travel. Dank had connected the chair by a heavy orange electric cord to an old clock radio that he'd improved by the addition of a three-pronged outlet in its face, beside the digital display. The other end of the orange cord disappeared under the seat of the chair. (The clock's original ungrounded cord was plugged into a wall socket.) The chair was also fitted with a rear-view mirror and a bicycle horn—a red rubber bulb fitted onto one end of a chrome-plated steel tube that flared at the other end like the bell of a trumpet—though I never learned their purpose. Neither do I know just what was under the seat that needed so much juice, but when Dank strapped me in (there was a seat belt), set the clock's alarm, and threw the time machine into gear with a tug on the lever that used to make the chair recline, it felt like I was sitting on a big joy buzzer. Exactly (?) two minutes later, the radio woke up in the middle of a James Taylor song, and Dank slammed on the brakes by tugging the lever again. For the rest of the day, overwhelmed by gratitude and perhaps a dawning sense of the terrible sacrifice he'd just let me make on his behalf, Dank was embarrassingly kind—constantly clapping me on the back, cooking me a special dinner, calling me his "only real friend," and so on.

He was right, of course, about the "only real friend" part, if the only other candidate was Hirt—who, by the way, has been awfully quiet lately. No? If I'm not mistaken, he hasn't flung his excrement at Dank for a couple of weeks now, not counting one or two unimpressive feculae aimed at our author from the coward's safety of the footnotes. He must've found some other outlet for his rancor. Maybe someone gave him a new magnifying glass and he's busy burning ants. Or dousing them with Campari. Or maybe he can tell that I've had just about enough of his ingratitude toward the most admirable man I've ever known, and so he thought it prudent to lie low for a while.

But I digress. I'm happy to report that *after* dinner, Dank dragged himself upstairs, slept for fourteen hours, and came back down around midnight convinced that he was back in sync with the rest of his time zone—leaving me all alone in the near future as, a few years later, his death would do again.

"Time Vandal": It's 2087 and there's a time machine in every garage, but these "Chrono-Recreational Vehicles," or CRVs, are equipped "for safety's sake" with special "regulators" that permit travel only to and from the future—never the past. After the tragic death of his son, though, a grief-stricken CRV repairman overrides the regulator on *his* time machine and puts it in reverse. He heads back to the Pleistocene and purposely disrupts the past in any way he can—swatting bugs, stomping flowers, tasing mammoths, setting fires, sharing his era's technology with cavemen, inseminating their (big-breasted and improbably good-looking) mates, and so on. The idea is to alter history. He's convinced that his is the worst of all possible worlds, so any throw of the dice is bound to yield a better present than the one he knows.

Yes, it's a pity about little Phoebus Jr., and far be it from me to suggest that Dank was cynically "milking" a private calamity for the sympathy vote that can make all the difference to an author's sales. But the infant mortality rate in his fiction *is* ridiculously high, especially since his talents were better suited to dead-baby jokes than to *Kindertotenlieder*. Our agent once persuaded him not to publish a story about a child-killing mother who "grows her own," giving birth again and again so as to have a steady supply of victims. As an author Dank behaved exactly like that troubled mother, never bringing a child into the world of his fiction except with a view to killing it. (OH)[*]

"The Tiresias Formula": In this gender-bending variation on Jekyll and Hyde, a "top biochemist" concocts a "special hormone" that enables him to change from a man named Jack to a woman named Heidi. Ho ho. The transformation has a way of wearing off abruptly, inconveniently, and "unpredictably," as for instance in the women's locker room at Heidi's gym. The plot, of course, is nothing but a pretext for the sort of cheesy voyeurism found in teen sex comedies, and Dank did in fact urge our long-suffering agent (Hi, Tom!) to interest Hollywood in the film rights. But it would be wrong to assume that the story was written for sordid monetary motives. *Au contraire*, "The Tiresias Formula"—an all-

---

[*] I don't know about the reader, but I'm getting pretty sick of all this *schadenfreude*, sarcasm, and outright cruelty. One reason I rashly agreed to Hirt's offer to help with this guide was the hope that he'd provide all kinds of information about the twenty years between his first meeting with Dank in 1971 and mine in 1991. If we then enlisted Jane as a third collaborator, we'd have Dank's whole life covered, with on-the-spot observers of its every stage, even the prenatal. Well, I soon abandoned the idea of enlisting his— sullen, illiterate, bigoted—sister, and I clearly could have managed without Hirt as well. We're now up to the "T"s and he hasn't yet supplied *a single anecdote* I hadn't heard already, from Dank or else from Hirt himself, in the sad course of the interviews we held, or rather waged, in his breakfast nook in 2006. In fact, there's not a single sentence in this book—not even (say) in the part about the era when they lived in the same house—that I couldn't have written myself . . . though of course I'd never *want* to write Hirt's sentences, since I'm so far from sharing his sentiments. (BB)

too-typical product of Dank's sex-deprived middle age—is first and foremost a printout of a cherished and, ahem, long-standing masturbation fantasy.

Ah, poor Dank. Tonight I can honestly say I feel nothing but pity for him—and, no, that isn't the Campari speaking, though my fiancée and I just made short work of a bottle out here on the terrace of her palazzo. The wedding won't be here but at her country place, since it has so many more guest bedrooms. (OH)

Tischman, Tyler: A well-meaning journalist unwittingly responsible for a series of catastrophes. In July 2005, a nationwide newsmagazine commissioned him to write an article on neglected American writers. When Tischman called to say that Dank would be one of the featured neglectees, Dank persuaded him to feature Hirt as well—an amazingly generous act, when you consider that the former friends hadn't spoken in four years. (And when you consider that there were many other, more deserving writers whom, ahem, Dank might have named instead, if he hadn't been so fucking—but *de mortuis nil nisi bonum*.) Nor did Hirt show any gratitude to Dank for his good fortune now, but it's possible he didn't know that Dank had had a hand in it. In any case, it is safe to say that Hirt was thrilled at the prospect of his inclusion, of the belated recognition it would bring him (though by that point he'd officially quit writing), to judge by his violent reaction eight months later when the scheme fell through. I had the misfortune of interviewing him the day after Tischman called to tell him that the article—aptly named "Sins of Omission"—had exceeded its allotted space, and that the part about Hirt had been cut, though he'd be glad to know his friend Dank was still featured.

Several times that winter I'd gone over to interview Hirt for the biography, and considering that he and its subject no longer spoke, he had proven surprisingly willing to speak to me *about* Dank.

Once or twice I even sensed that Hirt regretted their falling out and wanted a rapprochement he was too proud to ask for, and that by justifying (or even, almost, once or twice, apologizing for) his past behavior toward Dank, he was speaking to his former friend through me. Or thought he was. I took care not to repeat any propitiating words to Dank, or what was left of Dank (see WHAT NEXT for a description of Dank at that point in his final decline), since I knew that if the ex-friends ever patched things up, there'd be no room for me in their friendship. For the same reason, I'd been alarmed to learn from Dank, the previous summer, not long before he stopped going outdoors, that he and Hirt had taken to nodding when they passed on the street, and sometimes even pausing to say a few words. So in a way it was fortunate that at that point Dank's agoraphobia placed him under house arrest, before he and Hirt could resume their infuriating friendship.

On the day in question, anyhow—the day of our last interview, March 3, 2006—Hirt was *not* in one of his propitiating moods. "Oh Christ, it's *you* again," he said, when I rang his doorbell at the appointed time. "Kiss any good butts lately?" He slurred his words, and stank of alcohol—even if he hadn't answered the door with a bottle in hand, I would have known he'd been drinking. (Not a "people person" to begin with, Hirt had become positively misanthropic since his falling out with Dank, and I gathered that booze was what kept him company now.) I should have left and come back later, but I was curious about what revelations Hirt's bad mood might move him to, if I could get him to focus on Dank. And he did aim some put-downs at Dank—after leading me to the breakfast nook where all our interviews took place, and where several empty bourbon bottles stood in silent homage to his drinking problem—but mainly to emphasize how pathetic *I* was for devoting my life to the man and his works. There was no trace, that day, of Hirt's usual urbanity (or of Campari—this was clearly a no-nonsense binge). As he glowered at me like a belligerent wino, I felt that for the first time ever I was face to face with the *real* Hirt, even if his face was half obscured by the big bushy beard he'd embarked on right around the time of the quarrel. (Since that was also when Hirt renounced his vocation, it may be that he'd been channeling into his beard all the energies he'd formerly channeled into his poems.) What seemed especially to bother him, that day, was my biography of Dank, though that book was the whole reason for our interviews.

"I've got news for you, Boswell—no one wants to read a biography of Dank."

"Yeah, well, that's your opinion."

"It's everyone's opinion. No one wants a book about Dank. Especially not by a jackass like you."

"Are you some kind of expert on what people want to read?"

"No, but I do know a jackass when I see one. Too bad *you* don't. You're writing a book about the second-biggest jackass in town."

If Hirt was getting the better of me in this duel of wits, that's because he was so angry that I didn't dare provoke him by retaliating. Ask any drill sergeant, wife beater, gym teacher, bully, or cop: One of the perks of inspiring fear is that you get to be the only funny person in the room. I barely dared to parry, much less riposte. So instead of scoring an easy point ("Well, maybe when that book is done I'll write another book about the *biggest*, if you let me"*), I said, "If Dank is

---

* (October 2007) Since that day, I've toyed with the idea of writing a biography of *Hirt*, since Dank himself never got around to writing a biography of a total nobody. I've found the perfect epigraph in Ben Jonson—"There be some men are born only to suck out the poison of books"—and the perfect title: *Born to Suck.*

such a jackass, why were you two friends for so many years?"

"You tell me—you're the novelist. Don't you make a point of understanding strange behavior?"

"I never understood why Dank liked *you*."

"I suppose that's why you're writing his biography? Did you realize that you're too stupid to write novels? Too stupid about people?"

"One of these days, my novels—"

"And *I* never understood why Dank puts up with *you*. He doesn't seem like he would need a full-time sycophant."

Hirt continued to insult me in that vein for several minutes—longer, reader, than *you* would have stood for. Maybe the reason I didn't lose patience sooner was that for first time ever he was taking me seriously. After so many years of silent contempt, his open hatred was a welcome change, though it made me reluctant to drink the lemonade he poured me, as if he might have poisoned it in a desperate effort to silence Dank's biographer. And eventually the insults went too far. Hirt was standing at the sink with his back to me and struggling with an ice-cube tray when he spoke the last words I would ever hear from his lips: "You know, I've met a lot of people who kiss ass as a means to an end, you're the only one I know who kisses ass as an end in itself. Is that what you do instead of sex?"

Even for a man of my patience, that was too much. I grabbed an empty bottle and broke it over his head.

Like a puppet whose strings have been cut, he dropped to the floor. "Hah!" I exclaimed, pumping my fist in a sort of Black Power salute. But my exultation soon gave way to fear: Hirt seemed ominously still, even for a minor poet in a drunken stupor. His chest wasn't rising and falling, and when I knelt down to check, I couldn't feel a pulse. I took the pitcher of lemonade and poured it on his head, but nothing happened.

Not only did that prove, at least to my satisfaction, that Hirt was past reviving, but it gave me an idea for disposing of the body. I hope readers won't realign their sympathies with my fellow commentator—as if Hirt and I were lawyers arguing Dank's case before the tribunal of posterity—when I say it never even occurred to me to call an ambulance, much less to call the police. (I also hope, and trust, it goes without saying that I hadn't been trying to *kill* him, only to hurt him—to pay him back, in one lump sum, for a dozen years of unwavering disdain.) No, I moved from ascertaining Hirt's death (though, as his this encyclopedia makes only too clear, I ascertained wrong) straight to wondering what to do with the body. There is a deep and murky lake in an abandoned quarry a few miles out of town—the lake where Dank had been arrested once for skinny-dipping—and I couldn't think of any final resting place more appropriate for Hirt than the muck at its bottom. The trick would be to get him there.

Unlike Dank, Hirt didn't have a garage built into his house. Rather than risk someone seeing me leaving that house with a corpse, I dragged the poet down to his basement and, with difficulty, through the tunnel he'd never deigned to enter while alive. When I reached the other basement, I rested for a minute. Dank was stranded in his bedroom by obesity and dread, and little better than a vegetable (this was the era—described in WHAT NEXT?—of his final psychosis, his last and most heroic feat of passive resistance to reality), so Hirt and I were safe from interruptions. When I'd caught my breath, I dragged my fellow commentator through the basement and into the garage, where my El Camino waited. It wasn't the first time I regretted buying an El Camino, one of those things that look like a cross between an ordinary car and a pickup truck. The bed in back does carry bigger payloads than a car trunk, but affords them much less privacy. I debated whether to belt Hirt into the passenger's seat or to lay him in the open bed in back beneath a tarp. Finally I decided on the tarp—and the cover of night, which had fallen by the time I pulled out of the drive. If Hirt stirred or moaned back there, en route to the lake, I didn't hear him.

On reaching Lake Granite, I was able to back the car to the very edge of the cliff where randy teenagers parked on Saturday nights, and off whose edge the more reckless dived on summer days. This was a Tuesday in March, though, and I had the place to myself. After buttoning the seedy old corduroy jacket that Hirt had worn for our last interview, I loaded its pockets with stones as a suicide might. Not for nothing had I supervised the factory that assembled PERSONAL WORST, one of Dank's bloodiest bloodbaths.

As for the shove that sent him into the lake, that was harder than I'd expected. Though as far as I knew the damage was already done, I had to override a silly inhibition, as Dank had had to do the time he wet his pants on purpose (see VOID WHERE PROHIBITED). I sat Hirt up at the edge of the tailgate and sat down beside him like a man and his dad in a heartwarming commercial for life insurance or beer. I gazed out over the water, thinking how much better off we'd both have been if stupid Hirt had just been nice to me. I remembered our first meeting, at COFFEE TOWN, in 1991, and how he'd made up his mind about me the moment we met. Had it been my nervousness? My ingratiating manner with Dank and Dank's sophisticated friend? The cocoa I had ordered?

The plop of a frog brought me back to my surroundings. I took a deep breath and heaved the poet over the edge, into the lake, where he made a bigger plop. I didn't wait around to see him sink, but for the next week I watched the local news each night. There was no mention of a corpse in Lake Granite, so I assumed I'd gotten rid of Hirt for good.

Titles: One reason that the titles of Dank's fiction often fail to suggest his true originality is that most of his works were printed under different titles than the ones he gave them. Throughout his career, his publishers high-handedly renamed his stories and novels, as if a title were no more than a marketing device. Here are a dozen of Dank's published works and their original titles:

> *The Academician* = *The Martian Who Liked Wine and*
>   *Cheese*
> *Amnesia* = *Are You My Husband or Something?*
> *F for Fatal* = *Grade Book of Death*
> *The Mystery* = *The Man Whose Toothbrush Drove Him Insane*
> *The Pageant* = *Ten Kinds of Pretty*
> "The Suicide Man" = "Never Let the Actuary See You Cry"
> "The Tiresias Formula" = "The Woman Who Left the Toi-
>   let Seat Up"
> *The Wilson Twins* = *The Man Who Was Also His Brother*
> *Void Where Prohibited* = *To Boldly Go*
> "What Next?" = "The Pill-Popping Fetus"

"The Toe": A writer of Dank's genius can draw inspiration from anything, even a stubbed toe. In "The Toe," a yogi trains himself to take his mind off chronic back pain by focusing entirely on his big toe, turning his attention to that body part all the way up on the mixing board of consciousness, and turning all other sensations way down. It works. And since he pampers the toe—gently massaging it, anointing it in oil, dusting it with talcum powder, swaddling it in silk—his life is one of Oriental pleasure. The *rest* of his body he neglects outrageously, forgetting to eat because his brain no longer acknowledges messages from his belly, and not even conscious of an abscess in his molar that would've incapacitated anybody else. None of that matters, though, because he's living in his toe, and living the life of Reilly . . . *until* the day he drops an anvil on his privileged digit (having withdrawn all perception from his hands, he's a bit of a butterfingers), and dies of shock.

Though (as Mark Twain said of Wagner's music) "The Toe" is better than it sounds, it would be an easy piece to ridicule, and I'm surprised that Hirt didn't stomp on it. I've been letting him decide, as we go along, which entries to write—i.e., as it's turning out, which monuments he wants to vandalize. He volunteered to focus on Dank's weaker works, and that is how we've been dividing the labor, though it has the effect of suggesting a bigger gulf than really exists between Dank's more and less successful outings, because Hirt's entries are so relentlessly savage. Often, though, as far as I can tell, the resulting "runs" of Hirt and welcome Hirtless interludes have as much to do with fluctuations in his day-to-day hostility level as with the fluctuations in Dank's output or the happenstances of alphabetical order. Ups and downs in Hirt's financial situation may be a factor too, since I'm paying him by the page (wiring money from Dank's estate to a Swiss bank account). If so, we can be grateful that the fugitive isn't more desperate for money: I've written most of the entries, and most of Hirt's are mercifully brief—not much more than stagy yawns or angry snorts. He already wrote *his* commentary in blood. His entries in this volume are really just a series of unapologetic footnotes to, and elaborations on, that first terse statement of violent disapproval.

"Tough Guy": The adventures of a charismatic brawler as wistfully recounted from his jail cell, where he awaits the hormone therapy that will turn him into a regular pussycat—i.e., a neutered one. In the namby-pamby future Dank imagines, excessive maleness is treated by a sort of pharmaceutical emasculation, especially when that maleness results in someone's death. Tiger, our narrator, got a bit *too* tough in his last fist-fight, and though that fight took place in a lonely parking lot and not a crowded bar, he wasn't as successful at hiding his crime as I was at keeping up appearances—see THE WILSON TWINS—after the killing I thought I'd inflicted, one afternoon by accident, in a certain poet's kitchen. Can poor Tiger escape with his manliness intact?

I myself, by the way, was once arrested for brawling, and I share Dank's disapproval of castration as the answer to rowdy behavior. What I find disturbing about his story, though, is that it pictures male violence not as real problem in need of a saner solution, but as a positive good that only an insanely puritanical regime would seek to abolish. (To see where Dank stands on the issue, it's enough to know that the same regime has also outlawed singing, dancing, alcohol, and chocolate. Violators of *those* laws incur harsh penalties too: Dancers, for example, have their kneecaps broken; chocoholics are arrested and subjected to a month of satiation therapy during which they eat *nothing* but chocolate.)

"Tough Guy," in other words, is the sort of unreflective glorification of violence that Dank used to write under pen names like Dirk Manning, Steve Rockhard, and John Slaughter. He signed his own name, though, to this one, as if proud of its pulp-fiction ethos, or willing anyhow to be confused with its two-fisted narrator. Or was the confusion Dank's? If, as Valéry said, Victor Hugo was a madman who thought he was Victor Hugo, it may be that Dank, for a while there, was a madman who thought he was Steve Rockhard. Maybe he forgot that he himself was *not* a tough guy, and that his persecution, as an adolescent, by hooligans like Tiger (or their adolescent counterparts), was precisely what had driven Dank to the safe haven of science fiction in the first place. In the eternal war between the brawny and the brainy, Dank forgot which side he was on. Life reminded him soon after "Tough Guy" was published, but he really shouldn't have needed a reminder, since by the time he wrote the story he was scared to leave his house.

Elsewhere I've recounted the Moped Episode and the Pit Bull Incident—scares that exacerbated Dank's agoraphobia and sped the inward spiral to which his murder finally put a period. (During a discussion of marine biology in 2004, I was amazed by, and failed to sway, Dank's contention that the chambered nautilus—the mollusk that produces the celebrated seashell—spirals *inward*, starting in the open, dwindling as it goes, and dying when it reaches the innermost chamber.) There is one more chapter to the tale of how our author, after half a century of functioning—reluctantly—outside the womb, ended life as little more than an overgrown fetus.

After he was attacked, or "attacked," by a dog in spring 2005, Dank vowed never again to set foot outside. I'd heard a lot of crazy vows from him over the years, and I didn't take this latest seriously. Six weeks later, though, he'd yet to break the vow. Well, he *had* made one excursion out to the front porch. But that wasn't far enough. And his recollection of the last time he'd gone farther seemed to be getting more and more horrendous, to judge by his daily retellings—the dog bigger, the fangs longer, the eyes more demented, the slobber more rabid. Finally I resolved to lure our author "out there" (as he now referred to the part of the world not contained within his house) before it was too late. Specifically, I wanted Dank to go as far as Coffee Town, or just around the block. He wouldn't even have to walk—I'd drop him off, then park the car and join him. There are no pit bulls in coffee houses, I reminded him, and even if there were, I'd be there to protect him. His actual exposure to the great outdoors—his Extra-Vehicular Activity, as spacemen say—would consist of four brief dashes (insofar as a three-hundred-and-fifty-pound man can ever be said to "dash"): house to curb, curb to coffee house, coffee house to curb, and curb to house again.

I chose Coffee Town because it was close and because it had always been one of Dank's favorite places, even back before his world shrank to the compass of a single block. Lately he'd been having a recurrent dream about the place—a dream where his house and Coffee Town turned out to be connected underground (as his house and Hirt's were in real life) by a private tunnel. The tunnel led directly from our basement to the handicapped stall in the men's room: All Dank had to do was wait until the stall was vacant, flush, and emerge nonchalantly.

So he liked the coffee house. Still, it took two weeks to wear down his resistance—it might have been easier just to dig that tunnel. When the big day finally arrived—a Tuesday, June 14—he stood for several minutes in the front doorway, while I waited at the curb, engine running, until two stroller-pushing housewives who'd happened to meet in front of our house stopped comparing babies and finally moved along. Then he tiptoed out to the edge of the front porch like a runner leading off first base . . . and froze again, scanning his environment for threats. And this was the man who just a few weeks earlier, in the last and most two-fisted interview he ever granted (Ruefle's accident had forced the public Dank out of retirement), had told the cute brunette from *Author* magazine that he liked a good fistfight but could no longer find one because word had gotten around about his black belt in karate.

But back to the front porch. Just a few seconds would elapse between his leap from that porch and his dive into my El Camino, if he didn't trip *en route*, but those seconds were a long time coming: I'd been waiting a good quarter of an hour when he finally made his move. He made it to the car okay (though with a comically panicked expression), but we had to go through the same business again on reaching Coffee Town, where more of those mothers were loitering out front. They too moved along at last, and Dank burst from the El Camino like a novice parachutist bailing out of a plane. I circled the block in search of parking, wound up in front of our house again, and walked back around to Coffee Town, taking my time. I'd promised to be with him every moment, but for this outing to be a success, Dank had to realize that he could still fend for himself in public, at least in the unthreatening environs of the local coffee house.

Except that he couldn't. When I reached the coffee house, I knew something was wrong: the sunny front room, always crowded, was deserted. So was the microwave room, where the Melvilleans met, though with a queasy feeling I noted that their table was strewn with twice-neglected manuscripts, and that the room stunk of Wagenknecht. Everybody seemed to be in the smoky, windowless, and always-empty back room, and I knew that somehow Dank must be the reason. Sure enough, there he stood without his glasses, in the middle of a ring of patrons, face to face with Plinkett, the ex-weatherman who'd always had it in for him. Dank had his dukes up like an old-time pugilist, but that hadn't stopped his foe from landing several punches: Dank was bleeding from both nostrils and the corner of his mouth. He also appeared to be crying. Plinkett (even bigger than Jablonsky) was feigning punches and laughing. Among the onlookers were all the other Melville regulars—I'd forgotten that they met on Thursday afternoons. As far as I could tell, they were rooting for Plinkett. "Hit him again, Jim!" said Dawson. Wagenknecht concurred: "Don't just fake it, Jim, hit him for real!" Plinkett obliged, though with a body blow that can't have done much damage to someone so well padded. Then he turned to Dawson to say something jocular about Dank's obesity, and Dank seized the opportunity to hit Plinkett in the Adam's apple. Plinkett fell to the floor with his back to Dank, who promptly kicked him in the rump. "That's what you get!" he added, as if in explanation. He wanted to continue kicking Plinkett, but I was eager to get him out of there: The police, in my experience, don't like it when you punch somebody in the throat. And it was just possible that the Melvilleans still standing would gang up on us, though I think they'd always been a little scared of me (I understand that they referred to me, behind my back, as "Travis Bickle"). Somehow I steered Dank through the crowd and out the door, where I recalled that I had left my car back at the house. Our author, though, was so exulted by his upset victory ("Did you see that? I literally kicked his ass!") that he swaggered back around the block without a flicker of anxiety.

His phobia returned, though, with a vengeance, as soon as he was back inside his house. Dank wouldn't talk about the incident at Coffee Town, but from other sources I gathered that Plinkett had seen that pugnacious interview in *Author* and had called the interviewee's bluff by picking a fight. Dank feared that other readers too were waiting out there, like so many after-school bullies, for a chance to call his bluff, and since in its latest edition that bluff involved a hyper-manly love of fistfights, Dank stood to lose teeth as well as face if he ever went outside again. And so he didn't. Well, he did take one more walk around the block, in the year remaining to him, but aside from that brief and unseasonable blossom of normal functioning, the next time he left his house was in a hearse.

"Toughie": Dank's fiction constantly reminds us not to underestimate the handicapped. The very fact of its existence is a tribute to the human spirit: Who would think a novelist with an IQ of eighty-nine could publish all those books? But nowadays the road to publication is not only wheelchair-accessible, but wide enough to let a short bus overtake on the shoulder.

"Toughie" is even dumber than average—even for *Dank*. Based on a fantasy dating back to his much-persecuted adolescence, the would-be-inspirational tale packs such a wallop of sheer stupidity that if you insist on reading it at all, I suggest you wear protective headgear. Born without arms or legs in a pitiless near-future where the handicapped are barely tolerated, much less published, Timmy ("Toughie") Tufferson takes a lot of pummeling before he finally figures out how to fight back via telekinesis. Toughie's psychic "punches" are as powerful as any able-bodied boxer's, and—since they're invisible—impossible to block. Because, like Dank, he's also extremely well-padded with fat, and because he boasts such timeless qualities as moxie, mettle, chutzpah, grit, and pluck, Toughie soon parlays his special talent into a world heavyweight title, though not before enduring a brutal title match during which his psychic powers desert him for several rounds. (OH)

A B C D E F
G H I J K L
M N O P Q R
S T U V W X
Y Z

Understanding "The Author": In the spring of 1999, Dank announced that he was "nothing but" a character in a novel. He even thought he knew its title—*The Author*—though he couldn't say who'd written it. Sunny Thanker? Rebus Blank? August Traurig? Phineas Duck? Some third-rate metafictioneer, in any case: Dank himself would not have stooped to the stale postmodern gimmick of having a fictional character suspect his own fictional status. And yet in real life he was not above behaving like just such a character, doubting his own existence and experiencing himself as another author's figment. Maybe because his friends were all writers, and his waking life consisted of little else but writing, he tended to think that there were just two kinds of people: the kind who write novels and the kind who populate those novels. And of course it's possible—though not a good idea—to be both. In the spring of 1999, Dank decided *he* was both.

That conviction led to his quixotic attempt at a critical study of the novel whose hero he believed himself to be. Before losing interest at the two-hundred-page mark, Dank summarized, interpreted, and criticized *The Author* in impressive detail—tracing influences, pointing out structural flaws, pouncing on clichés and continuity errors, deploring lapses of taste, finding fault with certain characters' psychologies (I, for one, was deemed "implausible" and even "incoherent"), patronizing his creator's "bountiful imagination," arguing persuasively that parts (his second heart attack) should have been cut and others (his third honeymoon) expanded, and even speculating about the missing ending the way Kafka scholars do with *The Castle*.

Dank's delusion of being just another author's creature was the kind of folly not susceptible to refutation (what would have counted as evidence against it?), but like most of his delusions it subsided of its own accord, after a month and two hundred pages of frenzied exegesis. The readiness with which he relinquished such delusions makes me think that Dank never really fully embraced them in the first place—even if he *thought* he did, even if he never understood the difference between owning a conviction and taking one for a joyride.

Though we think of delusions as either/or propositions, there are infinite shades of credulity. Science fiction writers in particular have a strange relation to the more preposterous things they claim to believe—a mixture of the hazy truth-ignoring wishful thinking of a happy drunk, the cynicism of a venal televangelist, and the demiurgic ambitions of a physicist with a particle accelerator. "Granted that I'm *not* a Martian [I can see Dank thinking], let's see if I can't convince myself I *am*, for just a second, before truth reasserts itself and annihilates that particle of unreality."

As for his conviction of being a fictional character, I'm emphasizing its tepidity, the first time around, because the delusion flared up again at the end of Dank's life, but without a trace of skepticism. Not until he'd really lost his mind did I come to see how basically sane he had been up to then.

The Unsent Letters of Phoebus K. Dank: Like most of us, Dank found it easier to say imprudent things in writing than in person, so it was good that he lived several blocks from the nearest public mailbox. Especially after he stopped driving, the distance gave our author—not the quickest second-thinker—time to think twice about some of his letters. This volume (still in preparation, but presumably in print by the time you read this entry), collects the many letters that he thought the better of.

Not that his second thoughts always arrived in time. Dank would sometimes pick up his pace *en route* to the mailbox, if he felt good sense approaching, so he could reach the mailbox and drop his letter through the slot—with the little thrill of irreversibility he always felt at that instant, even if only paying a bill—before his better judgment overtook him. Most of his neighbors had seen him, at one time or another, hastening up to the mailbox with a letter in his hand and then either veering away at the last moment or else mailing his letter and immediately looking horrified at what he'd done. A few weeks after Gabriella left, Dank was arrested for attempting to set fire to the mailbox at the corner of Empedocles and Elder. It seems he'd been lighting and "mailing," one after another, several dozen wooden kitchen matches: He'd thought the better of a long hate letter he'd just mailed, and knew no other way to intercept it.

Mostly, though, he thought the better of his more outrageous letters before he dropped them through the slot. As a result, the ones he *didn't* send make better reading—and luckily for us he saved them, probably telling himself, each time he refrained from mailing an ill-advised letter, that even if its first addressee never saw it, posterity would. He made sure of that: His will ordained this posthumous collection, and his estate is footing the bill. Among the goodies in the book are a letter to his mother blaming her for his sporadic impotence; a letter to MacDougal diagnosing and deploring the latter's "short-man complex" and enclosing a coupon for elevator shoes; a letter to Pandora telling several shameless lies (as to the size of his savings account, the remarkability of his childhood, the likeli-hood of his receiving a Nobel Prize, and so on) calculated to make her regret that she'd opted not to spend her life with him; and a long letter to McNeil Pharmaceuticals, the makers of Immodium, offering, for a mere thousand dollars, to men-tion the product "frequently and positively" in the novel he was writing. It is interesting to imagine just how Dank would have worked in that drug so frequently and prominently, if McNeil had deigned to answer his letter.

A B C D E F
G H I J K L
M N O P Q R
S T U V W X
Y Z

Virtually Immortal: Dank's last novel. In October 2003, his father developed the rare and deadly species of INSOMNIA—worsening and finally total, so that the afflicted seem to die from simple lack of sleep—that ran in the family. Crazed by wakefulness and with nothing else to do, Edmund Dank spent the long nights of his last winter typing up the story of his life, or so he claimed, but showing no one the results. He refused his son's dutiful offer to write that story for him like the as-told-to "memoirs" of pro athletes, rock musicians, movie stars, and other celebrity illiterates.

Dank the elder died in March 2004, but not before producing reams of gibberish on the old word processor his son had given him. His widow wanted that son to edit the manuscript into a semblance of sense, but she was asking the impossible: Edmund's apologia for his (lazy, wasted) life, his final message to posterity, consisted of some fourteen hundred pages of keystrokes in no discernible order. Often, said Dank, who knew a "qwerty" when he saw one, it looked as if the memoirist had used his whole hand, or the side of his arm, to fill a page as fast as possible. Now and then Edmund had managed a word, or a near-word ("insomia"; "shoess"; "argicultur"), but otherwise it was all nonsense. After skimming that appalling manuscript, Dank had nightmares in which his father came to him with the expression of a man with something urgent to say, but when he opened his mouth what came out was the spoken equivalent of his typewritten gibberish. Dank hated and dreaded those dreams like the visits of a ghost, but isn't it good that the living dream about the dead? Our persistence in dreams may be all the afterlife we get,* and about as much of one as Edmund merited.

But it wasn't enough for Dank, and *Virtually Immortal* was his way of coping with his father's death, which made his own seem so much nearer. The book is as close as Dank ever came to "hard" science fiction, fiction based on plausible extrapolation from existing science or technology. For most of 2003 Dank had been addicted to electronic CHAT ROOMS—so addicted, for about a year there, that it largely took the place of writing fiction (though most of his online chat was fiction too). When, chastened by his father's fatal illness, he finally logged off and went back to work, the book Dank wrote was one that got a lot of mileage from the simple observation that more and more people are relating to their fellow humans largely through the Internet. Dank had noticed that he wasn't the only one spending most of his waking hours online, and seeming to experience separations from his computer—to eat, to bathe, to sleep—as interruptions or suspensions of his real life. It was a commonplace that such addicts *had* no life to speak of away from their computers. In that case, reasoned Dank, they could be said to live on after death if their computers could be programmed to relate to other people, or other computers, in the same way the deceased had while alive. If you knew you had a year left to live, and nothing better to do with that year than what you'd been doing already—growing older in front of a computer—that would be plenty of time to give your CPU

---

* Or it may be just another meaningless phenomenon, like the growth of hair and nails after death. (OH)

all the information it needed. Especially if you have the luck to live in a future where the demand for this cyber-afterlife is sufficiently widespread that entrepreneurs develop software for the purpose, like tax-preparation software.

With the help of such programs, it's easy for the dying to input data about their personal history, their likes and dislikes, opinions and dreams, and what Dank calls "modes of electronic self-presentation." In order for the software to produce a truly lifelike imitation of you after death, you can't hold back any secrets: The computer needs to know whatever St. Peter ("in that other, now-discredited afterlife scenario") would find under your name in the Book of Life, which in a way is what you are writing. But only a fraction of that data will be revealed to others (and all sorts of protections, legal and cybernetic, exist to prevent people from hacking into the database). A man might have electrocuted his best friend's worst enemy, or tried to kill a surly bitter alcoholic poet by cracking him over the head with a bottle of the whiskey that was killing him already (though those examples aren't the ones Dank cites), and if so he needs to tell the computer. But he also tells it never to release that information, not even to his psychoanalyst. (In the future Dank envisions, there's no need for psychotherapy to end just because the patient has died: Those with the money to waste might choose to stay in analysis long after death, gambling; maybe, given a century or so to explore the repercussions of infantile traumas, the cure will finally cure someone.)

Somebody must keep the loved one's database updated— keep it abreast of current affairs. For news of general interest, online services provide regular and automatic updates directly to the loved one's database. News of more personal developments—of friends and family—demands a bit more effort from the living, especially since it can't be added to the cyberperson's fund of knowledge on the fly. (That is, you can *tell* a cyberperson that his sister has just been arrested for stealing a spaceship, and if programmed right he'll react appropriately—but he won't remember it, next time you talk, unless you've also taken the trouble to enter the data in a special format on a special form.) But of course the whole technology exists for the living as much as for the dead, whose frantic last-minute efforts to program a passing simulacrum of themselves is often no more than a dutiful favor to those who will outlive them. As a rule, survivors appreciate the favor, and just as they'd keep the loved one's cemetery plot in good condition, they are moved, by gratitude and guilt, to keep his or her database online and up to date. Even in the old days people used to visit graves to tell their loved ones about weddings and graduations and cancers. Now, when they commune with their dead and bring them up to date on such events, the living are repaid with feedback that gives the illusion that their loved ones hear and understand the news.

As with most "hard" science fiction, *Virtually Immortal* is less about its characters and plot than about its high-concept technology. But if Dank never lets us forget that his futuristic premise is the novel's real star, at least that premise has the virtue of suggesting many parallel or intersecting storylines. One subplot concerns a custody dispute for control of a dead man's database, since his children by his first wife think his second has been misinforming him. Another storyline involves a dead avant-garde author whose executor must keep him apprised of new developments in fiction so that the author (modeled on *me*, of all people) can continue from beyond the grave to write cutting-edge work.

My favorite subplot, though, involves a young widow who for a while conscientiously updates her husband's database and spends several hours a day in "conversation" with him. As time goes by and life goes on, though, she neglects him more and more—especially when, after a year in mourning, she meets another, living man. At one point she neglects her dead husband for more than a month. When she finally boots him up again, he bawls her out. Chastened, she resumes their daily conversations, but no longer bothers to keep him up to date—to do the brief but tedious inputting she would need to, to inform him of their son's promotion or their daughter's second child. And her husband notices that she no longer logs on in the evenings. He seems to know that she has met another man. One day they quarrel so rancorously (he calls her a "gold-digging slut") that she destroys her computer in an effort to delete her husband from the world in a way that death itself has failed to delete him, but by that point (2022) it is no longer possible to delete a cyberperson: Inerasable backups are stored on central servers. The widow settles for blocking e-mails from him, so that he can no longer contact her, and she goes for several years without accessing her ex-husband again. When she finally does, she's overwhelmed by guilt to find him not only pathetically grateful for another chance, but pathetically uninformed about everything that has happened in the meantime, in her life in the larger world.

"The Visionary": On the regrettably brief and infrequent occasions when Dank was feeling "blocked," he still managed to scribble little stories about fortune-tellers losing their ability to see the future—a metaphor, he said, for his own difficulties picturing a future in which to set his fiction. It was one of Dank's better metaphors (not saying much!) in its unconscious admission that, as a soothsayer, he was as much of a charlatan as any storefront psychic.

During the stoppage of 1998, Dank wrote "The Visionary," set in a future where fortune-telling is a legitimate profession, with its own union. Our protagonist, a certain Madame Fia Wollheim, forgets to pay her union dues, and from one day to the next the images on her crystal ball are "scrambled," like premium channels on cable TV, for those who haven't paid for them. That, too, is Dank's metaphor, not mine—and you can tell what kind of things are really on a writer's mind by where he gets his metaphors. All too often, Dank's reflect his television habit. Where a real writer might unwind, at the end of a productive day, by reading fifty pages of *Paradise Lost* or *Being and Time*—since even the hardest reading is easy compared to serious *writing*—Dank lumbered back and forth between his study and his living room, between computer monitor and television screen, as if channel surfing. Never stretched, his neurons never needed to relax, and the brainless trance in which he watched TV was less a vacation from than a variation on the brainless trance in which he wrote his books. (OH)

Void Where Prohibited: An unlikely "true crime" book (modeled on the ones I kept in a box beneath my bed—my "guilty pleasure," as pornography was Dank's) about a truly minor crime: public urination. The book was Dank's response to his arrest for that infraction one night in August 1999, as he was walking home, alone, from the dive where he spent so much time that summer because it was a favorite hangout of Pandora's.

Dank's book begins, like most books of its genre, with a brief but lurid account of the crime. Then he backs up to give his whole life history and milieu, with special attention to extenuating circumstances: an absentee father, a smaller-than-average bladder, a head full of the punk-rock show he'd heard that evening, by a group called Adolph and the Attitude, whose lyrics featured exhortations to "fuck shit up," to "do whatever the fuck you want," and, yes, to "piss on the System." From there, the book slowly works up to the night of the crime, slows down even further to redescribe the act itself from every conceivable angle, and then reconstructs the painstaking process by which the perpetrator was identified and brought to justice. (Dank hadn't been surprised in the act, but stopped a few blocks farther on—his fly still damningly unzipped—by a squad car responding with admirable promptness to a complaint from the old lady in whose birdbath he had urinated.) There is a tense interrogation sequence culminating in a dramatic confession, and then, as a sort of coda, followups on the criminal and his victims—on all the lives he affected. It sounds like an extended joke, but Dank viewed it as an artistic challenge, the serious application to a misdemeanor of a genre usually devoted to high-concept felonies.

What Dank's accuser found especially inexcusable had been his choice of her birdbath as the destination for his urine, a choice she saw as transforming his from a simple if untimely draining of his bladder into outright vandalism. Dank insisted that he hadn't meant to defile the birdbath, that he'd just been pissing on the lady's dogwood tree and hadn't even noticed the nearby receptacle, though he left a damning puddle of evidence in its basin. Had I been called as a witness for the defense, I could have testified to the poorness of Dank's aim—so poor he'd recently had the downstairs bathroom remodeled, paying a carpenter to replace the hardwood floor with institutional tile, a plumber to install a storm drain in the center of that floor, and another plumber to rip out the toilet and replace it with a regulation urinal, though that meant that Dank now had to go upstairs to defecate. But he liked the idea of having separate rooms for the two functions—he seemed to think it was classy. The downstairs bathroom was also where he kept the bathroom scale he'd bought in 1997. (Till then, whenever he suddenly wanted to know what he weighed— most often after an especially massive bowel movement—he'd been content to go to Wal-Mart and weigh himself on one of the scales in the housewares department.) Since he always kept his scale right in front of the urinal, I surmise that Dank liked to weigh himself as he urinated, probably enjoying the illusion of sudden miraculous weight loss. In 2003, though, he painted over the dial of his scale with opaque black paint, though he still stood on the scale for a minute every morning: He felt obliged to weigh himself ("for health reasons") but didn't want to know how *much* he weighed. (For a week or two he tried the same thing with the dial of his wristwatch.)

A few nights after the Birdbath Affair, on another drunken stagger home from the same bar (the Alibi, later the site of his second heart attack), Dank wet his pants, on purpose, under cover of the night, in the name of Science. He'd once read an article in *Popular Psychology* claiming (on the basis of a laboratory study whose logistics he'd forgotten, though you'd think they'd be as hard to forget as they are to imagine) that few adults are *able*—try as they may—to override that particular learned inhibition, the one against wetting their pants. He told me all this almost boastfully the morning after, though he hadn't seemed so proud the night before, on his return from the bar, as he hastened through the living room where like a fretful parent I sat waiting up for him, and hurried upstairs with his hands over the dark spot on his khakis. As far as I'm aware he never tried to replicate the results of his experiment, but he continued for the rest of his life to take a mild pride in his ability to do something that most healthy adults cannot. The artistic ego is so insatiable that even artists as accomplished as Dank are always looking high and low for further proofs of their remarkability.

A B C D E F

G H I J K L

M N O P Q R

S T U V W X

Y Z

"Wacko!": Another of Dank's variations on the Jekyll-and-Hyde theme—as most readers would have guessed when informed that the story's troubled hero is named Jack L. Hyde. Jack consists of two warring personalities, each with its own agenda. One is a respectable accountant with a steady job, a tidy lawn, a restful marriage. The other is a beatnik, though, who wants to live and paint like Jackson Pollock, and to hell with squares. Each self knows about and does his best to sabotage the other, but neither knows about the other's sabotage. The beatnik can't imagine who keeps getting into his locked studio somehow and slashing all his paintings, while the burgher doesn't understand the dirty looks he keeps receiving from his neighbors and co-workers.

Though Dank sometimes wondered what it would be like to be a normal money-making family man and not a lonely artist, he was not afflicted by the ruinous ambivalence—the inner civil war—he visits on his hero. Something in Jack's plight, however, must've struck a chord with *me*, since from the day I came across his story, as an adolescent, in a magazine called *Shocking*, the piece has had a fascination for me no mere synopsis can convey, much less account for. It was the first thing by Dank I ever read, and in a sense the reason I went on to read the rest. If I'd happened to catch hold of his elephantine corpus by some other protuberance, I might have let go and continued blindly groping around for an author I could call my favorite.

My collaboration with Hirt has given a new pertinence to "Wacko": None of Dank's stories better conveys the essential *silliness* of envy (the least enjoyable of the seven deadly sins), probably because it was written right around the time its author first became aware of Hirt's envy disorder. And only a friend as trusting as Dank, and as innocent of the sentiment himself, could have taken so long to notice what after all was Hirt's ruling passion.

God knows *I* have more right to be bitter than Hirt. He at least he got his stuff published, though there could scarcely be less demand for my novels than for Hirt's sestinas. Since those novels are more worthy (not saying much!) than many that do find their way into print and onto the shelves of your favorite chain, I'm forced to conclude that the Club of Published Authors is as arbitrary and unfair in its admission policies as the secret club established by the other children on Dank's block, when he was nine or ten, with the sole purpose of excluding him. (Dank tried to retaliate by starting his own club, the Astronauts, but nobody wanted to join.) Hazlitt, in his suspiciously hard-to-find essay on Patronage and Puffing, put it best: "Reputation runs in a vicious circle, and Merit limps behind it, mortified and abashed at its own insignificance." But sooner or later my novels—*The Ancestors, The Arithmetic of Life, Hypersensitivity, Lost in the Supermarket, Three-Point Perspective, Wired for Truth,* and *A Word to the Wise*—*will* be published. They may not be runaway bestsellers, but there's a place for limpalong shelfwarmers too.

In the meantime, though, you don't see *me* begrudging Dank's success. And what's my secret? "Confronted by outstanding merit in another, there is no way of saving one's ego except by love." That's Goethe. And if *Goethe* could eat humble pie like that, I'll take another slice myself.

"What Next?": A psychopharmacologist develops a prenatal anti-anxiety drug. He reasons that a sentient creature gradually developing all sorts of specialized equipment for which, in its current environment, it has no special use, will also, by and by, with so much time to think, develop a dread of the world those organs imply—i.e., a fear of being born.

This early story, written during Dank's first wife's ill-fated pregnancy, doesn't have much of a plot, but I find it one of his more poignant pieces in light of the stillbirth of his son a few months later, as if Phoebus Jr.'s prenatal dread had culminated in a decision *not* to be born—not to let them take him alive from the paradise of the womb. And it seemed like such a perfect emblem for the smartest science fiction—a fetus dreading, and trying to envision, the world that awaits it—that I borrowed the title of the story for the academic journal I started soon after the death of our author, to spread the word about him.

The story also sheds some light, I think, on Dank's later attempts to return to the womb, which is how I understand his bouts of pathological laziness, sleepiness, morbid ideation, and agoraphobia. After his scuffle with Plinkett (see TOUGH GUY), Dank spent a week in the basement, floating in the jumbo womb that was his swimming pool, and floating better than ever—though finding it harder to climb the basement stairs—because he was getting fatter and fatter. He spoke of moving down there for good, but one day while floating and feeding from the little mini-fridge he'd set up poolside, he accidentally tugged the fridge (the same one that features in THE BIG BOOK OF PROBLEMS) into the water. Though the shock he received wasn't as deadly as the one that rid the world of MacDougal, it was bad enough to ruin the pool for Dank as a place to relax, a place to pretend that he hadn't yet been born.

So he moved his show up to his bedroom—under his own power, after the mechanical lift overheated and broke. By the time he finally reached his bed, Dank was panting so alarmingly that when I found him there a full day later, I thought better of exhorting him to get back out. And by that point he'd developed an infirmity more crippling than obesity.

Unlike his rugged PUBLIC IMAGE, Dank had never been an outdoorsman, so his inability to leave the house at all now—and reluctance, lately, even to leave his bed—was not as end-of-the-world tragic as it must sound to my mountain-climbing, scuba-diving, bungee-jumping readers. No, what ended the world for Dank was a recrudescence of his all-time silliest delusion: that of being nothing but a character in someone else's novel. As mentioned in another entry (UNDERSTANDING "THE AUTHOR"), Dank had entertained that delusion before, but not to the point of letting it upset him. Minutes after moving the locus of his torpor from his basement to his bedroom, though, Dank fell asleep and had what ever after he described as his all-time worst nightmare: He dreamed he was the hero of a comic novel about a third-rate author. In the dream, he met the author of that novel and they argued about who'd imagined whom. Dank lost the argument. They also argued about which of Dank's most cherished memories were real and which ones were merely "implants," though you'd think the question, so urgent for so many science-fiction characters, would lose its urgency for those who've realized that they themselves are only fictional. Evidently not: Dank and his author had repeatedly consulted the index of the novel—the novel had an index—to check the status of specific memories.

Though he summarized the dream at length, I still don't know what made it a nightmare for Dank—the sheer fact of being a fictional character, or the *kind* of character he happened to be, or the kind of *author* luck had saddled him with, or the kind of *book* that author was using him in. I guess you had to be there.

Neither do I know why Dank took the dream so seriously. After all, it was only a dream. Or so I kept reminding him; *he* kept insisting that he'd had a glimpse of his "true nullity." He'd already had a glimpse the week before at Coffee Town, he told me, during the fistfight, when for a moment his humiliation, hatred, fear, self-pity, and pain gave way to a sense that nothing mattered, not even a punch in the nose, because he (like Plinkett, and me too presumably) was "nothing but a figment." And who hasn't felt, in a moment of crisis, the solace of schizoid detachment? It's a circuit breaker to protect you from high-voltage surges of reality by letting you experience them as *un*real. Usually the circuit breaker resets itself after a minute or two, but Dank's never did reset itself, probably because he *preferred* to experience the life as unreal, if he had to endure it at all. He probably saw that as the next best thing to not having been born.

So my theory is that Dank made such a fuss about that dream because it gave him a way of explaining the sense of unreality he'd already vowed to cultivate. Dank denied it hotly, or rather with what little warmth he could muster now that he knew he was nothing but a fiction. He insisted (from his bed, where he'd been driven by that knowledge, as by a crippling illness) that far from being a convenient pretext to withdraw from life, the dream had been a rude awakening, a trauma as jarring as birth. He had been expelled forever from the fool's paradise of assuming he was real (as even the sharpest of fictional characters tend to assume). He was stuck in a novel and knew it. As for his apparent decision to spend the rest of the novel in bed, Dank seemed to see that as passive resistance.

He knew he could never evade his author's surveillance or anticipate—in order to thwart—his author's intentions, but as a novelist in his own right, Dank knew a thing or two about recalcitrant characters. He knew that no author wants a protagonist just to lie in bed page after page, stolidly refusing to do or say or feel or remember or imagine anything. By his own refusal, Dank hoped to salvage a scrap of dignity from the humiliation of being nothing but another author's creature.

So he claimed. All we know for sure is that, whatever the reason, he did stay in bed. Twice a day he dragged himself across the hall to the toilet, but otherwise he barely stirred except at meals. His appetite was now enormous, and I was too busy with classes to feed him, so I rehired the woman who had cooked for us during the LA-Z-BOY crisis, which had ended so recently that I'm tempted to view this last chapter of his life as a relapse.

To make his bedroom still more womblike (already I'd replaced the window shades with heavy curtains), Dank asked me one day to shut the shutters—as I did, with difficulty, from inside. When I returned from campus the next day, I saw two big patches of red where Dank's bedroom windows had been. I'd known from an old snapshot that the house's sky-blue shutters had been red once, and now I saw that back in 1992 when Dank repainted them, he had painted only the side exposed when the shutters were open.* Shutters, after all, are always open. Some don't even shut. Dank had just shut his, though, exposing red backsides that still looked freshly painted. Had they even *been* red, all that time, with no one to see them? They were red now, anyhow, and so jarring that a rumor spread throughout the neighborhood: 107 Empedocles harbored a dangerous maniac.

---

* The sort of corner-cutting characteristic of bad artists in every genre, from housepainting to science fiction. (OH)

And there *was* something scary in there, though it hardly posed a danger to the neighborhood. Dank came more and more, in his final year, to resemble the things in his aquarium, so unresponsive and rooted in place that, though classed as animals, they were easier to think of as plants. If I'd merely been his lodger, not his friend and keeper, I would have moved out at this point. I'm ashamed to say I might have moved out anyhow, if I'd had anywhere better to go. Not that I regretted putting all my chips on Dank. Far from it. The trickle of movieland interest that has since become a torrent was already beginning to swell. My colleagues had been treating me with more and more respect: It turned out that the World's Leading Dankian wasn't such a dinky title after all. Dank's reputation was looking better than ever.

But Dank himself was now defunct. Like the artist in "The Transfusion" (one of many stories that don't rate entries in this guide because they were written not by Dank but his assistants), a painter who dies on completing a uniquely lifelike self-portrait, Dank had put himself entirely into his art. *That* was where to find him now. And it looked like there'd be no *more* art from him: Even fantasy, to be any good, has to be inspired by excitement with the real world, and Dank had lost all interest in the real world.

In the last year of his life, I grew more and more reluctant even to visit his sickroom: There was really no one there. More and more I caught myself speaking of Dank in the past tense. ("He was one of the most inventive people I knew." "He wrote several stories about false memory.") What remained of the man I'd met in 1991 was still capable of rudimentary metabolism, but wasn't otherwise alive in any meaningful sense. As for what exactly died on June 14, 2006, I'm not sure *what* to call it, but since it did still manage to squeeze out a few more stories, and produce a few more twitches and spasms of selfhood, we'll continue for simplicity to refer to it as Dank, and to its death as murder.

What Next?: The Journal of Dank Studies: To be published quarterly starting next month (June 2007) by the Dank Studies department at Hemlock College (which currently consists of me, though there has been talk of hiring a TA to help with the large intro course), *What Next?* will be the only journal dedicated to the serious scholarly discussion of Dank's oeuvre. Notable articles in the inaugural issue will include "Bonk!: The Head Injury as Epiphany in the Later Fiction of Dank"; "No Vaccine: Dank's Subversive Fictions as Filter-Passing Viruses"; "Minus Seven, or Why You Haven't Read Dank's Greatest Novels"; and "Model Moms: The Housewife as Temptress, Martyr, Witch, and Madwoman in the Works of Phoebus K. Dank," all by the present commentator.*

I had lobbied for a Dank Studies program ever since I came to Hemlock College back in 1994. You'd think the local college would be thrilled to celebrate the writer who put Hemlock on the map, but academics are famously reluctant to recognize the merits of living writers. If there'd been a college in Stratford-on-Avon circa 1600, it's safe to say the professors would have resisted any attempt to add that upstart Shakespeare to the curriculum, at least as long as he was still alive. A grim irony: Only the tragedy of Dank's death made possible the program and the periodical I had dreamed of for so many years. If I believed in Providence, I might try to solace myself

---

* (October 2007) I'm pleased to report that that issue was *an unqualified* success. So was the second issue, just last month (Sept '07), with its two long essays, "No Pain, No Gain: Why Dank Makes His Characters Suffer So Much," and "Keeping it Up: A Feminist Reading of Dank," both by this commentator.

with the thought that Dank died at the right time (as Nietz-sche exhorts us all to do). He had written himself out, and by staying alive was only hampering the spread of his reputation and the growth of Dank Studies.

"Where Does Dessert Come Before Dinner?": Where? In the diction-ary—and in this ridiculous story about a police state whose citi-zens are forced to do everything in alphabetical order. They learn to dance before they learn to walk, learn to sing before they learn to speak, study calculus before they study trigonometry, engage in kissing only after intercourse, and, if arrested for a violation of alphabetical order, serve their sentences *before* their trials.

Lest it be said that I don't enter into the spirit of the stories I discuss, I'll add that this one is awkward, bathetic, callow, de-mented, embarrassing, fatuous, geeky, ham-handed, illiterate, juvenile, kitschy, labored, mealy-mouthed, overblown, prurient, queasy, retarded, sophomoric, tedious, unreadable, vapid, wordy, xenophobic, yawn-inducing, and zzz-evoking. (OH)

***The Wilson Twins*:** A sort of mirror-image of THE COLLABORA-TION. Like the brothers in that story, Will and Phil are identical twins. One day, on a hike, Will accidentally or semi-acciden-tally causes Phil's death (a somewhat absurd one, otherwise unwitnessed, involving a long argument about the books of Cordwainer Smith and then a shoving match on the lip of an active volcano). Will knows that their aging, ailing parents wouldn't be able to handle the death of a son, so he keeps it from them by impersonating Phil, both over the phone and in person, though now of course only one or the other can visit their parents on holidays.

The impersonation soon takes on a life of its own, which means that Will starts leading two, and maintaining two households. He even works two jobs—and the impersonation itself, after all, is a bit like taking on a coworker's duties in addition to his own. His initial motive, again, is to spare his parents needless grief. As soon as they die, he plans to kill off his alter ego and get back to his normal life. But when, after years of this elaborate imposture, he loses both parents in the space of a month, Will can't bear to lose Phil too: Theirs was a very close family, and now Phil is all he has left. And so for the rest of his life he keeps Phil "alive," or keeps "Phil" alive. In any case, he keeps up two e-mail accounts (as well as two bank accounts), sends messages back and forth between the brothers daily, buys presents for each from the other on their birthday, and so on. He even avenges his brother's grudges, since the brother was an angry, maladjusted loser. Will was always the easygoing one, and yet he has no trouble occupying his twin's anger, any more than he had trouble, after his wife left him, in occupying the closets and bookshelves once allotted to her.

The cleverly structured novel begins with Will's own death, at forty-six, in a car accident involving the tiny Toyota registered to Phil (Will himself drives a Lexus), on the way home from Phil's part-time job at the DMV. Police can't understand why the surviving brother, Will, seems to have vanished into thin air at the instant of Phil's death, and when a dutiful postmortem fingerprinting reveals that the corpse is Will and not Phil, they're still a long way—a whole novel away—from knowing the whole story.[*]

---

[*] (October 2007) *The Wilson Twins* dates from 1979, when I was thirteen and had never heard of Dank (nor he of me, of course), making even sillier Tom's already ridiculous suggestion that Will was modeled on yours truly. Yes, his full name is William, but that's all we have in common. And if Tom had paid attention thirty years ago in his Intro to American Lit class, he'd recognize the story as an updating and rethinking of Poe's great doppelganger story, "William Wilson."

Dank and *his* twin, of course, were about as far from identical as two well-fed grown-ups can well be. That had been
one of his main grievances against her, growing up—that she
"wasn't identical," and so was no good for the zany deceptions
that twins are always pulling on sitcoms, much less for the
elaborate deception depicted in *The Wilson Twins*. And such
deceptions are so central to our culture's mythology of twin-
ship that even Dank, who knew the drab reality, preferred to
daydream about the sitcom version. As we all do. When I was
young I had an imaginary twin whose activities I pictured in
great detail when dissatisfied with real life, as I almost always
was. Lucky (as I called him) didn't have to go to school, and
though I couldn't send him in my place (any more than Dank
could Jane), I got through long dull classes by thinking about
him, picturing him popping wheelies, reading comics, climbing trees, tormenting bugs, setting off M-80s, or whatever
my current idea of fun was. Sometimes in the winter he won
snowball fights or built imposing snow forts, but more often I
sent him to Florida, where I'd never been but only heard about
from classmates, and where he could continue to pursue the
warm-weather pastimes I preferred to wintry ones.

So instead of saying—as I planned to—that *The Wilson
Twins* gave me an idea, maybe I should say it revived an idea
that had been in remission for decades. In March 2006, I found
myself in a predicament a lot like Will's after my interview with
Hirt got so acrimonious as to leave me thinking that I'd killed
him. And predicament it was: My hatred of Hirt was a matter
of common knowledge. The year before, I'd even *threatened*
to kill him—not in earnest but, alas, in public (in the deli section at Food Planet, where he'd picked the wrong day for an
idiotic quip about "braunschweiger for brown-nosers"), and at
the top of my lungs. That we later patched up our differences,
at least to the point where he let me into his house (the bet-

ter to go on insulting me), wouldn't be enough to clear me of suspicion. I thought I'd gotten rid of what I thought was a corpse, but that didn't solve all my problems. When it was noticed that Hirt was missing—as sooner or later it would be, though what with his reclusiveness it might take a while— I would certainly hear from the police. And I couldn't face another week of interrogation like the one after MacDougal's death. (Once the police had ruled out Dank as MacDougal's killer, I was the prime suspect—either because, upset about the critic's book, I'd gone for a long soul-searching drive that night, or simply by default. But there was no real evidence to tie me to the crime.) No, even though Hirt's death had been an accident, or at most an overstatement of my real feelings, I would either have to kill myself or leave the country.

While I weighed the options, I took advantage of the tunnel connecting our houses to buy time by creating the illusion that Hirt was still alive. For the next two months, in fact, I led a double life, as myself and as my neighbor. Whereas, for a while there, Dank had shared or subcontracted some of the chores involved in being himself, I—like the surviving Wilson twin—had rashly taken on a second self and his chores in *addition* to my own. But being Hirt was relatively easy because the real Hirt had been such a loner. He hadn't associated with anyone during the last few years of his life, and toward the very end had been almost as housebound as Dank, though what kept *Hirt* indoors was not agoraphobia but sheer misanthropy. For the past year he'd even had his groceries delivered, by a borderline-retarded man who left the bags at Hirt's front door and may never have laid eyes on Hirt himself. It also helped that lately Hirt had sported a big bushy beard and that, the day after our altercation, I'd found a phony one that looked just like it in a costume shop in Chico. So it didn't take much effort to keep up appearances. Once a day I would crawl through the tunnel to his house, turn on a few lights that had been off, turn off a few that had been on, take in the mail if any, take in the groceries if it was Monday, and show myself at a few windows with my fake beard in place.

On one of my crawls through the tunnel, by the way, I noticed an extension cord running stealthily through the dark from Dank's basement—from an outlet hidden by one of the retired La-Z-Boys—to Hirt's. There the cord came out of hiding and ran to the laundry room where Hirt had typed his Notes from Underground on a computer powered, it turned out, by Dank. Hirt had been notoriously frugal, by the way: Back when he taught at the college, there had even been a scandal, gleefully reported by the student newspaper, in which he was caught by a maintenance man in the act of stealing two rolls of toilet paper from the men's room in the Humanities building. Hirt's motive, though, for stealing electricity was probably symbolic—a fantasy of plugging into Dank's artistic power. It's safe to say that if Hirt had ever found a way to do *that*, the hair-raisingly high voltage of Dank's imagination would've fried the dainty microcircuitry of Hirt's "good taste."

So for a while, as I say, I maintained two selves. It didn't hurt that Hirt and I were built the same, and roughly the same height—even *Dank* had mistaken me for Hirt, once or twice, from behind. I kept a faucet in Hirt's upstairs bathroom running day and night, at a level meant to simulate a bachelor's modest daily consumption of water. I paid the utility bills.

In April, though, after a month of this routine, I got so depressed that I could barely bring myself to keep up the duties of a single life, let alone a double. As my initial fear of getting caught subsided, I was overwhelmed by the full horror of what I had done (or thought I had done)—not the wild blow struck in the frenzy of the moment, but my calm disposal of the corpse. As if for years I'd lulled myself to sleep, night after night, by visualizing Hirt's murder and tidy removal. Of course, we've all done that from time to time, imagining the murder of an enemy—the venue, the weapon, the disposal of the corpse—and may have even acted on, or acted out, a few of those imaginings, but somehow this was different. As much as I'd resented Hirt, I hadn't meant to *kill* him, hadn't *really* meant to kill him. He'd intrigued me for so long, by dint of the awe he inspired in Dank, that I almost felt as if I'd killed a brother, even a twin, and not just a haughty neighbor.

As my mood grew blacker, my "Hirt" impersonation grew more perfunctory. I installed cheap anti-burglar timers (the same ones I'd once used, with Dank's endorsement, to make our own house seem more lifelike in my absence) to turn the lights on and off at Hirt's house so that I wouldn't have to do so myself. I cancelled his weekly grocery order and let the local gossips wonder what Hirt was doing for nourishment now. I went for days on end without going over there to be Hirt, and once or twice when I did go I didn't bother with the tunnel, which I'd come to hate, but just walked out my back door and over to Hirt's by way of the back yards, cutting through Jablonsky's (he was out of town that spring), and listlessly adding my fake beard *en route*, so hard was it becoming for me to care anymore if my crime was detected.

But then it soon dawned on me that it wasn't my alter ego I was sick of, but myself. Sick of my colleagues, sick of my students, and sick especially of Dank, who in those days was not a thousand laughs. After a month of slacking off, I found myself spending more and more time next door, behind my big Hirt beard, and not for the sake of the imposture, but because I was sick of being Boswell. Dank—whose book, again, had given me the whole idea—never suspected a thing. He was not a noticer, and in any case he was too busy passively resisting his fictional condition—his indentured servitude to an unknown and malevolent author—to think about much else, or even to get out of bed. If he thought of me at all in that demented era of our lives, I'm pretty sure he didn't think *me* capable of the bizarre behavior so common in his novels, and to which Dank himself, as we have seen, was not immune. He didn't seem to find it odd when I dragged my desk and mattress down to the basement (which in the summer was not only quiet but cool), putting my official whereabouts two floors away from Dank. I hooked up an intercom between his sickroom and the basement, and an extension at Hirt's, so Dank could page me if he needed me, or if I had a caller. One night I slept over at Hirt's house, and from then on, I made that house my home base and Hirt my home persona: I only went next door once a day to keep up the illusion that Boswell was still around.

As soon as I defected to my alter ego (sometimes I even forgot for a moment who I "really" was, and who I was only pretending to be), my depression lifted. After all, I was starting a new life. I was no longer indifferent to getting caught and bitterly regretted my former laxity (though it seems to have gone undetected), vowing to be more careful in the future. Impersonating Boswell, though, was a lot more work than impersonating Hirt. Where before I'd rigged up a buzzer to sound in my bedroom if anybody ever rang Hirt's doorbell (no one ever did), I now had a buzzer in Hirt's kitchen, one that went off several times a day. The buzz was my signal to drop what I was doing, whisk off my fake beard (and I could have been well on my way to no longer needing a fake, except I didn't dare to grow a real—didn't dare let Boswell sport the same facial hair as his neighbor), run down to the basement, scamper through that fucking tunnel, and run upstairs panting and puffing, pretending I'd come from no farther than *Dank's* basement. Finally I destroyed the intercom in a rage that might otherwise have been directed at Dank, whom I'd come to think of as a tormentor—why couldn't he just leave poor Hirt alone? In my lucid moments I reminded myself that it wasn't Dank's fault, that he had no idea of my exhausting double life.

Or did he? Once or twice, on my dutiful visits to his bedside, I caught him looking at me narrowly. He'd actually exhibited an increase in activity since I'd taken to living at Hirt's. It was as if my reassuring presence in the house had been what let Dank settle into the vegetative state in which he'd squandered almost a year, and now that I was never there he was beginning to revive. Once or twice he'd gotten out of bed, waddled downstairs to his study, and turned on his computer. And once I found him standing almost wistfully at the threshold of the wide-open front door, with nothing between him and all that wasn't Dank but a flimsy screen door with a big capital "D"* set in the middle of the corroded wrought-aluminum scrollwork. So I guess it's possible that once or twice, on failing to reach me with the intercom, he had ventured a descent to the basement after all, had found the tunnel hatch ajar, and put two and two together. Could it really just be a coincidence that he wrote YOURS TRULY (which concerns a double life even odder than my own) right around that time, and could I really have imagined the unusual intensity with which he watched me the day—April 26, 2006—he gave me the story to read?

In any case, that was the day I decided to kill off Boswell, or at least to prune him way back—decided it was time for him to move out, and out of Hemlock. And so, not quite two weeks later, on May 8, I loaded my belongings into a U-Haul, went upstairs to say a sincerely tearful farewell to Dank (who

---

* Like a shamefully inflated grade for the life he was flunking. (OH)

looked sincerely embarrassed, insofar as he was still capable of emotions), and drove away, or sort of drove away. Probably the wisest course would have been to leave town altogether at that point, but then Hirt would have vanished at the same time as Boswell, which might have looked suspicious. So I'd decided to phase out my two selves in two installments: Boswell first and Hirt a few weeks later. I drove to the new Stor-Mor on the edge of town—on the main road *out* of town, and I was tempted to keep going. I stashed all but a carload of my favorite things in a locker where they would remain throughout my months in Clackamas, since I wound up leaving Hemlock in a hurry two months later, and the fears alluded to in other notes prevented me from sneaking back to fetch my stuff. Then, pausing only to reward myself (or, as I recently scolded a student for writing, to "incent" myself) with a snack cake from the 7-Eleven just across the street from Stor-Mor, I drove back to U-Haul, where I'd left Hirt's Toyota. (The week before I'd sold the guilty El Camino to Jablonsky.) After transferring the rest of my things to the car, I returned the truck, put on my fake beard and glasses, and drove back to Hirt's as Hirt. A few days later, I drove up to Portland (which had the distinction of hosting, or boasting, the only semi-well-regarded literary magazine that had ever published one of Boswell's stories). I didn't remove the glasses and beard till several hundred miles north of Hemlock. In Portland, I rented the first ugly hovel the realtor showed me—I was that eager for a refuge. It was hard enough to wait another month, but I had to wait because my rent-a-hell wouldn't be available until June 15.

Boswell had officially left Hemlock, but he hadn't severed ties with Dank. I even got a cell phone (after years of denouncing those obnoxious, overrated walkie-talkies) so that they— so that Boswell and Dank could stay in touch, since after so many years in the same house, I found myself wanting now and then to talk to what was left of Dank. It wasn't clear how much he wanted to listen, but he frequently answered the phone when I called and let me rattle on as long as I liked. And if, unnerved by his silence, I interrupted my babble to say "Dank? Still there?," he grunted an affirmative. It would have been cheaper for me to use Hirt's land line, but the phone on Dank's bedside table had caller ID, and how could I explain what I was doing in Hirt's house without explaining what I'd done with Hirt? Maybe I *would* have told Dank my secret, sooner or later, but on the night of June 13–14, my insanely envious, unkillable co-commentator snuck into Dank's house and murdered him in his sleep.

"Woogie": Brian makes a joke of saying cruel things like "Time to have you euthanized" to his two pet cats in a friendly tone, and friendly things like "Dinnertime!" in a cruel one, since of course cats respond more to tone than to words. One day, though, he adopts a fat gray cat who pays no heed to Brian's tone but only to his words. When the words are simple ("No" or "Who wants some tuna?"), the new cat's behavior is easy to explain, but things get really scary when it proves to understand—regardless of the tone in which they're uttered—tricky Jamesian constructions like "Although your persistent appetite, as announced by your no-less persistent caterwauling, strikes you as demanding an immediate response from your too-frequently taken-for-granted enabler, his own appetite will always—at least as long as he's the only one in this apartment with the wherewithal to open the refrigerator—be acknowledged and satisfied first." The result is a surprisingly effective horror story.

The story's fat gray cat was based, as far as looks, on Dank's cat DOOKIE, and the human was modeled on me, since I did have a game of saying hateful things in a loving tone to the uncomprehending animal. I never made up my mind if liked Dookie. Sometimes I would scratch his head and play with him and talk to him in the falsetto that seems to be *de rigueur* when talking to a cat for any length of time. "Who's a good boy?" I would ask, in a Rudy Vallee voice, stroking Dookie's massive belly (as an adult he was fatter than Dank). "Are you a good boy, Dookie? Are you a big fat loverboy? With a little tiny head? Who's got a little tiny head? Does Dookie have a tiny head?" But my affection felt arbitrary—I could just as easily have chased him out of the room. And some days I did, when I wasn't in the mood. Sometimes my mood would change in midstroke, and it took an effort not to shove him out of my lap, where he lolled in a state of utter trust. Mostly I restrained myself, not wanting to prove unworthy of that trust, or to seem inconsistent (though Dookie himself had no such qualms, and would go without warning from lazing in my lap to attacking my hand). In the interests of consistency, I used the falsetto only when I was feeling friendly, and Dookie soon learned to steer clear of me the rest of the time. He probably thought we were two different people (as different, say, as your two commentators): the nice man with the high voice and the mean one with the low one. Sometimes *I* thought I was two different people.

Sometimes the mean man teased and tormented Dookie, when his owner wasn't looking. Once I took Dank's record albums out of their stolen plastic milk crate, turned the crate upside down over the cat, and set an open can of tuna just outside his prison. Once I stuck a bunch of little yellow Post-Its all over Dookie and turned him loose to race around the house, trying to elude the little yellow pursuers. On that occasion, I recall, poor Dookie retched, or tried to: He knew that somewhere or other there was some kind of foreign matter making him unhappy, but couldn't figure out if it was outside or inside. Once when Dank was at the supermarket, I fetched the frilly pink-and-purple baby bathing suit I'd bought the day before at a discount store, and, after cutting a hole for Dookie's fat gray tail, stuffed him into the suit and made him wear it till Dank got home and made me take it off. Our author spent so little of his waking life away from his computer, and so much of that little was now lavished on the newcomer, that I guess I felt a little jealous.

I know it wasn't nice of me to torture Dookie, but to readers who would call my actions unforgivable, I say: *Au contraire*, Dookie himself forgave me, forgave and forgot. Or maybe just forgot: No matter how much I teased him, he kept coming back for more, just as no matter how long I held him yowling in my arms while he strained and struggled to get free, as soon as I did set him down he'd flop over at my feet, inviting me to rub his belly. (His favorite game was to sprawl spread-eagled on the kitchen floor and have me scoot him around the linoleum with my foot, like a big dust mop.) Like his owner, he had an almost saintlike inability to learn from experience.

Dookie disappeared on Christmas 2001, about a week after his catsitter quit. I was glad to see him go—I'd never been especially fond of him. I even have a frequent dream in which I gleefully strangle the cat and bury him in the yard, at the very spot where Dank once buried a time capsule. The dream is so vivid I'm tempted to dig at that spot, just to convince myself once and for all that it's *only* a dream. But why look for trouble?

Word Game: Still unaccountably unpublished, this brilliant eight-hundred-page *tour de force* features just one word per page, now in one place on the page and capitalized to suggest the beginning of a sentence, now in another and perhaps italicized, or followed by a question mark or a close-parenthesis or a pair of inverted commas. Read in rapid sequence, the eight hundred words might seem not to mean much, but if the reader extrapolates a full page for each word (I recommend fifteen minutes per word), the result is an immense and riveting saga of love and hatred, friends and lovers, parents and children.

I admit that the sort of formal experimentation so triumphantly brought off by *Word Game* is more typical of my own fiction than of Dank's. But it's absurd for Tom to insinuate that I wrote the book, and to decline on that account, as well as on account of "feasibility" (his mantra), to shop it around. After all, I've made no secret of my belief that the very books whose authorship Tom doubts are the best Dank ever wrote— books that *any* writer would love to have written. If they *were* mine, why on earth would I disown them? It doesn't add up. And how does Tom explain the fact that several of them (like THE BIG BOOK OF PROBLEMS) are based on the events of *Dank's* life? Sure, I might throw in a character modeled on Dank now and then, but does Tom really think I'm so obsessed with Dank that I would keep writing biographical novels as if I were Dank writing autobiographical ones? Or would take manuscripts that have been yellowing and gathering rejection slips for years and retrofit them with Dankiana so I could pass them off as Dank's? But why would I want to pass them off as his?

"The Worst of All Possible Worlds": Dank's initial title for the short story he ended up calling TIME VANDAL, and a title I've borrowed for this entry, as I might have for my own life story, if I'd been casting around for a title for that on the night of June 13-14, 2006. Instead I'd been sleeping serenely, *chez* Hirt and *qua* Hirt—and little suspecting that two doors down, the worst of all possible crimes had just occurred—when the sirens woke me up. When I went out to investigate, joining a crowd surprisingly big for three in the morning, as if it were an all-night bacchanalia, a block party, and not a private tragedy, I gathered from the babble that Dank had just been murdered—bludgeoned to death in his bedroom.

After a few minutes of skulking in the dark at the edge of the crowd, I returned to my—to Hirt's—house, pretty sure that no one had gotten a good look at me. I knew I was in trouble, or rather that "Hirt" was. So far as anybody knew, *Boswell* was in Portland minding his own business. And he and Dank had always been the best of friends. Dank and Hirt, however, had wound up bitter enemies. *I* knew, of course, or thought I knew, that Hirt couldn't be the killer, since at that point I still thought that I'd killed *him*, but a wise instinct advised me that it was time for "Hirt" to leave town in a hurry. The police were still milling around in front of Dank's house when, by the dawn's early light, I put on my phony beard for the last time and drove out of Hemlock, after removing my papers and a couple other incriminating objects, but leaving the food in the fridge, the dirty dishes in the sink, and so forth, to make it look like Hirt had in fact been living there till the night of the murder. Though I hadn't planned it that way, his sudden disappearance no longer cast suspicion on me, but on him, which after all was where the suspicion belonged.

That night, in the most depressing part of Portland, in the small brown living room of the tiny ugly house I had so hastily rented the month before—what the hell had I been *thinking*?—and had just prevailed on the landlord to let me move into one day early, I caught something about Dank on the local news. According to the anchorman, the murder weapon had been found in the *Fahrenheit 451* wastebasket in the upstairs bathroom: It was the signed first edition of *The Moon Is a Harsh Mistress* that Dank had lent to Hirt in 1999, just days before the two stopped speaking to each other, thus preventing Dank from ever asking for it back. It occurred to me that you'd need to be a whole lot angrier to kill somebody with a *book* than with a crowbar, say. More to the point, though, it occurred to me that Dank had been clubbed to death, or booked to death, by his old friend Owen Hirt. Any doubts I have had were dispelled a few nights later by another bit of info from the same newscaster: The police had found Dank's blood on an old raincoat his neighbors recognized as Hirt's, though the coat had been discovered, by some wino, in a dumpster outside a convenience store at the edge of town.*

When I realized that Hirt was still alive (his plunge into Lake Granite must have resurrected him, even if a pitcher of lemonade had failed), I wasn't sure if I should laugh or scream. It meant I wasn't guilty of his murder—and he was in no position to press charges for or even to report whatever lesser crime I *had* committed that day by bonking him on the head and dumping him in the lake. But it also meant I had a homicidal enemy on the loose. For all I knew, he had broken in to murder *me*, and—finding my room vacant, and little suspecting that I was two doors down, in *his* house, sleeping peacefully in his own bed—had settled for Dank as a consolation prize.

A week later, newly installed in my tiny, barely furnished hideaway in Clackamas (I'd been too eager to get out of Hemlock to stop by the storage locker, though I stopped at the neighboring 7-Eleven for coffee and doughnuts), I received the e-mail mentioned in my entry for THE COLLABORATION.

---

* (October 2007) A follow-up article mentioned that the cross-cut shredder in Dank's study had been used "recently," whatever that means and however they knew. No doubt some drudge in Forensics is still trying to piece together those shreds and so reconstitute poor Dank's last words. ("MacDougal was right"?) Better the drudge should read the millions of unshredded words that preceded those last.

In addition to proposing that we work together on this encyclopedia—and I know it was insane to go along with that proposal—Hirt said not to worry, that he'd left the country, and that anyhow he'd forgiven me for what he'd known all along to be an accident, and for my panicked attempt to hide the crime I'd thought I'd committed. He didn't say what he'd been up to in the meantime, during the months when I'd impersonated him and usurped his house, but he alluded to a bout of amnesia he blamed on his head injury.

Dank had said in our last conversation that he hadn't slept in several days and was half-convinced that he'd developed the disease that had already killed his aunt and then his father. In any case, he'd developed a tolerance to ordinary sleeping pills. But he'd just prevailed on his doctor to prescribe some stronger pills—he said he thought they were the same ones frat boys use in their pharmaceutically assisted rapes. So he was looking forward to a little rest at last. He got more than he bargained for.

But I digress. One benefit of heading the Dank Studies program, and editing its magazine, is a lighter course load, which I find especially fitting since my loyalty to Dank has led to some bad feelings in the classroom, where I make a practice of failing any student who writes or speaks about my author other than respectfully. (I do take a more democratic approach in the few non-Dankian classes I'm still obliged to teach.) As I see it, I'm there to tell them what to read and what to make of it. I'm not paid to sit back and let them tell me what they did and didn't "like." As I insist several times a semester, it's a classroom, not a coliseum. The fate of a writer shouldn't be determined by a thumbs-up or thumbs-down verdict from the mob.

"A Writer Reconsiders": This distressing thirty-eight-page essay—a long and disenchanted look at his own *oeuvre*—was the last thing Dank wrote, and in my opinion it was one too many. Pulsing with self-hatred and bristling with self-libels, the essay made me sadder than any other words I've ever read, not excluding pink slips, Dear John letters, or obituaries. I'm happy to say it no longer exists.

About a month before his death, or right around the time I moved out of his house and pretended to leave, Dank experienced a miraculous recovery. For the past year—ever since the scuffle with Plinkett that scared our author back into his house for good—he'd been deteriorating. He so seldom left his bed that I'd forgotten he could walk, and he'd been so busy mutely wrestling with whatever demons he'd held at bay with his fiction till then that I'd almost forgotten he could talk. That spring I'd been so busy with the double life entailed by the need to dissemble Hirt's death that I'd left Dank wholly to the care of a nurse, went for days on end without visiting his sickroom, and felt about him what you feel toward a loved one dying in some dim and stuffy corner of your house: sorrow, guilt, impatience, irritation. Dank wasn't *officially* dying, or not of the disease he thought he had, but his bedfast way of life was so unhealthy, his heart so bad, and his morale so low, that for months I'd been telling myself it was only a matter of days.

So I was astonished when he called me, on the evening of May 9—the day after "Boswell" left town, though I trust that that was a coincidence—sounding better than he had in years. After asking if I'd liked my drive to Portland (where he thought I'd gone, and where I really did go a month later), Dank announced that he'd "recovered."

He'd not only left his bed that afternoon but left his house and—unsteadily, he granted—shuffled around the block to Coffee Town, where he had found Plinkett, apologized for punching him in the gullet, and admitted that the weatherman had been right in ridiculing Dank. They were "friends again," he assured me, though they'd never been friends in the first place. He'd told the nurse he didn't need her any more, put himself on a strict diet, and made inquiries about liposuction. Best of all, he'd started a new book, though the subject, he said, was a "secret."

I heard all this with mixed feelings. I was astonished, as I say, and as I'd been two weeks before when Dank pulled himself together enough to write one last story, YOURS TRULY, like the final spasm of responsiveness—the swan song—of the bumblebee I just this day (May 28, 2007) nudged with a knuckle as it lay, belly-up, on my windowsill, apparently already dead but in fact still dying. And of course I was happy for Dank, and pleased to see that he still had some life in him. At the same time, it was safe to say that his newfound love of life would prove as fleeting as all of his other delusions. Like the protagonist of THE SUICIDE MAN, who quits his job at the suicide hotline when he decides it's cruel to prolong the ordeals of chronically unhappy people, I'd made up my mind by then that Dank would be better off dead. And I had to admit to myself, as I do now to my reader, that in some moldy basement corner of my mind I'd been "counting" on Dank's death, and even—as much as I would miss him—looking forward to it, as a precondition to his posthumous canonization. As long as he lived, he'd never gain the recognition he deserved, there would never be a Dank Studies program, and—worst of all— the unpublished manuscripts would remain unpublished.

Still, it was fascinating to follow his accounts of slowly booting up his life again—pedaling on his exercycle, sticking to his diet, and even placing a personal ad (though by the time it appeared, the advertiser was dead, which was just as well since Dank had understated his weight by more than a hundred pounds). Had he finally gotten over his delusion, then, of being nothing but a character in someone else's book? Or had he just resigned himself to that odd fate, and vowed to be a happier and more productive character? I thought it wiser not to ask. In any case, Dank was busy again writing a book of his own, and though he still refused to talk about it, he did talk about others he wanted to write. After a month of that, I'd almost gotten used to the new born-again Dank, and had pretty much resigned myself to his sticking around.

But then he wrote "A Writer Reconsiders." He wrote it on the last afternoon of his life, June 13, 2006, and showed it to me via e-mail, since again as far as he knew I was in Portland. He often showed me shorter works the minute they were finished, though I was never sure if he wanted my honest opinion or the sort of unconditional love that no sophisticated reader can give *any* writer. With pieces he was really proud of, he awaited my once-over as a playwright awaits a premiere. I know next to nothing about the Internet, but I'm pretty sure that, in order to reach me at Hirt's, two houses away, Dank's final piece of writing had to leave Hemlock, which strikes me as somehow emblematic of the final chapter of our friendship.

In any case, "A Writer Reconsiders" was the subject of our final conversation, which occurred hours after he sent me the piece, and hours before his bloody death. The conversation was an ugly one, because the essay was the first thing Dank had written that I'd ever violently hated. It's safe to say that Hirt would hate the essay too, if it were ever published (and it never will be), though for different reasons. Certainly it helps to explain his murderous envy of Dank, and clarifies the difference between the two authors.

Hirt always thought he was writing strictly for the love of Art, but in the end he found that that wasn't enough. When the world didn't give him any of the other, less lofty incentives for which writers hope—fortune, fame, a full professorship—

he quit: His real motives for writing had never been as lofty as he thought. Nothing shocking about that: Writers, as I say, excel at self-deception. Harder to explain is that for decades Dank believed *his* motives for writing to be *less* lofty, and more sordid, than they were. He thought he was in it for the money, the glory, the sex, but when none came his way, or next to none, he kept on going anyhow. It took him thirty years to see that writing had a different function in his life—not to help him "get ahead," but to give his life a meaning and a purpose. And that, I think, is what Hirt finally found so maddening— not that Dank was more successful (and Dank *wasn't* more successful, really, not when you divide each author's allocation of "success" by the number of books he wrote, or the hours he squandered on his art), but that he was more *serious*. It had always gone without saying, between the two, that Hirt was the more serious, the higher-minded, the purer of heart. The truth, though, is that Dank was the one who would have kept writing on a desert island with no hope even of posthumous rescue and readership.

So far, so good—I didn't have a problem with any of *that,* which infuriated only Hirt. What infuriated *me* about the essay was Dank's self-denigration. He'd always been too modest, but up till now he'd still found time for at least a touch of that grandiosity all artists share, and without which everything is pointless and unbearable. Now, though, he seemed to be insisting on his mediocrity, his lack of talent—and with a kind of hysterical relief, as if finally facing a horrifying fact that had lurked all his life at the edge of his vision. What his essay seemed to be saying—but *couldn't* be saying—was that he'd never written anything worth reading and had no reason to write except the sense of "purpose" it gave him, just as a lunatic in an asylum might find his purpose weaving tunics out of used dental floss. And in that case, there was certainly no reason for an honest scholar to devote his whole career to Dank. So he *couldn't* be saying what he seemed to be saying, right? When I phoned, though, to beg for reassurance, he just repeated the same distressing sentiments.

"The point is, I *like* to write—even though I'm not successful."

"Not successful in worldly terms, you mean. But neither was Melville. Or think about Kafka—"

"No, I *don't* mean that. I mean I want to go on writing even though I know I can't. Even though I know I'm crap."

"Have you gone crazy?"

"No, I've gone sane."

"What are you talking about? You're the greatest living writer in America!"

"Look, it's nice of you to always be so positive, but we both know I'm a hack."

"Dank, don't ever say that again." It was the last thing I wanted to hear. I'd devoted my life to his writings, and it was a little late in the day to decide I had backed the wrong horse. "If you do, I'll never talk to you again."

"Okay, okay, calm down. Listen, I need your advice for the title. For the book I'm writing now."

"A title?"

"Yeah, it's going to be a book about my other books—about what's bad about each one. I can't decide if I should call it *My Bad* or *MacDougal Was Right*.

"MacDougal was *right?*"

"Yeah, I thought that one was better too. Plus that way I won't look like a plagiarist if I say what *he* did."

"Dank, you've got to be kidding."

"I'm not. I've already got, like, fifty pages." (I'm glad to say those pages are no longer extant: I shredded them—together with "A Writer Reconsiders"—at my first opportunity, and

I've never regretted the act. Nor, though this guide has entries for some of Dank's unfinished books, does it award one to—ugh—*MacDougal Was Right.*) "You should hear what I just wrote about *Aromarama.*"

"You're out of your fucking mind."

I slammed down the phone, angrier with Dank than I had ever been with anyone. I felt like a member of a cult who'd given up everything—his family, his friends, his profession, his life's savings—to follow its charismatic leader, only to have that leader decide to come off it and manage a Denny's instead. Sometimes, as I think I've said, Dank was honest to a fault. It is *never* right to be brutally honest, not even with yourself. Because of course the brutal truth is that the world is a steaming ball of shit, and everything we value—culture, beauty, ethics, learning, love—is an heroic effort to forget that fact. And so is Dank's fiction. If, like everything else in the world from a baby's laughter to a Beethoven quartet, that fiction could be proven, spectrographically, also to consist of shit, that was no reason for its author to dwell on the fact, much less to rub *our* noses in it. As I've emphasized throughout this guide, Dank's whole art consisted of transcending, transforming, and ennobling an ugly reality. But now his magic transmogrifier was stuck in reverse, turning his silk purses back into sows' ears.

It is true that in my darker moments, like a priest with Doubts, I'd been fighting back my own misgivings on the question of Dank's greatness, and even his goodness. My misgivings, though, just made me more intolerant of other people's criticisms. And Dank's own misgivings, of course, were especially hard to take. In a way, I had more at stake than he did in the postulate that he was a great writer, since he couldn't help being Dank, but I had *chosen* to devote my life to singing his praise.

"Writer's Block": It turns out that writer's block is a contagious disease, transmitted by—you guessed it—a new virus. Scientists announce the news, and writers start avoiding one another ("like the plague," writes Dank, exhibiting that special flair for simile his readers know so well). Any writer who hasn't published lately is shunned.

The story spelled an end to one of Dank's own regrettably infrequent bouts of writer's block—not the one we have to thank for the slowdown of 1998, but the one that led him three years later to quit the MELVILLE BROTHERHOOD, convinced that all that contact with so many other losers was sapping his "powers."

It might seem that "writer's block," in Dank's case, could mean only carpal tunnel syndrome, since it's hard to see what *else* could stop him—what knack or craft or inspiration could conceivably be lacking that isn't also lacking in his published books. Yes, there are the famous "premises," but there were enough of those in his notebooks for several lifetimes of indefatigable hackwork. Was he having problems expanding those premises into full-grown fictions? But nothing prevented him from continuing to recycle the same stock descriptions of people, places, objects, and actions that he'd been so frugally reusing for decades. Was he having trouble thinking up new characters? But his characters—even those based on himself—had never been more than stick figures, and if the hand that drew them was shakier than usual, Dank's diehard fans were bound to prove as forgiving as ever. Almost as forgiving, that is, as Dank himself had always proven where his own faults were concerned. Was it the effort of animating those figures that was suddenly too much for him? No one will think so who has read Dank's fiction and seen just how jerky the animation is. Maybe he couldn't he get them to talk? But that would be a blessing, since every one of his novels is blighted by huge tracts of expository dialogue—the "maid and butler" kind where two characters tell each other things they both already know. Was he having trouble hitting the high notes of his own customary voice? Ha ha ha. Well then, had he simply said all he'd had to say? But he'd never had *anything* to say, and that had never stopped him in the past.

No, the truth seems to be that, in order to write, Dank needed a (false) sense of inspiration, or at least the illusion of knowing what he was doing. For a week or two in 1999, he lacked that illusion. What he considered writer's block was actually a lucid interval. (OH)*

"Wyatt's Party": This unfortunate story—one so bad not even Hirt could do injustice to it—is ostensibly the work of a troubled young man with the unlikely name of Wyatt Swilliam (naming was never one of Dank's strengths). As we learn in a clinical afterword by a fictive psychiatrist, Wyatt suffers from what was once known as a "split personality," and later "Multiple Personality Disorder," but is now called "Dissociative Identity Disorder." (Now as I write, that is— by the time you read this, the condition will no doubt have been renamed again, or dropped from the menu altogether.) Wyatt's story involves a small but rowdy party, almost an orgy, and is narrated from half a dozen viewpoints, those of Wyatt and his five guests, who in the trick ending prove to be his alter egos. Turns out that Wyatt was told by his psychiatrist to write the story as a form of therapy, an effort to reintegrate the different facets of his personality. (Wyatt's illness, like his story, reifies those facets as independent individuals: the bully, the nebbish, the highbrow, the joker, the creep.)

Even Homer nods, and even Dank wrote stories concerning which not even I, his biggest fan, can find a friendly word. "Wyatt's Party" is one of his worst, and one I'd gladly delegate to Hirt (as the good cop might hand over an especially heinous felon to the bad cop without even *trying* kindness). But I've muzzled Hirt (see final note to WRITER'S BLOCK) and now am on my own. And I, for one, believe that Dissociative Identity Disorder will soon go the way of brain fever, demonic possession, seminal intoxication, and all those other quaint misdiagnoses now banished to the attic of psychiatry. Already the psychology on which Dank's piece is premised is about as credible as the chemistry by which R. L. Stevenson "explains" Jekyll's transformation into Hyde. No doubt our author got the idea from some TV miniseries or after-school special or movie-of-the-week about someone with DID. In the story's "Afterword," Dank rehearses all the tedious mythology surrounding the disorder: how patients may have just a single

---

* I hardly know where to begin with this insane tirade. Hirt seems to have gone around the bend completely, though I always knew he was headed in that direction. In fact, though I've been too kind to say so until now, I've always thought of him as a cautionary example of a man driven mad by sheer envy of his betters. I could refute his libels point for point, but by now, I trust, the reader has learned to correct for the sickly greenish tint that Hirt's envy imparts to every book he describes. Or perhaps a better metaphor—though envy is clearly a factor—would be to think of Hirt as a demented curator running amok in a museum and daubing the master-pieces with his own feces. I could restore those paintings myself, despite my promise not to tamper with his "prose," but I think I'll let the reader have the honor. (BB)*

---

* Though I've been too nice to say it before now, the real reason Boswell is so threatened by my candor is that on some level he's aware of his own insincerity, aware that his unflagging pro-Dank stance (unlike my anti-) is not a verdict but an *axiom*, like the positions arbitrarily assigned to high-school debate teams (Solar Power: Pro and Con) regardless of what they actually think. One imagines that the most successful debaters know they can't afford to think at all—can't afford to cherish their own convic-tions, deep down, distinct from their public opinions. So with Boswell:

extra personality or as many as a hundred; how the transition from one to another is usually abrupt but sometimes takes hours; how the different personalities may or may not be aware of one another, and of one another's actions; how they

---

Like all career apologists, he no longer *has* a "deep down," if he ever did. He's a hollow man. Or rather, he has *just* enough of an authentic self to know, however dimly, that his praise of Dank is compounded of humbug, flim-flam, eyewash, claptrap, lip service, sophistry, thimblerig, and poppycock. That's why he protests so much, and why he can't forgive me saying what he too believes, deep down. (OH)*

---

* Rubbish. Hirt is like those people whose fear of opera, pungent cheeses, roller coasters, or pop art—with all of which Dank's fiction has affinities—convinces them that anyone who *claims* to like those things must be a liar. In other words, Hirt treats his own complacent and provincial tastes as the measure of all that is tasty. He reminds me of a bumpkin strutting, full of indignation, through a modern art museum, scowling at each painting, *determined* not like it for fear of being hoodwinked, and hating all the patrons who can savor what he can't. (BB)*

---

* See how he evades the issue? What's in question, Boswell, isn't *me* or *my* capacity for pleasure, but the authenticity of the loud, long-winded orgasms that you keep faking on these pages. Never mind *me*, Boswell: The point is that *you* don't like Dank, *you don't like Dank,* and you're too insane to face the fact. My attitude toward him is the same as yours, only minus the Positive Thinking, minus the sycophantic flourishes—minus the paraphs, perhapses, and serifs of chronic insincerity. (OH)*

---

* What the hell is your problem? It's not as if I haven't admitted at several points in this guide that Dank's work has

may have different IQs, different voices, different handwriting (and no doubt may favor different fonts for their word processing), and even different eyeglass prescriptions; how they may be either pure inventions or impersonations, personalities borrowed or stolen from actual people, dead or alive; how, according to the bean counters at the American Psychiatric Association, the affliction (or is it a blessing, like owning several houses, even if it means working several jobs?) is three to nine times more common in women but not unheard of in men, and so on. Fiction, though, ought to *invent* mythologies, not

---

its flaws. And you forget you haven't read his seven greatest books: THE BIG BOOK OF PROBLEMS, HOW JOHN DOE GOT HERE, A KNOCK ON THE HEAD, PANTS ON FIRE, PLANET FOOD, THREE-WAY BULB, and WORD GAME. Even *you* will have to recognize their excellence, as soon as the publishing industry does. (BB)*

---

* Don't hold your breath, Bill. That "industry" already knows who really wrote those seven books, even if you're too crazy to know it yourself anymore. I suppose I ought to pity you, but pity is *your* outlook. Sometimes I think we'd both be happier if I'd killed you and not vice versa. (OH)*

---

* All right, this demented stichomythia has gone on long enough. As has this no-less-ridiculous collaboration. As of today (June 8, 2007), I hereby remove Hirt from the project once and for all. Readers who have grown as sick of him as I have will be glad to know that I'll be writing the rest of this guide by myself. Let Hirt crawl back under his rock, and that's one stone we'll leave unturned. I've blocked all e-mail from his address and eagerly look forward to never hearing from him again. (BB)

just take ones that are well on their way to being debunked . . . and *re*bunk them.

The title character of this unfortunate story first reared his head in the year 2000 in a brilliantly abandoned Agent Harder novel, *Which of Me?* ("Wyatt's Party" dates from later that year.) *Which of Me?* was (mis)conceived as an avant-garde whodunit: There's no question as to who done it. Wyatt has done it, and done it on camera. But what with Wyatt's many personalities, Agent Harder has his work cut out deciding which to pin the blame on (a question that is supposed to matter to Harder—and so to the reader—because not all of Wyatt's alter egos have been read their rights, not all of them are old enough to sentence as adults, etc., etc.).[*]

---

[*] (October 2007) In a recent unsolicited submission to *What Next?: The Journal of Dank Studies*, some lady I'd never even heard of argued that those characters, those aspects of Wyatt, correspond to warring factions of Dank's own personality, "even if his psyche wasn't quite as Balkanized as Wyatt's." Since its author never even met Dank, the article was idle speculation, and I rejected it with no regrets. So far, in fact, the journal's articles have all been written by this commentator, though I trust that sooner or later other *qualified* scholars will come forward.

A B C D E F

G H I J K L

M N O P Q R

S T U V W X

Y Z

"Xeroxes": Set in a future that has perfected, or almost perfected, the teleportation of matter, this story concerns a strange degenerative personality disorder afflicting frequent users of the new means of travel. Hailed as the greatest advance in transportation since the wheel, the matter transmitter has made it possible to travel almost instantaneously from one point to another—New York to LA, say, or Earth to Mercury—so long as the traveler has no objection to being translated into a digital signal and reconstituted on arrival. The process *seems* to be safe, and after a maybe-too-hasty test period during which subjects neither report nor exhibit any ill effects, it is approved for general use. What everybody fails to take into account is that now and then a photon goes astray, and so an infinitesimal fraction of the information in the enormously complex signal is lost on every trip: The person who materializes in the reintegrator is a very close but never-perfect copy of the one disintegrated at the other end. And each subsequent trip yields a copy of a copy. The change from one trip to the next is negligible, but small change adds up, and frequent fliers finally become a little "woolly," writes Dank, "like a Xerox of a Xerox of a Xerox."

Dank began the story in 1981, but didn't finish it for twenty years, having let a lot of other fiction "play through" in the meantime. Not counting his bouts of abulia, he was always a hard worker, though it wouldn't have seemed so to "Xe-roxes," if stories had hurtable feelings. When Dank appeared to neglect a promising project, it was usually on purpose, to let it grow in secret, the way I once neglected a twenty-pound bag of potatoes for months to let them sprout the pallid and poisonous tendrils I was going to substitute for bean sprouts in the very special chop suey I planned to cook for Lips. As it happened, he moved out before I could harvest my crop, but a few weeks later, at that winter's potluck dinner, several of my colleagues developed florid though non-fatal stomach pains.

A B C D E F

G H I J K L

M N O P Q R

S T U V W X

Y Z

"You're Me": A stranger comes up to Jim on the street and says "You're me" (the first words of the story). Jim offers him eighty-four cents to go away, but the man says he doesn't want money. What he wants is recognition as Jim's double. When Jim tries to walk away, the stranger pursues, insisting that he, too, is Jim, and so has a right to go where Jim does. Except that both have beards, he doesn't look a bit like Jim, but he bolsters his absurd, nightmarishly insistent claim with evidence that makes it harder than it should be to dismiss him as a simple lunatic. He's privy, for example, to secrets Jim has never shared with anybody, like the time in childhood he killed his sister's gerbil.

The story dates from 1988 and has three parts. The first, told from Jim's point of view, begins with the scene above and ends, a week later, with Jim's capitulation: "Maybe I *am* you." The second is told from the stranger's point of view, begins a year before part one, and traces the conception and growth, in a once-sane and well-adjusted man, of the impossible conviction that he is someone else, or rather (and the author stresses this distinction, which I'm still not sure I get) that someone else is *he*. In the third part—the zany cross-country escapades of Jim and his now-acknowledged double in an old red Mustang stolen by the latter—the genre switches unaccountably from a metaphysical thriller to something more akin to a "buddy" film. Or unaccountably unless one knows that Dank decided, two-thirds of the way through, to write a story Hollywood might option.

"Yours Truly": A newly single mother, Willa, gradually becomes convinced that her ex-husband has been sneaking back into the house they once shared, and—in an effort to drive her insane?—leaving little signs of his intrusion. Not a day goes by without a calling card: the toilet seat left up "the way a man would leave it, typically" (and the only other member now of Willa's household is her baby daughter); the TV tuned to—and receiving, loud and clear—the Playboy Channel, which her husband used to watch but which she canceled the day he moved out; the sudden odd behavior of Cookie, the cat, whom her husband always hated, and who on close inspection turns out not to be Cookie at all, but an imperfect lookalike. Some of these nasty surprises are made even worse by Post-It notes bearing the phrase, "in an inexplicably familiar hand," that gives the story its title. Inexplicably because it's not her ex's writing, and in any case the police ascertain that he was out of town when many of the "calling cards" were left. Gradually, the reader realizes—though poor Willa never does—that the truth is even scarier than she suspects: She herself, deranged by loneliness, has been leaving "evidence" to simulate her ex-husband's intrusions, though she always does it in a sort of fugue state, so that later she honestly thinks it's *his* doing.

The story bears a striking resemblance to THE ACADEMICIAN, all the more striking when you consider that THE ACADEMICIAN was the first thing Dank wrote after I moved in, and "Yours Truly" the last he wrote before I moved out. It was, in fact, one of my reasons for moving. Both works reflect Dank's uneasiness with his lodger, a sense that he had let an odd, unknowable, and possibly demented stranger into his house. That uneasiness is more perplexing in the second case because Dank by then had had a dozen years to get accustomed to me.

The story came to mean much more to me, though, about a year after Dank's murder, when I experienced the special primal fear you feel when your house is violated by an unseen intruder, especially one whose motives are not as reassuringly clear as an ordinary burglar's. At two AM on June 22, 2007, or about a week after finishing this guide* and two weeks after bidding farewell forever (see WRITER'S BLOCK) to its pathologically angry co-author, I went into my study and logged on to the Internet to see if I had gotten any e-mail. I checked for messages so often that I'd made my inbox my home page, but now to my astonishment I found myself staring instead at *Hirt's* inbox. It was a surprisingly effective way to let me know that he was back in town, probably planning to kill me, and for all I knew there in my house at that instant. Or perhaps he hadn't meant to let me know he was back, but had broken in for some other reason, probably to murder me, and had paused, before or after learning that I wasn't home, to check his e-mail, just as burglars have been known to interrupt their burglaries long enough to raid the fridge and make a sandwich. The only thing I knew for sure was that *Hirt had just been in my house.* On moving back to Hemlock, I had sealed off the tunnel, but stupidly never considered that Dank's old friend and neighbor might well have a key to the front door.

---

* (October 2007) About a week, that is, after handing the manuscript to Cynthia, who of course wanted some changes. Her main request—and one I found myself oddly reluctant to comply with, though to a point I *have* complied—was to "tone down" Hirt's entries. Cynthia actually wanted me to purge Hirt altogether and rewrite those entries from scratch, but there was no question of that: I'm a busy man these days. And I've come to see this guide as—among other things—the story of why an innocent writer was killed by an unbalanced "friend." To understand Dank's life and death, you need to understand the rancor he provoked in less-gifted people.

The terror I felt as I stared at that screen, that list of messages from me (his only e-correspondent, it seemed) with subject lines like "Footnotes not a good idea after all?" and "Re: 'Sight Unseen'" and "Judge not lest ye be judged"—that terror was what Willa must have felt on finding Cookie (the real Cookie) in a Tupperware container in her freezer. Or what the third victim in PLUS SEVEN feels when the water in her shower suddenly goes scalding hot, as it only ever does when someone elsewhere in the house flushes a toilet—and she's home alone, her husband out of town.

I grabbed the crowbar I had bought for home defense the year before in Clackamas, and gingerly explored my house, but Hirt had vanished. There was nothing left to do but call a locksmith. I also e-mailed Hirt, repeatedly, to ask what the hell was going on, but I never heard from him again.

So it was with deep relief, as well as deep bewilderment, that I learned just yesterday (October 30, 2007) that some divers found a corpse at the bottom of the lake where I left Hirt for dead last year. And then I learned this afternoon that the coroner has identified that corpse as Hirt, or at least its dentition as his.[*] I can think of lots of reasons why Hirt might want to kill himself, but there's something unspeakably chilling in his choice of a final resting place (or semi-final, as it happened, thanks to the meddling of some teenage scuba buffs):

---

[*] (October 2007) Since I promised Cynthia to give her my revisions today, October 31, by five PM, and it's 4:41 right now, I can't do much more in response to the news of Hirt's suicide than to mention it here. There may be some passages, elsewhere in this guide, that will strike the reader as needlessly harsh now, in light of Hirt's final despair, and that I might have tempered if he'd had the sense to kill himself sooner, but considering how merciless he was toward poor Dank's memory, I can't feel all that bad about disrespecting Hirt's. I do regret, though, that there isn't time to change all mentions of him—even his own—to the past tense: That would be a positive pleasure.

the very spot *I* chose for his disposal back in March 2006, when I thought that *I* had killed him. He even wore the same ratty corduroy jacket.

I still ask myself if the head injury I dealt him, that day in his kitchen, was what prompted Hirt to murder Dank. Hirt of course had envied Dank for decades, and Dank's unawareness of envy only made it worse, but there's no denying the unprecedented surge of malice in the last twenty months of Hirt's life—the sudden emergence of a murderous resentment so hidden till then that not even he, perhaps, had been aware of it. And his injury may well have played a role in the eruption of that resentment, or in the withering away of the tiny sector of Hirt's brain that until then had prudently concealed his hatred of Dank. Whatever the cause, Hirt really did become a different person around the time of our scuffle (though, as his entries in this guide make all too clear, he retained some of the old Hirt's least endearing traits, among them arrogance and snideness). Doubting Tom, my former agent, who was Hirt's and Dank's as well, and who knew them both from college, told me (last winter, mere minutes before we stopped speaking forever—see PALS and PLUS SEVEN) that he didn't recognize his old friend in the entries followed by Hirt's initials. Tom insisted that Hirt "may not have suffered fools gladly, but he was never gleefully contemptuous." (*I* say *Tom* didn't see Hirt that day in the kitchen.)

The blow even impaired Hirt's memory. At least, Tom insisted that some of my collaborator's recollections are "disturbingly inaccurate." In his entry on the NOMENCLATURE PROJECT, for example, Hirt claims he accompanied Dank to the party where, in the vicinity of a certain newel post, they encountered Dank's third wife with her new lover and his agent, Tom himself. As Tom reminded me, however (and it's the *only* thing that he was right about in the course of our whole awful conversation), it was I and not Hirt who accompanied Dank to that particular party. (I hadn't noticed the discrepancy myself because my memory, though generally reliable, is badly overloaded: Dank's life and work tie up so many synapses that there aren't enough left over for my own.)

So much, then, for Hirt's memories. Like his opinions of Dank's writing, his "eyewitness" recollections should be taken with a grain of salt. Not that Tom himself is any golden yardstick of reliability. He claims, for example, that Hirt always hated Campari—and that clearly *isn't* the case (see THE CONSEQUENCES, THE HOUSE, THE TIRESIAS FORMULA). Tom also claims that in his final chat with Hirt—by telephone, in February 2006—my collaborator expressed regret at his estrangement from Dank (once more denying he'd written the review to blame for that estrangement), as well as "sincere admiration" for Dank's fiction. Sincere admiration? I'm forced to conclude that Tom's bullshit detector doesn't work over the phone. In any case, that last talk of theirs predated Hirt's head injury—and as any real fan of Dank's fiction can attest, after a good knock on the head, all bets are off. And I must have given Hirt a good one: The brash but hardly homicidal blow I dealt him, that day in his kitchen, left enough of a bruise or a bump or a crack that a year later the coroner mistakenly named *it* and not drowning as the cause of death (he also got the *time* of death all wrong), evidently failing to notice the stones in Hirt's pockets!

I still haven't set foot in Dank's bedroom, or not since the day I returned, and then only long enough to grab its inward-swinging door and tug it shut with a bang. I'm trying to forget the room, as if that would let me forget that Dank was killed in there. Last month I went even further and dust-sheeted the entire second floor, since every time I passed that door I envisioned the murder—the killer's shouts, the spray of red, the different thuds and thumps the murder weapon made as its different facets hit different parts of Dank, the way the book gradually battered his face out of all recognition, the way the heavily sedated author, who some would say had sleepwalked through his life, slept through his death as well—as vividly as if I'd been there at the time.

No one who has worked in academia will be surprised to hear that my best friend in Hemlock—now that Dank is gone—is not some tenured colleague but my neighbor Jock Jablonsky. Why play *verbal* ping-pong with some arid deconstructionist when you can play the real thing in your next-door neighbor's basement? Why should I speak to my colleagues at all, for that matter, when they just make fun of me and imitate my walk and call me "Polonius Maximus" whenever I enliven a dull department meeting with a timely sentiment from Emerson or Goethe? What's so terrible about quoting Goethe? Sometimes I come up with something quotable myself, though not—or no longer—at those meetings, where I no longer deign to open my mouth. In recent weeks I've even taken to preserving the best of my *bon mots*, just as that other Boswell did in his *Boswelliana*, a monument to those infrequent intervals when Dr. Johnson gave his megaphone a rest and let someone else get a word in edgewise. (In case the reader wonders, there is in fact a legend in my family, as perhaps in every well-read family with our surname, that we descend from Johnson's Boswell, the man who wrote by far the greatest of biographies—certainly a greater book than any of his celebrated subject's.)

In addition to a ping-pong table, Jablonsky's rumpus room features a dart board, a bar, and a full-sized Foosball set, and though I'd never been especially fond of Foosball, I've learned to like it lately: According to my calculations, when we play we stand directly over the tunnel that once connected Dank and Hirt. When Jock and I face off down there, I get almost nostalgic for the days when I was Hirt as well as Boswell—when I shuttled back and forth between my two identities without quite inhabiting either, changing personae as abruptly as the foosball changes possession. When Jablonsky makes a goal and I stamp my foot in annoyance, I can even hear, or think I hear, the hollow beneath us. One of these days I'll put my foot through the floor, and then the jig will be up.

Though he didn't die a rich man, Dank's stock is on the rise, as I can say with confidence as his executor. As mentioned elsewhere, movies based of several of his books are in development, and publishers have been contacting *me* (a real ego boost, I have to say) about reissuing Dank's works, since several of the best are out of print. The best of all, of course, have never even been published, but I'm confident that that will change soon, now that there's a minor "Dank sensation" in the air. It's a shame he isn't around to enjoy it, to enjoy the fact that his books are now more publishable, simply by virtue of bearing his name on the cover, than even better books by less-established and still-living authors. Though offhand I can't *think* of any better books by any living author than the seven not-yet-published masterpieces that Dank's readers will, if all goes well, soon have the privilege of admiring.

I have several other Dank-related projects in the works, including a Phoebus K. Dank cookbook with recipes for meals eaten in his novels; a page-a-day Dank calendar with a thought-provoking quote for every day of the year; a self-help book applying the teachings of Dank (as gleaned both from his books and from his conversation) to life's little trials; a selection of his dreams with my interpretations; and a classroom-ready critical edition of that much-maligned extravaganza, THE LIFE PENALTY, complete with preface, annotations, excerpts from the note-books, sample bad reviews, and several articles by me—articles insisting that even Dank's worst novel isn't really all *that* bad.

A B C D E F
G H I J K L
M N O P Q R
S T U V W X
Y Z

The Zoo: Written during Dank's incarceration for drunk driving, and reflecting his annoyance at the lack of privacy in jail, this novella pictures a near future where the state defrays the cost of jailing felons by *displaying* them, or at least the most exotic—a serial rapist, a killer of children, a double parricide, and so on—in an old-fashioned zoo setting. Like most zoos, these new ones charge admission, and people gladly walk around gaping and jeering, rattling cages, snapping photographs, and tossing peanuts. Inspired by the profitability of the new zoo, several other institutions, including an insane asylum and a home for the deformed, follow suit and open zoos of their own. A hospital even reconceives its coma ward as a living wax museum.

Somehow I never minded the lack of privacy myself when I spent a month in jail back in 1991, after a drunken scuffle—see THE ILL-ADVISED AND THE INADVISABLE—was absurdly misrepresented, by an ex-friend's lawyer, as aggravated assault. (If my sentence had been any stiffer, I'd have missed the fateful conference where I first met Dank after reading the paper I'd written about him in jail. Later I avenged myself by using my ex-friend as the model for the obnoxious, litigious graduate student in one of my novels, *Three-Point Perspective*.) I minded everything *else* about that ordeal—the food, the uniform, the boredom, my opinionated cellmate, the pathetic "library" without a single book by Dank—but I felt a little thrill each time another felon asked what I was "in" for. Fighting for what I believed in, I always responded. And would I do it again? Oh yes. I would do it again.

ACKNOWLEDGMENTS

The author would like to thank Lydia Davis, Minden Koopmans, Sarah McAbee, Cal Morgan, Mark Poirier, Eric Simonoff, Elliott Stevens, Deb Olin Unferth, and Brad Verter. I'm also indebted to Lawrence Sutin's *Divine Invasions: A Life of Philip K. Dick*.

About the author

About the book

Read on

Insights,
Interviews &
More . . .

Dueling Theremins
Two Authors Disagree About Which One Imagined the Other

A darkened bedroom—a sickroom, to judge by the bed tray, the bedpan, the intercom, the home defibrillator. Phoebus K. Dank is in bed, on his back, snoring loudly. Christopher Miller stands by with a clipboard. Suddenly, with an apneic snort, Dank opens his eyes.

Phoebus K. Dank: Great. I'm awake again. If only I'd never been—(*Gives a start.*) What the—are you the doctor?

Christopher Miller: I'm the author.

PKD: The author? *What* author? Who let you in? Who are you? Go away.

CM: My name is Chris. You're scheduled to interview me.

PKD: Oh. I am? Today? My memory . . . Okay, no problem. I'm going to stay in bed, though, if it's all right with you. You can sit on that hamper over there.

CM: (*Sits.*)

PKD: Okay. Um . . . so . . . I don't know, what kind of pencils do you use?

CM: Here, just ask the questions on this sheet.

PKD: Oh. Okay. "I'm told that you, too, were born prematurely?"

CM: Yes. As a matter of fact—

PKD: "In the wake of 9/11, how can the novel—"

CM: Hold on! I'm still answering the first one. My birth was pharmaceutically induced because the obstetrician wanted to get it out of the way before he went on vacation. I always say that that's why I hate to be rushed.

PKD: You *always* say that? That's a kind of goofy thing to *always* say. I mean, do people see you coming and go, "Uh-oh, there's that guy that always talks about his birth"?

CM: Just ask the questions on the sheet, okay?

PKD: "Your first novel starred a bad composer modeled on a great musician. Your new novel stars a hopelessly bad writer modeled on a major modern author. Why keep reimagining giants as midgets?"

CM: I guess I've always hated geniuses and the way they wreck the grading curve. Just kidding. But I'm a comic writer, and genius isn't funny. Greatness is no laughing matter.

PKD: Plus, if you did write a novel about a great man, readers would keep noticing how *not*-so-great *you* are.

CM: Right. So instead I wrote a novel about you.

PKD: A novel about *me*?

CM: I told you I was the author. (*Chuckles.*) Phoebus, Phoebus, don't tell me you thought you were *real*?

PKD: Oh. So that's how it is, huh? (*Gropes for intercom.*) BOSWELL!

Bill Boswell (*panting*): Here I am, sir! I came running when you called, just like you told me to! ▶

Meet Christopher Miller

Marlene Sauer

CHRISTOPHER MILLER is the author of *Sudden Noises from Inanimate Objects*, a *Seattle Times* Best Book of the Year. A former technical writer who has also worked as a counselor in a psychiatric group home and a night attendant in a homeless shelter, Miller studied philosophy and English literature at Columbia College in New York. He currently teaches at Bennington College in Vermont. ❧

Dueling Theremins (*continued*)

PKD: Good boy, Boswell. Boswell, did you let this lunatic in?

BB: No sir. I was reading in the bathroom. (*Holds up* 101 More Ways to Kill with Your Bare Hands.)

PKD: Well, this guy claims to be an author too.

BB (*narrowing his eyes*): Great. Just what the world needs—more reading matter.

PKD: He says I'm just a character in his new novel. And a midget. And a hopelessly bad writer. Make him go away!

BB: You heard the man.

CM: Wow, you're even creepier than I imagined.

BB (*sizing him up*): How much do you bench?

CM: Excuse me?

BB: Never mind. It doesn't matter. (*Flips through his book, apparently searching for a particular page.*) I know all kinds of pressure points and secret grips.

CM: You do, huh? (*Takes out Palm Pilot and jots a few words.*) I always forget how to spell "aneurysm."

BB: Ow! (*Drops book, clutches head, crumples to floor.*)

CM (*to Dank*): See? You're not the only author who kills off annoying characters.

PKD: Oh, my God! Oh, my God! This isn't happening!

CM: Let that be a warning to you. I once had a—are you doing Kegel exercises?

PKD: No.

CM: Are you—should I get the bedpan?

PKD: No!

CM: You sure?

PKD: I'm trying to wake up, is all.

CM: Oh. I forgot. You think this is a dream. You think I'll go away if you just stop believing in me.

PKD: Right.

CM: But that only works if I'm imaginary. In the words of one of *your* annoying characters, "Reality is that which, when you stop believing in it, *doesn't* go away." Italics mine.

PKD: Who said that?*

CM: Never mind. Let's get through this interview and *then* you can wake up, okay? I'll even *wake* you up.

PKD (*glumly*): I doubt if even you could. The other night I realized that people are designed to wake up only a certain number of times. I used up mine by taking all those naps, back in the old days. Once you use up all your wake-ups, boy, you're up Shit Creek. It gets harder and harder to wake. In the end you'd sleep right through your own electrocution.

CM: Hmm.

PKD: Like how it shortens the life of a lightbulb if you keep switching it on and off too many times. ▶

*Philip K. Dick, in *How to Build a Universe That Doesn't Fall Apart Two Days Later.*

Dueling Theremins (*continued*)

CM: I see. Let's get back to the interview.

PKD (*sighing*): "I understand that you teach at Bennington College?"

CM: Yes. A Bennington education holds several principles in creative tension: freedom and responsibility; individuality and community; independence and—

PKD: "Do you enjoy teaching?"

CM: Yes. The kids are great. Some of the grown-ups are a little hard to take.

PKD: "How long have you been there?"

CM: Seven years. Before that I worked with the mentally ill for a decade, first in a group home and then in a shelter. I also worked with the developmentally disabled, if that's still what you're supposed to call them. I even worked, though briefly, as a janitor. One of the narrators of the novel I'm working on now is a janitor too. He listens to Slayer and Cradle of Filth. His prose is even worse than yours.

PKD: Being as this is a dream, I'll ignore that. You claim I'm a figment of your imagination, but I say *you're* the figment. You're just an uppity projection of my own self-doubt.

CM: Or *you're* just a projection of *my* self-doubt.

PKD (*after a moment's confusion*): I know you are, but what am I?

CM (*mockingly*): "I know you are, but what am I?" Whatever this is, it isn't a dream. And if it *is* a dream, that *proves* that you aren't real: Real people don't have dreams like this. Trust me, I've been trying for a decade now to write a book on the representation of dreaming—in novels, movies, music, paintings, poems. I know a fake dream when I see one.

PKD: I thought you were writing a janitor novel.

CM: Yeah, well, I go back and forth between the two.

PKD: Oh. Like changing channels when there's different shows you want to watch at the same time.

CM: Exactly. Or like crop rotation.

PKD: Crap rotation?

CM: Crop rotation.

PKD: Tell me something. Have you ever been in jail?

CM: Never.

PKD: Ever try to kill yourself?

CM: Not yet.

PKD: Ever overdose on Sharpie fumes or Robitussin in an effort to unleash your inner demons?

CM: Why would I want to do that?

PKD: Ever wet your pants on purpose, to see if you could?

CM: Can't say that I have.

PKD: I didn't think so. Here's what I'm thinking: Truth is supposed to be stranger than fiction, right? So if you're so real and ▶

Dueling Theremins *(continued)*

I'm so fictional, how come your life is so boring?

CM: Touché.

PKD: Has *anything* interesting happened to you? I mean *since* you were born?

CM (*sadly*): That was certainly the high point.

PKD: Any other claims to fame?

CM: Well . . . let's see . . . My mother placed third in the National Spelling Bee once. She went out on "sarsaparilla." Though that was before I was born. But when I was one I had an operation on my skull, to keep the plates from fusing prematurely. If not for modern medicine, I'd be a pinhead now.

PKD: Far out.

CM: I grew up in Cleveland. I collected beer cans back in junior high and have a recurring dream about finding a coveted can. In seventh grade I studied the trombone. My brother Mike plays trumpet in the Cleveland Orchestra. In high school I was on the wrestling team and got so many nosebleeds that I finally had my nostrils cauterized. Then off to Columbia, where my brain was cauterized by the likes of Stanley Fish and Edward Said. After college I moved to Seattle, and throughout my twenties I shared a house with other young underachievers. At one point I believed that a housemate—a graduate student in physics—was beaming a death ray at me. Through the wall. Later I moved to Brooklyn, like everyone else, and for a while I shared a loft in a converted girdle factory—

as good a place as any for a formalist, I used to say.

PKD (*gives a start*)**:** Sorry—guess I nodded off there for a second. (*Brightly.*) You say you collect beer cans?

CM: *Used* to. Now I collect canned meat products, but there has to be a picture of the living animal on the can. Preferably looking reproachful or angry.

PKD: I'll bet. I would too.

CM: I'm also fond of novelties and laff-getters. For a while I tried collecting phony dog shit, but there seem to be just three varieties "in print," and each is highly stylized. One looks like a pretzel, one an asterisk, one an ampersand. I guess the phony-dog-shit factories felt that, with the real thing so plentiful, it would be redundant to make artificial feces without ennobling and improving on the real thing. Too bad.

PKD: Too bad? I thought you were a formalist.

CM: Where fiction is concerned. When it comes to phony dog shit, I'm a realist. I guess that sums up my sense of what each tradition is good for.

PKD: Whatever. Listen, if you're finished telling me about your stupid poo collection, tell me more about your novel. The one you claim I'm only a character in.

CM: What do you want to know?

PKD: Does it have every single thing that ever happened to me?

CM: Of course. If it happened at all, it's in ▶

Dueling Theremins *(continued)*

the novel. Where else could it happen, since you're just a character?

PKD *(angrily)*: Then your book must be infinity pages long.

CM: Nah. Closer to five hundred.

PKD *(sputtering)*: But—but—I have *way* more than five hundred pages of memories!

CM: Yeah, the rest are only implants, I'm afraid.

PKD: Oh.

CM: Sorry.

PKD: Does it have the Lobster Incident, at least? Your stupid book?

CM: I think so. I could check the index.

PKD: There's an *index*? To my *life*? So you mean—okay, see it if has that time I saw Cher at Home Depot. In the checkout line. Was that an implant too? Is this stupid dream an implant? See if it has the time I left my laptop on the bathroom floor and Boswell thought it was a scale and stepped on it. See if it has the time I . . . ❧

Index

Compiled by the Author

About the book

Index *(continued)*

Author's Picks

Books by Dick

Philip K. Dick was a much better writer than Phoebus K. Dank, and no less prolific. Not even the two fat volumes published recently by the Library of America can accommodate all the Dick worth reading, but they're a good place to begin. Each of the novels collected in those volumes is also available as a trade paperback. Start with *The Three Stigmata of Palmer Eldritch*.

Philip K. Dick: Four Novels of the 1960s. Includes *The Man in the High Castle*; *The Three Stigmata of Palmer Eldritch*; *Do Androids Dream of Electric Sheep?*; and *Ubik*.

Philip K. Dick: Five Novels of the 1960s & '70s. Includes *Martian Time-Slip*; *Dr. Bloodmoney*; *Now Wait for Last Year*; *Flow My Tears, the Policeman Said*; and *A Scanner Darkly*.

Time Out of Joint. An ingenious early novel that may have inspired—and certainly anticipated—*The Truman Show*.

A Maze of Death. I may be the only Dickhead who prefers this book to *Ubik*.

Valis. One of Dick's last and best. Its exclusion from the first two Library of America volumes suggests that a third (*Three Novels of the 1980s?*) is in the works.

The Selected Stories of Philip K. Dick. Start with "Faith of Our Fathers."

Dr. Futurity. Even Homer nods, and even Dick's amazingly excitable imagination had its refractory periods. This early novel served (along with works by Henry

Darger, Theodore Dreiser, and Lionel Fanthorpe) as a model for Dank's prose.

My Favorite Books About Imaginary Authors

Start with *Lint* by Steve Aylett—another transposition of Dick's life into the key of fiction. Aylett strays even farther from the facts of that life than I do, and the result is very funny, inventive, and strange.

Sartor Resartus, Thomas Carlyle
Cakes and Ale, W. Somerset Maugham
Orlando, Virginia Woolf
The Third Policeman, Flann O'Brien
Chronicles of Bustos Domecq, Jorge Luis
    Borges and Adolfo Bioy-Cesares
Loitering with Intent, Muriel Spark
Breakfast of Champions, Kurt Vonnegut
Concrete, Thomas Bernhard
Mulligan Stew, Gilbert Sorrentino
The Information, Martin Amis
Shining at the Bottom of the Sea,
    Stephen Marche

Paragons of Pitilessness

Being as sweet as Mother Teresa, I found it hard to make Hirt so consistently unkind. Here are some exemplars I consulted again and again to fortify myself for the distasteful task. Start with Disch, who was not only a novelist but a poet and a brilliant critic.

The Dunciad, Alexander Pope
"Epistle to Dr. Arbuthnot," Alexander Pope
A Fable for Critics, James Russell Lowell
"Fenimore Cooper's Literary Offences,"
    Mark Twain
"Warren G. Harding's Inaugural Address,"
    H. L. Mencken
Against the American Grain, Dwight
    MacDonald

Author's Picks *(continued)*

Deeper into Movies, Pauline Kael
As of This Writing, Clive James
The Castle of Indolence, Thomas M. Disch
The War Against Cliché, Martin Amis
Nobody's Perfect, Anthony Lane
The Irresponsible Self, James Wood
2000 Insults for All Occasions,
Louis A. Safian ～

Don't miss the next book by your favorite author. Sign up now for AuthorTracker by visiting www.AuthorTracker.com.